M000211830

EX
LIBRIS

James Jeffrey Thomas

HEAT LIGHTNING

Persephone Book Nº 101
Published by Persephone Books Ltd 2013

First published by Coward-McCann, New York in 1932
© The Estate of Helen Hull
Preface © Patricia McClelland Miller 2012

Endpapers taken from 'Memories of the Alamo' 1929, a plain
weave roller-printed silk by HR Mallinson & Co
© The Museum of Art, Rhode Island School of Design

Prelim pages typeset in ITC Baskerville by
Keystroke, Wolverhampton

Printed and bound in Germany by
GGP Media GmbH, Poessneck on Munken Premium
(FSC approved)

9781903155912

Persephone Books Ltd
59 Lamb's Conduit Street
London WC1N 3NB
020 7242 9292

www.persephonebooks.co.uk

HEAT LIGHTNING

by

HELEN HULL

❋❋❋❋❋❋❋

with a new preface by

PATRICIA MCCLELLAND MILLER

PERSEPHONE BOOKS
LONDON

PREFACE

✳✳✳✳✳✳✳✳

At the beginning of 1931 Helen Hull, a novelist and teacher at Columbia University, boarded the RMS *Majestic* in New York. She had with her a list of good but affordable London restaurants and a packet of encouraging letters from her longterm companion, Mabel Louise Robinson, one to be opened each day of the voyage. To keep costs down, they also devised a code for their twice-weekly telegrams during the coming months of separation when Hull would be working on a new novel. What remains of this exchange is a set of tantalising but opaque transatlantic messages, such as 'KESEP' and 'AHARY ITCER'.

Originally the 43 year-old Helen Hull had planned to use her six-month Guggenheim Fellowship to gather some background material in Ireland and England for a fictional family history and then settle down to write in France. As it turned out, however, she stayed in London and, as her diary from that period records, her disciplined writing schedule from February to May 1931 was interspersed with visits to the usual tourist attractions and to some less popular but memorable spots like the London docks. She also went to the

****

English Speaking Union, the Times Book Club and the Alpha Club; took in films, poetry readings and lectures on politics and literature; enjoyed outings to museums and art galleries; and attended the theatre, including performances of Rudolf Besier's *The Barretts of Wimpole Street*, Bernard Shaw's *Arms and the Man*, Aldous Huxley's *World of Light* and E M Delafield's *To See Ourselves*.

During those months of concentrated activity Helen Hull worked on *Heat Lightning*, her sixth novel. In some extant notes written in 1932, the year the book came out, she describes how its central concept became clear as she contemplated a 'cloudy beaker of thoughts about contemporary life':

> The idea was not astounding, nor was it new. It came from a chance sentence in an article and I have lost its precise phrasing. The content was this: here in America we stem from many races, we have no homogeneous roots, no common traditions. . . . I had decided that I wished to write a novel about the immediate present – this was the summer of 1930 – and I had been speculating about the way people were acting and feeling, about the difficulty of formulating any philosophy of life, or even of setting down any definite standards of behavior. The Depression was upon us, the Modern Temper was one of disillusion, positive standards for living seemed impossible to grasp. I remember a period of excitement while the casual sentence from the article acted as precipitant.

****

Although it focuses on domestic life, *Heat Lightning* is, at its core, a novel of ideas, even though not all of the book's readers would have recognised it as such. In Helen Hull's previous work – five novels published between 1922 and 1930 and over thirty short stories in magazines such as *Collier's*, *Harper's* and *Cosmopolitan* – several topics of interest to contemporary audiences had already recurred, such as the ramifications of marital and family structures, women's economic status, and the struggle to mature in the midst of what appeared to be far-reaching social change.

From the first beautifully crafted sentence of *Heat Lightning* – 'Now that she was back in the town of her childhood, standing on a corner across from the village triangle of green, a small pyramid of luggage at her feet, Amy's one clear thought, over the fluttering of unimportant recognitions, was, "Why on earth have I come?"' – Helen Hull anchors the novel firmly in the present; she creates a narrative pattern that controls the book, a constant weaving back and forth between present and past as granddaughter Amy Norton studies the large, memorably drawn cast of characters who comprise her family. In her notes Helen Hull later recalled Amy's emergence as the ideal protagonist. Working out her strategy for the novel:

> Gradually Amy came into life, a woman in her thirties, sensitive and receptive, with a serious emotional problem in her own affairs which she was struggling to resolve. Because she is searching for an understanding of herself and a code for her own life, she is hypersensitive to the personalities and the emotional

attitudes of the members of her family. At last I saw her standing on a street corner where the city bus had dropped her, fugitive, seeking illumination, and the story had started.

Part of the family group, but also removed from it by virtue of having lived in New York for years, Amy is a keen observer of the Westovers and of two matters vitally important to her: how couples manage their relationships and how women find a moral and philosophical compass for their lives.

Heat Lightning takes place during the drought-stricken summer of 1930 (the summer after the Stock Market Crash of 1929) in the small Midwestern town of Flemington, a fictional location reminiscent of the part of Michigan where Helen Hull herself grew up. Amy Norton is the protagonist but her grandmother 'Old Madam' Westover is the novel's most complex character who, despite her casual use of denigrating terms for some immigrant groups, has a long history of enraging both pretentious relations and townspeople alike by stubbornly championing the rights of the less privileged; nor does she have much patience with the hypocrisy of the affluent who attempt to dictate the behaviour of the poor at the same time as they themselves flout Prohibition and freely engage in dubious business practices. While the portrait of the Old Madam is neither idealised nor simplistic, most of her descendants appear feeble, self-interested and deluded in comparison with her vigour, unsentimental compassion and clear-sightedness – a dilution of family strength that Amy sees as a form of entropy.

****

When Amy turns to her grandmother for marital guidance, the Old Madam harrumphs, 'A lifetime's too short to find your way about another's heart, without blunderings and mistakes. That's why these folks nowadays are so foolish, rushing into marriage, out of it, into another.' It is her grandmother's understanding of the effort required for a good marriage that is both helpful to Amy and central to the novel. We realise that the real difficulty between Amy and her husband Geoffrey is how they interact emotionally (whereas her working and having children is, unusually for the period, rather taken for granted). Here is a dilemma common to many of Helen Hull's characters: how can women flourish when they are expected to make most of the adjustments in situations which really require the efforts of both men and women? Even her parents' marriage, which Amy admires, is dependent upon what Helen Hull described as Catherine Westover's 'imaginative endurance'.

Although Amy's problem while she visits Flemington is to sort out what to do about her own marriage, her deeper challenge is to determine who she is and what she believes. Initially Amy, like the country at large, suffers from a post-War loss of belief (exacerbated by the Depression) and an absence of clear-cut standards for behaviour; she then considers and dismisses the merits of biological determinism, modern psychology and religion as sources of authority or meaning. Despite Amy's confusion, Helen Hull suggests that she is capable of the kinds of insight associated with classical literary tradition.

✳✳✳✳✳✳✳✳✳✳

> If she could have patience [Amy thinks], could watch
> these shifting scenes with sympathy enough, out of
> them would come the wisdom she needed. It would, far
> more potent than any Aristotelian tragedy, constitute
> a personal catharsis, a purging of herself of blindness
> and other faults of vision – distortion, perhaps.

To this end, Amy intently observes her family, particularly her female relations. Although her grandmother is, in a sense, an anachronism, she gradually realises that the Old Madam's strength comes not only from age and privileged circumstances but also from inner harmony and integrity: she 'lived with sureness, knowing her own code.' Her mother describes a similar approach in her unsophisticated but plain-spoken and heartfelt advice to Amy. The first principle, Catherine says, is 'acting so I don't feel ashamed of myself, so I feel comfortable with myself.' The second thing of importance: 'People. Loving them. . . Not a general, vague love for everybody. But for your special ones.' As she searches for her own code, Amy also studies her off-putting Aunt Lora, 'a limp, unhappy, maternal octopus'; her indulged, busily idle cousin Sophie; her whining, self-deluding sister Mary; her cousin Laurance's bovine yet impulsive wife Emma, daughter of German immigrants; and her inquisitive, alert, and sensible French sister-in-law Felice.

In her notes Helen Hull singled out three dilemmas she had identified in the confusion and tension of heat-stricken America in 1930: lack of authority, miscommunication and, most important, the absence of a common tradition:

✳✳✳✳✳✳✳✳✳✳

The individual has nothing firm upon which he can lean, nor has he even any definite way of life against which he can rebel; he is under the necessity of determining for himself how he shall act and think. Next, he cannot communicate adequately with his friends, with the people beneath his own roof. All that uninspected part of his personality – his prejudices, his casual standards as to what he shall have about him, how he shall live, what he shall do with his leisure, what he shall expect in love, in marriage, in his relation to his children – all of this emotional equipment may differ completely from that of his neighbor. . . Then, [thirdly]. . .it might be true that in America we had no common tradition; that within one group you might find men and women a generation only from Sweden, Poland, Italy, France, or Ireland.

When Amy tries to account for the differences among her relations, she explores a range of explanations: individual temperament, stages of evolution, racial/national differences and motherhood. Eventually she realises that her family – into which 'foreigners' have married – is a microcosm of the larger society, each member 'with his own code, derived blindly from distant soil.' We are, she thinks, 'having to make a new code to live by.' The plot is driven by her struggle to identify values that persist, even though norms of behaviour may vary among ethnic groups, social classes or generations. What we might call Amy's moral or philosophical education, her *Bildung*, reflects Helen Hull's own belief in 'valor and tolerance and sincerity, the qualities of human beings which are developmental and constructive.' Amy's growth into this understanding of fundamental values lies at the heart of *Heat Lightning*.

One other female character is interesting in the light of Helen Hull's personal life and the changing political atmosphere: Amy's cousin Harriet, a tweedy lesbian who wears a tie, slicks her hair back and goes by the name 'Hal'. In her 1923 novel *Labyrinth*, Helen Hull mocks Freud and presents a lesbian couple as the most admirable example of marriage, but nine years later in *Heat Lightning* she gives us Harriet, a neurotic, 'shadowy lump' who hates men because her rejecting father liked only 'pretty' girls. Harriet represents, in an adulterated, parodic form, a way of life that, after the heydays of the 1910s and '20s, had been forced at least partly underground. Helen Hull was keenly aware of the growing political pressure to stigmatise and criminalise homosexuality both in America and in England, where Radclyffe Hall's *The Well of Loneliness* (explicitly referred to in *Heat Lightning*) had been banned in 1928 as obscene. Her use of Harriet is in fact nuanced – but too openly sympathetic a portrayal of homosexuality in the early 1930s would have ruined her reputation as a domestic novelist. Indeed, both her publicist and her editor at Coward-McCann talked about the difficulty of promoting Helen Hull and her work. Despite her track record as an authority on family life, the only thing that they could safely acknowledge about her family – which included her lifelong partnership with Mabel Louise Robinson – was her dog.

But Helen Hull was above all a professional writer. Aware

of changing literary tastes and shifting political and cultural landscapes, she was acutely sensitive to her audience and was, in the words of the critic Roberts Tapley, 'well equipped to voice the sentiments of a large group of intelligent readers' – precisely the sort of educated middle-class readership the Book of the Month Club targeted when their panel of five judges (including Dorothy Canfield Fisher) chose *Heat Lightning* as their April 1932 Selection. While Helen Hull's earlier books called for social change, *Heat Lightning* takes the more conservative stance of reaffirming traditional values in the face of social disruption – essentially a reassuring book published in unnerving times. Even though she intended this analysis of family life to be relevant on a larger scale, the 'solutions' here are individual rather than systemic: her novel offers a guide to individual integrity and personal relations rather than a blueprint for social and political reform.

Heat Lightning was published just as attitudes towards middlebrow domestic fiction were becoming both more pronounced and more negative among the literary establishment. When Helen Hull's earlier novels were described as 'women's books', reviewers meant that they were written on controversial topics from a woman's point of view. However, by the early 1930s, as domestic fiction gained in popularity, the term 'women's books' was used more pejoratively and referred not so much to perspective as to subject matter and audience. *Hardy Perennial* (1933), her next book, elicited a contemptuous response from the *New Statesman and Nation*, where Peter Quennell pronounced novels like hers silly and insignificant: they have 'a rather finicking and feminine air' which will appeal only to women and to 'men who enjoy girding on a nurse's apron.' On the other hand, the 1930s were a propitious time for her work: both the Guggenheim Foundation and the Book of the Month Club were newly formed, and just as the Foundation was the first to grant awards to women scholars and artists – thus making it possible for her to go to Europe to write – the Book of the Month Club helped make middlebrow fiction, especially work by women writers, more accessible, popular and profitable.

Following the success of *Heat Lightning*, Helen Hull sealed her reputation as a prolific and respected writer during the 1930s with the publication of four more novels, but in the 1940s her output slowed, and she produced only two more novels in that decade. Instead, in addition to continuing to teach full time at Columbia, she became more involved in the Authors Guild, stepping up to its Presidency in 1948 and co-editing two books about writing for the Guild. Two more novels would follow in the 1950s. Then, at the end of her career, Helen Hull shifted genres. Intrigued by a contest sponsored by Dodd, Mead for the 'Best College Faculty Mystery', she composed the rather unconventional *A Tapping on the Wall* (1960) as a diverting joke while she oversaw the care of Mabel Louise Robinson (whose health was steadily declining and who died in 1962). Having won the prize, she was then contractually bound to produce a second volume, when she was exhausted and rather bewildered. *Close Her Pale Blue Eyes* (1963) is an oddly eloquent and moving book, essentially the story of what it means to be old and dying. By the time of her own death in 1971, Helen Hull had published

****

a total of seventeen novels, some seventy short stories, and several books about writing – yet she died knowing that domestic fiction had fallen out of favour and that her once-popular work had faded almost entirely from view.

In 1939 Helen Hull broadcast a radio talk entitled 'Why I Write about American Family Life'. In it she lays out very clearly her belief that the family 'is the microcosm of the world'. The role of the novelist, she says, is not to indulge in fantasies but to *think*: to formulate 'if not a whole philosophy, at least a set of values about life', working with characters who are ordinary people, through whose lives we can explore basic human values. Helen Hull's list of those values echoes and expands the formula Amy Norton devises in *Heat Lightning*: a 'secret and devouring hunger for what we once called things of the spirit, an inner dignity, self-respect, fearlessness, tolerance, warm friendliness, a discipline of the self which holds it to standards of inner approval.' Decrying the tendency among contemporary novelists to choose protagonists at the extremes of 'degeneracy or genius', she argued that we underestimate the value of ordinary people, such as pharmacists or housewives, by calling them commonplace or average. On the contrary, she said, 'there is nothing commonplace about them' as they work better to understand themselves and others through their everyday struggles. It is, she concluded, 'individuals who have the capacity for feeling and for understanding' who are 'the most significant and the most potent for the future.'

Patricia McClelland Miller
Willimantic, Connecticut, 2012

xv

PRINCIPAL CHARACTERS

✳✳✳✳✳✳✳✳

Amy, née Westover, married to Geoffrey Norton

Alfred and Catherine Westover, Amy's parents

Madam Westover, Amy's grandmother

Mary, Amy's sister, married to Henry

Lora, Amy's aunt, formerly married to Tom (Senior)

Tom and Harriet, Lora's unmarried children

Laurance, Lora's other son, married to Emma, née Miller

Dewitt Westover, Amy's uncle, married to Isabelle, father to Sophie and Carruthers

Theodore (Ted), Amy's brother, married to Felice

Lulu, maid to Alfred and Catherine Westover

Curly, a member of Madam Westover's household

Lavinia, Madam Westover's housekeeper

Charley Johnson, Madam Westover's former chauffeur

HEAT LIGHTNING

Book One

NOW that she was back in the town of her childhood, standing on a corner across from the village triangle of green, a small pyramid of luggage at her feet, Amy's one clear thought, over the fluttering of unimportant recognitions, was, "Why on earth have I come?" The interurban bus which had deposited her along with the bags at the curb had already bumped its noisy elephantine way out of sight up the slight incline of the main street. She had forgotten, during all the years when her only visit home had been in winter, how summer felt in this middle western land, spread smoothly over town and country, tucked in at the horizon inescapably. Her coming had been a kind of flight, and like all flight, what she had run from had been far clearer than her goal.

Some one might have met her in the city, just one Westover out of the dozens this town held. Now she had not even a waiting room where she could leave the bags. Nothing but the pop corn stand in front of the Italian's. She couldn't carry them the blocks to the house, with heat wavering, full of unsteady motes, above the pale stone walks. The bags dragged at her consciousness, her thoughts bending under their weight, struggling through sunlight to the cross street where her father's house stood. But this was absurd of her. She could telephone. A little caustic in tone, she should be. Do you realize you have a daughter, or a sister, or a cousin, stranded on the corner? She scuffed the pyramid under the pop corn stand, and walked into the small shop.

It was dark after the street, and rich with fruit odors; in the gloom the banked fruit under pink netting gleamed like a strange aquarium, with globed sea creatures. Perhaps her head was swimming, fatigue-dizzy. From a room at the rear came a woman, like the fruit, with globed breasts and round, vivid face, gold rings swinging from her ears. Yes, the lady could use the telephone. There, beyond the bananas. The number leaped usefully to Amy's lips from a neglected corner of her mind, and she waited for a voice, the thick smell of ripe bananas pressing into her nostrils. Behind her sounded a scuff of small feet, a sh! a slap. The voice was strange, breathy,—a new maid. No, Mis' Westover wasn't home, Mister Westover, he wasn't home, nobody was home. To Amy's sharp, "Who are you?" a giggle answered, and, "Me? I'm Lulu," as if that should be apparent. "Mister Westover, he's to work, and Mis' Westover, she's to the other house, they got a new baby last night."

Amy turned. The woman, children clinging to her knees, burst into amiable volubility. "You are Mis' Westover's girl from New York, yes? I know. I see you Christmas time. Me, I come from New York." Strong teeth flashed in her smile.

"Could I leave my bags here, and send some one for them later?"

"Sure. My Joe could bring them. He got car."

"If it wouldn't be too much trouble."

[4]

Heat Lightning

"No troub'. We live close by your ma, same street, yes."

Amy remembered her mother's— "And an awful bunch of dirty foreigners have moved into that old Cole place, dozens of them."

"I'll walk along, then, if you'll send the bags."

Amy stood a moment at the corner. The single traffic light showed red, and a Ford chugged, waiting while nothing passed. Like a spell, an amusing spell cast over the almost deserted summer morning. A new red front grocery store on the opposite corner, and a chain drug store next, the windows a dusty replica of windows she had passed yesterday in Grand Central.

Her sister Mary's baby was ahead of time. Well, that arrival would overshadow her own. What had possessed her to come? The heat curled up about her ankles, pressed a straw odor out of the shantung silk across her shoulders. Even the drug store windows were a duplicate of the city. Traffic lights regulated automatically for all of life. This place would have no virtue for her, no wisdom for her need. There was the movie house her grandmother had built, and how the family had pounded against it! The Westover Block cut in stone over the entrance, garish posters on the boards beside the door. LAWRENCE TIBBETS IN "THE ROGUE SONG." Radios in the window of the furniture store, and a set of porch furniture with striped awning cushions and a sun umbrella, quite in the Long Island manner. Everything was a duplication of everywhere else. A sentimental whim had blown her hither. They would all wonder why she had come, where her husband, Geoffrey, was,— and the joke was that she didn't know the answer. She might say that she felt too rocky, after that slight operation, to go back to work, and the doctor advised a change, and she thought she'd like to see them all.

Here was the block. Her heart quickened, and her skin felt cold, at a subtle inner process of emotional absorption. Two great elms, the gray walk between them straight to the door of the square red brick house of her grandmother, old Madam Westover. The green shutters at the long front windows were caught under the ivy, the ivy lay over the face of the house like a shadow fastened there from the elms, under the roof the small windows of the third story squinted down, just as they had on her childhood. The lawns were a serer velvet than she remembered, from the drought. A row of privet marked the boundary, and next with maples in front stood her father's house, freshly painted so that the gray of the mansard roof gleamed silver in the sun, and the white of the lower stories slipped under her eyes, too white. Behind it was the green of willows, where the land dropped toward the small brook. Just across the brook, invisible from here, lived the Italians.

Probably her grandmother would be in, tapping briskly about the house with her silver-knobbed stick, supervising Lavinia. Amy walked slowly past, sniffing at a faint aroma,—what was it?—hot vinegar and spices. Pickles, of course. They always made pickles on a hot August morning. She didn't feel equal yet to the opening bombardment of questions which would compose Grandmother Westover's greeting, a rapid inquisition intended to bring matters up to date without delay. A man knelt beside a flower bed, green grass shears biting at the turf edge. He laid his palms flat on the earth and stared at her, a squat gargoyle in faded denim. Curly, his unwinking eyes blue even at that distance. Amy waved at him, but he did not move. She went hastily toward the next house, as if she were a little girl again, trying to hide her uneasiness about Curly under a dignified retreat. She could even hear her mother: "Why do you keep him around, Mamma? He's not good for the children." And her grandmother's, "Pfaugh! He's better for them than most folks. Curly is a good man." The children had made a mystery of his bent figure, his sun-bleached thistle-head, the strange noises instead of speech in his throat. Nobody knew where he came from, nor why Madam Westover kept him. There were stories— As Amy climbed the steps to her father's house, she thought: I might never have been away, coming back in the summer. I don't feel this way in winter, because I've come often, as I grew older. I have no grown-up summer self here to slip into.

"Hi, there, Amy!" The voice shrieked above the squawk of brakes, and she turned. Young Cousin Tom, flinging long legs out of the roadster, charging up the path with her bags, was at least no part of her youth. "I say, it's a rotten shame I missed you." He dropped the bags beside her on the veranda. "Rotten day for the bus. You must be sore, that kind of welcome." He extricated a tattered pack of cigarettes from a pocket, flicked a match with thumb nail, and puffed. "I'd a'made it, too, if that traffic cop hadn't butted in."

Amy shook hands with him. He looked more like his father each time she saw him; a hint of swagger in his gait and posture, now his shoulders had broadened to match his adolescent height; a kind of conscious maleness in his dark, heavy-lidded eyes, set not quite symmetrically in his long face. It would be queer to divorce your husband, as her aunt Lora had done, and then find him in your son. You couldn't divorce a son. He just was your son. Perhaps that was as true of a husband; hadn't you carried him beneath your heart as irrevocably as any child? But she wouldn't let Geoffrey in, not yet. "How is Lora?" she asked, and, "Did you drive in for me and miss me?"

"Oh, Mother's barging around as ever. Sure, I drove in. Your mother called me this morning. I'd just about got to bed, too. She was in a state. Mary was going to the hospital to-day, and she didn't wait. Or the kid didn't." He grinned up at Amy. "So every one was frantic, and would I drive in to meet you. First I had a flat, and then I had a traffic cop. I told him my cousin was having a baby, and he said not in my car, was she, and after some more wise cracks I got off without a ticket. So I hustled down here." He tossed away the half-burned cigarette. "I'll tote the bags up to your room, what?" He banged on the latched screen door, and from the rear of the house came the voice of the telephone, a "Ye-us? I'm com-in'," and then the maid herself, wiping red hands on her apron.

"Oh, Lulu, this is Mrs. Morton, Mrs. Westover's daughter." Tom pushed through the door, and the girl's blue eyes met Amy's an instant before they hurried back to the boy. "You got her room ready?" He rushed up the stairs.

"Mis' Westover, she say to tell you she be back quick."

"Thank you." Amy glanced in at the living room, unfamiliar in its dress of striped linen covers and hangings. "I'll have time for a bath before luncheon." She climbed the stairs, to meet Tom clattering down.

"Thanks for your trouble, Tom."

[8]

Heat Lightning

" 'Sall right. Sorry I missed you. See you later. Gotta date."

As she reached the hallway above she thought she heard the sibilance of a whisper and a hasty movement. But Tom was out of the door as she glanced downward. That girl had stared at him. She was pretty, with her soft, bland throat and wide face, but surely— Amy shrugged. She needn't think the boy was exactly like his father, for all the resemblance. Lulu watched at the door until the car moved away. Then, with a fearful glance up the stairs, as if she just remembered Amy's presence, she scuttled back to the kitchen. Amy, pulling off her silk coat as she walked along to the door of her old room, thought irritably about Lora, her father's sister, Tom's mother. She was so confoundedly ineffectual and fluttering, maintaining an ingenuous, tearful amazement when anything went contrary to her own schemes. She expected her picture of herself as a charming, helpless little woman to meet all difficulties. She would never in the world have come to a divorce if Grandmother Westover hadn't bullied her to it.

Then Amy dismissed that family and revolved slowly within the walls of her own room, exposing herself deliberately to impact of the past. Good of her mother to leave things so exactly as they had been, painted furniture, rugs, chintz at the windows, even to the old toilet set of amber stuff she had discarded when she went away. The windows looked out over the rear yard, with familiar disks of red and green in the apple trees, with denser green of willows beyond. Perhaps when she had bathed and dressed she'd feel less exposed. She had a quick vision of her sister Mary, caught in child birth, and with it a kind of tearing at the fabric of herself, as if for once it stretched painfully to include the selves of others,—all these other Westovers, going on living, each of them, as completely, as engrossedly from second to second as she did.

Each of them was as unaware of her own intense self, moving among her own experiences, as for the most part she was unaware of them, and her arrival wouldn't touch their lives more than the brush of a moth against a screen outside a lighted room. Amy dragged off her hat and pushed her fine dark hair up from a sticky forehead. She'd better hurry with that bath, or some one would be coming in. As she stripped off her few clothes, her thoughts ran on in desultory conversation with herself. You aren't a person to relatives. They all know too much about you, and too little. Tom didn't even see you, for all you think you're not so bad to look at. The mirror returned a white body, too thin, too tense, head with dark fluff of hair strained forward so that the cords of the slender throat made a shadow beneath the foreshortened lower face, and the dark eyes gave back an anxious stare. She probably looked an old woman to Tom's young masculine eyes. She wasn't old. Thirty-five might be, technically, from the Bible point of view of three score and ten, middle age, but middle age certainly sounded older than she felt even at her rockiest. Tom just had a concept of cousin, female, old; he didn't see her. No relatives saw you; they all had concepts. Well, didn't she have them all lined up?

She pulled a gay silk coolie coat from one of the bags, felt for a moment an illusion of coolness at the touch of silk folds against warm skin, scuffed her feet into brocade mules, and went down the hall to the bathroom. As she walked, she had a swift, wordless realization: she could put away her present life here, for nothing contained it, neither place nor people nor people's thoughts of her. The escape she sought lay in that very absence of provoking associations, and her stretching out to include these others was a part of escape from her troubling self. Suddenly she laughed, as the bathroom opened like a green cave to enclose her, water lilies dangling along the border. She remembered her mother's letter: "I've had the bathrooms redecorated, and your father hates them. He says some things (guess what!) ought not to be painted a color."

Later Amy inspected her mirrored self again. Well, that was better. She fastened a scarlet belt about the white silk frock, and brushed dark hair back from her forehead. It lay sleek for a moment and then eased forward in waves. She sighed. In strong light that cowlick over her left temple looked quite gray. What did it matter? If she were twenty, she'd have to let her hair grow and cultivate a small waistline. A touch of lipstick, just to confirm the opinion of some of the relatives that she led a wild life in New York. Perhaps the red heels on her sandals would aid that opinion.

As she started languidly down the stairs she heard her mother's voice somewhere in the house. She stopped, listening. It was strange, when a voice so held the essential quality of a person, that you couldn't recall it, like a detail of face or movement. You could think around it, but you couldn't hear it. At the sound, the words indistinguishable, low, full, a hint of overtone, Amy felt, in a sharply isolated moment, the double quality of her relationship to her mother. Part of her swung, warm, hurrying, submissive, child-Amy, rushing toward her. Part of her retreated, alert, alarmed, erecting barriers against submergence.

"Amy dear, where are you?"

"Hello!" Amy ran down the stairs for her mother's cool, unhurried greeting, a kiss, and firm hands on her shoulders, holding her a moment. Her mother was like her voice, a well made instrument with depth and resonance. Geoffrey had given her a phrase: "You're alike, you and your mother, only written in different keys. She's pitched lower, with *andante, legato,* as indications. You're staccato with variations."

"Did Tom meet you? I am so sorry. I would have wired, but your train had left." At Amy's, "It didn't matter, really," her mother frowned. "That boy! I knew it was another of his mornings after. Well, come in here." She led Amy into the darkened living room and drew her down on the wide divan. "You're thin."

"Just tired. Having tonsils out is a bore, at my age."

"When you were a baby, they weren't snipping things out as they do now."

"But what about Mary?"

"Isn't it just like Mary?" Mrs. Westover smiled, and settled more comfortably in her corner. She pulled off her white hat, and Amy looked with affection at the hair drawn back from smooth forehead behind small ears into a knot at the nape of the neck, from which little resilient gray curls escaped. Her mother had worn her hair just that way forever. "Here she had a room engaged, at the hospital, and nurses and doctors, and to-day we were to drive her in. She was quite indignant when I asked if she was sure about the date this time. And then last night when she was taking a bath—" Mrs. Westover lifted her hands in a tolerant, amused gesture. "Poor Henry lost his head—you know how he is—I suppose he was afraid the baby would arrive before any one else got there. Dr. James said it was too late to drive her into town. But the nurse came out, and after all the baby wasn't delivered until eight this morning. Another girl. Imagine, not a thing ready. That's the trouble with planning on a hospital."

"I suppose you've been up all night, and you look fresh as a daisy. Is Mary all right?"

"Seems to be. She thought she was dying, but the doctor says she's fine. Henry—well, he seems normal until there is some strain, and then he flies apart. He'd be pitiable if he weren't such a nuisance. Of course Mary knows how to handle him, but she wasn't thinking about him last night. The war is certainly long enough ago so his nerves have had plenty of time to get over it. Why, most of us have forgotten there was any war."

"No doubt all the cripples remember."

"That's just it. He's perfectly well. You wouldn't be so tolerant about him if you lived in the same town. Although I must say Mary is wonderful. But there's no use our starting that old argument." Her smile at Amy was so sly and humorous that Amy laughed.

"I suppose I never forget that first meeting, when Geof and I went over to Hoboken. Henry crawling up that gangplank— But that is a long time ago." What she did remember was Geoffrey's comment, one of the remarks he tossed aside, casually, not caring how much it meant, and Amy picked up, dusted off, stowed away, and looked in at occasionally with reflective wonder. "The trouble with those men," he had said, "is that they've had a dose of concentrated essence of life. Most of us get small doses, administered at intervals, until we develop some immunity to the horror, the futility, the cruelty at the bottom of

this sweet world. Like Mithridates—he died old."
And at Amy's protest, he had added, "We couldn't
any of us endure an instant, if we knew everything in
a gulp." But her mother was talking, asking about
Geoffrey. "Oh, he's fine. He's gone fishing in Canada
somewhere. The children are in camp. I don't mind
your being busy, if you just let me loaf around a week
or so."

"I just meant I should have wired you to wait a
few days. It's nice to see you. Did you stop at
Mother's? You better run over before lunch, then.
Tell her I took Mary's children out to the farm.
Emma never minds a few more." Mrs. Westover
rose, glancing at her wristwatch. "Your father will be
in for lunch at one. Whatever you do, don't ask
him how business is."

Amy walked with her mother to the door, enjoying
the quiet, easy movement of the older woman, the
straight, alert carriage of the small head. In the
bright sun of the doorway she saw a faint network of
fatigue lines at the corners of the dark eyes, from
nostrils past the curved mouth, like cobweb spread
over the smooth, clear skin. "You better take a nap
till lunch time," she said, kissing her.

Amy crossed through a gap in the hedge to her
grandmother's house, the sun laying metallic fingers at
the roots of her hair. The long hall was warm and
redolent of pickling, heavy clove and allspice, the
thin, permeating odor of heated vinegar. She went
back to the kitchen. It was empty, the range shining
black, but in the summer kitchen beyond, Lavinia,
smaller and more dried than ever, was scrambling
dishes into a pan at the sink. She jumped around at
Amy's voice, and her face, the color and texture of a
peanut shell, creased into pleased wrinkles. "Why,

it's Amy! I declare!" She darted at her, clutched her hand in a damp claw. "We been looking for you. Your grandma's sitting on the side porch, peeling peaches. We thought we'd fix some of her spiced peach conserve while we was at it."

"You look smart and well." Amy pointed at the stone crocks ranged on the table. "You've done all that this morning, in this heat?"

"Good canning weather, I always say. Takes a warm spell to do good canning."

"This is hot enough to cook without any stove, I should think."

"Humph, this isn't so hot." Lavinia darted at her sink again, with brittle celerity, and Amy strolled through the dining room, its heavy oak furniture bulking ponderous, the same silver caster sets on the sideboard, the same linen centerpiece with crocheted edge on the table. A door opened to the side porch, with the remembered screen of morning glories, the fragile trumpets drooping in the noon sun. Grandmother Westover was there, her knees wide to hold the pan into which peelings dropped from her dexterous knife. Her bright dark eyes gleamed up at Amy from deep sockets, and her smile was a peremptory flash between her proud hooked nose and her square projecting chin. "I thought you'd forgotten you had a grandmother. Come here and kiss me. I'm too much a mess of peach to touch you. They're ripe. Too ripe." Amy bent over her and kissed the firm, dry mouth.

"I was so dirty I had to clean up a little first." She sat down on a small wooden chair beside her grandmother, and with an automatic reversion to her youth, said, "Do you want me to help you?"

"No use your getting all juice too. I'm getting along." The silver knife flashed swiftly, while her old eyes inspected this granddaughter. Her skin was like unpolished ivory, stretched snug over the high forehead bones, over the long line of jaw. She didn't look thin, thought Amy, so much as properly old, as if her age had dispensed with flesh, leaving the hard bones, beautifully shaped, close against the skin. Her hands were the same, quick, lean, with veins very blue over the knuckles. "You look peaked," she said, and her voice was a powdery vibration without resonance. "What you been doing to yourself? Where's that husband of yours? You run away from him and your children, eh?"

"I'm all right. Not so smart as you are, working this kind of weather. Yes, I ran away, alone."

"How's Mary? Your mother might have stopped in here. Another girl, I expect." At Amy's nod, "When they had four already, and can't make ends meet. Well, it's their lookup, not mine. Here," she dropped the peach into the white enamel kettle at her feet, "you take that out to Lavinia and tell her I want the other basket of peaches."

Amy, moving briskly on the errand, reflected in amusement that her grandmother kept her flavor. I'm not really afraid of her, now, but I might be. She doesn't really like any of us. She likes Lora's children. Perhaps a mother never cares too much for her son's family. They're farther away, the distance of another woman. The summer kitchen was empty, and in the space against the dim ochre of unpainted wood the odor of simmering vinegar took shape, thin spirals shining and pointed. Amy heard Lavinia's dry voice outside the shed. "You, Curly! You know what Mis' Westover told you. Don't go throwing stones at them Eyetalians. I don't care if they did. You stop it." Did Lavinia really know what Curly's queer sounds meant? His jerking arms conveyed quick wrath. Amy looked about for the basket of peaches, and Lavinia pattered in. "They make him awful mad, those kids." She shook her head, gray hair flying. "Teasing him and calling him names. But he might hurt one of 'em, and your grandma says they got to live, even if they are a pest. They mock at him, making noises in their throats."

"I thought Curly liked children."

"Just his own folks. He likes them. He's too smart to stand being made a mock of. What you want? You tell your grandma I don't need no more peaches this morning. I got just enough syrup for these."

Amy delivered the message to her grandmother, who sat, fists on her knees, the knife gleaming in readiness.

"Humph. Might as well do them all to-day." She dropped the knife into the pan at her side. "If Laviny won't, she's set. What she hollering about?"

"I judge Curly was repelling an Italian invasion." Amy thrust a forefinger into the silken crumple of a morning glory blossom.

"Curly doesn't approve of immigration." Madam Westover made the small clucking noise against her upper plate with which she always pointed a joke. "No more do I. Too many foreigners. Too many right in our own family. Sit down, child. You can't stay here for lunch. We don't eat when we preserve. Where are Mary's ewe lambs?"

"Mother said—what did she say?"

"Emma's, no doubt. Yes, I thought so. They'll tear all over the farm and eat green apples and chase chickens and when Mary gets them back she'll complain because their manners have been ruined. They all take advantage of Emma, and Laurance doesn't like it much."

"How many children has Emma?"

"My Heavens, Amy, don't you remember your own family affairs?" Madam Westover stared at her, her long eyelids folding back. "Two, of course. Little Emmary, the one they named for me, looks like a German haus-frau, all pink and yellow and round. They're nice children, and the farm is doing well."

"Queer to think of Laurance as a farmer. He was so elegant."

"Elegantly nothing, he was. I tell Lora she's a fool, sighing about her poor dear boy. Emma's had her own mother visiting her most of the summer, and Lora keeps away." Madam Westover's eyes glinted with malice. "I tell you, the old lady must have given Lora a piece of her mind."

Vague images floated in Amy's mind as her grandmother talked. Emma's mother, Mrs. Miller, firm-busted, tight-corseted, a faded switch pinned like a pancake on top of her round head, features tight, hard, high-colored. She spent her year visiting around among her three married daughters. And Lora, Laurance's mother, drifting about in melancholy curves, as if her bones were too soft. Not much like Grandmother Westover. They would make a queer combination.

"They eat breakfast in the kitchen, with oil-cloth on the table, and when Lora cried about that, Mrs. Miller told her such things had made a man of Laurance, and she'd best look out for a good girl to do the same for Tom. Lora'll never forgive her that remark, the more so that she is worried about young Tom."

"I saw him this morning. He looks like his father, doesn't he?"

"Pfau! Not at all. Not a shred of likeness." Madam Westover scuffed her soft shoes angrily. "He's every inch a Westover. What are you talking about?"

Amy smiled slyly. Of course. Grandmother hated Tom Blake, Senior. She'd driven him out of town. But young Tom was her grandson.

"Don't you believe what they say about Tom." The tracery of veins over the finely modeled temples grew more prominent. "They're jealous of him. He's a handsome young fellow, full of life. Half of the family have forgottten how it feels to live. I haven't. I tell you Tom's all right."

"I haven't heard a thing, darling. I just came." Amy laid her hand a moment on the impatient fist her grandmother beat against her knee. She liked the brief contact; in the firm structure under the dry skin lay a hint of the essence of the woman. "You're a grand old thing," she said, knowing as she spoke that after a few days in town she couldn't make a personal remark to her grandmother. She would be drawn back into a more habitual family relationship, in which she might even cease to think personal remarks. She was still free of that old pattern, having so recently come.

"Stuff and nonsense!" said Madam Westover, but her hand relaxed. "There's your father. I hear his car. You better run along. He pretends to be in a terrible hurry at noon, although the factory's quiet as a nut. If you didn't paint your lips, you wouldn't look so white, I should think. Tell your mother I want to hear about Mary." She clambered stiffly to her feet, extending a hand for her cane. Amy brushed a finger tip against the smooth silver knob, and placed it in the outstretched hand. The engraving had worn almost invisible; for a moment the silver had felt cool. "This dampness makes my knee stiff," grumbled her grandmother, getting slowly into action. "You haven't told me a word about Geoffrey."

It isn't damp, thought Amy. The poor darling hates being stiff—she seemed much older as she moved. "I'll be over again soon," she said.

"I must see what Lavinia's up to." Her grandmother turned toward the kitchen, and Amy went languidly through the midday sunlight to her father's house, wondering what Madam Westover would say about Geoffrey— She liked him. She appreciated men when they were tall and clever and gallant. She'd no doubt say, "Don't be a fool, Amy. He's full of life." Amy shivered in the heat, and her red heels tapped a staccato irritation across the veranda and into the hall.

"Well, well, Amy!" Her father's crisp mustache brushed her cheek. "This is fine, having you here in the summer. I'd just started to call you. Lunch is ready. Business men have to eat and run, you know."

Luncheon in the quiet dining room, the green chintz curtains drawn a little against the outdoor light, sweet peas spraying in a crystal bowl, iced tea in black-footed amber glasses,—it was all very pleasant. Amy's glance strayed along the plate rail for familiar bits of china and silver. The pewter things were new. Pewter hadn't been in when she was a child. Her mother, in a fresh white frock, presided with tranquil alertness. She had an easy competence, thought Amy; she could train a maid like this rather sullen Lulu, and she knew when to have pewter and colored glass. Her father talked little; he offered a few questions,— how was Geoffrey, and the children, were they well?

Heat Lightning

Was it hot in New York? Could she stay long? Amy felt that his attention to her answers was perfunctory, not because he was so absorbed in his own thoughts as that his imagination didn't include a clear enough picture of her life outside his house to make details matter in the least. But that's as true of me, she thought, in hasty apology. I don't know anything, really, about him. She looked more sharply at him. He was a sandy Westover, and he looked as she always remembered him, slightly florid with bushy light eyebrows and stiff lashes, with scanty fair hair,—or was it gray, now? Perhaps his cheeks sagged a little, and that trick of pulling one side of his lower lip between his teeth was a new one. He looked,—well, nice. That blue shirt and darker blue tie, with the gray suit, looked smart. "I should think you'd take off your coat, weather like this," she said.

"If you begin to try to keep cool, you feel all the warmer." He poured cream over sliced peaches with an air of wisdom. "I pay no attention to the temperature."

"You're marvelous, then." Amy laughed. "The train last night was an inferno. Too bad Dante didn't know about sleepers in August."

"Why don't you take a nap this afternoon, and to-night, when it's cooler—even your father notices that! —we'll drive around and see folks." Mrs. Westover folded her napkin. "You are tired. You ate almost nothing. I must run over to Mother's. She will wish to hear all about Mary. Then I'm going back to Mary's. As long as you can't see her yet—"

"I must say I think Mary was most inconsiderate, putting all this extra burden on you," began Alfred, his bushy eyebrows pulling together.

"Now, Father! Mary couldn't help it. I don't

mind, it's all come off so well. Must you go back to the factory at once?"

"Yes, I must. Even if—" He stopped, looked across at his wife, and then pushed back his chair. "You take it easy, then, Amy, and to-night I'll drive you wherever you want to go. We haven't seen your brother this week. Might run over there." He bent over his wife a moment, kissing her forehead. "So long." He left them, the important masterful air of a busy man in the stiff angle of head and shoulders.

Amy looked at her mother, whose fingers moved idly along the edge of the green linen plate doily, eyelids down.

"Is he awfully worried?" she asked.

Catherine Westover looked up, her dark eyes thoughtful. "When things are rather bad, he has to pretend to be very busy, you see. I don't know how much he convinces himself. Now you have a good rest. I'll be home again before dinner."

2.

Amy lay motionless on her bed, her head turned against the pillow. If she could sleep! Never, until the last few months, had she thought about sleep. It had been an easy part of life, like breathing. Of late she had learned that it was a mystery, that it was a tricky, elusive, longed-for unconsciousness, a delicate fabric she had grown too clumsy to weave for her own wearing. She knew how it came, rising about her like mist, with tiny fragmentary images along the margin of its approach. If she could lie motionless, her inward gaze relaxed, not fastening upon any single hint of image, then sleep would flow into her and about her, black, silent, warm. But if from those marginal images one lingered, enlarged, gained substance, so that she grew tense in her effort to lie without moving, without looking at one thing, then too often she had lost the spell. Thought would begin again, holding the image fixed as its starting point. She had lost the trick of letting it drift past her, and once any of the random images was fixed, even for a moment, the lovely, engulfing movement of sleep was broken. Always thought dragged her back to Geoffrey, and feverish confusion.

To-day, in this room where nothing outside herself evoked any Geoffrey association, with intense fatigue dulling every sense, she dropped at once into sleep. The sound of crickets in the dry and breathless August afternoon rose dimly like remote hylas of some forgotten spring.

Much later the dropping sun came under the lowered shade, caught in a mirror and spread crimson over Amy. It woke her, and she stared an instant, startled, at the queer light. It's a cruel color, she thought, a Waste-Land color, all barren drought and heat. She held her hand into the light, watching the color dye transparent crescents between her fingers, run like a gilded serpent along her thin wedding ring. That was a trick of Geoffrey's. "See how easy you are to see through!" She sat up, her head heavy with sleep, and her bare feet fumbled along the rug for her mules. "Go away, Geof. You can't come in," she said, standing up and shaking her silk coolie coat loose from her heat-moist body. "You don't even know where I am, and you know you don't give a damn. Let me alone, you!" A cold bath, and then a note to the children. The house had not a sound in it. Her mother must still be at Mary's.

Heat Lightning

As Amy let herself down into cold water, she wished she could escape a visit to Mary. The house would smell of antiseptics and talcum powder, it would have the sounds of a nurse's rustle and quick step, of the thin, intermittent rhythmic wail in which a new-born child protests against its emergence from the dark warmth of the womb. Mary herself would look up with smug exhaustion. Amy stretched flat in the tub, head cocked a little. If she sank, as she'd like to, her hair would be a mess. Funny how hard Mary worked at feeling superior to her. As a fat litttle younger sister, she had tagged after Amy, an admiring nuisance. They had shared a room until Amy went away to college. When she came back, the next summer, she found a new Mary, bristling with critical hostility. "Don't mind her," their mother had said, at Amy's distress. "She's just feeling her age. She'll get over it." But Mary never had swung back to any middle ground. The assertion of her own personality continued to demand a divergence from Amy equal to her former adoration. She found Geof too clever, she was sure Amy neglected her children. Oh, well. Poor Mary. Amy stood up, dripping delightfully, and reached for a towel. She'd been only eighteen when she married Henry, she'd had her first baby before Henry came back from that awful winter at Archangel, and since then— No wonder she did herself up in smugness. Amy dried herself slowly. Those green walls and the drooping water lilies did look cool. I've had lots more than Mary. Oh, have you! her mind jeered back. Mary's got a kind of safety. Who wants that? I'm not going to argue with myself this hot afternoon, cried Amy, and the jeering voice of the under part of her mind subsided.

When she had dressed, she took her writing case

from one of the bags, and propped on the dressing table the leather folder with its photographs of Geoffrey and the children. She'd like to take out Geoffrey, so he wouldn't look at her with that lean half grin. It was an enlargement of a snapshot she had taken one day at the shore— She hung a handkerchief over that side of the folder. Removing the picture would expose her to troubled inquiry in her mother's face. No use starting that.

Buff and Bobs. She paused, thinking of each of them in camp. Would they mind her not coming to see them this next weekend? Buff had told her solemnly, "You mustn't come too often, the councilor says, for it disturbs the atmosphere if parents hang around." She did hope Bobs was happy. Little, skinny brown boy. Camp was supposed to be good for him just because he didn't get on easily with other boys. His first time. Buff loved it. Silly name. Bobs had made it out of his early attempt to say Elizabeth,—Elizabuff. She wrote a note to each child. When she had finished she sat there, her pen scratching idly on a fresh sheet of paper. Letters were unsatisfactory. You couldn't see the need of your reader at the moment the letter came, as you could when you talked. When she wrote to Geoffrey, she labeled the letter. Early morning note. Not to be read until you are through with the day's work. Keep this one till you know you miss me. But she wouldn't write to Geoffrey. Not yet.

She thought about the children and their father. Buff was volatile, articulate, loving Geof in an easy, untroubled way for which she found countless expressions. Bobs was difficult. Much too sensitive under Geoffrey's impatient moods, too resentful of his sarcasms. Oh—she flung down her pen and dug her fingers into her hair, her palms hard against her cheek-bones. She couldn't straighten herself out with regard to Geoffrey, not alone and clear. Not that any one believed nowadays in sacrificing personal happiness even to children. All those dangerous scars left. What did any one believe in? Wasn't that the horrible empty chasm to the edge of which your feet carried you no matter where you started?

At a knock on the door Amy sat up hastily, and hunted for stamps for the letters. "Oh, Mother! Come in."

"I thought I heard you. Did you have a good rest?" Mrs. Westover sagged against the door, dark circles under her eyes. "Your Aunt Lora is here." She smiled at Amy's grimace. "I asked her to stay for dinner. She's in a state because Harriet's got a new affinity."

"Female, of course?" Amy grinned. "My cousin Harriet's awfully modern, isn't she?"

"Harriet's an awful fool for a woman of thirty, I think. But if Lora would let her alone—"

"Lora can't possibly let her children alone. She isn't wise, like my mother." Amy crossed quickly to her mother, tucking a hand under the relaxed arm. "What you been doing now, to get that very tired look."

"Lora hasn't as nice children as I've got." Mrs. Westover enclosed Amy's fingers in her warm hand. "I've just come from Mary's. Oh, she's quite all right, and so's the baby. But there seemed to be all sorts of odd jobs. You know how a hired girl and a nurse always get on! Come on, now, or Lora'll be sure we're talking about her. Are those new photographs, or did you have them here Christmas?"

Amy's hand darted out to shake the handkerchief

from the folder. "They are new, I think. Enlargements of some snaps we took in May, one weekend." She held herself stiff against betrayal under her mother's interest. "Buff's grown. Bobs hasn't, much. Geof not at all." She laughed, returning the folder to the dressing table. "Now let's go." Was she too casual? "It's an experiment, sending Bobs to camp. He didn't say much, as usual, but I know he hated it in advance. They have this wonderful schedule, all sorts of outdoor things, and he'll have to do them with other boys. He rides and swims so well: that gave him some confidence." Together they walked slowly down the stairs. "They—I mean child specialists and all—make such a point nowadays of social adjustments. Children ought to grow up better than their parents, don't you think?"

"Parents always have counted on that. You don't do what you meant to, yourself, but you think, 'Oh, well, my children will go on from here.'"

"Um. Sort of lets us out." Amy tugged at her mother's arm. "Does it ever really let you out? Wait a minute." They stood at the foot of the stairs, and Amy saw her mother's gaze press down on hers with intentness. Her pulse quickened in recognition that a casual word had dropped far beneath surface communication, into a secret and real current of the older woman's life. "I mean—(ah, a delicate finger on a dial, not to lose that rare and distant wavelength—) it doesn't really let you off an instant, what I am, or any of us, from yourself, your own urgencies—" Her mother heard her, the intent and darkening eyes an evidence of the precision with which the question fitted into her own feeling. "Oh, damn!" Amy flung her hand aside, as Lora swooped upon them, a flutter of silk and little ejaculations.

Heat Lightning

Amy listened and replied with the brittle gayety her Aunt Lora inevitably produced in her, and meanwhile her thought brooded over that lost moment. You couldn't make that kind of moment. It came, and you spoke, you heard a naked and real word. Lora had ruined the moment, barging in like that—like so much static. Her mother betrayed herself so rarely; she offered you the quiet decorum of her visible hours. "I almost learned something," thought Amy, "about both of us." She turned at Lora's sharp, "Amy, I asked you if you didn't think Tom's looking well? He was really very busy to-day, but he laid it all aside to drive in to meet you."

"Yes," said Amy, "only he didn't—" She stopped, at her mother's tilted eyebrow. "Yes, he's looking very fit." Funny, how every one protected every one from Lora's knowing anything! Even Tom's failure to meet her. And why did Lora always wear too many bangles? Two strings of beads and ear-rings with that figured silk. Her narrow, pale face had a rapacious mournfulness, and her white fingers with heavy rings lingered automatically over the methodical waves of her hair. She certainly touched it up: purple in the high lights.

"He's been working frightfully hard at summer school. Of course it was a shame he had work to make up, but some of the courses are just unreasonable, and he does want to finish this next year. He realizes how heartbroken I was that Laurance's career was ruined."

"I hear Laurance is doing very well." Try as she might, Amy had to bait Lora a little.

"But when I think what he might have been! But with the war, and then the marriage—" Lora's gesture indicated complete destruction. "Wait till your boy grows up and you'll understand better. Where are your children?"

"In camp." No use rising to that implied accusation, that something must be wrong behind this midsummer appearance. "Geoffrey's fishing in Canada."

"I notice many men fish in Canada now, although they say the regulations make it hard to drink too much. You'd think there wouldn't be a drop left they run so much of it across the river. But most of it's cut, of course."

Amy let her head drop back against the high back of her chair, and crossed her ankles, displaying the red heels. Lora stared at them, her short-sighted frown adding a line to her face. Suddenly Amy's irritation dissolved in a kind of pity without tenderness for the woman. Lora had to run on because she was such a mess inside. Tom drank, and Lora prattled about bootlegging. Laurance had escaped her, and she lamented his ruin. And Harriet—her one daughter—they hadn't come to Harriet yet. Lora was all loose ends; her bright strings of colored stones, her ear-rings were a symbol. Walk past a counter with trays of loose beads at a five and ten cent store, and you had Lora. Her string had broken when she failed with Tom Senior.

"I was telling Catherine I wished you would talk to Harriet. She'll be home later this week. She might listen to you. She thinks they do things better in New York."

"What about?" Amy dangled her black enameled vanity case by its chain.

"Harriet doesn't understand. She ought to get married. Instead she falls into the clutches of some unscrupulous woman, older—I don't mean—" Lora sat up straight and with a long breath plunged into terrific boldness— "I don't mean quite the 'Captive,' you know." Oh, yes, her smile said, you see we do keep up with things out here. "But it takes all her attention, and makes her almost queer."

"I doubt if Harriet would listen to anything I might say." It was certainly time for lipstick. Amy pursed her lips into the small mirror. "I don't—" her words twisted out, amusingly—"care about interfering."

"It's scarcely interfering to speak to a person, is it?" Lora trembled, her beads falling from her hand with a rattle. "I heard they weren't using so much make-up now, nice women."

Amy moistened a finger tip and smoothed one eyebrow. Over her mirror she caught her mother's warning. Poor Mother, she put up with Lora the whole year round!

"I hadn't heard that." Amy laughed, good-humoredly. "I want to look at the gardens, now the sun's most down. What time's dinner? Half past six? Right-o." She fled.

If Lora was what a woman turned into, when she shook off a husband, Amy would hang on to Geoffrey. She dug her heels into the neatly graveled drive, crushing Lora's words under them. Pf! gnats, mites, to be brushed away. There seemed fewer flowers than she remembered from her youth at home. Probably she rememberd the whole procession of them compressed in time into one mass, snowdrops and crocuses straight through to dahlias and asters. Gladioli spiked the path, stiff and gaudy. A single bud was lovely, with its strong thrust out of the sheath, but she didn't like the flower. She crossed the grass, liking its matted feel beneath her feet, toward the small formal garden enclosed by shrubbery. Her mother had made that only a few years ago, and Amy had never seen it except as a design in snow with brown stalks to mark its pattern. She pushed through the low white gate. It was a pleasant recess in the subdued light, stretching to the willows along the small brook, with green grass paths, flower bordered, a trellis vine-covered hiding the willow trunks, a bench at the far end under an arbor, where late roses clung to the ramblers like tissue paper flowers. "It's been such a drought," her mother had said. "We've had to conserve water. The garden shows it."

After all, Amy wasn't interested in the flowers. She made her. way listlessly to the bench and sat down. She heard her father drive into the garage. She heard Lavinia shrilling out for Curly, and his throaty, indistinguishable answer. She could see the two houses, over shrubbery and through trees, capacious, sheltering, enduring. They looked from where she sat, obscuring any further horizon, like—she smiled a little —like bulwarks of society, like places where people would live wisely, comfortably. As if the houses knew more than their inhabitants. And yet—her consciousness spun out tiny separate threads toward the members of the family, Lora, her mother, all the rest of them. They moved under her thought like bits of glass in a kaleidoscope. So many of them, radiating from that old woman, the grandmother. What had Geoffrey been explaining—that increase of disorganization, of the random, shuffled, scattered elements of life, which was all of life— Oh, entropy. That was the word. Constant increase of randomness, and never decrease. They couldn't, if they liked, all go back into Madam Westover. Amy moved restlessly, harassed by an idea she couldn't pursue. Geoffrey hadn't explained enough of it. He always grew impatient if a listener lagged. Suddenly, at a sound behind her, beyond the shrubbery, she sat rigid.

"Now, see here, Joe, you can too!" That was young Tom, surely. She glanced around, but the olive green and brown interlacing made a close wall. "I tell you, I'll have some money next week. You know me."

"Sure I knowa you. Your ma, she come in store this morn', yes? What she say? She say she make da trub for me. So I no give you any, yes?"

"See here, she won't know, I tell you. I gotta have the stuff. I promised these fellows, see, and it's a party they're pulling, and they're good friends of mine. You don't want to lose all that good trade, now, do you, Joe? Aw, come on, be a sport!"

Amy stood up and moved silently across the grass, out of the garden. She looked back from the clear space of the lawn. Of course. The old Cole house, where the Italians lived, was beyond the brook. She remembered floating paper-sailed boats with the Cole boy. The backyard ran down almost to the next street. She whistled under her breath as she walked to the house. So Joe was an enterprising bootlegger, was he? Probably kept his stuff in the brook down which their boats had drifted. She could sniff the damp moldy odor of straw around those bottles Geof had gotten at the shore.

Her mother stood waiting on the flagged terrace beside the house. Amy hesitated briefly. Should she speak of her eavesdropping? Then, with the faintest shrug, she dismissed it.

"Don't take Lora so hard," Mrs. Westover said, quickly. Ah, she'd been waiting just for that. "You have to get used to her again, that's all. Dinner's waiting."

Heat Lightning

Amy shook herself into decent brightness. Her father looked weary, and he always tiffed a little with Lora, as if surprised that he should have such a sister. They'd all had a harder day than Amy, she thought. Lora and the bootlegger and Harriet, her mother and Mary, her father—and what?—a fading business? She worked diligently at pleasant small talk, and finished dinner with approval of herself. The telephone rang. Her father came back. His brother Dewitt had called to see if they'd come in for an evening of bridge.

"I don't play." Amy could escape that, at least. "Must we go there to-night?" She'd like to put off that relative until another day.

"How about you, Lora? We might drop you there. We're going to drive a while, and stop at Theodore's so Amy can see her brother."

"If you prefer. I'm sure I don't mind. Felice won't be disappointed, I'm sure, if I don't go."

"We'll be glad to have you come with us, Lora." Mrs. Westover raised her voice slightly, and Amy watched with amusement. The thin spot in her mother's patience with Lora concerned Theodore and his French wife, Felice. "The last time you were at Ted's, you know you said you were bored to sleep, and you do enjoy bridge."

"I wasn't bored," complained Lora. "But Felice insists on talking about things she knows no one could be interested in, politics and—oh, what she calls ideas. Anyway, I know when I'm not welcome."

"You would prefer bridge, then." Mrs. Westover was actually curt. "I'm going to ask Mother if she wishes to go."

As the screen door clicked behind her, Lora rose, her beads jingling. "I don't know how Catherine puts

up with Felice. Oh, you needn't look at me that way,
Alfred. She's not your style and you know it. I'm
going to Dewitt's, and I'm going right now. No, I
can walk." She trailed across the hall with impressive
martyrdom.

"You never walk that far, Lora. Don't be silly.
I'll drive you over in a minute." Alfred groaned as
Lora continued her disappearance, not so rapidly that
she couldn't be overtaken. "Well—" he met Amy's
smile and laughed. "I'll go chase her in the car and
deliver her. Anything to keep her away from Ted's.
Felice won't humor her. That's the only trouble."

"As I recall, Ted never lost much love over her."

"No. And Felice just shrugs her plump shoulders
and spits out a French phrase, and Lora gets mad
because she doesn't know what Felice said, and it's
just as well, if you ask me. Felice is a nice girl,
though."

"Felice is a realist." Amy laughed at the way that
remark drew her father's heavy brows together into a
puzzled frown. "Run and catch Lora before she's so
furious she won't get into your car." He was tired, she
thought, watching him lumber out of the room. His
muscles hinted at sluggish discouragement. Business,
of course. Lulu came in to clear away the coffee tray.

"It's cooler this evening," said Amy. Did she
imagine it, or was the girl's stare at her edged with
hostility?

"Yes'm." Lulu loaded her tray. Her movements
were clumsy, like her flat, quiet tread. But under the
soft light her skin had a pale golden tinge, dark as
honey against her white uniform, and her smooth hair
twisted at the nape of her thick throat was the same
color, in a darker, duller tone. Pretty was the wrong
word. Amy thought of that brief suspicion at the

moment of her arrival. She'd be nice to paint,—still life, with a bowl of pears on her knees, faded amber pears. No inner light. There was a dull, fruity quality about her. Would that be seductive? Amy couldn't guess at young Tom's desires.

Amy moved restlessly about the living room, touching familiar objects, straightening a pile of magazines, sliding a metal cigarette box along the table. It was a way of escape, this heightened awareness of other people. You couldn't think so much about yourself if you laid yourself open to receiving them. Hadn't she come for just that kind of distraction? Her hand closed about the slender stem of a brass candlestick, one of a pair on the mantel over the fireplace. She and Geoffrey had found them, years ago, in a little antique shop—where? Somewhere in Maine, the summer they had their first car, that funny old Ford. No, distraction wasn't her purpose. She had enough of that. She wanted its opposite, whatever that would be.

"Mother doesn't want to go out." Mrs. Westover came quietly in. "She is in bed, for a wonder. Says she's cooler there, her solitaire board on her knees. She sent her love, and wants you to come over for luncheon to-morrow."

"She is a wonder, isn't she?" Amy's voice was gentle. At her mother's inquiry: "Father went forth to rescue Lora, who started on foot, trailing woe."

Catherine Westover sat down on a straight ladder backed chair. Crimson touched her cheekbones, as if she had rouged, and her eyes were bright. "The real trouble, of course, is that Lora keeps comparing Laurance and Ted, and Emma and Felice, and she'd so much rather have a clever French daughter-in-law, than a solid, cheerful, worthy German haus-frau, that

[35]

she can't be decent about it. Felice is clever. She's—well, a little hard, perhaps."

"So are bones and gold and lots of nice useful things. There's Father." The light from the car made a bold white swath through the soft light in the room as he swung around the curve and stopped.

"You need a wrap. Yes, my dear, you do! I'll give you a coat."

"No, I'll be esthetic if I must mind my mother." Amy kissed her cheek as she ran past and up the stairs. She shook out the fringes of a scarlet shawl, tipped face down the photograph holder, and ran again down the stairs.

"Your father says Ted and Felice are out. Funny, when they knew we might come over."

"I'm just as glad." Amy sank into the rear seat of the car. "This is an enormous family to do up in one day."

"We'll drive around a while. Show you how the town looks in summer. It's grown a lot." Mrs. Westover was hesitating.

"Oh, you sit by Father." Amy laughed at them. "He'd be too lonesome. Gives me more room." Suddenly she felt hot tears under her eyelids, as her mother slid agilely into the front seat. The darlings —oh, the darlings! "This is a nice coupé," she cried, shutting her eyelids hard against the tears.

"It's a good size for us."

Through the opened windows the night air moved in the light breeze created only by their passage. Amy let her fingers twist in shawl fringes and watched the two, so familiar, so foreign—the solid bulk of her father's shoulders, his ears laid firmly against the mass of his head; the slope of shoulder into neck of her mother, light catching in the escaping fine curls of hair. Her father spoke, pointing out new houses, changes in roads. Presently he ceased to be guide, and drove in silence through the dark country around the town. At times a car behind them shattered their isolation with a funnel of light splintering against the windshield. At times they passed a car, first a distant glow, then a clash of light against light, almost audible. Her father muttered things about dimmers. At a crossroads he slowed the car. "How about the country club? Shall we show that off to Amy?"

"Not to-night, Alfred. She's tired. It'll keep."

Pleasant to be driven endlessly through the night. The car was a microcosm, enclosing the three. It defeated, almost, that entropy of Geoffrey's, almost it defeated the separation, the breaking up into smaller particles. Father, Mother, child. She was losing herself, carried softly on with them, lulled into wordless, thoughtless quiet. They talked, her father and mother. She heard their tones without letting the words enter, her father's low, but not deep enough, not full,—as if part of him held back. Her mother's lighter, varying its cadences, always tender, sustaining.

"Well, Amy, you asleep back there?" The gravel slid with a chur under the wheels. Home again.

"Such a nice drive." Amy hated to move, hated to lose this drowsy spell of nothingness. She wound her scarlet shawl about herself, spell and all, as she stepped out. "I'm going straight to bed before I wake up." She took their good-night kisses, still their child. "Good-night."

3

She woke after a long night of sleep from which not a shred of dream remained, to lie motionless, savoring still the delight of that profound sleeping. Voices pricked in, her mother's, Lavinia's, the latter shriller, more excited than usual. She rose, stretching lazily, and went to one of the windows. Lavinia was excited, all her jerkiness exaggerated.

"Hello!" Amy sat on the window-sill, calling down. Her mother stepped from the porch into view. "What you talking about?"

"Nothing. Nothing at all." Lavinia kept an entertaining indifference to any added years in the grandchildren. "You better get dressed. Your grandma's expecting you over."

She darted off toward the rear of the other house, a wiry, agitated figure. Presently, as Amy dressed, she heard her mother on the stairs.

"I hope we didn't wake you, Amy."

"How nice you look." Amy touched her shoulders, let her hands drop to enclose her mother's wrists. "I haven't seen a dimity dress for years."

"It isn't dimity. Dotted mull."

"That blue is just right for you. Come on in while I finish my nails. What's the matter? Lavinia thought I was too young to hear, evidently."

"She's upset. She says Curly wasn't home last night."

"What?" Amy snapped open a small manicure set. "Not the faithful Curly?"

"She's sure he was in his room when she locked the house. But he's gone."

"I thought he never left the yard."

"That's just it. I think I better call your father, but I hate to bother him."

Amy peered at her mother. "You know a lot more than you're saying. What is the mystery?"

"I don't know much more. I didn't write you about it, this spring—so many small things—I can't write them all. Curly vanished once before. Some of the boys got him drunk, Amy. I was shocked. Like getting a dog drunk, or a young child. Lavinia found him in the country somewhere. She was half crazy that time, not knowing what had happened."

"But who ever—Mother, it wasn't Tom?" Her mother nodded. "Oh, what a rotten trick!"

"It wasn't really Tom's idea. Some friends of his. Oh, I suppose they were half seas over when they did it. Tom was awfully ashamed. I can't think he'd do it again."

"But what—" Amy puzzled—"what would Curly do, drunk?"

"Nobody knows, exactly. Tom swore he couldn't remember much."

"He must have been tight." Amy was scornful. "Is he an awful souse?" That snatch of dialogue last night, behind the arbor!

"Ted was here, and he drove Lavinia around until they found Curly, asleep. It was a miracle he hadn't been run over or something. He was way out of town. They got him home. But I shouldn't stand here. Of course he mayn't have done that again."

"Have you called Tom?"

"Lora said he spent the night with friends."

Amy seized her mother's arm. "Come on, let's find him. Does Grandmother know?"

"No. Lavinia doesn't want to tell her."

"I've never known whether Curly's mind was as

tongue-tied as his speech or not." There was a kind
of horrid drama about Curly drunk, Amy's thoughts
ran on, as she ·and her mother went down stairs.
"Grandmother always said he was smarter than most
folks, I know. Where did she ever get him?"

"He's always been there."

"Well, he came from somewhere. But, you
know"— Under her words leaped, unsought, a quick
thought— Geof would like this theory! "Curly,
sober, being simple minded, is like ordinary people
when they are drunk. Isn't he? Just impulses, clumsy
actions. So what would Curly be, drunk?"

Her mother obviously had no concern in theories.
"I think I'll call your father and just tell him I want
the car. He can send it—"

Breaking off her words, filling the pleasant morning
with the sudden dread at which the listener's blood
hurried to deep centers of the body, a tumult rose from
somewhere, down back of the house. Amy and her
mother gave each other a quick, startled glance, as if
each asked, "Did you hear that? Did I dream it?"
and then both ran through the hall, out the side entrance, toward that noise. Lavinia was running, too,
like a puppet, and shrilling, "Curly! Curly!" as she
ran.

Amy flung herself after Lavinia—how could she go
so fast?—around the old stable, across the vegetable
garden, aware with horror of separate noises in the
tumult, screams of children, one long terrified shriek
that broke appallingly, and a kind of bellow like the
noise made by a sleeper who tries to cry out in a
nightmare. There, behind those bushes—an incredible
tableau at which Amy felt a scream perish, frozen,
on her own lips. Curly knelt, one hand holding down
something that kicked and struggled, a little boy; the

other arm uplifted, the sun flashing on whatever the hand grasped, a broken bottle! Dry leaves, mud in his bleached bushy hair, on the face he turned toward Lavinia's call. From his lips came that nightmare bellow, and beyond the muddy stream danced other shrieking children.

"My Lord above!" Lavinia hurled herself straight at him, clung like an angry sparrow to his outstretched arm. "You give me that, you bad Curly!"

His bellow died into throaty sounds of protest. Amy forced herself to walk nearer, to take the bottle from Lavinia's hand. "He'll hurt you, Lavinia! Wait!" Across the brook stumbled a man, clattering out hysterical Italian phrases. Curly sat back on his haunches, an uncouth and bewildered figure, and the child, freed of his grasp, twisted away.

"What is this? What is this?" Madam Westover, shaking off Catherine's hand, struck her cane sharply against the earth. The Italian poured out a torrent of phrases, of wild gestures, and Curly whimpered like a dog.

"Where is your boy, Joe? Let me see him. Curly didn't kill him, if he could run away. Where is he? He must have done something. I told you he must stop tormenting Curly. Lavinia, you take Curly into the house. Go along, Curly."

Streamers of green slime clung to his faded blue overalls and shirt, his whole left side was dark with water. Had he slept in the brook? A dejected Bacchus, he shambled after Lavinia.

"He had this, Grandmother." Amy held out the bottle. The neck had been smashed off, and the water-stained label clung to her fingers, peeling away from the glass.

"This is yours, isn't it, Joe?" Madam Westover nodded. "Did you give it to Curly?"

Voluble protests, denials, accusations.

"He found it, then. You hide your stuff here, in the water? Yes. He must have seen you. Where's your boy? I want to know what happened."

Out of the excited and incomplete explanations of the children, out of Madam Westover's persistent inquiries, they made at last a picture. Curly, asleep on the bank under the bushes, empty bottle in his hand. The boys discovered him, poked at him with sticks to wake him, to hear him mouth at them. Waking, Curly had rolled into the brook, and in a fury had caught at the first boy, Louis, Joe's son. He hadn't hurt him, thanks to Lavinia's speed. Joe would tell the police. The boy had been near death.

"Yes. And I'll tell the police about your whisky. Think it over." Madam Westover folded both hands on the knob of her stick and looked calmly at Joe. "This brook's on my property, too. Curly never harmed anything in his life. You want to go to prison for bootlegging?"

"Me, I have good stuff. All your men they buy of Joe. Your man—" He implored Catherine for help against this implacable old woman. "Tom, he buy. Other Mist' Westover, they buy."

"That's another matter. You let my poor Curly find whisky and drink it. You let your boys torment him. Come out here, boy!" She had spied him, creeping up behind his father to listen. "Are you hurt? Where?"

"Naw." He strutted, arching his skinny chest. "He ain't hurt me any. I hollered so he wouldn't dast."

"You see, Joe? Now you let Curly alone. He

served you right. If you tease a dog, you ought to get bitten."

Joe's dark face twisted, eloquent of his attempt to solve the complications of this affair. "He ain't safe," he insisted, his hands dramatic. "You shoulda put him somewhere."

"Stuff." Madam Westover waved him to silence, and proceeded slowly back to the house. Amy saw curious observers behind the trees. It was a wonder the whole village hadn't turned out. Her own knees had quavers as she walked with her mother behind the erect back of Madam Westover.

Lavinia was scrubbing the steps, her face grim.

"Curly was sick," she said. "He can't stand it, drink and all that excitement. He's laying down."

Madam Westover tapped past her without a word, through to the side porch, where she sat down, reached for her knife, and went on with the peaches she had abandoned. Catherine sat on the chair near her, and Amy leaned against the railing.

"Can't you rest a minute, Mother?" Catherine was troubled. "After a scene like that?"

"What do I want to rest for?" The peach slid under her swift fingers. "I hope, Catherine, that you won't say anything to Alfred. He'd take it too seriously."

"It is serious." Amy felt the burden of an old discussion in their quiet words. "I must tell him. Joe is right. You can't keep Curly. It was one thing when he made no trouble. But now—"

"He won't do it again. I'll see to that. Who's coming, now?" Voices approached, the shallow, plaintive sound of Lora, and a deeper tone—why, that was her father!

"There ain't a thing to fuss about," Lavina's protest shrilled after them as they came out to the porch.

"You'll have to get yourself some chairs, if you've come to stay," said Madam Westover, selecting another peach.

"What has happened, Mother?" Lora twisted her hands as if she washed them. "Lavinia says Curly is found. After she called up, I was wild. Tom was in town. He didn't have a thing to do with it. I got Alfred—"

Alfred brought a straight chair from the house and seated himself deliberately. "I heard about it, Mother. Lulu told me. I'm thankful nothing worse happened. You might have been hurt, or Lavinia. I hope you realize now what I've been saying since last spring."

"Will some one please tell me—"

"Oh, hush, Lora!" Madam Westover pointed her knife at her daughter. "Curly got drunk again and frightened one of those dago boys who torment him all the time. That's all."

"You might add," said Catherine, steadily, "that Curly would have smashed the boy's head with a bottle if Lavinia hadn't arrived in time."

"Stuff and nonsense. You might as well add he'd have killed all of us if it wasn't that he didn't."

"I looked up that Home for—"

"This is Curly's home." Madam Westover laid her knife carefully in the pan of peach skins, spread her hands firmly on her knees, and stared around at each of them. The nostrils of her strong hooked nose flared, white dents visible in the ivory of her skin. "You're all at me again, except Dewitt. You better send for him and make it a family session. You can't budge me."

"Now, Mother." Alfred jerked his chair forward. "You can't sacrifice all our comfort, our ease about you, just for a feeble-minded hired man you've kept years and years." His voice cajoled her. "After all, you have some responsibility toward your own children. Curly can be cared for, safely, comfortably, in a home for such men."

"That's just what I say." Lora's bangles jingled.

"Did you put Tom in a home because he got drunk, Lora? He's no doubt sleeping it off right now. Maybe Curly saw where he got the whisky for his spree, and that's how he knew."

Lora's face was scarlet. "But Tom's my son, and just a boy. Curly's no one——"

"Listen to me! You blind fools. Curly has as much right as any of you. Oh, you've pretended not to know it."

"Just what do you mean, Mother?" Alfred had lifted one hand, to press back into silence words that should not be spoken. Amy saw sunlight catch in the tufts of sandy hair along each solid square finger; she thought the moment before her grandmother answered was so long that she could see the pale flowers of the morning glory vine fade in the heat.

"He's a Westover, of course." Madam Westover spoke slow words, rusty, and corroded from long interment in her heart. "He's your brother. No, not my son. He was born a few months later than you, my first son, Alfred."

Alfred's face grew ruddy, until his bristling eyebrows and lashes looked white. He sent one distressed glance toward Amy. "Just why do you think this?" he asked, and from Lora came a dozen small sounds of rustling, clinking, gasping.

"You insist on further details?" Madam Westover put them all grandly in the wrong, as prying offenders. "I didn't know it until several years later, when his mother died. She was a girl in the lumber camp, one of several your father owned. Her father was a drunken French laborer. When I learned about the child, I took it. Your father wasn't real pleased, at first. Whatever responsibility you think I have for you is less than for Curly. He can't take care of himself, not away from home." She pushed herself abruptly to her feet, setting aside carefully her pan of peach scraps. "Now I hope you're satisfied. You had no business to bully me until I told you!" Indignant and unassailable, she marched away from them, and they heard her stick tap slowly up the stairs.

"I think Mother's losing her mind. After all, she's very old, and old people have queer fancies. Of course it can't be true—" Lora breathed rapid incoherencies—"asking me if I put Tom in a home—he doesn't really get drunk—"

"Lora, dry up, for God's sake!" Alfred got to his feet. "Of course it's true."

"You needn't swear at me. Our own father! A few months younger than you— Oh, I've heard that men—"

"Let's go home, Alfred." Catherine laid her hand on his arm. She had, Amy thought, forgotten everything else in her alertness to her husband's disturbance.

"Dewitt must be told," chattered Lora. "It doesn't really alter matters except to make it more difficult."

"I think," said Alfred, somberly, "that we always knew it. But if you don't say it, it isn't a thing you have to consider." He went off with Catherine, and Amy had a childish desire to cry out, "Don't forget me! I want to come along with you!" Nonsense. They didn't want her.

Heat Lightning

She sat down in her grandmother's chair, picked up the knife, and attacked the basket of peaches. Lora fluttered about the porch for a few minutes, beginning sentences, breaking them off, and finally, with an exasperated, "I should think you might at least talk!" drifted away.

Amy's skin crept a little. She hated the dry fuzz of peaches. If she took a firm hold she felt it less. Grasping nettles. That was her grandmother's way of life, wasn't it? She pried cautiously with her imagination at those past years. Taking your husband's illegitimate son into your household—why, Curly had been conceived while the old woman carried her own first child. That was what Lora had meant. Had she taken Curly as a thorn to hold always in Grandfather's side? Amy shook her head. As she recalled her grandfather, he had given no impression of a man among thorns. Nor was her grandmother a deceived, unhappy female. Not she. Oh—Amy pounded one hand, peach and all, against the other fist. If she could see it, how they felt, what had evolved between them,—surely there was wisdom there. It was just what no one would tell that might give a glimmer about how to live.

She peeled more peaches, and then suddenly her wistfulness located itself precisely. She was hungry! She'd forgotten her breakfast in the early morning drama.

Lavinia, with little *tchks* of pity, hurried to make fresh coffee for her, and toast. Amy sat at a corner of the kitchen table. "I'd rather stay out here and watch you," she said.

"Not much to watch here. My lands, I ought to hurry." She rattled fruit jars in her dish-pan of scalding water. "Your grandma ought to be getting those peaches done. We're going to preserve some whole for sauce."

"She's probably used up." Amy crunched at her toast.

"Not her." Lavinia sniffed. "You'll see. She just went off to stop the argument. There she comes, now."

There she was, indeed, a mocking caution in the glance she sent into the room. "They all gone?" Her chuckle had a note of rich amusement, as if she considered that she had routed them all triumphantly. "It's a wonder they left you, Amy. They'll be having a solemn family conclave. You see!"

"Lot of good it'll do 'em." Lavinia laid her hands each side of her spare waist and admired the old woman. "They might of learned by this time. You going to finish the peaches?"

"I'll help." Amy drained her coffee cup. "That was grand coffee, 'Viny. Give me an apron and a knife."

She and her grandmother sat together again on the porch, working. Bits of sentences tugged at the leash of Amy's tongue, straining for speech she dared not give them. Tell me, Grandmother, what it felt like, discovering that child, taking him. Knowing your young husband's faithlessness. Living with him. Bearing him more children. What was it like? She tried to reconstruct a young man out of her images of her grandfather, a sturdy, choleric old man with a square beard that kept a sandier tone than the bristling white eyebrows and snowy thatch of hair. Why, of course! Curly's blue eyes were like her grandfather's, except that Curly's eyes were those of a child. Every morning Grandfather had driven off to his factory. She could smell the queer stuffy odor of the

black brilliantine coat he had worn in the summer.
He had died that last winter of the war, just after
the Armistice, while she was still in France. Now
her father went every morning to the factory, but
with a difference. She had never considered that
difference before. Her grandfather had gone with
the air of the Lord stepping out to take a look at the
universe he had made. Her father just went to
business. The older man had created the works.
Westover Plows, Westover Farming Implements.
Grandfather's love, aside from the factory, had been
for his male descendants. But he tolerated admiration
from his granddaughters.

The warmth of the morning flowed into the en-
closure; it seemed to come in little crescendos and
diminuendos like the hum of the bees among the morning glories. Alpha, the Persian cat, stalked out, made
a shining black scimitar against Madam Westover's
foot, purring like the bees, and then chose a distant
corner for a nap, circling twice with little tinkles of
the silver bell on his collar before he settled.

"I was thinking about Grandfather," said Amy,
boldly.

"Yes?" Her grandmother's eyes, under wrinkled
lids, were inscrutable. "So was I. He always liked
a warm summer morning. Said it warmed up all his
juices and tasted sweeter. He'd stand out there—"
she nodded toward the lawn, yellowed with sun—
"with no hat, just soaking in the summer." She selected another peach, snipped out deftly a bruised spot,
and pared away. "But he liked winter, too. He
could enjoy himself. Sometimes I think you young
people have forgotten how to enjoy yourselves. Look
at—" she broke off, thrusting her chin forward, her
smile flashing an instant. "I was going to say mean

things, about some of you. I won't. But you, Amy, you look as if you'd lost your own zest. Peaked, and too full of thinking."

Amy's nerves rippled in alarm. She had planned an onslaught, and here she received one. Trust her grandmother!

"Tonsils, Grandmother." She made a wry face. "They leave you melancholy when they go."

"Humph. You don't look happy."

I'm not! I'm not! Amy kept back the cry in her throat. "I forgot to put on any make-up this morning. That gives me a pensive air."

Lavinia was in the doorway. "I need a kettle of peaches," she said, sternly. "I suppose you been chattering instead of working. And Lulu says your mother wants to know if you'll go over to Mary's with her now."

Amy rubbed her peach-moist fingers and rose. "I suppose I must," she said. "You know what these new mothers are—"

"Give her my love, and tell her she might have had a boy this time. And there are your peaches, Lavinia."

Amy found her mother waiting in the car.

"I drove your father back to the factory," she said, "and kept the car so I could take you around. Did you have any breakfast?"

Amy nodded. "And then I earned it, peeling peaches." She liked to watch her mother drive, she did it so gravely and conscientiously.

"Did Mother come downstairs before you left?"

"Oh, yes. Hours ago."

Catherine's face was drawn into earnest lines. "Did she seem upset?"

"Not a bit."

"I'm sorry this had to come up, while you're here such a little time. Curly, I mean. Your father is terribly distressed. Dewitt is in town, but to-night they'll have to make some arrangement. You know—" she turned for an instant to look at Amy—"I've always suspected that about Curly. Once I asked your father. He resented it. It seemed an insult to his father, I suppose."

"What can you do?" Amy discovered that, in spite of the brief horror of that scene beside the brook, she was aligned with her grandmother. "You can't force Grandmother to let him go. After all, he isn't violent unless he's drunk, and I don't see how he's to get drunk often. This was an accident, the other time was a trick of Tom's. You know, Tom may be in this yet." She told her mother of the snatch of dialogue she had overheard. "Curly may have heard them, too."

"Mother's won you over," commented Catherine.

"She didn't say a word!" Amy had to protest against her awareness of partisanship. "But imagine her taking Curly as a little boy! How did she do it? I mean, how did she feel about it? Whatever she felt, she couldn't possibly let him go, now."

"I haven't the slightest idea how she felt." Catherine disapproved of that line. "And she must be protected, even against her own wishes. She is a stubborn woman, for all she is so remarkable."

"At least she didn't do it just to make Grandfather wretched. I can remember him well enough to know that. Did women expect infidelity then?"

"My dear Amy!" Catherine grazed a tire against the curbing as she drew up in front of Mary's house. "I don't know."

"And nice little girls don't ask such questions, eh?"

[51]

Heat Lightning

Amy hugged her mother's arm, laughing softly at her, and they went into the white frame house.

"You wait here a few minutes." Catherine left Amy in the living room.

Amy glanced about, her nose quivering faintly in distaste. Mary's house always looked untidy, for all it was so bare. Everything seemed to be in the wrong place. The room had an uncherished look, as if the dwellers in the house never saw it, as if they came in, sat a while, and went away with no concern for their shell. It wasn't lack of money, exactly. Mary couldn't manage the details of her existence. Amy straightened the magazines: *Literary Digest, National Geographic, Ladies' Home Journal.* Exactly. On an imitation Persian tapestry, from a department store basement. Poor Mary!

"Amy!" her mother called, and Amy climbed into the odor of drugs and antiseptics, into the shaded warmth of the bedroom. The nurse rustled past her with a professional smile, and her mother stood at the foot of the double bed. Amy noted that bed, as a last sardonic touch, and then forgot her critical survey in an unexpected rush of old tenderness.

Mary looked so young, her soft short hair spilled against the pillow like a child's, her eyes large, shadows of pain under them.

"Why, Mary!" Amy bent over her, brushing her cheek in greeting. Perhaps that odor,—scent of powder, faint echo of chloroform,—revived moments of her own weakness. "How's the girl?"

"Glad it's over." Mary's words crept out. "Have you seen the baby?"

"Not yet. I wanted to see you." The words were true. Briefly, perhaps, but perfectly for the moment Mary was her younger sister, loved in that early

[52]

mock-maternal way, as if the old relationship between them still lived and shone up now through layers of later years superimposed upon it. "Don't try to talk this morning. Too much work. You sleep and sleep." Amy kissed her again, feeling almost apologetic.

"We'll drive out to Laurance's this afternoon." Mrs. Westover nodded approval at Amy—for her tenderness, or her advice? Amy wondered. "To see what your family's up to out there. I'll stop at the drug-store for that formula."

"Then Henry won't have to walk down in the heat." Mary let her eyelids close, and Amy, with a little pat to smooth a wrinkle in the sheet, walked softly away.

She sat on the porch railing, swinging one foot idly, waiting for her mother to do some diplomatic work between the hired girl and the nurse. Was it sentimental, that flooding up of tenderness? Or was it real feeling, in a different time level? She didn't know—nor care.

She heard her mother in the hall, talking with the nurse. Henry hurried around the street corner, a thin, shabby figure in the bright sun. His hand, limp and unwilled, touched Amy's and his eyelids twitched.

"Glad to see you, Amy," he said. "Is Mary all right? You been up to speak to her?" Poor Henry; his very hair looked dingy, too thin on top, receding from high temples. He pulled a crumpled handkerchief from a pocket and rubbed it over his face. "She had a hard time. I don't mind saying I was frightened. But things seem to be all right now." His twitching eyelid added an incongruous wink. "Each time I think I'll know what to expect, and not mind, you know." As Mrs. Westover came out he turned suddenly toward her with a shift of his whole body, almost leaning on her as proxy for Mary. "Oh, Mother! Everything okay?"

"Mary's asleep, and so's the baby. Effie's got your lunch all ready. Now don't creak up the stairs and wake them." Mrs. Westover patted his limp shoulder. "You might take a nap yourself."

"No, I won't wake her. You couldn't come in, have lunch or something?"

"Not now, Henry. I promised Mary to take a look at the children."

Mrs. Westover frowned as she drove away. "It's too bad Mary can't nurse the baby," she said. "More expense—experimenting with foods." She sighed. "Bottles are such a trouble, too, and Mary's not good at that sort of thing."

"It will leave her much freer."

"Mary doesn't want freedom. Not from her babies."

"No. Even Henry's breast fed, isn't he? Oh, I'm sorry." Amy caught the real shock in her mother's glance. "I suppose she can't keep the nurse on long." That complete dependence of Henry stirred a violent antagonism in her blood. Perhaps—she peered down a dark alley of thought—because Geof escaped her as completely as Henry clung to Mary.

"They can't afford the nurse long. Mary managed with no maid at all until a few weeks ago."

"What's Henry doing now?"

"Selling insurance. Trying to. He had a good position last year, with an advertising firm in the city. But the force was cut down, after the slump started, and of course Henry was one of the men they let go. He tries hard enough." Catherine drove along the main street, hunting for a parking space. "I'll have to stop around the corner and walk back." She left

Amy, who watched her out of sight. How well she walked, with supple, erect carriage, her head with its curly knot carried a little proudly. Well, all the Westovers stepped out with pride. They felt as if they owned the town. They had, once, but now— Amy could remember, as a child, walking with her grandfather, conscious that every one knew who passed. There goes Alfred Westover and his granddaughter. You know, Westover Plows. Now so many Westovers walked or drove through the streets that their passing must be unnoted. And so many other new people. She didn't know any of them.

Her thoughts moved back to Henry and Mary. Probably her father gave Mary an allowance. Henry had wanted to be an artist just enough so he didn't care to be anything else. Mary said he still longed to paint, but his hands were too unsteady. Nerves. Amy sank down into the seat, her hands wound about her knees. What would it feel like, nursing your husband? She tried to stand Geoffrey up beside that picture of Henry, and she could see only his hands, long, with strong, jutting thumbs, the forefingers short against the other fingers,—and an ache like physical pain began to beat in the rhythm of her heart. Suddenly she was out of the car, running after her mother.

"I want some money, Mother. To send a wire." She was breathless. "Where do you send wires? Oh, yes—" Back to the corner, and past the new shops in the hotel arcade. *Dear Geof, I love you.* The girl took a pencil carefully out of the formal curl over her ear and counted the words, not a ripple of amusement. Sending the message eased that beating pain. Would it reach the camp,—perhaps to-morrow?

4

Catherine drove swiftly away from the business blocks, along an abandoned street-car track, past the small railroad station—(Amy saw that suddenly in winter dusk, snow in drifts along its dingy window ledges, trampled over the platform, swirling, in the glow of headlights as an engine chugged up the slight grade drawing the train to take her away—she could feel wet fur of her coat collar under her chin. When was it?) But they drove into the factory yard, and the recollection dropped beneath memory. The parking field for the men had a scattered border of Fords and Chevrolets. Two box cars, released by a yard engine, rolled slowly along the incline of the spur track.

"You can see there's not much doing," said Catherine. "I'll see if your father is ready." She was back at once, Alfred behind her with a tinge of petulance suggesting that he had been waiting.

"I'll have to rush"; he settled himself at the wheel. "My morning's been shot to pieces so."

Catherine sat beside him, her shoulder touching his. He leans on her, thought Amy, only he's not supine, like Henry. Mother's too clever to let him fall over. Or even to let him know he leans. Queer, how her own desperate need of light seemed to throw such brilliance over the affairs of the members of her family. She carried her need like a many-batteried pocket spotlight, illuminating emotional corners in other people, but she walked in darkness behind it. Her wrist wouldn't bend to turn it on herself.

Luncheon was rather silent. Alfred answered the telephone once, and explained that Lora had located

Tom, and that Tom swore he hadn't even seen Curly the previous day. As he talked, Lulu lingered, her hands clutching the green Chinese salad bowl, until Catherine lifted disapproving eyebrows at her. When the door closed upon the maid, Catherine sighed. "I suppose she must have heard all about this morning. She'll never learn that a good servant has no ears."

Amy hoped that only curiosity had halted the girl, and not the news of Tom.

"I'll see Dewitt to-night. I'm sorry you were dragged into this." Her father looked heavily at her, and then went off. Through the opened French doors Amy could see Curly, squatting at the edge of the drive, green grass shears moving like a lazy crocodile in his hand. She pointed to him.

"Do you suppose he feels repentant?" she asked.

Her mother shrugged. "Who can tell? Mother insists he'd break his heart if she put him away anywhere."

"I've heard of animals dying of that malady. People don't. I can't decide which Curly is."

"Do you need a rest before we drive out to Laurance's? Father's sending the car back at once."

"I'm crumpled. Don't I need a clean dress?"

"Not to call there. Save it for Dewitt and Isabelle to-night." Catherine gave her a droll smile, in which the farm, with Emma and her mother, were lined delicately beside Isabelle's languid elegance.

Amy strolled out to the terrace, and dropped into the Gloucester hammock under its gay striped canopy, to wait for her mother. She felt her telegram to Geoffrey like an arrow, sped straight through space, between huge tree trunks, seeking out his heart. He would be bending over a camp fire, skillet in hand, frying speckled trout, and the arrow would astonish

[57]

him. Her hands lay gently together, palms and finger-tips, and she could see the long line from his ear down to the opened collar of his brown hunting shirt. I feel different already about him, she thought. Presently she would take out all the disorderly fragments, to see what she could make of them. Not yet. But if you thrust your own life as far beneath the surface as you could hold it, ignoring even the bubbles that floated to the surface, you had more eyes for other people, surfaces and sub-surfaces. Almost you took advantage of them, not explaining that you had turned your back on your own affairs. And then—vaguely Amy felt the beginning of a strange catharsis, a purging of herself. She had done well to come, although she had not known why she came.

At her mother's summons she hurried upstairs to run a comb through her hair, to stare a moment at the queer detached Amy who looked from the mirror at her. She dangled her vanity case from a finger, shook her soft waves of hair forward, and joined her mother.

The afternoon at Emma's and Laurance's had the unreality, the swift irrelevance of scenes, the touches of comedy and grotesquerie that belonged to an ani-mated cartoon in motion pictures. Emma had been shy at first with this cousin from New York. She was letting her hair grow, and it escaped in yellow strings from the bun at the base of her sun-burned neck and fell over her round pink cheeks. In her sleeveless much-washed print dress, her round arms burned, her white cotton stockings rolled over her plump knees, and wrinkled into her lop-sided canvas pumps, she looked like one of her own children. Laurance was down in the orchards; the men were picking early apples. The children were no doubt there, too, helping and hindering. One side of the white house wore a wild trellis of scaffolding, empty of workmen. They were building a new wing, kitchen and porch, when the men found time. She spoke as if her world contained countless men. She had just finished washing the dinner dishes; would they like to see her new dish-washer? She lost her shyness as she exhibited her possessions. Electric ice-box, ironer, washing machine. "Laurance is wonderful. He buys everything I speak about."

"I should think you could hire a woman to work for you for less than all these machines cost," said Amy.

"I don't want one. What would I do?"

They drank cold fresh buttermilk, with its clear delicious pucker. Mrs. Miller came out, in fresh gingham, her hard round cheeks shining from recent soap. In her harder, tighter, rougher version you could trace the earlier presence of an Emma. She was voluble about Curly. Yes, Lora had been out that morning to consult Laurance. Catherine's reserve had no effect upon Mrs. Miller, who sniggered in contentment at Lora's outraged disgrace. They had walked down to the orchard, to see the children, past gardens that made lovely fan patterns with their long rows of green stuff between rows of soft brown cultivated earth, rows so long they seemed to Amy to swing on a distant and invisible axis as she passed. "They cultivate every morning, because there's no rain," explained Emma. "Laurance works hard, but he's well." Cows raised their long faces and stared, unwinking, as they followed a lane past fields. Then the orchard, small, sturdy, young trees, men on ladders handling each apple in careful, curved fingers. The children rushed at them. "These are mine." Emma sorted out two tow-heads, product of her fairness and the sandy Westovers. "Mary's are all girls. They act sort of crazy, being in the country for a visit."

Emma found the ladder on which Laurance stood and laid a hand on it, jarring it. Amy caught the look that swung down from Laurance, a weathered, straight Laurance, lean of back and thighs; swung up from Emma to meet him, a look of clear pleasure, as if, even casually, they couldn't each one see the other without complete recognition. She made some bantering greeting and turned away, trembling a little. She'd been,—yes, face it!—feeling superior to Emma, who smelled definitely of the perspiration that stained her armpits, and who used indifferent English.

She walked back with Emma, her mother going ahead with Mrs. Miller and the older children. She noticed Emma's easy, balanced tread, her feet liking the earth. "You're happy, aren't you?" she said.

Emma had just set her white teeth deep into an apple. "Sure." Her word was apple-juicy. She mastered her enormous bite. "I get mad sometimes, but I get right over it." She lagged, increasing the distance between them and the little procession ahead. "Sometimes Laurance's folks get me crazy. They're his folks, and I try to be nice. But that Harriet! And his mother—only she doesn't boss me so much any more. Laurance told her she needn't. You're lucky, living so far away. Your husband's folks don't live near you, do they?"

"He hasn't such a raft as Laurance. No one in New York at all."

Emma slipped her arm into Amy's in childlike friendliness. "He didn't come with you, did he? Don't you miss him? I couldn't go off without Laurance. Why, I'd almost die if I had to sleep alone." Her eyes stared, round and sly, at Amy, and her warm, apple-fragrant breath seemed about to hurry on into garrulous confidences as to sleeping with Laurance. Amy felt the bare arm against her own flesh swell a little, as a flood of well being expanded Emma's whole person, sunshine and earth and love-making taken in a bite like an apple. "Mamma thinks I'm awful, liking it,—you know. She says it's just a nuisance. She was glad when papa stopped. My goodness, I hope Laurance and me never get that old. Oh, pshaw, they're waiting for us, just when we started to have a good talk."

One of the children came rushing back, swinging on Emma's free arm, and she released Amy, holding the half-eaten apple for the child to bite. The other children danced around in colts' play, and Amy could walk on, aware of a tingle in her sense of reticence at a threat whisked quickly away. Emma was simple, amazingly. Didn't that ease which made Laurance so different from the cousin she remembered, that lack of strain, come from that very simplicity? Emma made him her world, but only receptively, without possessive demands. She had burst out to Amy as a child might, unhindered by any adult fear of Amy's attitude.

"Come out again," Emma urged, as she stood beside the car. "Come out and stay all day. I'd love to have you. It's nicer in the country in summer, and then we could have a good talk." She cuffed good-humoredly at her small boy, and Mrs. Miller shrilled farewell advice about Curly.

Catherine smiled obliquely at Amy as she drove down the dusty lane to the road. "When Emma takes a fancy to any one," she said, "she's a babbling brook."

"It must be wonderful to feel like that,—clear and simple as a brook."

[61]

"Well—" her mother was tolerant—"she seems to suit Laurance."

"Hard to see what the children will be like, with Tom Blake and Lora on one side, and Frau Miller on the other. It's racial intermarriage, isn't it? Purify the bloodstream by peasant stock. Thrifty, family-bound, simple German housewife. How *could* Lora get on with her!"

"She complains chiefly against the standards of living. They lack—civilized elements, perhaps."

Amy could feel that warm, pressing arm. "Huh! She's alive and she loves Laurance. Lora better not meddle."

"She can't." Catherine set that fact down baldly, and added, sighing, "I rather wish she hadn't talked Curly over with them. She probably couldn't get Laurance by himself. Mrs. Miller would see to that. She thrives on Lora's misfortunes." She stopped the car in the drive at the side of the house. "You've time to bathe and dress before dinner, if you like."

Amy glanced eagerly at the hall table before she started up the stairs. Geof might have answered. "I'd die if I had to sleep alone." Emma's warm amorousness stirred danger nerves in Amy, and she stripped and laid her body in cool water, working to pull back her garment of apathy, to push far, far under the surface every trace of her personal life. Then she began to cry, slowly, so that she had to sit up lest she choke. She leaned her forehead uncomfortably against the convex edge of the tub and cried, the water moving gently against her body. What are you crying for? Geof— Lost, lost beauty. Crying because you aren't like Emma? Poor fool! She bent her head between her knees, face down in the water, eyelids trembling, as long as she could hold her uneven breath. Cry a tubful! Suddenly she laughed and sprang to her feet, splashing. You didn't cry when your face was drowning, because you couldn't feel a tear. Enough of that kind of foolishness.

She dressed herself in smart white chiffon with tricky narrow bands of dark fur accenting neck and sleeves, and weighting one long point of the skirt. "Very chic, my dear," she said, leaning to the mirror with lipstick in hand. "You'll make your Aunt Isabelle shiver with desire." She brushed her hair behind her ears, pulling it forward in points, and screwed on long onyx ear-rings. She hadn't worn them since the doctor'd snipped out her tonsils; the light tap as they swung seemed to hurt her throat. But she'd risk them to-night. Isabelle had to be ridden down.

Her father stood at the buffet in the dining-room, filling a glass from a siphon. "Oh, hello, Amy." He held up the glass, tinkling ice. "Will you have one?"

"No, thanks. I just got cooled off."

"Um. This is going to be a hard evening. Here's to you." He drank quickly.

"That some of Joe's? Does he get good stuff for you?"

"Fair. Say—" Her father grinned at her. "If I'd known he kept it right there in our brook, I could have saved quite a few bucks." He sobered. "Shame, though, for Curly to run into it. I saw Tom this afternoon. He and another fellow went there last night, and helped Joe get it out. He thought Curly might have been in the bushes. Says Joe was uneasy, thinking he heard some one." He nodded. "That's how it happened. But that makes no difference." He was firm, although slightly mellowed. "Mother's got to listen to us, when we all agree what's to be done."

After dinner they drove off, stopping first at Mary's.

Heat Lightning

Mrs. Westover had to tell her about the children, and Emma wanted more stockings for them. She let her own run barefoot, but Mary wouldn't stand that.

The approach to Dewitt's house was impressive. The curving drive led between poplars, like cypresses in the twilight, and the air hinted at flowers somewhere over the stretch of lawn. "I'd like to know what Dewitt paid for his trees, alone," said Alfred. "Isabelle couldn't wait for them to grow, and so they set out dozens, each a truckload to itself. He'll be wishing he hadn't sunk so much. You'll see." In the light from windows and doors the house stood out clearly, pale stucco, exaggerated sweep of roof line from chimney down and out over the hidden garage. Mongrel Spanish, Geof called it.

Isabelle's greeting, in her ostentatious southern drawl, had, as always, a specious warmth. "Why, Amy! How wonderful to see you! You're looking perfectly marvelous. Come in, all of you. Come right along in."

The large living room, with block linen slip covers in green and black and shaded lamps with modernistic angled bases of bright metal bore the stamp of interior decorator, 1930. Isabelle, still drawling phrases, watched to see how Amy took it. And Amy, as usual, was taking it and her aunt with amusement. Isabelle looked a little plumper. Her small childish features remained unchanged, imbedded in a matrix of increasing years and pounds, small nose, small mouth, dark eyes which had been much admired in Isabelle's youth, and which she had a trick of holding wide open, so that a tiny edge of blue-white above the iris caught the observer disturbingly. "What a charming frock, Amy! Do turn around. I suppose there are marvelous bargains this time of year in New York shops.

Heat Lightning

I'm in rags. I haven't had a new thing for ages. I tell Dewitt even the newspapers tell us we should spend, if we're ever to have anything but these dreadful hard times. But we mothers have to learn to sacrifice, don't we, Catherine?"

Dewitt strolled in, cigar between nervous fingers, his dark face cut by deep lines of perpetual irritability. As he took Amy's hand a moment, she thought that his eyes, behind the thick bifocal spectacles, had the same harassed withdrawal from the scene she had suspected in her father, except that Dewitt's look hinted at an immediate rather than a general cause. They chatted aimlessly a while,—idle questions, how was Geoffrey, how and where were the children, wasn't it frightfully warm? Isabelle's daughter was visiting a school friend at Southampton,—did Amy know the Porters? Such lovely people, charming house, oh, all sorts of money, oil, you know. Amy considered the case of Isabelle's daughter, Sophie. She had gone away to school, to college, to Europe for a year, and then come back home at her mother's urgency. "What does Sophie do with herself when she's not visiting?" she asked.

"Oh, my dear Amy, she's terribly busy. Bridge, country club,—she plays a marvelous game of golf, you know. Committees,—she belongs to several clubs in town. She's a great comfort to her mother, too. She had an idea for a while of going into social work, but as I said, when there are girls who must earn a living, you mustn't take bread and butter out of their mouths. Especially when your own social position demands so many things of you."

Poor Sophie, thought Amy. The girl must be almost thirty. Funny she hadn't married.

"Well." Dewitt cleared his throat, swinging one

leg over the other knee, deep in his armchair. "We might as well get down to what you came about."

Alfred leaned forward, selecting a cigarette from the black lacquer box at his elbow. "Mother said you were in to see her before dinner." Amy lifted her head slightly; her father's voice had irony unwarranted by the simple fact he had stated, and her mother had made a quick movement, like a warning.

"I did see her. And I'm compelled to say I don't see any reason for making such an issue about Curly. Mother's an old woman, and if she wishes to keep the fellow, who are we to oppose her?"

Alfred ground his cigarette against the jasper tray. "Just what," he asked slowly, "has given you that point of view?"

"Dewitt," began Catherine, softly, "you didn't see Curly this morning. Amy and I did. It wasn't—pleasant."

"That won't happen again. Joe'll see to it he caches his stuff where a half-wit can't find it."

"You agreed with me this morning, when I called you," insisted Alfred. "You might explain this enlightened vision."

"For one thing," Dewitt's full lips sucked in, making of his mouth a hard downward crescent between deep lines from nostrils past the corners, "Mother says she'll publish the little fact of Curly's identity. How would that smell in this town, eh? She'd do it, too."

The two brothers stared at each other, Dewitt's face all sharp, hard lines, Alfred's a relief map with surfaces of concentrated inquiry. Alfred brought his palm down smartly against his leg.

"You want something out of her. You're borrowing again. She won't advance you a cent unless you side with her in this affair. Good God, Dewitt, have you no scruples?"

"This is a nice family party." Dewitt settled more deeply into his chair. "I don't mean to discuss my business here. I have scruples enough, about washing dirty linen in public, for instance. I don't intend to have our father's name smirched. I have scruples about keeping my head above water, too."

"I saw where that stock dropped again, to-day. You can't save it. Mother must be mad to give you anything more. She bribed you, that's all."

"If Dewitt doesn't agree with us,—" Catherine tried a drop of oil on ruffled waters,—"there's no use arguing about it."

"That's exactly what I was thinking." Isabelle fluttered into speech. "Men always shout so about money, poor darlings, and I always say such things should be kept outside the home. Now I'll run out and get us all a nice cold drink. Dewitt, honey, you come help Isabelle carry in trays—"

"Don't bother, please." Alfred rose. "We'll move on. You're quite right, Isabelle. This isn't a proper social call." He frowned at Dewitt, still intrenched in his deep chair. "If something like this morning, only worse, happens— You realize that if Lavinia hadn't been damned spunky and quick, Curly would have killed the boy. What about family linen then, eh?"

"I could put you a few ifs while we're about it." Dewitt pried himself up to his feet. "If you hadn't agreed with me last fall this stock was good, if you hadn't unloaded yours last March—"

"I told you then I couldn't cover any margin. I had to have cash for the factory." Alfred's eyebrows bristled but he responded with a shrug to Catherine's hand on his arm.

"I'm sorry." Dewitt's hand was ice against Amy's. "Sorry you were dragged into this. But Alfred never can forget he's an elder brother. Admonitions and all that. Good-night."

As they drove homeward Amy waited, rather tense from the clashing undertones of the scenes, for whatever her father or mother might say. Catherine spoke, presently. "Is Dewitt losing much money?"

"The poor fool thinks he can save himself by throwing thousands after what's already gone. He acts as though I made the slump, by clearing out early. I told him what I was doing. He's helping that precious son of his, too." The car spurted ahead, sharing Alfred's temper, and Catherine made a little warning sound. "Just because they've made easy money these past years, they won't believe what's going on. 'This is the bottom, and now's the time to buy. To-morrow everything will shoot up.' Bah! I'll bet we won't see that to-morrow in our lifetime."

"It certainly hasn't improved Uncle Dewitt's disposition, has it?" Amy stretched, savoring the release from tension. "I suppose Isabelle isn't much of a hand at retrenching."

"Not she." Catherine looked over her shoulder at Amy. "Dewitt's made a lot, but how she has spent it!"

Alfred stopped at the entrance to the house. "I'll put up the car," he said. "Isabelle's going to have a taste of retrenching. Why, Dewitt's got mortgages on that place thicker than the stucco. All the same—" in the faint light reflected back from the headlights his face sagged, a melancholy mask—"it was a dirty trick, reneging about Curly. He knows Mother wouldn't be hired to tell who Curly is."

Heat Lightning

He drove off, and Catherine stood in the soft darkness a moment, her hand in Amy's. "I'm not sure she wouldn't, if it meant keeping Curly," she said. "I hate having your father bothered this way."

Through the trees, dissipated gently by the thick leaves, shone a light from the second story of the next house. "Grandmother's not asleep yet," said Amy. "It was smart of her, now, wasn't it?" She thought of the old woman, the light beside her bed shining down on the bold modeling of her ivory face. She was like an old knife, worn from long use into a thin and lovely curve, bright, sharp at the blade's edge.

"Sometimes I think no one has ever forced her against her will to anything." Catherine sighed, looking toward the window. "And yet no one could live that long without some yielding. It won't be smart if she lets Dewitt throw away all her money. Well, I wish I could see what to do about Curly."

Alfred was returning, the gravel sliding with little noises under his feet. They entered the house, Amy reluctant to leave the leaf-hidden window. "I should think she'd be asleep," she said.

"I've seen her light all hours." Catherine moved quietly about, snapping on the lamps. "She says she can't waste time sleeping. (A long sleep coming soon, thought Amy. Is that it?) She has a way of dropping into sleep any minute, and out again, refreshed. She's changed, this last year. She seems to need less of everything,—sleep, food, people. She talks more about her early life. Sometimes,—" Catherine hesitated, glancing at Alfred. He had picked up a newspaper and was twitching the pages rapidly. "Sometimes it seems to me she's making a full circle, rounding back upon herself, as if she had to enclose everything before she left it."

Alfred rattled his paper. "Your mother's got the liveliest imagination I ever heard," he said, looking up at Amy. "Mother's the same as she always was. Not caring how she gets her own way, as long as she gets it. Circles. I don't know what you're talking about."

"Never mind, Father." Catherine rubbed his sandy hair as she paused behind his chair a moment. She sat down by the table, her hand reaching for a book. "I always know what I mean." The telephone rang. "You go, Amy. If it's Lora, don't tell her anything. Say we haven't decided what to do."

It was Lora, her voice too close, its plaintive notes whining along the wires. "But what did Dewitt say?" she insisted, and finally, "Well, I'll drop by in the morning. We must do something at once."

"Good work, Amy." Her father nodded at her. "Lora'd be wild if she knew Dewitt had got anything more out of Mother. Her own income's been pared a lot this year. You ought to be thankful you and Geof live on what you make, not on what money's supposed to make."

"Some advantage at last in belonging to the working classes." Amy stood at the doorway, watching the room, her father and mother. There was an ease about it, a pleasant dignity as unobtrusive as Catherine's manner. She made her house an extension of herself, of her own way of life, with taste and civilized comfort and affection for what had long been familiar. Isabelle's husk had to be redone every few years lest she miss the latest style. "Do Lora and Isabelle still have battles about their children?"

"Lora plays good bridge. So they mostly leave

the children out. Sort of 'thin ice, danger!' label, you know." Catherine smiled. "Harriet and Sophie don't move in the same crowd at all, and of course Tom is younger than Carruthers."

"Um." Amy yawned. "I'm going to bed, folks. This has been quite a day for midsummer." Ah, they wanted her to go! She caught that upswing of Catherine's face. Of course, Alfred wanted to be comforted. As Amy climbed the stairs she remembered, from her childhood, that murmur of low voices from the room next hers, her father's and mother's room. She had gone off to sleep hundreds of times, held secure from a strange world beyond the house by that sound, with its rising, falling, two-toned cadence, little waves of the relationship between those two in which her childhood found its safety. She wondered, abruptly, what her own children would remember, of her and Geoffrey. You made, inevitably, some solution, a mixture of the two, in which the children were suspended. Well, at least they hadn't quarreled, in loud, angry tones, when Buff and Bobs were home. As she undressed she went on with her thought, shifting the figure. Her father and mother had, together, made a warm light in which the children dwelt, unconscious that there was light. She and Geoffrey— unsought came a recollection of one evening on Riverside Drive, with the sky a warfare of crossing, clashing, opposing shafts of light from the ships of the fleet, moored along the Hudson. She had taken the children to watch the display, and Bobs had clung to her hand, trembling with excitement. The widening shafts of light blunted themselves curiously against low clouds, they moved against each other, and Bobs said, "I think I hear them fighting." She knew what he meant; she could hear that clash of dizzy atoms, a thin, metallic ringing. Ah, wasn't that the kind of light she and Geoffrey furnished, not spectacular and brilliant, but all the same disturbing?

She was so tired she could feel her forehead pressing down against her eyeballs. She couldn't think to-night. She couldn't even go back over the day, with its weight of many people. Later, to-morrow, another to-morrow, she'd look at them, see what they meant for her.

5

Her first thought in the morning was, "I should hear from Geoffrey to-day." Yesterday had been expanded to hold so many different encounters that she felt months had gone since she left New York. At least she heard no agitated words from Lavinia under her window this morning. To-day she would see Theodore and Felice. They had driven off on a sudden decision to look at a cottage near a small lake. Felice's note had explained that they'd just heard of it, a great bargain, and they were afraid they'd lose it if they waited. After them, Harriet would appear, probably in tweeds no matter what the weather, her hair slicked back, her eyes a little small in her plump face nibbling at you warily to see what you thought of her. What a family! It was queer so many of them had stayed near the Westover nucleus. They whirled about in their own orbits, but they helped make up the nebula, never fully escaping. They drew in strange elements from other—what did you call the core of a nebula? Amy smiled to herself at her picture. She must remember it, to tell Geoffrey.

From the small window at the stair landing she looked out. Another brilliant day. Curly shambled across the grass, with Alpha the black cat stepping daintily at his heel. He stopped, and Alpha rubbed an arch against his boot. Curly reached a dangling hand to the cat's back before he went on again toward the gardens behind the house.

Amy breakfasted alone. Her mother, Lulu explained grudgingly, had driven Mr. Westover to the factory, and was going shopping before she came home. The girl's under eyelids looked swollen, and she set forth orange juice, toast, coffee with resentful thuds, not distinct enough to be rebuked in words.

"Has the mail come this morning?"

"Yes."

"Nothing for me?"

Lulu relished her "No'm." Perhaps she merely disliked this serving an extra breakfast. "Where do you live, Lulu?" Amy mocked at herself as she questioned the girl. Absurd to find her breakfast flavored by a maid's bad temper. A form of vanity, Geoffrey assured her, that desire to have the moods that touched her even casually pleasant ones.

"I lived across the tracks with my folks. I don't go home now."

"Below the factory? Oh, yes, I know."

"My pa, he worked to the factory." She spoke in a loud, flat voice; as she moved past the opened French doors the sunlight laid patines of palest gold on her smooth hair and cheek and throat.

Amy speculated idly about her as she crunched thin toast. Her voice probably was the result of a crowded little house, full of children, yelling. She was either very dull, or so absorbed in some affair of her own that she hated the interference of her ordinary tasks. She's behind a hedge, her race, her own life, like all the rest of us.

Heat Lightning

Amy glanced at the table where the mail lay. Letters couldn't follow her as yet, of course. But time felt so much longer than it was!

She strolled across to her grandmother's house. Alpha, under the lilac hedge, stalked an invisible prey, a lovely rhythm of vibrating destruction from his laidback ears to the tip of his plumy tail. Amy watched him a moment. It would be nice to have one's body synchronized like that, completely expressive of emotion and intent. Too revealing, though. When man began to have conflicting impulses he stood up on his hind legs, put on clothes, and practiced concealment. She tried to wave her arm and fingers like Alpha's tail. Couldn't do it.

Tom met her just inside the door. "Hello, Cousin Amy." He illustrated her thesis, hurrying to put off that crestfallen look, to swagger a little. "Well, how you getting on with all the relatives? Want a cig? No, I suppose not, to call on the Madam. Mother had a bad head this morning. Sent me around with messages. I say, Curly did pull a stunt yesterday! Have to keep that boy on the wagon." In the morning light the boy's face had a cheesy look. "Well, I must tootle-oo. Cheer'o. Say, Amy, is Aunt Cathy home? No?"

Amy turned to watch him, pitying him a little. He threw off such blustering fragments from his brittle, spinning youth. Lora no doubt wept and jangled bracelets and clutched at him. He sauntered out to the roadster at the curb, stood there to light a cigarette, and then, with a glance at the doorway,—she probably was invisible, there in the dusky hall—made a dive for the other house. Amy felt several uncertainties pull together. He knew Lulu was there alone, Or was she a suspicious busybody? No one else seemed worried. Perhaps she was too alert; she had escaped the current of her own affairs, and stood on a bank watching the others drift past. "I might go after him," she thought. "Then I'd just interrupt, without any knowlege to use on the affair. Tom's no doubt kissed her once or twice. With all you hear about the willingness of girls, you'd think he could pick on his own kind. Oh, Lord!"

She found her grandmother in the kitchen, inspecting rows of golden peaches.

"Aren't they beautiful?" Amy laid a finger at the base of one jar, in the globule of amber light where sun shone through.

"They'll do very well." Madam Westover had the air of a satisfied creator. "You might attach these labels for me." Name and date in fine Spencerian script. "I like them to ripen a few years before we use them."

Amy remembered the shelves and shelves in the cellar, with their rows of glass jars, remembered too being sent back because she had brought up the wrong vintage; the date had been dimmed by the film of gray dust. More than several large families could ever use, but when preserving time came, Grandmother and 'Viny were seized with preserving madness.

"We meant to do pears this morning, but the fruit Hawkins sent over was no good. Too ripe. I sent it right back."

"Gives me a chance to brush up the upstairs." Lavinia bustled through the kitchen, dustcap awry, armed with ʻbrooms and mops. "I finished the downstairs now. Curly wants to turn on the sprinkler, but I told him he shouldn't, not till evening. This sun would boil the grass if you put water to it."

"It does seem as though it would have to rain some-

[75]

time." Madam Westover reached to straighten a label Amy had not affixed quite true. From the yard came the whir of lawn-mower blades, and Curly passed the window, fine spray of grass falling back into the canvas hood tied to the handle. "Curly made that himself," said Madam Westover proudly. "He saw one somewhere. He's smart about such things." Her glance had sly inquiry, probing into Amy's knowledge of the enemy's location and plan for attack. "You went along to Dewitt's last night?"

"That's the last one." Amy looked at the rows, labels straight enough for her grandmother's exigent eye. "Yes, Grandmother." She stood up from the table, and her eyes met the old woman's gleam. "You're a wicked old person!" She laughed at the delighted triumph under the drooping lids. "You ought to be in Tammany politics. You'd be good there."

"Family politics keep me busy." She walked ahead of Amy, her stick on the polished floors making an accent in a little march of victory. "Not much happened, did it?" She retrieved a basket filled with balls of gay yarns and long bone needles, and marched on to the side veranda. "Your father,—" she settled stiffly into her chair,—"is a good man. He's so good I have to outwit him by other channels." She chuckled softly. "I made a blue jacket and boots for Mary's baby, so it would be a boy. Now I have to make a pink one. Didn't work."

Amy shoved a low wicker hassock near the railing and sat down, her shoulders against the lattice. Her grandmother was staring over her head, needles arrested. "Is that—what's Tom doing over there?"

Amy peered through the vines. At the front door of her father's house was Tom, in a curious posture, as if some one clung to his hands. He pulled away and ran down the steps, leaped over the door of his roadster, and with a violent whir of the starter, had his car in motion. Amy's quick glance at her grandmother found the old face secretive, the mouth puckered between strong overhang of nose and jutting chin.

"Is your mother home?" she asked, and at Amy's negative shake, "So that's it. Humph." Her needles moved rapidly in her fingers. Old ivory, almost an extension of the fingers.

Amy huddled comfortably on her stool, hands clasped about her knees.

"You always could keep your mouth shut and your eyes open," said her grandmother, harshly. "Have you seen anything? I mean that girl."

"I don't know. I—well, I had wondered. She looked this morning as if she'd been crying."

"Crying! Humph. If that young fool—" Madam Westover knitted steadily, the soft pink tone of the wool an incongruous color beneath the mood of her face. "He came to see me this morning. He wanted money, and he wouldn't say why. The allowance I make him is ample. I thought he'd been losing at poker. But that clod of a girl! He must have been drunk."

"You think—" Amy looked at the firm mouth, tucked in at the corners until the faint etching of mustache had almost vanished—"you think, then, that he's really mixed up with Lulu?"

"That bit of pantomime we just saw looked like it. Amy,—" she laid down the pink fluff—"I had to buy up three women before Lora got rid of Tom Blake, Senior. I always thought it was a mistake, but Lora had the three children, young then, and wouldn't let go of Tom. Not at first. No, I think young Tom'd better squirm a while. He'll have to come out with it before I'll help him any." She lifted her knitting again, and set to work, the needles moving in a different rhythm, steady, deliberate. She had made up her mind, and, amazingly, dismissed the matter. "Tell me about your children. You might have brought them along."

Amy, jerking herself away from Tom's melodrama, hunted for stories of Buff and Bobs. "Perhaps next Christmas I can bring them with me."

Her grandmother listened, with dry comments and chuckles. Above them were thuds and rattles, Lavinia's attack on dust, and in the vines the plushy tumbling of bees. Catherine knocked on the screen door.

"No, I won't come in now. You look like a nice gossip party. Will you have dinner with us to-night, Mother? I have a young turkey, just large enough to roast."

"That girl of yours hasn't sense enough to roast a bird."

Amy laughed at Catherine's mild surprise. So, grandmother had been thinking all the time, had decided Lulu was alone to blame. She rose, stretching lazily. "I must go and write to my children. They've all forgotten me. I haven't heard a word."

"You will come, Mother?" Catherine coaxed. "I'll keep an eye on the bird."

"I'll bring a bottle of wine Joe brought me this morning." Madam Westover glinted maliciously. "Apology for the way he talked yesterday."

"That's better than our sending him flowers for a funeral." Catherine spoke quietly, and Amy guessed at the communication beneath those two speeches.

Heat Lightning

You see, said Grandmother, Joe's sensible. And we haven't settled things yet, answered Catherine.

"You better bring your writing things down to the porch," suggested Catherine, as they walked across to the other house. "The cleaning woman's upstairs now."

"I meant to ask how you managed with just one maid."

"Mrs. Maguire comes in three days, cleans, washes, irons. It saves quite an item, and that pleases Alfred. I suppose that's why Mother says Lulu can't cook. She didn't like my change. She thought it reflected on the way the factory was doing." They stood a moment at the door, watching a flock of goldfinches about the stone birdbath. The air was full of flashing petals of bright yellow, full of the repeated single note, thin, high, a twang of stretched catgut. "I must clean and fill that bath. The birds need a special attendant this summer. It's so dry they all use my baths." She returned to the earlier thought. "Mother's pride is involved in every detail of that factory, in spite of the years since Father died. It's an insult that there's less work. If she had her way, she'd run it full tilt, making plows no one would buy. She'd keep an extra maid rather than admit hard times included the Westovers." The little triangle between her brows and the fine bridge of her nose crinkled; she didn't frown often enough to make a wrinkle, thought Amy. "Alfred doesn't talk about it with her. He had to, at first, but when she disposed of her stock, when the estate was settled, you know, then she didn't have any need to know. Any real need, I mean." Catherine rubbed a forefinger between her eyebrows. "It was a relief to your father. He felt Mother was drawing a comparison between him and his father."

Amy could imagine a scene, the old woman emphasizing her words with her stick. "Your father never let hard times inside the factory gates!"

"As Alfred says, his father built up an industry during the years when hundreds of families were settling on little farms all through this part of the country, and Alfred took it over when their children were abandoning the same farms and moving to towns, where they bought autos and phonographs and then radios. Dewitt saw that, and sold out his share, to get into automobile production. What he didn't see was this year, when people have stopped buying anything." Catherine sighed. "I don't know how I happen to be talking so much," she added, "except that I've been thinking so much about these things. I can't do anything for your father except to have Mrs. Maguire." They walked into the house. "It's nice to have some one to talk to. I don't want your father to know I worry, and of course I wouldn't say a word to any of the family here in town. We all know too much about each other's business as it is."

After her mother had driven off, to see Mary this time, Amy sat on the porch, writing pad on her knee. She had wanted to stretch out in the hammock, but the terrace was too sunny in the morning. She wrote to Buff, about Alpha, about the baby jacket of the wrong color. Buff would think that very funny. "I hope a letter from you is running toward me very fast," finished Amy. "If one doesn't come soon, I may forget I ever had a Buff." She told Bobs about Alpha and his bell, about the goldfinches, about the drive to Emma's farm, and the way Emma's little boy had shown off, skinning the cat on an apple tree, and skinning his knee, too. "Write to me very soon, Bobs, and tell me what you like best in camp."

Getting away from your children for a while was a good thing, thought Amy. You realized them more completely as people when you weren't concerned with obscuring details about hands that needed washing and clothes that needed mending, and manners that, like the clothes, needed mending. No one had ever told her it would be such an absorbing and delicate and delightful task to be friends with her own children. It differed from friendship with an adult because of the subtle variation from day to day. They grew up by surprising jerks, and if you weren't alert, you were left behind where they had been yesterday and last week.

Her thought moved on to Geoffrey, and her face lost its softness. That relationship had changed, too, disastrously. She had fled before ruins clattered down to crush her. With children you expected to watch, to adjust yourself nimbly to a shifting personality. Didn't Geoffrey demand that very adjustment from her, with no return? This past year their attitude toward each other had been a tight-rope on which she struggled, with painful, awkward contortions, to keep her balance. And Geoffrey—he had jiggled the tight-rope! It was his fault. She saw his face, flashing up at her from the bag he was packing for his fishing trip—oh, he had been cruel, not caring that she was shaky from the silly operation, that she couldn't even talk comfortably.

She laid aside her writing things and walked across the porch, leaning against a pillar, staring at the little, meaningless movement in the leaves, her teeth set in her lower lip. Of course it wasn't all his fault. Nothing ever could be laid to one person alone. If she was still pitying herself, she wouldn't think about him. Before she shut him out, though, she'd send another wire. She went in to the telephone and jounced the hook in irritation at the slothful operator.

Do send me a wire hope you are well and happy and the fish bite.

Through the door into the dining room she watched Lulu, as she waited for the operator to repeat her message and to give her the charges. Lulu clumped around the table, laying the silver. Amy fumbled with the ear-piece, intent on the blue-ginghamed figure. If the girl was pregnant, she didn't show it. Even if Tom was mixed up with her, it might not be that serious. But her grandmother had assumed at once that it was. Amy reflected upon the old woman's attitude, as she walked back to the porch. She hadn't been shocked. She regarded possible trouble of that sort as a thing to be attended to with dispatch. Sharply Amy returned to a fragment of thought from the previous day. If she could have patience, could watch these shifting scenes with sympathy enough, out of them would come the wisdom she needed. It would, far more potent than any Aristotelian tragedy, constitute a personal catharsis, a purging of herself of blindness and other faults of vision,—distortion, perhaps.

From the front of the house came a chatter of several voices, like a flock of birds chirping in woods. Queer how sometimes that sound of approach made nerves shrink in a faint echo of a dark past when any approaching creature meant danger. Into the hall they came, her mother and father, and Theodore, her brother, with Felice.

"See what I brought home for lunch," called Catherine. "They'd just got home, and I thought it was time you saw each other."

How neat and compact Felice was, filling roundly the green knit suit she wore, her fine, intelligent, dark-fringed eyes expressive in her plain face. She pulled off a green béret, and her heavy cropped hair, gray-frosted, stood up like a cockatoo's crest. "Amy, it is good to see you." Her kiss was businesslike. "We ran away, but not at all from you." Theodore, sandy like his father, sunburned until his high forehead peeled, looked at her with friendly eyes behind his horn-rimmed spectacles, as he too kissed her hastily. He had been a funny little boy, with his nose in a book, paying small attention to his sisters. In fact, he had lived so satisfactorily in his own world that every one had been startled when he married. Amy remembered her mother's deep and unspoken concern. But Felice had gone straight into Theodore's world, had furthermore made a sturdy little dragon against intruders. She had spoken scarcely a word of English when she arrived, and she had, cleverly, kept through ten years the separateness thus launched.

"I hear Curly's been entertaining you." Catherine had gone out to break to Lulu the presence of two guests. "Mother's been telling us. And Dewitt won't coöperate." Theodore implied, in his dry, slow speech, his opinion of Dewitt.

"But me, I think Grandmère is a wise woman. And if Curly is her son, she must protect him."

"Not her son, Felice! Good God, don't make it worse than it is." Alfred grumbled at them all and strolled after Catherine.

"He is one harmless natural, yes?" Felice nodded. "But you, Amy, are you well after the little operation? And your family, yes?"

Heat Lightning

"What's Geof doing? I haven't seen an article of his for some time."

"He's fishing right now. Canada." Amy flew to Geoffrey's defense. He and Theodore never meshed gears smoothly. "It's been a hard year to sell his stuff. He hasn't done much except the advertising."

"We seem to be the only living souls not affected by hard times." Theodore jibed at himself and Felice. "It's a marvelous time for mathematics. Never was so exciting."

"You working this summer?" Amy was a little vague as to just what her brother did, aside from a small teaching job at the University. Last winter her mother had written that he had been offered a remarkable post with a firm of electrical engineers at a huge salary, and that he had refused. It would have left him no time for his own research, and Felice thought they had money enough. "I hope they are deciding wisely," Catherine had added. "I know money isn't everything, but they ought to look ahead. They make so little, and work so hard, Theodore shut up in that laboratory days on end, Felice tutoring in French and slaving over typing for Theodore."

"Oh, a little." Theodore never was expansive. "I had to have my glasses changed, so I'm loafing a little, getting used to them."

"You should tell your sister,—" Felice had a crisp pride in her accent—"that you have almost ready the monograph to deliver this fall before that august assemblage of philosophers and ancients."

"Amy wouldn't appreciate that honor." Theodore smiled at her. "Felice can't get over my being asked to read a paper."

"Why should I try to get over a pleasure?" Felice

lifted her dark lashes and looked at Amy with wide, calm eyes. "Your brother is already famous."

Amy thrilled at the serene identity of interests which shone through the restraint in Felice's words. "Come along, children," called Catherine. "Luncheon's ready." As they seated themselves, she added in a quick undertone, "Lulu says there's not enough, and how could I expect to have enough for two more all of a sudden."

"The Lulus cannot understand that it is more important we see each other than to eat largely." Felice sat erect, a pleasant eagerness about her small head, her solid throat and shoulders. As the talk ran on, Amy listening, adding comments, had a secret busyness with little asides to herself. Felice had a quality of making conversation seem unusually interesting. She had an inquisitive, alert mind, and more than that, a concern with what any one said to her which flattered the speaker into a belief that he spoke wisely and wittily. Ideas for Felice were never thin disguises for her own prejudices, they were on another level where emotion did not penetrate. She had no desire to coerce another to her way of thinking. Look at her drawing out her father-in-law until he actually forgot to worry about his factory in his discussion of kinds of unemployment insurance. Amy would never have suspected him of thinking so consecutively about the matter. Sardonically Amy imagined Lora there, jingling her beads through her fingers, waiting to interrupt with some sharply personal remark. Or Emma, —what would Emma do? Was the difference between Emma and Felice merely temperament, with Emma instinctive and female? Or did Felice represent a different stage of evolution? Was the difference racial? Amy sighed. I must stand somewhere between the two, she thought. Felice had as intense a personal life as any of them, didn't she? With the capacity for keeping that a private affair, and extending herself about that as a core into a larger world? Perhaps because she had no children. She had had, some years ago, a bad miscarriage which had left her ill for months. "We won't try it again," she had told Amy. "Theodore couldn't stand it, he says. I'm more use to him without children, I say to myself."

Amy snapped back to the present. Theodore was laughing at her, slouched comfortably in his chair. "You still wool-gather, old Amy? Where were you then?"

"I was thinking about all of us," admitted Amy. "How different we are." That sounded fatuous, she thought, but Felice turned toward her with a long, humorous glance in which Amy's words stood up, shook off their superficial obviousness, and revealed a little of her real effort toward appraisal.

"You see it more clearly, coming from away," Felice said, wisely. "I think it must be"—she paused to feel for a word—"enlightening, to come back to this huge family."

"I don't know about the enlightening part." Theodore rose, and drew back his mother's chair for her. "Some of us are in a mess."

"No, but when you are with people,—" Felice followed her, a fine intentness over her eyes and mouth as she hunted for this idea,—"you strike a balance between yourself and each of them, and forget then, what each is like."

"You certainly know what to expect, if that's what you mean," said Alfred, dryly. "Couldn't very well go about being surprised at everybody all the time."

"And yet,"—Felice dropped her voice, let it travel

just to Amy,—"they continue to be a surprise, is it not?"

Amy nodded at her, grateful. Later, when she and Theodore had driven off in their noisy Ford, and Catherine had driven Alfred away, Amy went back to her consideration of Felice. Perhaps that quality of charm, of apperception, came only from inner security. Felice had no anxiety, no wobbling of personal intentions. You might conclude she was too absorbed in her husband, too without any life of her own, and then she confounded you, in spite of ideas about women and their independence, with this quality. She was free-floating, not hemmed in, not moored fast in mud. Emma, now, was absorbed, but with a difference. Like a flicker of summer lightning at the horizon flashed a trace of explanation. Each of them satisfied herself because she lived true to her own code, without conflict or rebellion. And I—Amy moved restlessly— I don't know what my code is.

6

When Catherine came back, she went out to the kitchen. Amy, stretched on her bed, unable to forget how heavily the heat pressed down upon the still, dry earth, heard her voice. She was being firm about something. Tom? But Grandmother would scarcely have complained, at least not to Catherine. She might sail into Lulu directly. Amy twisted uneasily. Probably her mother was discussing the turkey, pride now being involved in the success of its roasting.

"Hello," Amy called, as she heard her mother walking cautiously along the hall. "I'm not asleep. Too hot."

Heat Lightning

Catherine came in and dropped wearily into a wicker chair beside the bed. "It really is frightful." She sighed. "I feel the way my poor flowers look, no juice left in me."

Amy propped her head up on one hand, elbow crooked.

"You run around too much," she scolded.

"I'm not running this minute," said Catherine, thrusting her feet out before her, wriggling her heels free of the canvas pumps. She looked at her daughter tentatively, and then went on, "Do some days ever seem ominous to you? You haven't any good reason for the mood, but the very air has a threat in it? Perhaps it's just the weather, drying up my disposition."

"Do you feel that way about to-day?" Amy hitched up on the bed until she could prop a pillow behind her shoulders, relieving her stiffening elbow. "I thought it was just me, being edgy or something."

"Nothing's really the matter, that I can put my finger on. But Lulu's so cross. She used to be quite different. I asked her if she felt sick, and she laughed, most disagreeably. And Dewitt was telephoning your father from town; the call came just as I went into the office with him, for a drink of ice water. Alfred didn't tell me what he wanted, but what language! I told him they'd take the 'phone out if he wasn't careful. And then Curly." Her hands, usually so quiet, made restless encirclings of each other in her lap. "Your father talked with Dr. Bates this morning. He's made up his mind—your father, I mean—to put Curly away. I agree about the wisdom of it, but I don't see how we can defy Mother. Dr. Bates pooh-poohed the whole thing, and that didn't help any. Just made your father furious. He's going to see a lawyer this afternoon. I know it's too bad of me to sit here, pouring out my grievances, when you're here to rest." Her lips trembled an instant before she drew them into a rueful smile.

"Then you ought to add that you've been midwife and mainstay to Mary, and Henry's been hanging on your skirt, and I'm no good—"

"Gracious, you'll make me sorry for myself! But here the whole summer has gone along, fairly pleasant, except for the uneasiness about bad times. I haven't minded that, except as it worried Alfred. Maybe there's a bad feeling abroad in the air. After all, nothing's wrong enough to have all this queer tightness about." She laid her hand between her breasts in an involuntary gesture. "To-morrow I'll wonder why I was such a fool. Won't I?" She waited, urgently, for Amy's reassurance.

"Those aren't entirely imaginary difficulties," said Amy. "I think, though, if you'd rest a while you'd put them farther from your chest, the way you usually do. What countless tasks have you planned for this afternoon?"

"Nothing. I did tell Mother I'd go with her to see Mary and the baby."

"I can do that." Amy swung herself upright, bare legs dangling. "I can drive your bus."

"Oh, Mother goes in state. Hadn't you heard? You know Charley Johnson, the chauffeur she had when she kept her own car? He's opened a garage. Mother financed him, and when she wants to drive, she calls him up. He comes around with a Lincoln and drives her himself. He has a special cap he wears for her, but he never washes his greasy face, and it's so funny. They go along with Mother listening to his yarns about the business, and I expect him to drive up a tree."

"I know Charley. But I thought he left town."

"He did. The State Troopers caught him with a truck load of liquor. He sent for Mother. She went bond for him, and somehow got the case postponed. And then, in spite of her children,—oh, weren't Dewitt and Lora furious!—she started him in the garage business. She said we were all to blame, that we made bootlegging the only way a poor man could get rich quick, and then rushed him into jail if he got caught delivering our own orders."

Amy laughed. "She must have had an elegant time, defying her respectable children."

"She did. She enjoyed it thoroughly. Charley's made a success, too. Nobody asks what his sideline is, now he owns a garage. It's so confusing, Amy, when some kinds of lawbreaking are quite the thing to do. I find the world rather mixed up."

"Darling, if you will rest this afternoon, part of it will straighten out. I'm going with Grandmother and her ex-bootlegger chauffeur." Amy took her mother's arm and propelled her gently to the door of her own room. "You disappear for at least three hours. Promise." She closed the door upon her.

As she dressed she thought over her mother's recital of anxieties. Was trouble swinging toward them? Perhaps this heat and drought contracted the spaces between spinning atoms, so that they bumped together more disastrously. What was that old Indian way of capital punishment?—tying the victim up in a fresh skin, and leaving him in the sun to dry, the thongs and skin shrinking steadily. She shuddered; her own skin felt too tight. She thrust her arms into the pale yellow silk sheath, held them over her head and let the dress slide down. At least she looked cool. No make-up to-day.

In the hallway below she hesitated a moment. But what on earth could she say to Lulu? The girl would resent, and justifiably, any attempt of hers to edge into whatever existed between Tom and herself.

Madam Westover was in her kitchen, a checked apron tied over her gray silk, arranging stalks of flowers in tall vases. She had a pailful of them, gladioli, snap dragons, old-fashioned spicy pinks.

"See how crisp they are." She laid a stalk in Amy's hand. "Curly cut them early and set them down cellar. They keep better that way. You might put this vase in the hall."

Amy carried the vase with its flame-hued spears of gladioli to the hall table. Snap-dragons for the living room, pinks for the center of the dining table. Grandmother dried her hands on the roller towel, untied her apron. "Where's your mother?"

"I made her lie down. I'm going with you." No hint of any foreboding in her grandmother's calm face. "This heat is trying, and Mother's been gadding about at a great rate."

"I'd just as soon have you." Grandmother took her stick from the corner and started through the house. "One advantage of being old is that hot weather doesn't bother me. Don't notice it. No flesh to melt." She opened the closet door and took down from the shelf her familiar panama with its black velvet band. "Your grandfather brought me that"— she held it out on a finger tip—"when he went to the World's Fair. It's been a pretty good hat." Amy watched her pull it over her thin white hair. It had the same ivory tone as the face it framed, and it wobbled a little. She had forgotten that summer hat;

she used to drive with her grandparents behind two black horses, grandmother's hair blowing out from under the brim of that very hat. "Where's that Charley? I told him three. Ah, there he is."

There he was, jumping down from the shining gray car, holding open the door, a sunburned Swede, striped shirt sticking to his broad shoulders, sleeves rolled above grimy elbows, and visored cap askew on thick fair hair.

"Just on the dot!" He grinned at Madam Westover, strong white teeth startling in his red face. "You feel pretty good? I ain't seen you for most a week."

"I been too busy to go driving." Charley's roar of laughter marked that as a repeated joke between them. "I have work to do." She clambered into the car. "You remember my granddaughter, Mrs. Norton?"

"Sure." Charley laid a finger to his cap. "I won't shake hands. Never shake hands with a garage man, Mis' Norton." That was funny, too.

Amy sank beside her grandmother. "Isn't this a nice car," she said.

"Pretty good. She's got a fair engine." Charley rubbed his shoulder against imaginary dust as he closed the door. "I let all the windows down, but if you feel too drafty, you just say so. Where you going?" His face hung at the door, a round sun.

"I'm going to see my new great grandchild," boasted Madam Westover.

"That baby lost me one job," confided Charley. "She come too quick, see? Her papa hired me to drive them to the hospital, and I lost the job."

Madam Westover nodded appreciatively. "You better watch out. I can't have you losing money for us."

Heat Lightning

Amy relaxed in relishing of the talk. What a good time her grandmother had! Charley loved her. This bantering wasn't pale gratitude because Madam Westover had rescued him from a tight place; it was ruddy affection.

"Now get along, Charley. And don't drive with your head back here, for you'd make Mrs. Norton nervous. She doesn't know what a smart driver you are. If we get through in time, we can take a real ride."

He could drive well, and the engine was good. They swung luxuriously out of the drive and along the village street.

"He's doing real well," said Grandmother, waving the head of her stick toward Charley. "I never heard of any man who was smarter about engines. He could tell blindfolded what ailed one. Most folks like him, too. He's put in a new hearse, and a new station bus, and he's talking about a big motor bus for trips. The folks all thought I was crazy, starting him out." Her nose and chin moved toward each other in sharp triumph. "He's made me money."

She leaned forward as they passed the motion picture theater. "I haven't seen that picture," she said. "We ought to go to it." She smiled. "We'll go Sunday. I make a point of going that day, ever since we had the fight about it. All the folks in this town with no day but Sunday for amusement, and the folks who don't have to work hard through the week making long faces about desecrating the Lord's Day. Bah!" She pounded her stick on the floor, and Charley turned his head. "I'm not talking to you." Grandmother brandished her stick, and Charley looked back, shouting something at a man on the corner.

"You've got your finger in almost every pie in

town, haven't you?" Amy counted on her fingers the various pies. "Charley's garage, the Westover Theater Block, the office building,—"

"You wouldn't have fingers enough, so you needn't count 'em." Grandmother looked pleased. "I got a scheme now for a new library, with a room where clubs could meet. There's a young architect in town making up some plans. But don't you breathe a word of it. That starts the family talking. Here we are." As she climbed out, she added, "Most of our family hasn't any imagination except for trouble, and they have too much of that."

Henry met them at the door, coatless, suspendered, dejected, his eyelid twitching furiously as he greeted them. "Excuse me, I didn't know you were coming. I'll run get a coat."

"Stuff and nonsense, Henry. You needn't roast yourself for us."

Amy was sorry for him, trying to stand up to his fear of this old woman. His inner cringing made him clumsier, dowdier than usual.

"I've been home a day or so, keeping an eye on Mary." (Why must he try to justify himself?) "I expect to get a line on something good next week."

"Um. We'll hope so." Grandmother sniffed, and started to mount the stairs. "I suppose we can go right up?"

"I think so. Perhaps I better see. You wait a minute." He hurried past her, catching his toe on a step and recovering his balance with a contortion of his body.

Madam Westover looked at Amy, her eyebrows lifting wrinkles in her high forehead, and sniffed as if she saw the pity Amy was feeling.

"Mary says come right up." Henry's voice was

loud, granting them this privilege. "The nurse will bring the baby in, too." He stood aside as they passed him. "It's nice it's another girl," he added, defiantly. "It can wear all the clothes that are left."

"Stuff and nonsense," muttered Grandmother, going into Mary's room.

Mary at least wasn't afraid. Her cheeks had more color to-day. Or had she heard Henry, and blushed for him? Grandmother bent over the bed, her whole bearing altered suddenly into gentleness. "My dear child," she said, "you're looking very well."

"It's good of you to come. Such wretched weather." Mary's voice was stronger to-day, too, without that undertone of recent pain still held in fatigued muscles. "Find some chairs, please. Henry's been so good,"— she offered this boastingly—"he fixed up that electric fan, but the whir bothered me. It's lucky for me he can stay home just now."

"Lucky for him you feel that way," said Madam Westover. "Where's the baby?"

"Nurse will bring her. She's been fretting a little. I think they ought to let me nurse her." Tears of weakness filled Mary's eyes, intensifying the deep blue of the iris. "Prepared food isn't ever right."

"You'll find it much easier, Mary, dear." Amy laid her hand over her sister's fingers.

"But I like to nurse my baby." The tears slid down, and Amy patted the damp streaks with a handkerchief. "I'm not really crying, you know," sniffed Mary.

"In my day," said Madam Westover, "women nursed their children because there was nothing else to do. I shouldn't wonder if before you girls die you'll see them making babies by machinery."

"If men had to bear them, they might do something about it," said Amy.

"But they don't." Madam Westover's glance at Mary had a reminiscent sharing of birth. "Here comes the baby."

The nurse settled the thin pillow carefully on Grandmother's knees, and the new baby, not yet smoothed nor bleached, lay there, an animated frog beneath the strong old face that bent over it. Amy held her finger for the tiny, clutching hand, and she and Grandmother smiled at the mock-smile grimace of the puckered little face.

"She looks like Henry," said Amy.

"Just that she's bald," said Grandmother, her forefinger brushing the dark tuft on the soft skull.

"She's got lots of hair," cried Mary. "Give me my baby. You shan't call her bald."

"Glu-up!" said the baby, and the nurse hastened to mop her chin.

"She ought to go back to her basket, Mrs. Chester. She's just been fed." The nurse lifted the pillow with a dexterous slide of her arms. "She'll lose it all again if I don't keep her quiet." And off she went.

"That's all I see of my own baby," murmured Mary, tears bright in her eyes again.

"That's plenty," declared Grandmother, getting to her feet. "I'm going to send you calves' foot jelly. That'll strengthen you. Now you go to sleep. Takes lots of sleep to get over a hard job like a baby. Don't you let Henry come mooning about all the time." She walked briskly away.

Amy kissed her sister's damp cheek. "She's a sweet baby," she whispered. She felt a tremulousness in her throat, a mixture that might be sentimental, of Mary as her little sister, of babies clinging to her finger with that bite of tiny claws. "Good-by."

Madam Westover, in the hallway below, was warning Henry. "A man can be a great nuisance about the house such times. Mary ought to sleep hours and not be worried about you."

"I don't worry her." Henry squirmed visibly. "I don't want to be here all the time. What am I to do? She's glad I'm here."

Amy laid a hand on her grandmother's arm. "Mary will hear you," she said. "Don't distress her."

"I'd find something if I was in your shoes," muttered Grandmother, stumping out of the house. "He makes me mad," she added, as Amy followed her into the car. "Why doesn't he keep a job? I never knew a man like him. Drive out the river road," she told Charley.

"Couldn't Father give him something at the factory?"

"He did, and Henry couldn't get on with the men. He goes around with so many chips on his shoulder he hasn't time for anything but seeing to the chips. I offered him a job myself, ticket seller at the theater, and you ought to have heard Mary! He couldn't be cooped up in an airless booth all day, right here in this town where every one knew the Westovers. He was too good for that kind of work. He'll have to find his own job now, for all of me. Mary's got pluck, but she lacks sense. Especially where he's concerned."

"At least he's good to her," offered Amy.

"Humph. Too sweet for a man." Grandmother waved her stick. "I don't like him."

"He's not your kind, you old Tartar," said Amy, and her grandmother looked at her, eyebrows up in startled anger an instant before she laughed.

"That's it."

"You like 'em bad and bold, don't you?"

"I like your man, Geoffrey. Why doesn't he come

along with you? He's not bad, but he's bold enough."
She peered shrewdly at Amy. "You haven't said much
about him. What's he been up to?"

"Figure it out." Amy shifted away from the sharp
old eyes, trying to hide her sudden stiffening of muscles
under a glib tone. "You ought to know what bad,
bold men do."

"Humph. I suspected as much. You'd like me to
stop prying." She was silent a moment. Charley
drove along the wide state road, so swiftly that telephone poles rushed and retreated in dizzy repetition.
"It's funny," she went on, in a quiet monotone, the
words smooth from frequent turning in her mind,
"that what an old woman knows can't help her, her
life with a man being over and done with. Nor can
it help a young woman, for she wouldn't listen if you
could tell her all you know. No, we have to go it
alone. But I'll tell you one thing, child. A lifetime's
too short to find your way about another's heart, without blunderings and mistakes. That's why these folks
nowadays are so foolish, rushing into marriage, out of
it, into another. They never do anything but make
a beginning, and then make the same beginning again.
They think there's nothing else, besides that crazy
excitement at the first."

"Yet it was you who made Lora divorce Tom
Blake."

"Oh, Lora!" Grandmother snorted. "She may be
my daughter, but she has less idea than a rabbit
about living with other people. All she did was moan
and wring her hands, and she got Tom to hating her.
They're both better off."

Amy was silent then, pressed back into her corner.
Her grandmother's words were a handful of pebbles,

smooth and cool, which she must finger, one by one. A lifetime's too short—too short—

"Stop a minute, Charley!" Amy jumped at her grandmother's sudden shriek. "No, by that next lane." The air within the car made a pocket of dead heat as they paused, the faint breeze of their motion gone. "See that grove that runs down to the river?" Madam Westover pointed with her stick. "Your grandfather wanted to make an amusement park there for picknickers. I haven't got around to it yet, but maybe next year I shall. Two years ago Dewitt was after me to sell the trees. Some furniture company wanted them. They're the biggest in this part of the state." She leaned back. "That's all, Charley. You better turn around. It's too hot for any use, even driving."

"When you start your park, Mis' Westover, I'll run a jitney bus out here." Charley's teeth flashed. "Folks'd enjoy a place like that."

"What do you have to do to start it?" Amy climbed hastily out of the abyss into which her grandmother had driven her. "And how do you find so many projects?"

"Well—" Grandmother had the faint, malicious glint that was so frequent in her eyes. "I'd have started sooner, only I had a fight with the Country Club. Their land touches this. In fact, Dewitt sold it to them. Part of his inheritance. And they couldn't see a public park next door. Some wop might swipe a golf ball, I suppose. They tried to stop me by law. You ought to hear them go on, Amy, it would make you scream. All these folks trying to pretend they're too good to rub elbows with common people. Country Club! The only kind of country club their parents ever heard of was a woodshed and a shillelah. I told my lawyer to tell them this was the United States of

America and to read the Declaration of Independence. Anyway, I beat." She chuckled. "A public park isn't a public nuisance."

Amy laid her hand over the old knuckles that clutched the silver head of the stick. "You're just swell," she said.

7

After a final word of praise for the car, which pleased both Grandmother and Charley, Amy went quietly into her father's house. But her mother, instead of being asleep, sat at the telephone.

"How late will you be? Oh, Alfred! Isn't it terribly warm in town? Yes, I suppose so. I wish you'd tell me what— All right. No. No, I won't say anything. But, Alfred! Al—" She waited a moment, in the vain emptiness of a severed connection, and then replaced the instrument slowly.

"Hello, Mother." Amy could see her wipe off the worried abstraction, pull a brisk smile over her features. "Didn't I send you to bed?"

"I did sleep. Lulu just called me to the 'phone. Did you have a good ride?"

"Yes. Grandmother bullied poor Henry. But she was sweet to Mary. Sort of one woman to another air."

"If Henry would stand up to her she'd think more of him."

"He tried to, but his feet kept slipping. Then we drove out the river road, as far as Grandmother's public park." Amy laughed at the face her mother made.

"Did she tell you about that?" They went into the living room, where the unstirred air had a dim green shadowiness from the drawn shades. "I think it's cooler here than on the porch. Did Mother tell you about the law-suit?"

"Just that there'd been a battle and as usual she won."

"Isabelle was behind it, hidden back of a club committee, but Mother knew she was there, all right. They tried to prove that a public park would bring undesirable characters into the neighborhood of the Country Club, lessening the exclusiveness, and also the value of the bonds. I didn't hear the young lawyer Mother hired, but people said he was marvelous. I am sure some of his remarks came from Mother. 'Was a man an undesirable character because he drove a cheap car and drank lemonade instead of synthetic gin and played ball instead of golf?' You can imagine how the case went. And you know, I have a feeling Mother is right. Her schemes always sound so wild, but she always puts them across and then sits back and watches them succeed. Like the motion picture house. I don't want to be too catty, but I am afraid Isabelle wants to keep Mother from spending anything. Wasting the estate, is her phrase. As if Dewitt hadn't already had more than his share. Isabelle is long on exclusiveness, too."

"She's no match for Grandmother Westover, though." Amy ruffled the pages of a magazine, her gaze discreetly away from her mother. Poor dear, talking so busily, piling words on top of the snatch of telephone conversation, and all the time that harassed look showing through the thin gauze of her smile and chatter. Father had gone in town, and she wasn't to say anything. Amy's thoughts picked out another item to lay beside those. Dewitt had telephoned earlier, and her father had been excited.

"Do you want to read a while? Oh, here's the postman." Catherine rose, embracing the interruption.

Amy waited, trying not to allow eagerness to swing her so high that a fall would hurt; she could not control the quickening of her heart beat. Geoffrey wouldn't have written; there hadn't been time. He hadn't even replied to her two wires. She heard the postman's feet heavy on the porch, and then her mother came back.

"Here you are, my dear." Her anxiety had vanished for the moment, as she looked at the envelope. "Which one of your children can print so beautifully? And look, it says, 'Care of Grandma Westover.' Isn't that adorable?"

"That's Bobs." Amy held the envelope, reading the neatly made address. "They teach printing instead of writing, and Bobs handles a pen very well." She laughed, running a finger under the flap. "He would add *care of*. He's a cautious young man."

She read the letter slowly, letting images of the boy drift through the words. The top lines were straight, and then they tobogganed riotously toward the end of the page. She read it aloud, an amusing record of things most vivid in his few days at camp, and nothing of any importance. Except for the last, a postscript on the back of the sheet. "I remember what you said about how to act if I felt lonesome in my stomach. It works pretty good. Your loveing son Robert Norton." Amy's eyes misted.

"He sounds as if he liked it," said her mother. "I wish Buff had written, too."

"She's probably tearing around having such a wonderful time she can't bother with letters. You know, she's something like Grandmother Westover, isn't she?"

"Is she?" Catherine puzzled a moment, as if her imagination could not bring the child and the old woman close enough for comparison, with that gap of seventy odd years between them. "I never thought of it. In a way, she'd be lucky if that's true."

"Yes, she'll have a good life." Amy laughed. "It may be overwhelming to be her mother. I'll have to ask Grandmother how she was managed in her youth."

"Her own mother died when she was a little girl. I have heard her talk about caring for her younger brothers and sisters, even when her father married again. They moved to this state from the east just before the Civil War."

"What a short time a long time is," said Amy. "All those years gathered up in one life."

"Was you going to fix that dressing, Mis' Westover?" Lulu glowered at them from the doorway.

"Yes, Lulu. Presently." Catherine's forehead puckered as she looked after the vanishing Lulu. "I wish I knew what's wrong with her. I don't like to scold her if she's sick or bothered."

For an instant Tom's name moved in the cords of Amy's throat. But why add a grain to the anxiety her mother confessed? Not without some more definite clew. "Can't I help stuff the turkey? Maybe Lulu's just cross at the idea of cooking anything this kind of day. Set it out on the sidewalk in the sun, why don't you?"

"She uses the electric stove in the summer kitchen, and it isn't hot work. No, you certainly can't help in the kitchen. I do wish Alfred could get back, he's so fond of turkey." She sighed a little and went off.

Amy tried to read, but although her eyes moved down the lines of print there was a wall between the small black marks and the meaning they should click off. She closed the magazine and slouched more deeply in the chair, head back against the smooth linen cover.

She'd have to follow her advice to Bobs about feeling lonesome in his stomach. But Geoffrey might send her a wire. It was unlike him to hold anger long, and never had he held it past the moment when she waved the smallest flag of truce. Of course, since the quarrels or strains were always his fault, he would be ready to pick up a sign of peace. Amy found a crumb of paper in her fingers, which she rolled and rolled. They were his fault, weren't they? Suddenly dark crimson burned her cheeks, and she pushed herself upright in the chair, her fingers laced till the knuckles showed white. She'd been saying that a long time. She'd come out here, in a way, to discover the truth of her saying. That phrase Grandmother had offered her— "A lifetime's too short to find your way about another's heart without blunderings and mistakes." Was Grandmother as wise as she sounded, or was her wisdom applicable only to older days, older ways? After all, Geoffrey precisely didn't want her finding a way about his heart. She could see the sardonic hollows in his thin cheeks at the idea. Wasn't his plea that she should let him alone? "Every one has to have a private life, Amy. Go have yours. Don't poke into mine."

It had been easier, she thought, to live when you knew exactly what you believed, what was right, what you and every one else should do. Take Lora. When Tom Blake gallivanted with too many ladies, Lora divorced him. She knew what a husband should do. Not that Geof was like Tom. But wasn't it ridiculous not to be sure where resentment should begin, not to know whether you were a selfish prig, or—well, what?—an injured woman? That was a swell, antiquated phrase.

At least—Amy released her tight fingers and watched in dull curiosity the speed with which blood flowed back into the green-white compressed flesh. Why, what was happening to her! Some pressure had been released, and slowly, not at the same speed as blood, she was beginning to think, instead of moving round in a treadmill of emotional catchwords.

The clock on the bookcase dropped one note into the still air. Amy heard the faint preliminary chur of metal cogs, and the widening, diminishing ripples of the low sound. Only half-past four. She thought how different time felt here, compared with her days at home. Once you took yourself out of your accustomed life, into a setting where you had no tasks and no habits, you found time a series of definite hours, one after another, with divisions sharp as lines on a chessboard, and yourself a pawn moving from one square to the next, continuously conscious of each hour line as a barrier to be reached and passed, amazed at the number of them to a day. At home,—she tried to catch the precise feeling of time there. No watching of a silly clock. You had a varying rhythm for a day, you and time in counterpoint. You were yourself the hourhand, heels set against the steady rush, swinging through tasks and feelings of a whole day, without awareness of neat and arbitrary sections of time. Empty-handed people, hunting for things to do, must feel all their days like chessboards.

The telephone rang, and Amy strolled out to answer. It might be Geof. Sometimes he called her from the most surprising places. But it wasn't a long distance ring. Lora's voice made plaint against her ear. She had the most annoying telephone voice in the world. "No, this is Amy, Aunt Lora." Harriet had come home, and wouldn't Amy and her mother drive over for a cup of tea? Tom had the car somewhere, so unless Lora and Harriet walked in this awful heat— "I'll see, Lora. Wait a minute."

Catherine stood at Amy's shoulder, her breath quick. Ah, she had hoped it was Alfred. Amy laid her palm against the receiver, and explained.

"Ask them to come here for dinner. All that turkey— You could drive over after them. About seven."

Amy crinkled her nose in protest, but she delivered the message. Lora was delighted, if it wouldn't be too much trouble. She hadn't a thing in the house, as Harriet hadn't let her know when to expect her. "All right," Amy interrupted. "I'll be around pretty soon."

"Oh, that tremulo stop in Lora's voice!" She looked up at Catherine. "Aren't you too good to her?"

"It will be a simple way for you to see Harriet. I knew if Lora had a bad head this morning, she wouldn't have any dinner planned. Harriet and Tom are always appearing suddenly and vanishing as suddenly. I don't know how Lora could manage such a household."

"I don't blame them for vanishing when possible." Amy rose, rubbing her cheek against her mother's shoulder. "There, I won't be obnoxious. But you're too sweet."

"Harriet was to stay a week, I thought."

"She must have had a falling out with her lady love." Amy laughed. "Lora and her whispered, 'Not the Captive!'"

"You tell Lora Mother is coming, and she mustn't

say a word about Curly. Not at dinner. Tell her Alfred is seeing to the matter." Catherine jumped as the telephone bell clattered again. "Yes? Oh, Isabelle."

Amy climbed the stairs, bits of dialogue following her. "No, I don't *know* anything. Alfred just said he was in town. No. What? I don't believe it. Oh, no. But, Isabelle, Alfred would— What can I do? Really, Isabelle! You'll have to do that yourself. Certainly not."

So there was trouble. Amy had an amateur's vagueness about stock markets, and little beyond newspaper headlines in the way of knowledge as to what might be happening. Dewitt's son Carruthers had, she knew, gone from college to the gilded career of bond salesman. The trouble might be his, or Dewitt's. And poor Father was dragged in. Margins, pools, covering, all sorts of mysterious phrases wandered past as she changed into a fresh white silk.

She drove slowly through the village streets to Lora's, missing the corner where she should have turned, and circling a block or so, watching idly the pieces of slight activity she passed,—men driving home from a day of work, children playing on lawns, a dog barking as he chased a boy, a woman waiting on the steps of a screened porch. You saw much more of the way people lived, in a small town. In a city each family closed its apartment doors upon its life. You shot up in an elevator with strangers, guessing a little at the flavor of those whose hours matched yours, so that their contours and expressions grew recognizable. Here she supposed her mother could tell her intimate details, if she cared to, about each of the houses. Were you any wiser for all that knowledge? It was superficial, and you were as shut within your own walls, in your own affairs, as if you put chain and bolt on your box of an apartment.

Lora's house looked just as always. Buff colored, with chocolate trimming, a maple tree in the front yard already dropping crisp leaves on the yellowed grass, a bank of shrubs past their flowering each side of the steps to the square porch. Lora never had flowers. She couldn't tend them herself, she explained, and she couldn't afford a gardener. Grandmother had given her the house when she married and here she had stayed, the only change the ejection of Tom Blake. Amy touched the button on the wheel, and the horn squeaked. She might as well go in. They wouldn't be ready. Ming, the old Pekinese, met her at the door, his pop eyes age-filmed, his feeble intention belligerent.

"Here, Ming, come to Mother." Lora floated down the hall, picked up the dog, fingers smoothing his sable head. "Does he think he's a fierce old watch dog? Come in, Amy." Ming struggled under Lora's arm, his fore feet catching in a string of large amber-colored beads. He gave a violent kick, and with the clatter of small musketry the beads dropped from the broken string. Lora, Ming, Amy, all scrambled for them, Ming with restraint appropriate to his age. "He'll swallow them! Ming, oh, you bad boy!" Lora waved her hands agitatedly into corners, under rug edges. "I'll never find them all."

"What on earth are you doing?" Amy looked up, her hands full of round amber drops. Harriet lounged in the doorway, one hand in a pocket of her suit, one poising an extremely long cigarette holder. "Hello, Amy."

Hadn't she acquired a deeper voice? Amy smiled, showing her handsful.

"Don't just stand there," exclaimed Lora, her head under the console table. "Get us a box or a bowl, something to put these in."

"Jolly good thing that string's ruined," said Harriet, not moving.

Amy emptied a dusty chocolate cream from a glass bonbon dish and let her beads roll from her hands. "I think that's all."

"I'll tell the girl to look when she sweeps." Lora, still excited, poked a finger among the loose beads. "I'm sure the small ones aren't all here."

"Oh, never mind, Mother." Harriet preceded them into the living room, with a slouching sidle of wide hips and flat chest. Amy saw her gait as a physical symbol of the girl's protest against Lora. Her chronic irritation with her mother seemed nearer the surface than Amy remembered. "Don't fuss so over nothing. How did you happen to come to this awful town just now?" She confronted Amy with an air of, "Now that's a question no one could answer!"

"Oh, Ming!" Lora interrupted. "Look at the poor darling! Does him feel too unhappy? Come right here, darling. No, you aren't a bad boy. You are a sweet pet." Ming, with a faint twinkle of his worn feathered tail, followed Lora to her chair and waited to be lifted to her lap. Harriet puffed smoke violently from her nostrils.

The room had a familiar clutter of innumerable small objects; it had altered only by accretion. End tables, smoking stands, even a small painted bookcase with sky-scraper influence in its irregular angles, and all the surfaces loaded down with baubles. Small wonder Harriet slicked back her hair and went in for tweeds. Only why did she stick around if she felt that way? Amy remembered her as a small child, five years her junior, tagging about, a complaining limpet. She didn't like the games the others played, but she never invented her own.

"What did you come for?" she repeated. "I can't imagine any one coming here in summer unless he simply had to."

"I'm sure Amy wanted to see her mother and father." Lora made the remark imply comparison between Amy's motives and those of her own daughter. "Besides, lots of people like our pleasant little town."

Harriet grunted, and her abrupt gesture to dislodge her cigarette from the holder knocked ash tray and cigarette box to the floor. Ming lifted a disapproving flat face, and Lora sighed, "Really, Harriet—"

"Why must you be so awkward?" mimicked Harriet, before Lora had said it.

"Suppose we drive over," said Amy. She'd take these females to her mother, since the necessity for sharing their bickering came from Catherine's invitation.

"I must give Ming his dinner before I go." Lora set Ming gently on the floor, and shaking out loose ends of georgette, trailed out of the room, Ming padding his slow, stiff way after her.

"That dog must be awfully old," said Amy. "He walks like an old man."

"He's going to live forever." Harriet rubbed the palm of one hand over the sleek back of her head and then left it there, absently, fingers spread. "You think I'm terrible, talking to Mother that way. I saw it in your face. How would you like it—" off flew her hand in a wide gesture—"if you were picked at all the time? As if I were about ten."

Heat Lightning

Amy looked at her; colorless, undistinguished face, with stiff pale eyebrows and drab hair, with discontented mouth, nervous tension etched in lines about eyes and lips. "I don't see why you stay, feeling that way."

Harriet stared at her. "What else can I do? I want to take an apartment in town with a friend. I haven't any money. She won't listen to a word. I'm all she's got. You know the line."

"Earn some money," said Amy, coldly. "Most of us have to get it that way."

"But how? I'm not clever, like you. I—" she broke off, as Lora's high heels pattered in the next room.

As Amy stepped into the car after them, her toe was unnecessarily fierce against the starter. The car was too crowded, with that potential conflict on the rear seat. The trouble with Harriet—she swung down the street—was that the girl was lazy. She wanted to be kept, and she wouldn't pay for it, even by civility. But Lora, a limp, unhappy, maternal octopus, had clung to her, just when Harriet might have stepped out. College had been out of the question. Lora was just divorcing Tom those years, and Harriet had been violently her mother's champion. And yet—Amy poked among scattered odds and ends of the past, scarcely hearing the desultory words Lora kept bubbling—hadn't Harriet earlier been on her father's side? And Tom used to make fun of her awkwardness, her chunkiness. He liked charm and prettiness, even in small girls. Amy reached the doorway and a clear thought at the same moment, and stopped with a jam at the brake. All this man-hating stuff of Harriet's grew as scar-tissue on a wound! Funny how plain it was, once you saw it. Tom laughing at her, hurting her. Tom as false husband. Harriet had been forced into her mother's camp.

Curly trundled the hose cart around Grandmother's house, the creak of the roller as the hose unwound announcing his approach. Amy seized Lora's arm. "I almost forgot," she said, hastily. "Mother asked me to tell you. Don't say a word about Curly at dinner. Grandmother's to be here, too."

"But we ought to discuss it."

"No, Aunt Lora. Father's taking care of it, really. Now remember!"

They all three watched Curly unwind the final loop of hose and kneel to attach it to the sprinkler. As he plodded away with the empty cart, Harriet said, "He looks natural as ever. Why don't you let him alone?"

"You don't know anything about it," began Lora. "I'm sure—" but Catherine appeared at the doorway, and Amy delivered her guests.

Dinner passed in gusts of talk. Catherine and Grandmother Westover seemed to drop into abstraction, from which they bobbed to the surface splashing words about. "Funny not having any men here," said Madam Westover. "Where are they all? What's Alfred doing, in town as late as this? Well, where's Tom, then? Why didn't he come?"

"He's at the University to-day, working hard," affirmed Lora, and under Grandmother's eye Harriet looked down her own nose without an audible sniff.

Grandmother had brought her bottle of wine, and insisted on its being served. "Joe's going to make some more for me, out of my Concords," she said. "I hope it's better than this vinegar." She cocked her head at Catherine, defying her with the intimacy established between Joe and herself. Amy saw Lora's ruffles and beads heave visibly, but without result in words.

The turkey was satisfactory. "Alfred will laugh when he sees how badly I carved it. No, don't try to keep it hot for him, Lulu. Just set it in the refrigerator." Lulu had scarcely lifted her eyes through the serving of the dinner, after Amy had intercepted a queer stare at Harriet when the grape fruit came on.

"Now if you only played bridge, Amy." Lora fluttered into the living room. "What do you find to fill your evenings?"

"Too many things. You four play, and I'll read."

"I'll play if I don't have to be Mother's partner," said Harriet, fitting a cigarette into the holder.

"You can be my partner, but not if you wave that thing around." Madam Westover pointed a bony finger at the girl. Harriet shrugged, but dropped the holder into her pocket, and helped unfold the legs of the card table.

Presently Amy went quietly away, to sit on the bench at the end of the formal garden. The night was still and warmly dark; the texture of the sky had softness, like deep-pile velvet, in which the stars showed small as if the softness through which they shone muffled their brilliance. At first there was no sound near, not a voice nor a passing motor. Then high overhead, like talk of the stars, an irregular, repeated chirping, the questioning, valiant note of small birds in the dark, beginning their migrating flight. In the mood of the day and evening it was an alien note. Amy imagined that flight, dark, instinctive, swinging in a long curve over the surface of the troubled earth, obeying the seasonal rhythm. Winter was coming. How could they guess it, a night like this? Age was coming,—and how could you believe that, a night like this, with torment and distrust and longing at war within?

Along the garden path came some one, Harriet, unmistakably, from the heavy footfall and the wavering bright end of cigarette. Amy sat still, but her white frock gathered up enough light to betray her.

"Oh, there you are." Harriet felt along the bench for room to sit. "Mrs. Bates,—you know, the doctor's wife—came in, so I could run away, too." She swung one knee over the other, a heel gouging the gravel. "Thank God Mother likes bridge. She doesn't talk while she plays."

Amy was silent, resenting Harriet's intrusion. The girl didn't fit into the night. She didn't fit anywhere.

"I say, Amy. Would you do something for me? You said, at the house, that I ought to get away. You did say that, didn't you? Would you tell Mother you think so? You're so smart she'd listen to you. Anyway, you don't seem like a relative, now you live so far off."

"I said why didn't you go, not that you ought to go."

"Yes. I could manage on a small allowance, really. If you talk to her, she might listen."

"But, Harriet!" Exasperation lifted Amy's voice. "That's the kind of thing you have to do for yourself. I can't do it."

"She just doles money out to me." Harriet went on, and Amy realized that the girl listened too closely to her own thoughts to have an ear for anything Amy might say. "If she'd give me just a little regularly. Enough to pay my share of an apartment. I've got this friend—" She hitched along the seat and laid a hungry, clutching hand on Amy's knee. "She's wonderful, really. She's losing patience, waiting for me.

Heat Lightning

Another woman—" her voice thickened—"wants to go in with her. She's worming her way in between us. Amy, I can't bear it! Mother hates her, and I can't even bring her home with me. Tom does just what he pleases, and he behaves awfully. Mother's crazy about him. Laurance used to stand up for me, when he was home. He's jolly well out of it all now, with that dumb Emma of his. You always did what you pleased. Your mother's different from mine. It wouldn't hurt you to help me out. I tell you I can't bear it." Her hand transmitted to Amy the spasmodic quiver of her body, and Amy deliberately pried the fingers loose from her knee.

That chance remark of hers, combined with the second chance of this corner in the garden, dark and solitary, had let down the weak barrier behind which Harriet's emotions churned. "You're acting like a child, Harriet." Amy struck at her in sharp words. She'd be having hysterics any minute. "Stop shaking like that! Brace up. How can I help you out? Stop making that ridiculous noise. Here, give me a cigarette."

Mechanically Harriet responded to the request, and in the glow from the match Amy saw her face, clay-hued, fine beads of sweat glistening along the upper lip.

"Now light one yourself and quiet down."

"You don't know how dreadful I feel." Harriet fumbled with her holder, broke one match, lighted the next. "You always have that superior air about me."

"I know this, Harriet. If you can't bear a thing, you get out. What you mean is—"

"You see! You say get out. How can I?"

"How does anybody? Don't be childish."

"If I went to New York, would you get me a job?

I could write for a paper, I should think. But I don't want to go to New York. Nobody cares what I do."

"It's your own fault if they don't." Amy marveled at her own brutality, but Harriet didn't listen to her. She didn't listen to anything but the repeated phrases of her own self-pity. "When my daughter grows up, if she wishes me to support her, I certainly will expect her to do what I like. If she wants to suit herself, she can pay for it herself. You're soft, Harriet. Soft as wet putty." Amy moved lightly to her feet. "You wanted me to hold your hand and pity you. Yes, you did."

"You're shocked, that's all." Harriet's voice had an ugly defiance. "If I fell in love with a man, you'd think that was all right. I didn't think you'd be so narrow, living in New York."

"As a matter of fact, I hadn't thought about that." Amy looked down at the bench, at the shadowy lump that was Harriet. "I resent your trying to make everybody else responsible for your unhappiness, even me."

"I just thought you might talk with Mother."

"I tell you what I'd say, if I did talk with her. I'd say, 'Cut her off without a penny. Let her earn her bread and roof.' "

"I thought you might want to help me," went on Harriet, stubbornly.

"Oh, my Lord!" Amy walked hastily toward the house. She'd been tempted to lay hands on the dull shoulders, to shake her. That kind of deafness kept Harriet what she was. Nothing got in. Not one person in a hundred really listened to another. They all had their ears too close to the ground, attentive to their own familiar footfalls. I do it, too, thought Amy. She stood a moment at the door, trying to shake off a degree of chagrin at the irritation Harriet had provoked in her. The night had been so lovely, and Harriet had blundered into it,—like that Junebug which rocketed against the screen and fell and lay on its armored back, kicking its futile, silly legs. Amy turned it over, and as it whirred away, went into the house.

Mrs. Doctor Bates was just going. She shook hands warmly with Amy, her palm moist; she puffed chunkily, her round face pink. The usual queries about Geoffrey and the children. Amy must drop in some day. The Doctor always asked about her. She was one of his girls.

"She's a good woman, but she plays awful bridge," said Grandmother, after Mrs. Bates had gone. "I should think Alfred ought to be home." She reached for her walking stick. "Time I got back."

Amy walked across the lawn with her, arms linked, the old woman very careful not to lean toward Amy. At her door she stood in the yellow light from the lantern overhead, the same iron lantern of Amy's childhood, wired later for electricity.

"Your mother always thinks she must spare me," she said, dryly. "She knows more'n she'd say about what Alfred's up to. It doesn't spare me any to have to imagine in place of knowing, does it? What do you know?"

"No more than you do." Amy kissed the old mouth, surprised to feel a slight trembling. "I shouldn't worry. Some kind of business, that's all."

"Who said I was worrying?" Grandmother poked the door ajar with her stick. "Good-night."

Harriet and Aunt Lora were on the porch when Amy returned. They would walk home. Harriet, icily, preferred to walk and wouldn't dream of bothering Amy any more. Lora, departing, thought they had had such a pleasant evening.

Catherine yawned, a trifle ostentatiously. "I don't know when Alfred will come in. Guess I'll go to bed."

"All right." Amy's glance was tender. If her mother didn't wish to talk—

"I heard Lulu go off somewhere. She's not supposed to go out Friday night. I'm going to be obliged to talk to her."

"Not to-night. Maybe it will rain to-morrow." Amy climbed the stairs languidly. How long the day seemed, broken into bits among so many people!

8

Waking once in the night Amy heard the faint antiphonal murmur of voices, her father's and her mother's. She slipped her hand beneath her cheek and slept again. In the morning she thought she might have dreamed the voices. The house had no sound of her father's presence now. She wandered into the hall to peer down between spindles of the bannister. "Mother!" she called, and had no answer. Stretching her arms shoulder high she yawned, and went back to bathe and dress. It was the same kind of day,—flat disk of sun swimming in a colorless sky, not a cloud, not a stir of wind.

If she found no message from Geoffrey downstairs, would she hate him, or would she begin dire imagining of accidents, catastrophes, as reason for his silence? Hatred would, on the whole, be pleasanter. But why shouldn't he answer, if he had not been drowned, or injured, or lost? At least she could wait for an inspection of the hall table.

Nothing there. Amy felt alarm ripple through her nerves. She wouldn't worry. How often in the past had she made herself ridiculous, worrying about Geof, only to learn that his silence, his failure to appear, had from his point of view the most reasonable explanation?

She found no one until she reached the kitchen, where Lulu stood at the sink, her hands idle in the dish-pan. The girl started at Amy's voice, the china clattering with her movement.

"Sorry," said Amy. "I didn't mean to startle you. Where is everybody?"

Lulu didn't know (and didn't care, her heavy eyelids added), and there was no message for Mrs. Norton.

Amy ate the iced grapefruit slowly. She didn't want breakfast. What could have happened to Geof? To-day made the fourth since she had left New York, the fifth since Geof had gone. "I'd better begin feeling furious right off," she thought, "before I'm too frightened. He's just getting even. Perhaps my wires never reached him." That was the best idea yet. She could send another, demanding some evidence of its delivery.

Before Amy had done more than plan a message, firm, dignified, but not hostile, a Ford truck made a honking stop in front of the house. Emma, in sleeveless pink silk, climbed down from the driver's seat, held her arms up to the little girl, and leaned forward, child spraying over one shoulder, all waving arms and legs, to let Laurance kiss her. Then off he drove, the empty crates rattling.

"Hello, Amy. Did we surprise you?" They climbed the steps, the expression of each rounded, sun-pink face that of a delighted child on a holiday. "I brought Emmary to see Gran'ma Westover, and I came to spend the day with you. Laurance had to collect that shipment of crates for his apples, and ma said just to run along, she'd see to things. I haven't been away for a day for I don't know when."

"Do come in." But they were already in, looking about with curiosity. "Mother isn't here. I just had breakfast. I don't know where she is."

"Oh, we've been up hours. Just hours, haven't we, pet?" Emma moistened a corner of her handkerchief and applied it dexterously to Emmary's mouth. "You want to go see Gran'ma? You wait. It's nice here, I think. Some day, when the babies get older, we're going to fix up our living room. It wouldn't do any good now, the way they scramble over everything. Want drink water? You run out and ask the girl for one. She'll give it to you. Go on, you aren't as scared as that."

Amy, watching the child's plump jog-trot toward the kitchen, thought, this is appalling, a day with Emma. She needs her own setting. Fields and gardens, not decorous houses.

"You know"—Emma had lowered her voice, had quickened it—"I want to ask if you know what Tom's after. I didn't want Emmary to hear. You never know what kids will pick up. He was out last night, and he and Laurance had a real argument. I heard Tom yelling out, 'A fine kind of brother you are!' Laurance wouldn't say a word, except that he wanted money. What's he been up to, do you know? He had a nerve, trying to borrow of Laurance. He has done it before and never paid a cent back, and I made Laurance promise not to give him any more."

"I've scarcely seen Tom since I came."

"Nobody sees Tom except when he's after money. I knew his mother hung around here a lot, and I

thought she might have said something. She'd think
Laurance ought to help. 'His own little brother.'
Laurance was real cross last night, after Tom went.
He wanted to help him, and he wanted to please me,
too. I'd give in about most things. But I just tell
him a married man's whole duty is to his wife and
babies. Don't you think so, Amy? And Tom's just
wild and extravagant. Helping him is pouring water
through a sieve, that's all."

Amy smiled at Emma's open desire for reassurance.
Her naïve words drew a distinct picture of Laurance
suffering the discomfort which an unworthy seeker for
a loan can always pour over the worthy refuser.

"Marriage can't put an end to all your feelings about
your own family," she said, and then saw with a slight
shock of amazement the change in Emma's face; her
whole personality braced small hoofs deep in mud,
immobile, deaf to reason.

"It ought to put an end to any feelings that cost
money," she said, succinctly. "Laurance knows I'm
right, only he'd like to act as if he was a millionaire,
too. They all come asking him. At least, his mother
and Harriet don't any more. Tom must be in a tight
place to try again. I wish they'd leave us alone.
Laurance is never cross except such times."

"But, Emma,—" Amy pressed her finger tips together, disturbed by a need to justify Laurance, who
perhaps smothered a little in Emma's tight embrace.
"There is a family responsibility. I don't mean giving
Tom money, for he probably doesn't deserve it. (Her
thought included her father, drawn into Dewitt's
affairs, with Catherine aware of the obligation he
might feel.) You can't cut a man straight off from
the rest of his family."

"My mother says the more relatives a man's got, the

firmer you have to be. Me and Emmary and Lolly are his family now." Emma's face was pinker, but no shadow of any doubt touched it. "I guess you'd agree with me if your Geoffrey was all messed up with relatives." She sniffed audibly. Luckily Emmary came back just then, with a little running stagger that landed her safely at her mother's knees.

"Go see Gwam-gwam now?"

Emma wiped the damp chin and laughed, dismissing the argument. "She calls Laurance's mother 'Gwam,' and the old lady 'Gwam-gwam,' and my mother just 'Mwam,' because she hears me call her 'Mamma,' I suppose. All right, honey, we'll go see Gwam-gwam. Would she know anything about Tom? He gets money out of her often enough."

"You might ask her." Amy shared Laurance's mood, described as cross. Life with a simple vertebrate had some disadvantages, evidently. She stood at the doorway, watching Emma, the child clinging to her hand, the two of them fair and pink and alive in the sunlight as they crossed to the other house. What, exactly, did Madam Westover make of this granddaughter by marriage? Amy turned back to the living room, her irritation drooping. Funny, how Emma's invulnerability stirred her own Westover prejudice. With Laurance, of course, the clear devotion Emma felt would quickly melt any ice. Emma labored to make him all Miller, and he had to stay Westover in faint inclinations at times. Emma was fundamentally right. Or was she? Didn't she revert generations to a simpler social structure, when a family constituted an isolated fragment, walled against intruders? She lived according to her own code, and she drew that straight from another stock, a different kind of people.

Heat Lightning

Geoffrey would say, "She's a primitive anachronism, that's all."

Amy's teeth worried at her lower lip. She had to make Geoffrey say something! Emma had driven out of her head the satisfactory telegram she had planned. Reluctantly she walked to the telephone. If he had those earlier messages, she hated screaming after him with another. Anyway, there was her mother, stepping out of the car. She'd have to wait.

"Well, Mother!"

"Amy, dear." Her mother pulled off her white piqué hat, and patted her forehead with a folded handkerchief. "I'm sorry to run off this way."

"Oh, I don't mind. Emma's been entertaining me."

"Emma? Is she here?"

"She's calling on Grandmother. On Gwam-gwam, with Emmary."

"Oh, good Heavens! She always stirs Mother up, and this morning, of all times! Amy, you'll have to bring her right back. Your father and Dewitt want to see Mother. They're coming any time, now. Oh, it's too bad. If Mother loses her temper so early, she'll be edgy with them. I'll go right over."

"This sounds like a conspiracy," began Amy, following her mother. She dropped her light tone at the distress in her mother's face; Catherine had not turned toward her, but along her cheek ran a visible quiver and the corner of her mouth tightened. "I'm sorry, darling, but I'm completely in the dark."

"It's Dewitt. I might as well tell you. It's all coming out. They worked like mad yesterday, trying to save something. If it hadn't been for Carruthers, too— Later, Amy." She hurried into Madam Westover's house, and Amy waited.

It would be ludicrous, wouldn't it, if Emma had

[123]

accidentally made herself a spectator of this approaching call? She'd think Alfred reprehensible, wouldn't she, concerning himself with his brother's affairs, involving his wife? Would she think Gwam-gwam—the silly name epitomized, somehow, Amy's irritation at Emma, in its inadequacy—would she think Grandmother had any responsibility? Well, Mother was clever. Amy heard her. "I thought Emma would like to go with me to see Mary and the baby. I'm just driving over."

"I just got started on a good talk with Gwam-gwam." Emma's voice was loud and cheerful. "No, baby, don't pick up the kitty that way." Amy made a dart from the doorway and separated Emmary from Alpha just as the black sphere of fury unsheathed long claws.

"A tail is not a handle," said Grandmother, severely. Amy rubbed her fingers down Alpha's skull behind his ears, feeling the small bones through the silk fluff. He wouldn't purr, but he stared at her with topaz eyes in which the pupils were fine dark lines.

"Kitty, kitty!" insisted Emmary, beating her fists against Amy's knees.

"No, sir. Kitty's cross at you."

"He's not used to little girls, Emmary. Wait till you get home. Why, she can pick up our cat anyhow and he never minds." Emma stood up, pulling her dress frankly away from sticky places. "I'd like to see Mary and the baby."

"See baby?" Emmary abandoned her attempt to reach Alpha's swaying tail.

"No, you stay here with Gwam-gwam and Aunt Amy, like a nice girl."

"I'll take care of her," said Amy. "We'll take a

walk in the garden, and look at the pictures of my little girl and boy."

Emmary, with doubtful balance of emotions on her small face, watched her mother vanish. Quickly, before despair conquered, Amy set Alpha down safely inside the door, and grasped Emmary's moist hand. "Mother'll come right back," she said. "You go ask 'Viny for a cookie. She has cookies for nice little girls. When I was as small as you, she had cookies for me."

Emmary stared out of unwinking round eyes, and after a moment of wavering, decided on the cookie. Amy sighed faintly, and sat down opposite her grandmother.

"That young woman," said Madam Westover, clicking her teeth, "was rescued in the nick of time. No, I mean the mother." One hand tore off the pink paper from the top of a tall basket of pears beside her.

Amy laughed. "What was she doing?"

"I never saw such impertinence." She inspected the basket. "These look better than yesterday." Her long fingers moved over the globed fruit. "Asking if Tom had approached me for money! Telling me what I ought to do!"

"She isn't really impertinent, Grandmother. She just lacks finesse."

"Humph." Madam Westover's hands folded together in her lap, forgetting the fruit. "Is that what you call it?" Surprisingly her brilliant laugh flashed over her face. "You know, I really like her. If she weren't so stupid! That's what saves her from Lora, though. She's as thick as a turtle." She adjusted a bright flat pan on her knees, and reached for a pear. "If I don't get at these, Lavinia will be after me. I'll have to send for that Tom, I guess. You haven't seen anything? About Lulu, I mean."

Amy shook her head. "Mother says she's bad-humored, that's all."

"Probably got reason to be." Madam Westover's knife moved in bright ellipses about the golden pear.

Amy rose. She could hear the shuffle of Emmary's feet. Her thoughts shifted in bright fragments, like bits of glass in a child's kaleidoscope. You might think it a pity for an old woman to be badgered by all these problems of grandsons and sons. You couldn't present her with pity; it ran off her brave feathers. Too bad they weren't more like her, these others. Had her quality, broken up, disseminated among so many, suffered loss? "Did Mother tell you Dewitt and Father are coming in this morning?" It was only decent to warn her, thought Amy. I can't help it if they don't like it. All of them running to her.

The old woman looked straight up at her, the parchment forehead crawling into a wrinkle. "No, she didn't." She nodded her head deliberately. "I expected 'em soon," she added, dryly. "I keep an eye on the market reports."

"Walk?" teased Emmary, cookie crumbs on her pink chin. "Walk now?"

Amy kissed her grandmother, her lips lingering an instant on the powdery, wrinkled forehead. "I guess you're equal to them," she said.

When Alfred and Dewitt drove up, she and Emmary were sitting on the bench at the end of the enclosed garden; Amy had a stalk of tawny snap-dragon, and the child cuddled drowsily against her, watching the snap-dragon open its mouth between Amy's thumb and forefinger, and recite Mother Goose. Amy saw the glitter of sun on nickel as the car slid quietly around the house. That must be the elegant new model Isabelle had spoken about. Emmary slept, soft, warm, cookie crumbs in her fist.

Amy looked down at her, thinking, "How different she is, texture of her flesh, contour of her plump knees, from Buff or Bobs at that age. So obviously pretty little girl. She'll grow up to be like Emma. No subtlety, no imagination. Those qualities work from birth, like a sculptor's thumb, modeling flesh differently. Perhaps it's just glands, and Emmary's a rather dull child because she has more adrenalin than thyroid. Who knows?"

It was dismaying to think that you were all settled by the body you were born with. Not born *with*,— you were that body. You thought of yourself as changing, developing, degenerating. Weren't you, the essential, secret you, determined at the instant the sperm-arrow sought out the egg? All that struggle to become, to decide, wasn't that illusion? If you could relax, could wait, yourself would speak through without the folly of that effort. This life experiment continued recklessly, breaking up entities, scattering the bits in new combinations, hurling together random chromosomes, increasingly more remote from the oneness which presumably began it all, as if some day it might produce an extraordinary combination.

I'm getting beyond my depth, thought Amy, drowsily. If I relax and wait for myself, nothing happens. I don't know what I'm trying to say. If I could put my mind away, and just *be*.

Emmary lay heavy and warm against her thigh. Along the path came a young robin, larger than his mother, thrush-speckled, flapping his wings in prolonged infancy while his mother fed him, hunting out a worm for himself when the shabby older bird

flew away. Amy watched under sleep-heavy eyelids. Under the rosebushes sounded a tinkle, silver
bell so faint, so sweet it scarcely moved. Under
the rosebushes crouched danger, black and silky-
soft, or was it only a shadow of danger? The young
robin walked in dry grass, cocking his head most ma-
turely to detect a worm wriggling. Amy tried to lift
her eyelids, but sleep weighted them. The shadow
moved, the silver-sweet bell tinkled, and suddenly the
quiet of the garden was broken with angry wings, bird
shrieks of rage, of fear, of detection of a foe. Amy
darted to her feet. Emmary bumped her head against
the bench, the robins chattered in the trees overhead,
and Alpha, tail curveting, came to rub against Amy's
shoe, pretending that had been his one intention.

"There, Emmary." Amy set the child upright.
"You aren't hurt. I didn't mean to let you bump your
head, but—" she shivered, in spite of the enveloping
heat. And Alpha strolled so handsomely along the
path. "Let's go in the house, now we've had a nap."
From the door she could see the long nose of Dewitt's
car shining beside Grandmother's house. They were
making a long call. She had slept, and Alpha stalked
a bird, and Dewitt told what kind of elegy of business
affairs? Things went right on happening. And Geoffrey. He could go right on happening, too. She no
longer felt any urgency about the telegram. Apathy
dimmed her needs, like sleep reflected in a mirror. She
would wait, and see what had happened when she woke.

Mother and Emma were just coming across the
terrace.

"We had a flat." Catherine made a comical grimace.
"I left the car at the service station, and we walked."

"I can change a tire." Emma swooped deftly at
Emmary, and automatically moistened a handkerchief

to wipe away cookie smudges. "But not in my best dress this kind of weather. I'm swimming as it is."

"Your father hasn't come?" Catherine's gaze asked more, said, "Be careful in front of Emma."

"Not yet." Amy answered the query with a faint nod. Yes, he was still with Grandmother.

"Mary was sitting up when we got there."

"Gracious, it's four days. I was all ready to get up then after Emmary, but Laurance and the doctor were so fussy."

"I must see about luncheon." Catherine moved a bowl of nasturtiums out of a shaft of sunlight. "Does Emmary have anything special?"

"Oh, she eats anything the rest of us do."

"You'll find towels in the east bathroom, Emma. I don't know just when we'll have luncheon. When Alfred comes."

Emmary whispered urgently to her mother, and Emma, laughing, towed her across the room and upstairs.

"They are at Mother's?" asked Catherine, quickly. "Of course Emma will know later, if it turns out as black as Alfred fears. But I hate to speak about it. She tells everything to her mother, and Mrs. Miller has a hard tongue. She's never forgiven the Westovers because Lora didn't want her son to marry Emma. So she's especially pleased with bad news. I dislike gratifying her."

"Too bad Emma picked to-day for a family visit."

"Didn't she tell you why she came?"

"You mean about Tom? Yes. But why come here?"

"I don't know. There's Alfred! I must see him—" Catherine waited a moment at the door. Alfred stood beside the car, emphasizing with a fist in slow hammer motion whatever he said to Dewitt. Dewitt stared straight ahead, hands on the wheel. As he started the car, Catherine hurried out to meet Alfred. Emma could, if she happened to look out, see all this tableau from the bathroom window, thought Amy. She mounted the stairs, planning to detain Emma a few minutes, until Catherine had time to ease a little the burden of suspense which dragged at her.

9

The luncheon hour was, to Amy, a walk across a swampy valley, with Emma trotting cheerfully ahead on dry hummocks of talk, unaware that Alfred slipped often into mire of his own thoughts, that Catherine labored silently to extricate him, that Amy herself found it heavy going. Emma attacked each course with zest and speed, and having finished, sat back to chatter. She supposed she did eat fast, but the men were always in such a rush. Food she hadn't cooked did taste good.

"Did you and Uncle Dewitt settle what's to happen about Curly?" she asked. "Oh, I saw you over there." She was delighted at her own craftiness.

"Curly?" Alfred looked at her under bristling eyebrows. "Oh, no. No. We haven't done anything about him." His weariness laid dull blotches on his skin, as if his heart beat sluggishly.

"I know you have to be careful, for as Mamma said, the Westovers are good at keeping family scandals dark. I won't say a word."

"There's nothing to say," interrupted Catherine. "Is Laurance getting a good price for his apples?"

That sidetracked Emma for several minutes. Emmary, in a high-chair kept since Amy's childhood, and brought down from the garret, pounded her spoon against the shelf in delight at the ice-cream Lulu was bringing in, and Emma had to jump to rescue the glass of milk.

"I do wish some one could tell me about Tom," she said, into the pause while Catherine cut slices of the pink brick. "He'll be after Laurance again, and I always say forewarned is forearmed. Don't you know what he's up to, Uncle Alfred? It isn't as if his mother could do a thing with him."

Amy let her eyes move slowly to Lulu, standing behind Catherine's chair. The round silver tray quivered in her tight grasp, a weapon she might hurl, and her face, foreshortened as she ducked her head, suddenly hurt Amy with its broad forehead, its drawn-in, waiting look. Catherine had to speak to her before she came back from her own morass, and lifted the glass plate to the tray.

"How large a slice may Emmary have, Emma?" Catherine lifted her eyebrow at Alfred, who had glanced from Emma to his wife with an air of incredulous exasperation. "A whole slice? It's just frozen custard with peach. Lulu makes it in the electric refrigerator."

"I'm just learning some of those desserts." Emma was again sidetracked into a discussion of frozen delights.

When luncheon was finished, and Emmary had been lifted to the floor, Emma slipped her arm happily through Catherine's. "I just love coming here," she said. "Laurance's mother doesn't like it, my not going there when I'm in town. But it's just the idea of it she doesn't like, for we never have a really good time like this." She added, dimpling at Alfred, "It's because there's a man here. I tell Laurance that's what's the matter with his mother, and his sister, too."

"A man does make a difference." Catherine smiled, but her eyes hurried back toward Alfred.

"Don't you want Emmary to have a nap now?" Amy could at least free her mother for a few moments before Alfred went. She followed them into the living room, where the child was struggling with an Alpine ascent into a large chair, the round bottom of her white panties dust-smudged and conspicuous as she hoisted herself to the seat.

"No!" declared Emmary, reversing herself violently. "No!"

"Yes, yes, yes!" Emma swooped at her, hoisted her shoulder high with an easy swing. "I'll run upstairs with her. What a fat round tummy!" The child giggled at Emma's tickle, and they vanished.

"Why on earth did you have her here to-day of all days?" asked Alfred widely of his wife and daughter.

"Sh!" Catherine winced. "I didn't have her. She came. I am sorry, Alfred. But perhaps it was just as well. You had to eat without talking about things. Better for your digestion. Must you go right back?"

"I haven't been near the office for two days."

"I know. But you are so tired—"

Amy drifted away. As she climbed the stairs, she thought: "Now I should have said, 'You know I didn't invite that woman!' Then Father would have been still more furious. And when he said that about the office, I'd have roared back, 'What of it? Your old office can get along.'" Pride in her mother dropped through her like clear water. "She's wonderful with him. She meets him where he stands, not where she is, herself. She doesn't care about justifying herself to him. He's not really blaming her for anything, he's yelling about other things, serious things." She stood at the top of the stairs, her hand hard against the banister. "When Geoffrey yells at me, I holler back. Always. But why should I do all the work? I want Geoffrey to know where *I* am. Maybe you can't both know, at once, can't both see what's pinching the other into such unreasonableness." Amy ran her fingers through her hair, tips firm against the scalp. "I'm selfish, that's it. Mother—" That feeling of pride dropped like a swift cascade, bright in sunlight. "It's a gracious, finer thing, the way she behaves. And in the long run, she wins. Father always fundamentally knows where she is."

"What you going to do this afternoon?" Emma had closed the door upon Emmary's remonstrances, and intent on her reflection in a small mirror, wiped her nose vigorously with a dingy powder puff. "It feels hotter here than at the farm, I s'pose because I have time to feel hot."

"I haven't made any plans." Amy took the last step into the hall. "Don't you want to lie down and read a while?"

"I don't care about reading. I'll come sit in your room if you want to read. Emmary said you had some pictures of your children I'd like to see."

Amy showed her the folder of snapshots. If Emma tries to pry about Geoffrey, I'll smash her, she thought, fiercely. Some one ought to teach her ordinary manners. But Emma set the folder down with, "Your little boy looks skinny. Is he real well?" And for a long time, while Amy listlessly manicured her nails, Emma chattered on about illnesses of children, hers, Mary's, some of the neighbors, detouring for reminiscences of Felice and her miscarriage and how dreadful it was they couldn't have any babies, and Mary's miscalculation and her present state. Amy was vague about her own obstetrical experiences. "Oh, but I can remember everything about it!" declared Emma, and proceeded to prove that she could. Once or twice drowsiness crept through Amy's body, and only the sudden wrench against the insidious pull of gravity on relaxed muscles kept her awake. How queer it would be to have your mind full of pieces of experience, of sensations, and little else, each one ringing a tiny bell to summon an adjacent one. Emma was having a delightful time; her flushed cheeks bespoke real pleasure. She broke off as Catherine appeared at the door.

"Well, you two are running on," she said, tolerantly. "Lora just 'phoned, Emma. She heard you were in town, and wants to see you."

Emma stuck out a pink tongue. "Yes, she does. Laurance told me I should go over. Harriet's there, and we just don't get along, no matter how hard I try to be nice to her."

"You don't have to live there, you know." Catherine was firm. "When Emmary wakes up, you can drive over."

Emma inspected her pink silk stocking. A run beginning at a garter gaped over her plump knee. She moistened her finger and left a round, damp spot at the end of the run. "I ought to sew it up, though. I'm awfully hard on stockings, and this is my last good pair." She stripped it off, her pink Rubenesque leg thrust out before her. "I'm glad that fuzz is light colored. Some women's legs look terrible through light stockings. Oh, thanks." She took the needle and thread Amy offered.

Amy went into the bathroom to wash manicure lotion from her finger tips. That awful pink foot! She dried her fingers with nervous shoves of the towel, and as she folded and replaced it on the glass rod, she stared at the design, two plump, quaint trees with the monogram between, in dark green on the pale green linen. Fastidiousness. Emma hadn't a whiff of it. Amy could imagine her, if some one tried to explain what the quality was, saying, "Oh, yes, you mean being fussy."

Perhaps fastidiousness belonged only to tired, over-cultivated people. Yet Catherine possessed it. Reluctantly Amy strolled back. Emma drew the stocking up, patted the crooked seam she had made, and wriggled her toes back into the pump. "If I'd called on my mother-in-law with a run, she'd of said, 'Don't you think it pays to be careful of details, my dear Emma?'" Her mimicry startled Amy into a sudden laugh, it was so precisely Lora's tone, and Emma was gay as a child who has been clever.

"You come with me," she begged.

"Oh, no." Amy wouldn't. "I must write some letters. I've neglected my family."

"You just take the car, Emma. The man brought it over a while ago, all ready. Lora and Harriet were here last night. It's you they want to see." Catherine settled the discussion easily. "Amy came out here to rest, and she hasn't had a minute to herself."

"All right." Emma went off good-humoredly to scrub her small daughter.

"It's cooler down on the terrace," said Catherine. "There's a little easterly breeze since luncheon. If it would only blow up showers!"

Amy stretched herself in the Gloucester hammock, and her mother drew a wicker chair over the flags to sit near, a basket of sewing on a green iron stand beside her. Emma and Emmary stepped out to say good-by. The child's yellow curls were brushed up from her neck and tied with a pink ribbon, to fall in an amusing top-knot, and her face shone rosily. "You both look very nice," said Catherine.

When they had driven away, Amy said, "She's wearing on a summer day."

Catherine unfolded a damask square. "This is the last of a dozen I've hemstitched," she murmured. "I suppose it's a waste of time." She considered Emma, threading a fine needle. "Perhaps it's the day as much as Emma. Emma finds everything so simple that ordinarily she's a pleasant companion. But when you're finding things mixed up and disturbing, her contentment is a little, well—irritating."

"She talks too much." Amy thrust up her arms, hands under her head. She drew in long breaths, savoring the slight change in the air. It was less a breeze than a faint odor of moisture, wandering in gentle curves through the still heat. "At home," she said, "that would smell of the ocean. This is too far inland."

"Yes." Catherine sewed busily. "She does chatter. But she's so completely happy. It's interesting to watch Laurance change. She's been good for him."

"She makes him feel superior and masculine and looked-up to. I know." Amy dragged one knee up, and held her body taut against the slight creaking sway of the hammock. She'd better be careful. That sounded too hard. Her mother was eying her over the snowy square. "Well, hasn't Emma a Lord and Master attitude?"

"Not exactly. She's independent enough. But she does think Laurance is pretty wonderful, and he thrives on that,—that, and her calmness."

"Um." Amy wished the hammock chains wouldn't creak with her slightest motion. Was her mother

[136]

sliding advice to her under cover of discussing Emma? "Can you tell me about this morning?" she asked. "I mean Uncle Dewitt. I don't want to pry, like Emma." She smiled impishly. "But you are so worried."

Catherine's needle flashed, and she did not for several minutes lift her head. When she did, the triangle between her brows was puckered, and her eyes looked solemn, with fatigue smudges emphasizing their color.

"I'm worried because your father's being dragged in, and it isn't his fault at all. It's Carruthers and Dewitt. I don't understand all that's happened. Carruthers lost his head, I judge. He'd been making money hand over fist, ever since he went into that broker's office. He was going to be a millionaire any minute. Isabelle just strutted about him. He's engaged to a Cleveland girl. It's something about his clients' money. He didn't do anything criminal, Dewitt says. But he's lost thousands, not his own. He didn't follow instructions or something. Thought he knew better. Dewitt tried to help him out, and he had investments of his own, too. Yesterday they were afraid Carruthers would kill himself. He actually had a pistol, Amy, and they couldn't find him for hours. He'd lost money of his fiancée's father's, too. He's gone to pieces, completely. That's where your father was last night, finding him, and getting him into a sanitarium. Now Dewitt's trying to raise more cash, and Alfred thinks it's useless."

Amy pulled herself upright in the hammock, her arms about her cocked knee. "And Grandmother?" she asked. "Were they asking her for money?"

Catherine nodded. "It makes me feel so miserable!" She pressed one hand against her temple. "Your father gave Dewitt some securities to use. He says he can't put up more, as they are for me, in case anything happened. Dewitt is furious about that. He says he just wants to borrow them for a few days. Who knows what the end will be? A bank closed last week, one Dewitt was connected with. I don't pretend to understand the ins and outs, but Alfred does, and he says Dewitt's gambling on a rise in the market within a week, and it can't come."

"It's like headlines in the paper, isn't it?" Amy felt the curious, hurried pressure of disaster moving out of impersonal words into human, recognizable reality. "Stock broker ruined." She didn't know Carruthers. Isabelle had sent him east to a boys' school when he was quite small. "But Dewitt's got his own factory. He's not a broker."

"Motor accessories aren't making money this year. Anyway, he's raised every cent he can on that, too."

"And now he wants you and Grandmother to strip yourselves for him! As Emma would say, 'He has a nerve!'"

"Of course he turns to Alfred, his brother. And I—" Catherine folded her hands over the linen square. —"I told your father to do what he thought wise. Unfortunately Dewitt lost his temper this morning. He's frightfully nervous, of course, and Isabelle had been having hysterics before he left home. Mother's done lots for them, but she never quite forgave him because he preferred to get out of Westover Plows. Someway they've dragged that all up again. And Curly. She hasn't much cash available. She'd given Dewitt a lot just a few days ago. And when he said she could dispose of some of her property, I judge she didn't care what she said. She blamed Isabelle's extravagance. That injunction rankled, and she spoke of that. I mean her public park idea. Well—"

Catherine lifted her head to look up at the house. "I don't believe Alfred would mortgage this."

"Why should Dewitt expect you to ruin yourselves, even if he has done it for himself?"

"He's not in a reasonable mood."

Amy swung her feet to the ground, her hands flat at her sides against the tufted seat. "Grandmother's too old to be badgered like that," she cried. "For all she's so stanch and wise. She's an old woman. I think Dewitt ought to be ashamed."

"He's worse than ashamed, Amy. He's desperate."

"He could get a job, couldn't he? It would serve Isabelle right."

Catherine lifted her hands, let them fall, a gesture which admitted complete bewilderment. "I ought to go over to see Mother. I hoped she might send for me, if she cared to. Frankly, I'm half afraid to go."

"She won't bite your head off, darling."

"She'll want me to take a firm stand with Alfred, though."

"Want me to go? I'm out of it, except through you."

Catherine gave her a little wry smile. "Would you? I'd like to know she's all right, after the morning."

Amy stood up, smoothing down the crumpled sheath of her frock. "That looks almost like a cloud." She gazed at the pale bits of sky through the trees. "It's a different color."

"The clouds ought to come from the west, though, if they have any rain." Catherine, like Amy, lifted her head to taste the faint aroma of coolness that wavered through the heat. "I should have more compunction about sending you over," she added, "but if you will come home, you can't escape family affairs.

And Mother will be less—what shall I say?—you won't suggest so many reasons for being cross as I should."

They walked through the house to the porch on the opposite side, and Amy touched her mother's hand gently as she stepped out. "Don't be so anxious. It isn't your husband that's defaulted."

But Catherine was staring past her, with a quick intake of breath that lifted her shoulders rigidly. At what? Amy saw a small coupé dusty in the sunlight in front of Madam Westover's door.

"Oh, my goodness!" Catherine's breath ran out in the ejaculation. "Oh, oh! I ought to have known," she said. "Mother never nurses any of her feelings. She always does something. That's Walter Ripley's car. Her lawyer."

"Cutting him off without a penny?" Amy hesitated. "Shall I go over, or would it be indiscreet to interrupt?"

"I don't know." With a nervous gesture Catherine brushed stray curls away from her cheek. "I don't know."

"She can tell me she's busy if she likes." She'd copy her grandmother's technique of doing something for a feeling. Her mother looked so deeply wretched. "She can turn me out like a small child. I don't care." She went quickly across the lawn, and stood on tiptoe to peer into the screened porch. Nothing there except an empty pear basket. She stepped boldly into the house. The nectary fragrance of pears and syrup floated warmly toward her, and she heard Lavinia's sharp patter as she scolded at Curly.

"Hello." She looked into the kitchen. Lavinia swung around, arms akimbo.

"Oh, it's you. Now, mind you, Curly, I want all

those wide mouthed jars, like this one. You see? Now don't you bring me any others this time."

Curly answered with a "Hrrch—hrrch—" deep in his throat, and withdrew his head down the cellar-way.

"I never saw such a day! Everything's upset, and your grandma hasn't peeled me half enough pears. Folks coming in and getting her all het up."

"Where is she?"

"She's busy right now, and I don't know as she'd want to see you."

Amy turned slowly. "I think I'll go ask her, 'Viny." In spite of herself she made her tone placating. "Maybe I can help."

The door into the library, luckily, stood ajar, and Amy stepped in, trying to shake off a tinge of childish reluctance. Her grandmother sat at the old flat desk— it had been Grandfather's, and everything, inkstand, wire-spring pen holder, morocco corners on the blotting pad, was just as he had used them. In front of her stood Mr. Ripley, broad and stooped, a large mustache, a bald head, and serious pale eyes. Amy had an indistinct recollection of him.

"Are you busy, Grandmother?" The old woman looked at her, a firm, harsh stare which, after an instant, shed its hostility.

"I'm all through for to-day. This pesky fellow— Mr. Ripley, this is my granddaughter from New York, Mrs. Norton."

"Oh, yes. Alfred's girl. I remember." Mr. Ripley seized her hand as if she threw him a lifeline in a stormy sea. "Well, well."

"He won't do as I ask him." Madam Westover's nose and chin moved together over a hard mouth. "Thinks I'll change my mind when the sun comes up again. I'll show you." She lifted a folded document from the desk, tugged at it, unfolded it, and tore it, scattering bits of it on the desk, fragments of a red seal shining ominously among the shredded paper. "Now you think I mean what I say, Walter?"

"I ought to have left that in my safe. Tearing up a good will like that! To-morrow you'll want me to write another just like it. I tell you you can't make a better one."

"Better or not, I can make a different one."

"Will you come to my office to-morrow, or will I bring my secretary here? After you've slept on it—"

"I won't change my mind, I tell you."

"You want to make Alfred turn in his grave?"

"Walter, if my husband has been paying any attention to this family since he left it, he's been so restless in his grave he wouldn't notice one more turn. And anyway,"—Madam Westover brushed the bits of paper into a small pyramid, flattened the pyramid under her hand—"he would agree with me about this. Don't you think I know how Alfred felt?" She flung up her head as triumphantly as if her husband stood beside the chair with secret counsel. For her, thought Amy, the room must be close-tenanted with images of Grandfather; Amy could see him plainly at the desk, replacing his pen so violently that the coils of the holder sang, rolling his blotter up and down the sheet,—yes, the old roller still lay there, with fresh white blotting paper. She had loved that as a child. "I'll drive to your office at eleven to-morrow. And there are other lawyers, in case you still think you know my own mind better than I do."

Mr. Ripley pulled at his mustache, looked vaguely at Amy, seeing her not as a woman but as Alfred Junior's daughter, removed his spectacles and snapped them into a case. "You'll have your own way. But a good lawyer couldn't let you act in the heat of an impulse. At eleven in the morning, then." He bowed and went away with a slow lope of his large, loose body.

Madam Westover brushed the crumbs of paper over the desk edge into a wire wastebasket. "Walter's a good lawyer. But stodgy. He thinks me a bad-tempered old woman. Maybe I am, but I'd been thinking this over before I lost my temper."

Amy leaned against the corner of the desk, her finger tips crawling at the texture of the green baize cover. "What kind of plots are you concocting?" she asked. She admired the old woman, erect in the leather chair, the cords of her throat taut above the soft georgette scarf. Not a sign of fatigue, unless the hint of heightened intensity in hooded eyes and in tight muscles might be the present stage of weariness not yet admitted. Perhaps she likes conflict, thought Amy, because it gives a stronger dose of life, and mild doses no longer have any effect.

"I'm taking care of my responsibilities," said Madam Westover, smartly. "To your Grandfather, chiefly. That's all I'll tell you." She was silent, and from the kitchen crackled Lavinia's voice indistinctly, with an infrequent bass note, frog-like, from Curly. "I never believed much in trying to run everything from the grave. Alfred always said a dead hand on a living throat was a hated hand. But your father's too soft, Amy. Three things I have to take care of, Curly, the factory, and the Westover name. Now that's every word I'll tell you, and if any one asks you, you don't know a thing."

"Your brooch is unfastened." Amy leaned close, and slipped her finger tips under the georgette to fasten the heavy pin of garnets and pearls. Was that slow, faint beating under her fingers the rhythm of this intrepid heart?

"Thank you. Your grandfather gave me that, with ear-rings." Her eyes glinted. "A peace offering."

"Did you quarrel?" Amy's own pulse quickened. Why, she'd scarcely thought of Geoffrey all day, and no word had come from him.

"Of course we did. At first, especially. Two people have to wear off sharp edges before they fit together." She moved one finger slowly over the surface of the pin. "Then we made up. That was nice." Her smile flashed out.

"But quarrels do worse than rub off edges. They ravel out love." Amy spoke deliberately; if she could make her grandmother talk!

"Stuff and nonsense!" Madam Westover came briskly out of the bypath where her pin had led her. "Love isn't flimsy stuff to be raveled out. It's like everything else nowadays." She pointed a warning finger at Amy. "You expect things to wear out. No quality any more. Why, when I bought my wedding dress, I thought I'd be buried in it, too. I had it turned, and made over, and it's still in a trunk. Better stuff than I can buy to-day. When I fell in love, I expected that to last me a lifetime, too, and it did. You have to take care of it, or it won't last. Oh, I see young people jumping about, talking about freedom and all the rest. Just when men were beginning to have some idea about what love was, then women had to start acting like men."

"But men and women do make mistakes and find they can't live together."

"I'll tell you one thing, Amy. Any two decent ordinary people can make a match of it, if they work on it, and it'll be just as good as if they shuffled up a dozen times."

Amy looked down as Alpha brushed against her feet. With a barely perceptible adjustment of muscles he made an easy leap to the desk, and circling once in his own tracks, lay down in front of Madam Westover, his forefeet moving drowsily as he purred.

"Otherwise," said Grandmother, conclusively, "what they feel isn't love, any more than with Alpha here. He has his spells, but he doesn't want anything that lasts a lifetime. Folks ought to do a little better."

Amy stood up, cramped from her awkward slouch against the desk.

"They ought to," she agreed, bitterly. This assurance of Grandmother's might be true for her, for her generation. Not for Amy. "Who buys a wedding dress for its lasting qualities nowadays? You'd be dreadfully out of style."

"I don't know as it's stylish to be unhappy, even now," said Madam Westover, a strange, unprying tenderness in her voice, at which Amy's eyelids grew hot and she bent over Alpha, running her fingers through his silky ruff. Brusquely she shook back her hair and walked away from the old woman's shrewd eyes, to stand at the window. She couldn't talk about Geoffrey, any more than she could break her grandmother's reticence about her Alfred.

You couldn't, after all, turn into words your intimate relation to another human being. That relation existed at a depth to which words, poor light things, could never sink. Hadn't she and Geoffrey—she found her hands trembling against the window sill—hadn't they tried too hard to find words for themselves? And love was a deep-sea creature, exploding into bits if dragged up to shallow water?

"Oh, hang!" She turned from the window. "Emma's come back. She didn't stay long at Lora's, did she?"

"I thought that was where she must be going." Grandmother reached for her stick, patted Alpha, and got to her feet. Alpha leaped to the floor and followed her across the room. "That reminds me I meant to get hold of Tom to-day. They drove it out of my head this morning." She stood beside Amy, watching Emmary's bright tuft disappear into the next house. "The idea of his going to Laurance! Emma must have enjoyed telling Lora all about it. That's probably why she didn't stay long." She chuckled. "Tom ought to know Laurance isn't his brother any longer. He's Emma's husband and Mrs. Miller's son-in-law." She looked drolly out of the corner of her eye at Amy. "I know where I can catch the young scamp to-day. He'll be surprised." She waved her stick and left the window.

"Well, where?" Amy and Alpha trailed after her, the tip of Alpha's tail expressing discontent at these frequent moves.

Grandmother had headed for the dining room, where the telephone table stood so that Lavinia might hear the ring from the kitchen. She sat down on the chair, her eyes gleaming up at Amy.

"Joe told 'Viny this morning that he helped Charley get a car out of a ditch, and that the car was Tom's. He wasn't scratched but the car was, and Charley's fixing up the fenders to-day."

Amy leaned against the door, amused at the telephone talk. Madam Westover wanted Charley and didn't care if he was busy. She got him. First she left word that he should call at ten-forty-five in the morning. Then, confidentially, "When Tom comes for his car, you tell him he can't have it till he brings you a note from me. Yes, that's right. I want to see the young scamp."

10

Emma was uncommunicative about her visit to Lora. She said, "Oh, that Harriet!" and later, "Imagine telling me that Tom had a right to consult his older brother! I said right out that I'd consult him if he came begging again. She didn't like it, but I have to say what I think." Her soft, full mouth was sulky. She sat on the porch with Emmary pushing fretfully at her knee, looking like an untidy child herself, a careless dab of powder on her shiny nose, prints of Emmary's dusty shoes on her pink dress, hands and wrists as grubby as the child's. Like a child, her heedless vitality defeated neatness.

She jumped to her feet with unconcealed relief when Laurance made a noisy stop in front of the house. "There's Daddy, Emmary!" Instead of empty crates he had a load of children, jumping and shrieking in a youthful version of mob hysteria. "And all the kids, too! I'll be right out, Laurance!" she cried. "I just have to get my hat."

Catherine and Amy went out to the truck, Emmary running ahead.

"Keep still a minute, you Arabs!" said Laurance, and the children roared with laughter while Lolly, his small boy, tried to turn a somersault and tangled himself in the bare, scratched legs of Mary's girls. "They want to see their new sister," explained Laurance. "What do you think?"

"Up, up!" screamed Emmary, and Amy lifted her

[147]

to the seat beside her father. He hugged her and
pulled her dress down to her round and grimy knees.
"Not to-night," said Catherine. "No, Lucy." She
shook her head at the oldest girl, who made round,
woeful eyes over the edge of the truck. "In a day or
so, when you're all nice and clean, you can go one at
a time."

Emma came running, and hoisted herself nimbly to
the driver's seat. She looked down with a deep sigh.
"Well, I've had a good time." She reached a deft
hand backward, and pulled Lolly up for a quick kiss.
"My, what a dirty face! I guess you missed me."
Her glance at Laurance was eager, provocative, as if
she had been away weeks instead of hours. "Come out
and see us real soon," she cried back, as they drove
away, the children waving madly until the truck swung
around a corner.

"At least she got off before Father came home,"
said Amy. "Weren't you a wretch to send her to
Lora's?"

"No. Whatever they say to each other, Lora always feels much worse if Emma neglects a visit."

"Her only daughter-in-law," jeered Amy, as they
entered the house.

The telephone burst into a ring. "Now what?"
asked Catherine, resignedly. Amy went on restlessly
into the living room. She spun the dials of the radio;
nothing, and then a sputter and crackle, a harsh and
voiceless noise. She snapped off the switch. That's
the way the whole place feels, she thought. Every
one's buzzing with static. Perhaps there will be a
storm. The faint breeze of the morning had dropped,
and the heat stood up against the sky, pressing all color
out of it, until it fitted about the earth like a dull silver
casque.

"That," said Catherine wearily, "was Isabelle. She's coming right over. She's been in bed all day, but she must see me. Now don't you run off and leave me! And she mustn't go over to Mother's. She'd make a grand scene. Mother hates that. What does she think I can do?"

"More static," murmured Amy. "I suppose she's frantic. You can't blame her. I keep forgetting all this business of Uncle Dewitt and Carruthers isn't newspaper headlines. Why"—she puzzled, looking down at her mother—"I suppose losing money is the worst tragedy Isabelle could face, isn't it?"

"She would think so." Catherine leaned back in her chair, eyelids low, a faint etching of trouble at her brows and the corners of her mouth. "Just as she's always thought money was the most important part of living. Poor Dewitt."

"Don't look as if you were responsible for it all, darling!" Amy laid her fingers on her mother's forehead. "What's she coming here for, anyway?"

"She'll tell us soon enough."

"Is she here already?" Amy saw a change in the light that fell into the hall from the outer doorway. At the mincing falsetto, "Is anybody home?" Catherine rose, with an expression at which Amy whispered, "Oh, say damn! You'll feel better."

Mrs. Parsons and her daughter Jenny had heard Amy was in town, and thought they'd just drop in, if it wasn't dinner time, but it was so hot to venture out earlier in the day. They sat on the edges of chairs, Jenny in limp figured georgette, her mother tightly corseted under serviceable foulard. Jenny had wanted to see Amy for so many years, but Christmas was such a family time, and so they'd come to-day. They removed their white silk gloves to break bits of wafer and to sip at the iced ginger ale Lulu brought in.

Amy watched them, thinking: they're like a funny little nineteenth century skit, played well forward on a shallow stage, with the curtain dropped just behind them to conceal the real play. She remembered Jenny as a young girl in high school days, head thrust forward against the weight of great braids of dark hair, bearing an irritating and romantic flavor created by her mother's phrases, "Jenny is so delicate. I say her strength's gone into her hair." Her face, sharp and sallow, had the old angle above the harsh line of collar-bone, but the edge of gray hair under the too green hat showed that the braids had gone. She ran a quick tongue about her lips, crumb-seeking. She was still delicate, her mother explained. They wanted to give a tea party next week for Amy. Some of her old friends. What day would be best?

Amy tried to wriggle unobtrusively away. She had so few days, she didn't know just when she'd have to go back. But Jenny said, in her high, unresonant voice, "I told you, Mamma, she wouldn't care about old friends, living in New York." And while Amy was protesting that she didn't want to make them trouble, with the weather so trying, Isabelle entered, halting at the door with the air of a plump tragedy queen who has missed her cue and cannot deliver the lines with which she is bursting. The Parsons, pitifully, fluttered and thrilled at the encounter. Oh, yes, they had met Mrs. Dewitt Westover at the Church Bazaar, when Jenny had the candy booth. Didn't she remember? Isabelle patronized them, drawling (although she panted a little, straining against this unexpected barrier), "Oh, yes, you-all live in that yellow house downtown." She dropped into a chair, her small feet and hands restless, her face flushed even to the tip of her pointed nose.

"I heard last year you planned to sell, Mrs. Parsons." Catherine tried to manage this interlude smoothly, but the strained look between her brows showed how uneasily she listened to the real scene preparing behind the curtain.

"But it's so convenient." Mrs. Parsons exploded delightedly into a familiar speech. "Right in the middle of everything. We can't bear to sell. Of course, if we get our figure—things rush on so, you can't stand in their way. An age of progress, I always say."

"Progress!" Isabelle popped the word out like escaping steam. "You don't know what you're talking about. Progress! No, I don't want any ginger ale." She waved aside Catherine's interruption. "If you'd had any sense you would have sold when you could." She dabbed a handkerchief at her eyelids and forgot to drawl. "I feel quite faint. I walked—no car—" Even her plump ankles glowed pink through sheer hose.

"Here!" Mrs. Parsons whipped smelling salts out of her black silk bag. "I always carry them, Jenny's so delicate. Just a sniff—" She quivered with delight; this was an occasion, helping *the* Mrs. Dewitt Westover. But Isabelle thrust aside the bottle. Any minute, thought Amy, that slight protecting curtain would bulge open. The little Parsons had better hurry away. Isabelle, most apparently, was set at a nervous pitch where an external social interlude became impossible. Curious that you couldn't say, "Please go, we are in trouble." Later, if Dewitt failed openly, how they would buzz! "We thought she acted queer that afternoon. Bzz."

Heat Lightning

The Parsons were reluctant to go. Not often did they have such a pleasant call. Isabelle was silent now, except for tappings and shiftings of her steel-buckled pumps, except for being afraid she had an engagement for the Wednesday the Parsons settled upon as the day for their tea party. "Oh, of course. You have so many things to do. We read about the Country Club. I tell Jenny if she weren't so delicate, it would be nice for her to belong."

Finally, after several starts and delays, they went. Amy accompanied them to the veranda, and stood a moment as they minced away. They were a tiny back-water of the old village life, scarcely aware of changes except as they read the social notes in the weekly paper. Poor, arid Jenny,—why, she was no older than Amy.

"Now I snould go help Mother out." She could hear Isabelle's voice, beginning low and hurried, mounting steadily, until it ended in a muffled shriek. She saw, from the doorway, Isabelle fling herself down on the divan, pounding her fists against the cushions, her small features lost in a flood of scarlet, as she repeated, "But you've got to help us! You've got to. You can't stand by and let us be ruined!"

Catherine lifted her hands toward Amy in despair, and her eyes said, "This is even worse than I expected!" She laid a hand on Isabelle's bulging shoulder. "Isabelle! Don't shriek so. You just work yourself up."

Whereupon Isabelle burst into a torrent of speech. Alfred had taken advantage of his younger brother, always. He ingratiated himself with Mother West-over. He'd—what hadn't he done! And Catherine had always been jealous, because Isabelle had such lovely children, because she was an outsider, and yet

[152]

she'd made such a place for herself, socially. Catherine walked across the room and shut the door loudly.

"You don't know what you're saying," she put in, finally, when Isabelle stopped for a gasping breath. "What do you expect from me?"

"I'm saying what I think, what my poor tortured heart feels!" Isabelle sobbed heavily. "My son, my husband ruined! And you stand there calmly and let it happen! You can make Alfred help us. He does what you tell him to. Must we lose our home, our lives, everything, and you go right on?"

"It's no good arguing with her," said Amy, hastily. "Let's get her home if we can."

"That's right! Turn me out in the street! Ignore me!" Isabelle grew incoherent. She was for all the world like a kettle of boiling rice, under which hysteria turned the flame too high, so that separate grains, chaff and dust, churned and leaped to the surface, were sucked under, all in senseless disorder. Old grievances, petty details of family history,—why, it was unbelievable what could boil up from concealed levels. Then, quite as if she boiled over and put out the flame, she lay back against the pillows, beating at the air with her fists.

"Is there spirits of ammonia upstairs?" Amy fled to the bathroom, hurried back. "Now drink this." Amy spilled water on the round chin. "Drink it!" She held one hand firmly behind Isabelle's neck and tipped the glass until Isabelle swallowed chokingly. "Now you aren't going over to Grandmother's." That had been part of the bubbling. Isabelle would confront that hard and selfish old woman, would tell her for once what the family really thought of her. "I'm going to drive you home and see that you go to bed."

Heat Lightning

Catherine telephoned to Dr. Bates. They were going to drive Mrs. Dewitt home, and couldn't he drop in with a sedative? Right away? Then she brought the car around to the front door, and between them she and Amy dragged Isabelle, a moaning, heaving sack of meal, out to the step, shoved her in. Amy sat beside her, hands firm about the plump wrists.

"How about wiring to Sophie?" she asked her mother.

"No, no! Leave my poor baby alone. Her last happy moments." Isabelle grew articulate about her daughter.

Isabelle's maid, jaunty in orchid linen and ruffled cap and apron, let them in. "Oh, I told the Madam she shouldn't start off in this heat." The girl's small bright eyes had predatory curiosity, and Isabelle struggled to climb into her usual rôle of mistress.

Among them they undressed her, stripping off her elaborate confining armor of satin, lace, elastic, clothing her blanc-mange flesh in the exquisite hand-made gown the maid produced, getting her at last between maize colored sheets, her head restless among embroidered pillows. The margin of Amy's attention included countless details of luxury, silver and crystal on the dressing table, ruffled maize silk folded back from the four poster bed, chaise longue piled with small and elegant pillows. No wonder Isabelle had hysterics, with all this threatened. The doctor came, and Isabelle tried for a moment to open her eyes too wide, and then rolled over, crying feebly. He nodded at Catherine's brief, "She's had a nervous shock," and Amy wandered down to the living room to wait for her mother. The angled designs of chintz, the abrupt jutting lines of lamps and tables reiterated the discords in her mind, and she shut her eyes against them.

"Are you asleep?" Catherine smiled ruefully at her. "Dr. Bates gave her a hyperdermic. He's sending in a practical nurse. Let's go home."

Amy drove down the curved lane of trees. They did look as if they'd been there for years. "If they do have to give up this place," she said, glancing at her mother's reflection in the mirror, "Isabelle will be a great help, won't she?"

"I don't quite know how she will act. Dr. Bates said this was a worse attack than usual."

"My heavens, does she do this often?"

"Not at my house. But it's been her way of getting things. Isabelle's nerves, the family calls it. It's worked in domestic crises."

Amy drove along the wide main street of this new suburb, through the elaborate stucco and iron gate which announced FAIRVIEW. The gate to Isabelle's idea of Heaven, with no Saint Peter on guard. Was there a saint devoted to incomes large enough to build in this exclusive residential section, as the posters put it?

"She'll be asleep when Dewitt gets home," added Catherine, with satisfaction. "I'd be embarrassed to meet her the next time, but I suppose she won't recall much that she said."

"If there was an earthquake, she'd think she could stop it by throwing a scene, wouldn't she?" Amy swung deftly round a corner. "After all, this is a sort of earthquake. It's an outside force, nothing that will give in because of her nerves."

"It's hard to know what is fair." In the mirror Catherine's eyes met Amy's. About such a glance, projected beyond the individuals, caught at a point in space, there was an impersonal anxiety. "But if Alfred sacrificed everything, they wouldn't be much better off, and where would we be?"

"It doesn't seem hard to me, not the least bit." Amy spoke with hearty reassurance. "You needn't chop down your house, if theirs is wrecked in their own private earthquake. You've never demanded the kind of extravagance Isabelle likes. Look at the stuff in that bedroom! I never had a nightgown like that in my life. Nor did you!"

"Well." Catherine relaxed, letting Amy's words lie close to her own thoughts. "I did think of that. I feel as if I might develop nerves myself if things run on at this rate."

"Yes, you will!" Amy turned her head quickly for a warmly intimate exchange of glances.

The house was quiet. Alfred had not yet come in. Through the trees the horizon gleamed like old, thin gold. Almost in tangible pressure against her eardrums Amy felt the tension of the air; there must be an atmospheric change at work, approaching like a wall, contracting the still air into invisible density. Alfred telephoned. He couldn't get in for dinner, and he would stop to see Theodore. Catherine and Amy ate alone on a small table set on the terrace, with Lulu's secretive eyelids and slow feet protesting the additional steps.

"Have you heard from Geoffrey?" Catherine asked, after a long silence.

"No." How far away he felt to-night! "He's careless as a child about messages when he's on a holiday." She wouldn't add Geoffrey to her mother's full slate. "He always says if he knows he's all right, why tell other people." She hadn't sent that wire. To-night he seemed a figure in another planet, diminished from reality by her own immersion in the family concerns.

Lulu cleared the table, shook off the Italian cloth, and left them with the coffee tray. Darkness had crept into the yard, blunting the colors of flowers, intensifying the fragrance. From windows of Madam Westover's house the light stretched pale rhomboids on the grass. Hurried, irregular feet came along the sidewalk, mounted the steps next door.

Catherine strained forward. "Who's calling on Mother to-night?" They heard the click of the screen door, and presently a dark figure passed between the window and the light within. "Tom, I guess." She settled into her chair. "I do wish Alfred would come. He must be having a long talk with Theodore. I'm glad of that. Ted has a lot of sense, if he isn't a business man." A cricket spoke loudly in the grass near them, and remote as an echo, indistinct like a wagon on an old bridge, sounded thunder. "Did you hear that? We may get rain." She went on, gently, the darkness obliterating the barrier between thought and speech. "Your father's so proud of Ted now. He hated not having his son in the business with him, but he wouldn't insist on it when Ted wanted something else. He'd been too wretched himself."

"Father wretched?" Amy pushed to one side the sharp bite of curiosity about Tom and her grandmother. "About the factory?"

"Didn't you ever know that? He felt he must take it over, especially when Dewitt refused. It wasn't what he wished to do. He wanted to be an architect. He used to draw a little, and make sketches of buildings. But you children came along, and Mother depended upon him so much. I always felt I had to make it up to him as much as I could."

"Father!" Amy's thoughts ran down a long corridor, pushing at closed doors, dusting off old impressions of her father. "Why, I always thought he was a typical business man, successful, contented."

"Nobody's ever a typical anything. He has been a good business man. But it wasn't interesting, just taking over an established concern. Your grandfather made it. Alfred used to say he walked in other men's shoes and they didn't fit well. He wanted to make things, too. That's one reason I feel such resentment against Isabelle and Dewitt now. Of course your father dropped all his architecture ideas years ago. I don't mean he's suffered all his life. Of course not. It's just a secret feeling—he never talks about it— that he had never been fully used. Many men must have that feeling."

Amy listened, breathing lightly. The friction of the day had worn down Catherine's usual reticence, had thinned the texture of maternal fabric her speech to Amy often wore.

"That's why he wouldn't interfere with Theodore. For a while his disappointment made him stiff with the boy. I've been happy to see them come together again. Felice helped. She's really fond of your father. Ah, see that!" Lightning quivered above the trees. "I've always felt I had so much—that I must make it up to him."

"But what have you had that he hasn't?" Amy's impetuous question, deep from her own turmoil, was too like a quiver of lightning. It shattered her mother's tranquil mood. Amy heard her draw herself erect in her chair, pull on her habitual guard.

"My dear child, I have had everything I wished. How I have been running on! I'm quite as bad as Emma."

"Oh, please! Tell me more. I need to hear it."
Amy reached across to lay her hand on the rough
wicker arm. "It's as if I'd seen you both—oh, under
water, not clear, and you're just coming above the
surface."

"That's all. I had been thinking how unfair they
were to your father, you see. Even Mother. I
wonder what Tom is up to, staying so long."

"Never mind Tom. How are they unfair?"

"You heard Isabelle. Implying that because Alfred
had the factory he had everything. When Dewitt
really crippled Alfred, withdrawing his share in money
just when everything was so inflated after the war.
Now Dewitt's lost what he took, and Alfred still has
the factory. And Mother—when Alfred tried to reason with her about Curly, what did she say? That
Alfred, with control of his father's business, grudged
his own brother a home. Brother! She ought never
to have told us, after all these years."

"She did only as a last resort," murmured Amy.

"I know. But she's had fifty years to get used to
it. What other woman would have taken a child like
that? She made a model husband out of Father before
he died, but is it fair to hang Curly around Alfred's
neck now? Oh, he has had a bad week, and I don't see
how it's coming out. If Mother's making a new will,
be sure she has some clever scheme to manage all of
us."

The lightning ran up behind the trees from horizon
to zenith in quick, pale forks, not yet close enough
to throw light beyond its own tracery.

"It's like watching a play," said Amy, slowly, "in
which the lines are written, the scenes planned, even
to your own part, so that you just wait to see what
even you yourself will do and say next."

"I do feel helpless, if that's what you mean. Is that Lavinia?"

It was Lavinia, scurrying toward the kitchen door. Catherine called her, and she stopped, indistinct and huddled. "I want to see Lulu," she said, and Amy thought, "Here's another scene starting."

"If she's through with the dishes, she may be upstairs. I haven't heard her."

Amy heard her mother's chair creak in dry, rubbing notes of wicker. She was leaning forward, listening. Fainter than the sound of the chair came voices from the kitchen. " 'Viny never has anything to do with Lulu," said Catherine. "What can she want? Amy!" She rose quickly, straining across toward the lighted windows of Madam Westover's library. "It couldn't be Tom, could it?" A door slammed, and Lavinia slipped past close to the shrubbery. " 'Viny, come here! What do you want?"

Lavinia flung back a curt, "Nothing," and ran.

"After all," exclaimed Catherine, "Lulu's my maid, and I'm responsible for her." She got indignantly to her feet. "Wouldn't you think enough had happened!" she cried, as she went into the house.

Amy sat still. A splinter of wicker pricked her arm, and she slid a hand around to nurse the scratch. What a strange night, with that steady flickering in the sky, with this steady unrolling of the next scene in the play. The thought of Geoffrey moved in nerve-ends, as if his fingers, not her own, stroked her arm. No doubt that too was planned, what she and Geoffrey would say when they met. She had only to wait, to lay aside all folly of decisions and stands to take. Just wait, peering over her own shoulder to see what would happen. This is what they call perspective, she thought, with cool pride at her own astuteness. You see it when you read history or the life of a person who's finished. You don't often get that line on yourself. And you won't keep it long, jeered another thought.

There was a long flash of lightning, throwing blue radiance in which the lawns were garish velvet, and a rumble of heavy thunder. Amy rose. Things seemed to be happening more rapidly. Lavinia was returning, with Grandmother calling after her, "Tell Catherine to bring the girl over." Within the house some one turned on lights in the dining room, illuminating the terrace. Amy went in. Her father, for all his weariness, looked smoothed out; his talk with Theodore had shored up his esteem, his sureness in his own point of view.

"Hello, Amy. Where's your mother? I'm starved. Ted thinks he and Felice better go back before the storm breaks."

"It would be good to have a drenching." Felice was just behind them. "But this is my one best suit. We shall all feel better for a storm, I think." Her dark eyes inspected Alfred, and she gave a little nod as if what she saw pleased her. "Amy will make you a large ham sandwich, and you will sleep better tonight."

"Wait. I want you to see Mother. She'll appreciate your advice, you know. Where is she, Amy?"

"I'll find her." Amy went to the kitchen, closing the door carefully after her. What a pity if Father's brief respite had to be messed up with Tom and Lulu!

"I can't help it, 'Viny," Catherine was saying. "She's locked her door, and there's no sense breaking it down. She was sitting here with her eyes all swollen, and when I spoke to her, she flew upstairs crying."

"Your mother'll be right over and make her open that door," said Lavinia.

"Not to-night, please. We can't do anything to-night. Tell her it's true." Catherine's face was flushed in distress. "I told you, Amy, something was wrong."

"Cathy!" Alfred pushed open the door. "What you doing? Ted and Felice want to see you before they run home."

"Tell Mother I'll come over presently, 'Viny." Catherine steered Alfred quickly out of the kitchen. Amy heard Lavinia grumbling to herself as she flounced away.

"They don't want to get caught in a downpour," Father was explaining. "I've told them the whole affair and they agree with you absolutely. Think I've done all I decently should. I tell you I feel better, getting a new angle on things."

They chatted a moment, Felice repeating her sandwich advice. The windows shivered in a long roll of thunder, and she jumped to her feet, hooking an arm through Theodore's. "We must run!" she cried. But at the doorway they stopped, for, leaning heavily on the arm of a gray-faced, defiant Tom, her stick prodding at the rugs, Madam Westover met them.

"Now they don't need to hear it, too," said Tom, trying to wriggle free.

"It's family business." Madam Westover made a bony vise of her arm. "You can't go running off." Her face had the triumphant, wide-nostriled look of a warrior reaching straight for danger's fetlock. "We'll get this settled to-night. Alfred's the oldest man of the family." She brushed them all aside and took her seat erect on a chair near the door. "Can't you get that girl down, Catherine?"

Heat Lightning

"She couldn't help you, Mother." Catherine's preparation for trouble was her withdrawal into impassivity. She sat, her hands quiet in her lap, not looking at Tom, who lounged against the mantel in a miserable affecting of indifference.

"Is it something you wish us to stay for?" Felice stood at the doorway, her small head cocked, her eyes shrewd. "We were just leaving."

"I didn't know you were here, but you have a good deal of sense. We've got to see to this. Lora will just weep about it. Alfred, this boy's got your hired girl into trouble. He says she's had other men. But her father threatens Tom, says she was always a virtuous girl. He works in the forge. Now what do we do?"

"If you'd given me the money when I first asked, it would have been okay." Tom chewed his lip sullenly. "I had it all fixed. You know—to get rid of it. She went to a priest and got scared."

"So it's not your fault at all!" Felice broke in rapidly. "It is your grandmother's that she did not give to you the money, and the priest's, that he interfered! You are one big infant!"

"I say, now, I didn't ask what you thought, did I?" Tom's face moved in grotesque and nervous grimaces. "You all look as shocked as if it was a crime."

"What do you call it?" Alfred asked, harshly.

"I call it rotten luck, that's all."

"It is always rotten luck to have a consequence, is it not?" Felice observed, tranquilly.

"There's nothing to work up an argument about." Tom thrust a hand into the pocket of his white flannel trousers, and with a small convulsive jerk struck what, obviously, he hoped was a pose of nonchalance and charm. "The only point is her old man's after me, and he'll have to be bought off, and I haven't got a sou." He pulled out the pocket to show them, and pointed after the few coins that rolled, jingling, from the rug onto the polished floor. "So there you are. I can't prove I'm not to blame, though I jolly well know I'm not the only bet. Jeese, the reason the old Polack's so sore is that you fired him, Uncle Alfred." Tom offered that ingenuously. "It's because of the family Lulu dragged my name in. So the family ought to stand by."

"If you were my son, I'd put you to work. You're a preposterous loafer, and what Lora's thinking of— You're your father's—" Alfred's eyebrows bristled in a sandy thatch over his glare, but he stopped at Catherine's hand on his arm.

"Let's not waste time in bad temper," Catherine said. "What's to become of poor Lulu? I don't believe she was a bad girl, Tom. And the baby—"

Tom moved impatiently, as if reality touched him an instant with cold fingers. "Good God, you don't want me to marry a scullery maid, do you? Why, any fellow—" He glared at Theodore, at Alfred. "You're both so damned pious. Well, not all of us are that way. I say, look at Curly!"

Madam Westover brought down her stick with a whack, both hands crooked over it, and Tom swallowed visibly.

"I didn't mean to say that, Grandmother. But you all act as if I was a prisoner being tried, when all I need is a little cash. If I'd had it in time there wouldn't have been any need of this party."

Madam Westover got stiffly to her feet. "No. You would have added abortion to your other pastimes. Your grandfather was a man. Don't touch me." She knocked aside Tom's hand with a sweep of her stick. "Tell the girl in the morning that if she wants any help she must come to me. If the child is Tom's the family will pay for it, as he so ably points out." A blue vein swelled across the old woman's temple, and her mouth was a hard, lipless line between the hooked nose and jutting chin. She walked with strong steps across the room.

"Let me go with you, Grandmother." Amy obeyed the quick entreaty sent her by Catherine.

"I don't want any one," said the old woman. But as Amy took her arm, she did not shake her off, and as they crossed the grass her steps dragged. The lightning was almost continuous now, making an operatic unreality of shrubs and flowers, of red brick walls, as they approached the house.

Lavinia waited at the door.

"I was just coming to fetch you," she said, crossly. "You want to get soaked to the bone? Hear that wind coming up?" At the end of the hall crouched Curly, his head low between his shoulders. "She's home, Curly. Now you go to bed." He made a queer noise in his throat, not moving.

"It won't hurt you, Curly," said Madam Westover. "Lock your door and it can't get in." She smiled at Amy, a faint apology. "He's frightened when it lightens," she said. Then harshness sucked away her smile. "Tom shouldn't have said that," she cried. "He doesn't know!"

"You're so tired, dear." Amy drew her toward the stairs. "Let me help you up to bed."

"I'm not tired." But she started up the stairs, one step at a time, and Amy, feeling the dry weight yield involuntarily against her arm, had a fancy that the dark earth pulled hard at the old body, drawing

[165]

it down and down. It seemed a long journey to the upper room.

Lavinia had turned on the lights, had folded back the white counterpane, and plumped the pillows against the high head-rest of the wide bed. How small Grandmother must look, alone there in her frilled cotton gown. On the wall hung a framed crayon portrait of Grandfather, his beard very truculent. On the lower shelf of the table beside the bed, brass clasped and puffy, lay an album. Amy, as a child, had liked to turn its thick envelope pages, staring at the round-eyed ladies with bangs, at the fat babies on white fur rugs, photographs of the eighties. On the table beside the water jug sat the work basket, the pink yarn wearing its needles like antennæ.

"Can I help you, or get you anything?" Amy stood the stick in a corner.

"No." Madam Westover sat down in a low, armless rocker, and bent slowly to unbutton the straps of her soft, flat shoes. "Shouldn't you think—" her words unwound slowly from the spool of thought— "if that girl has money for a dowry, some man of her own class would be glad to marry her? There's quite a settlement of them. Lithuanians, I think they are. On the whole, I'd better see the father. Some man who wanted to start a little business—"

Amy hurried to the window as a gust of wind sucked out the curtains. Her hands on the sash tingled. "Shall I close it, or will you smother?"

"Just till the rain has passed."

"You'll probably even find the husband." She lowered the other window, pressing close to the glass an instant. Was that rain, or only the sweep of wind in dry leaves? "Suppose Lulu doesn't want a husband?" She must have loved Tom." She looked about, fearful at her temerity.

"She'll want one. With her father and the priest both after her." Grandmother pushed her feet into gray knit slippers and stood in front of the dresser, her fingers plucking at the brooch of garnets and pearls. She laid it gently in a china tray. "He shouldn't have said that about Curly."

"He didn't mean to hurt you, Grandmother." With the shades thus drawn the lights put back the night and storm. Amy longed to draw shades for this valiant figure against the buffeting turmoil that her sons and grandsons stirred around her, leaving her shut in safety.

"That's what he thought, though. But Alfred would have seen I had to speak out. About Curly. You must run home, Amy. Good-night."

"Don't let them worry you." Amy kissed her. "The way they all run to you!"

"I like that." Grandmother's dry laugh admitted herself, humorously, as an intentional lodestone. "Now run before the downpour."

Amy ran, down into a hall dim with the night light, hearing the door click shut behind her, across the grass, a dry leaf scratching at her cheek as it whirled, the thunder and the lightning blown away on the high wind. Felice and Theodore had gone, and Tom dashed past her as she opened the door. The house sounded with quick feet, the bustle of shutting all the summer-wide doors and windows against the storm.

"There, that's enough, I think." Catherine hurried down the stairs, her hair blown about her flushed cheeks. "Now I must get your father something to eat. Come along and help." She led Amy to the kitchen where Alfred stood, peering uncertainly into ice-chest shelves. "You sit down, Father, and we'll have a feast." She brushed back her curly hair. "Did Mother say much?" The white enamel of icebox and cabinet, the blue and white oilcloth on the table were suddenly eloquent of Lulu, moving slowly there, honey-colored, heavy.

"She's planning to give Lulu a dowry so one of her own race will marry her." Amy gave them that, triumphant evidence of Madam Westover's invincibility.

"Felice is right. Tom's one big infant." Alfred drew a chair to the table and watched Catherine slice bread. "I'm not going to fuss about it to-night. Why we should be responsible for his conduct!"

"Let's not talk about him any more. To-morrow's another day." Catherine creamed butter deftly. "I don't want to talk about anything!"

"I'm not hungry," said Amy. "I'm going to lie in bed and listen to the rain. Good-night, you two." As she left she knew her father reached for Catherine's hand, held it to his cheek.

When she had undressed, she knelt at the window to watch the rain, great black brooms sweeping the dry earth. Through the narrow opening she dared leave the water leaped in splashes against her face, and the strong sweet wetness filled her nostrils. A car crawled along the street, the rain splintering the lights into ineffectual haze.

That new sound was hail, tearing at leaves, bruising the flowers, assaulting windows and roofs. Under her hands which hugged her breasts she felt her heart race, its rhythm pitched to the storm and its excitement. And Geoffrey, infinitesimal in distance and in darkness—was he safe? She could see the storm tear away his small tent, hurl great limbs of trees down at him, till his lean, hard body stood out like a swimmer's, struggling for life through a great flood. She pressed one hand hard over her heart. Soon, soon she must find him. She put her face against the cold glass. The earth took the rain like a lover. A hasty, cruel, long-awaited lover. She stood up, her arms straight at her sides, not knowing whether rain or tears lay so wet upon her cheeks. Ah, she had been mad, thinking she and Geoffrey might make an end. In the darkness she stumbled toward the bed, and flung herself face downward.

Book Two

TOWARD morning Amy awoke, stifling in the stupid-sweet odor of stock and roses. The fragrance hung in the room, motionless and almost visible in the diffused light before dawn. Her eyes, sleep-heavy, came to the windows, focused there on something strange. Glass between her and the outer world. She had lowered them because of the storm. Cautiously, not to shake off the thin scarf of sleep, she moved her body across to the windows, and stealthily, not to wake any sleeper, she lifted them. Above the treetops in a raddled sky of clouds moved a swift lop-sided moon. The storm had ended, but the after-wind still blew, and from somewhere came the sound of running water. They hurry so, thought Amy, the moon and wind and water. She slept almost before she had fallen back against the pillow.

When she woke again she sat upright, with a sense of clear energy she had not felt for weeks. She stretched out her slim arms, liking the slide of muscles as she let them drop. What had happened to her? "It's that I've come out of thickets about Geoffrey. Or that the air I breathe has a different density. Who knows?" She would hurry, to have breakfast for once with her father and mother. A glance from the window showed an untidy world, clean-washed, but littered with torn leaves, twigs, bruised flowers, the driveway runneled from the rain. The sky stood out brilliant and blue.

She walked around the house, liking wet tongues of grass on her ankles, listening to the brook, loud even against the innumerable morning sounds of the town. The rain had been too violent; it had swept over surfaces and swirled off in the very swinging of the earth. Her mother spoke to her from the opened doors of the dining room, and she went in across the flags. "It's refreshing, isn't it? I slept so soundly."

"You look better." Catherine lowered her voice. "I didn't know what to expect from Lulu this morning, but she came down as usual. If she wants to go on working, I can't turn her out, can I? Even if it is— well, uncomfortable."

Alfred strolled in, faint reminiscence of shaving soap and powder about his ruddy jowls. "Well, see who's up!" He drew back a chair for Catherine and unfolded a napkin across his knees. "Did the rain spruce you up, too? Funny how different it makes you feel."

They talked of casual, pleasant things, the three of them in a conspiracy to hold time back, to keep this fresh awakening free of the rest of the day as long as possible. Even Lulu's step seemed less sulky; perhaps she took assurance from Catherine's silent acceptance of her this morning, now the secret was out. Perhaps—Amy glanced at her—she had just reached a further, less distressing stage of pregnancy. She brought in fresh muffins and crisp bacon like a tacit promise that she would do her best in the unwinding of her tale. The morning paper from the city was late; a tree down across the main road had delayed the bus. That, too, was pleasant; it kept breakfast intimate, without intrusion.

They had finished, and Alfred, with a sigh, folded his napkin, saying, "Well, I suppose Dewitt is waiting to hear—" when Lavinia appeared at the doorway from the kitchen. In her wrinkled face her mouth opened, gaped silent like a fish, buttoned down and gaped again. "What's that?" Alfred took a quick step toward her. "What'd you say?"

"Come over." She got the words out. "I don't know what's up. Curly won't let me in her room. I got up early to do some pears. Thought I'd let her sleep if she could, after all that stewing around yesterday. Fin'ly I went upstairs. Curly was there by her door. He wouldn't budge, and she don't answer me."

Alfred stared a moment, his eyes bulging under his thick brows. Then he plunged out of the doors, thudding across the terrace toward his mother's house.

Lavinia twisted her hands in her apron, her mouth fumbling again over unspoken words. "Curly might hurt him," she got out. "He's awful strong."

Catherine moved hastily, seizing Lavinia's arm. "Hurry up! You can manage Curly! Alfred can't. Hurry!" It was like a dream, all of them scudding toward the other house.

"Get away from that door, Curly! If something's wrong with Mother— Get away, I say!"

They pressed up the stairway, Lavinia shrieking, "Wait, we're coming!"

Curly crouched against the door, one hand on the knob, his other doubled in a threat against his chest, his face malevolent under the bushy hair, a low rumble breaking from his thick tongue and wide lips. Alfred, standing over him, had the awful tension of a man unused to physical thwarting, his hands quivering in aborted gestures.

"Curly, you let us in! You hear me! She wouldn't want you to keep us out." Lavinia chattered at him, darted under Alfred's arm to pluck at Curly's tight fist. He brushed her away, and as she stumbled against Alfred, the latter lunged for Curly's throat.

"Oh, wait!" Catherine gasped. "Mother! Do you hear me? Mother!"

Curly turned his dark face up at Catherine's cry, and they were all caught in a kind of trance, listening. Silence flowed out under the door, over the sill, and like a flood swept Curly down to his hands and knees, with a low cry more like a wild bird than a man. Over him Alfred reached for the door, flung it wide.

Amy knew what they would see. High against piled pillows, her hands rigid in the mockery of pink wool, her face secret and sealed, was Grandmother, the light on the table still burning, the shades at the windows drawn as Amy had left them.

The next hours labored in multiple confusion. Alfred rushed off for a doctor. "She doesn't need one," said Lavinia, prying the needles out of stiff fingers, setting aside the unfinished knitting. "I better leave her setting up, had I?" Her voice did not quiver. She glanced at the dressing table, and darted for a tumbler of water in which Grandmother's teeth gleamed. "She wouldn't like any one to see these." Lavinia carried them away.

"He'll be here at once." Alfred panted up the stairs. "Just caught him."

Curly crept along the hall to pluck at Catherine s skirt.

"Yes, Curly." Catherine looked down at him, tears in her eyes. "Nothing will harm her, Curly. Can't you find some work to do?" She steadied her voice. "The storm—broke the flowers. You have lots to see to." His face hung, dark and piteous, and his fingers twitched as if he felt her words between them, testing their truth. "No, don't go in there. Go out doors and work." He pulled himself to his feet, and without looking in at the opened door, made off slowly down the stairs.

Amy followed him as far as the doorway. A moment like that brought its own protection. It crashed on you like a muffled hammer, and you didn't have to know for a while what had happened. Lavinia scuttled down the stairs.

"Them pears will spoil if I don't see to them," she said, belligerently. "If anybody wants me, there I am."

The doctor came, and presently, very grave, went away again, and the door upstairs was shut. Catherine and Alfred were in the living room, making awkward motions, as if life apologized to death. "We should let the others know." A blood clot. Instantaneous death. Just what she would have asked for. Impossible that worry or shock could have caused it. That time last winter when she'd been ill—the doctor said she must have had a slight stroke then. He would send the undertaker.

It was more than two hours before Amy felt the first sharp pain from the blow. Tires slurred on gravel before the house, a horn sounded triumphantly, and looking out, she saw Charley climb down from his shining car, and cock his cap at an angle. She went out to tell him. After an instant he turned violently away from her, bending over the car, rubbing and rubbing with his elbow at the fleckless surface. "But she told me to come for her," he kept muttering. "At a quarter to eleven, she said. And here I am."

"Don't say that again!" cried Amy.

"No, ma'am." He hoisted himself to the seat, and his light blue eyes traveled over Amy's head to accuse the old brick house for standing so uncommunicative in the morning light. "A quarter to eleven," he repeated. "I had a job to make it, too." He leaned down toward Amy, eagerly. "You wouldn't like to come for a ride, would you? I could take you anywheres you liked to go. No." His hands gripped the wheel. "Just the sort of morning she'd of liked, too. Yeesus. She was an old lady, but I musta thought she would last forever." He stared ahead, his slow thoughts moving in the muscles of his throat. "I better get the funeral car washed and polished. If there's anything I can do for you folks— Don't you let that undertaker send to the city for a hearse, now, will you? She'd rather I drove her. She was used to me driving."

"Oh, yes, yes, Charley!" The intolerable edge of small finalities pried at Amy's control. "I'll tell them. Go wash the hearse!" She turned, and then as if to keep her balance on the thin wire of grief by swiftness, she ran across the grass to the other house. She would send for Geoffrey. He would surely start at once, knowing she had need of him. Her emotion broke in anger at the indifferent telephone girl. "If you'd listen you could hear me. Beauchamp's Camp. B-e-a-u— Mark it answer requested. How soon can I expect to hear?" The girl's voice had altered.

"Excuse me, but that isn't the old Mrs. Westover that's dead? I'll put this right through." Amy could hear chatter at an oblique angle before she hung up the ear-piece. If the camp could be reached by telephone, she'd hear within an hour. A messenger would take longer.

Still hurrying, she went to the kitchen entrance of her grandmother's house. The summer kitchen swam in thick smoke which stung her nostrils and throat. In the sink a white kettle bubbled sluggishly, and Lavinia scraped with a knife at brown scabrous stickiness over the stove.

"Yes, I burned 'em;" she flew around at Amy. "I know it. You needn't tell me. I never did such a thing before in my life." She stared out of smoke-reddened eyelids; her sparse knob of gray hair had slipped rakishly toward one ear. "They hollered for me to get some of her clothes." She fell to scraping madly. "She won't be bothered, anyway. She'd 'a' hated to waste them pears."

Amy watched the slow, volcanic action in the kettle. The house had sounds of slow feet and slower voices. "Who's come?" Amy blinked as Alpha jumped to the ledge outside the window over the sink and mewed at her, the bright triangle of his mouth plaintive and accusing.

Lavinia held open the screen door, calling him. "I never gave him his breakfast," she muttered. "Everybody's come. Undertaker's men, Dewitt, Lora. They're all in there. Here, Alphy, there's plenty oatmeal left this morning." She stooped to set his dish under the table. Amy listened at the kitchen door. How dreadfully busy it all sounded! A telephone rang. The doorbell rang. Feet moved heavily on the stairs. Voices. Was that Lora, crying? And all those cars lined before the house. A gray sarcophagus on wheels. Dewitt's elegant coach. A small coupé. The doctor had come back, too. She sat down,

[179]

her hands pressed together in her lap. Ridiculous, incongruous, all this busyness about death.

Catherine pushed open the swinging door, not seeing Amy just behind it. Her face looked gravely concentrated.

"Lavinia, what *are* you doing? You would be more help if you stopped that nonsense and answered the bells."

Lavinia whirled around, sticky flat knife wavering in her hand. The knife clattered across the floor, and she flung her apron over the ruck of wrinkles in her face.

" 'Viny, 'Viny, I'm sorry!" Catherine put her arms around the little dried figure, drew the apron away, kissed her. "But it's all so—" She caught sight of Amy. "You here?" She lifted a hand to brush back her hair, and the familiar, absent gesture brought Amy to her feet, guilty that she had even for so short a time slipped out of the busy necessities.

"I wanted to wire Geof," she said. "I can tend bells for you. 'Viny doesn't want to."

"I do too!" Lavinia stripped off her checkered apron. "I'll smarten myself a bit." She dragged open a drawer of the high yellow cupboard, unfolded a long white apron, tied it at the arc of her back. Her eyes beseeched Catherine. "She wouldn't have wanted that fruit to be wasted. It's ruint now, though." She laid her hands on her spare waist. "I can't be sitting down mourning. I got to busy myself." Off she scurried.

"Perhaps I better get some one in. Lavinia—" Catherine's fingers moved over her hair again. "What *will* she do, Amy? Oh, that 'phone again! How do people hear so quickly!"

They heard Lavinia shrill, "Well, she ain't coming, Mr. Ripley. She's dead. Yes, that's what I said."

"That was where Charley was to drive her," said Amy. "To make a new will." After she had slept on it, he had said. "She tore the old one up, yesterday."

Catherine did not heed her. That was the future, and to-day ran with distracted feet on futile, countless errands, breaking away crumbs of minutes as if its occupations might defeat the timeless finality of death.

The living room bulged with people. The undertaker, closing a notebook, beads of perspiration on his bald forehead, nodded at Alfred. "You'll be in soon? I have catalogues, and we can get a beautiful casket straight from the factory. Something with white satin, silver handles. You want the best, of course. The best is none too good for Madam Westover."

He went briskly away, and they all listened for the sound of his car. She should have white horses with plumes over their ears, thought Amy. Dewitt and Alfred would follow him, presently. Lora wanted to go. (Did she sleep in jingling beads and bracelets?) "Not unless you stop sniffling," said Dewitt, and Lora wept afresh. Harriet stood awkwardly about, a cigarette she didn't quite dare light between her fingers. Henry tiptoed in, rubbing his thumbs, pushing out nervous suggestions. The funeral should be in the church. No room here. The telephone again. For Amy.

Western Union calling. Mr. Geoffrey Norton was not at Beauchamp's Camp. The manager said he hadn't been there. They had two other messages returned just this morning. "But he is!" Amy pressed her mouth against the hard black rubber, imperative. "You must wire again. They may not have the name correctly. No, I'll telephone. They have a 'phone?

Heat Lightning

I'll call you in a minute from the other house." She couldn't talk here, with the low-toned, insistent argument behind her.

The minutes dragged, and her ear ached with the pressure of the black horn. Finally a drawling voice. Mr. Norton was not a guest at the camp. He hadn't been there since last year, August, 1929. No, he hadn't written about staying there. "I'm sorry, ma'am, but you got the wrong place. Sure, I know him. Tall fellow. He just plain isn't here. Too bad you had all this trouble. If he should come, I'll tell him."

Amy sat motionless, but within her body incredulity swooped in dizzy tail-spins. Not there! But where— her imagination fell back from this wall of not-knowing. Exhaustion tugged at her muscles, as if she ran through space seeking out all the places Geoffrey might inhabit. She picked up the telephone again, and it was heavy in her hand. A wire to the apartment in New York, another to the office. Geoffrey wouldn't be there. He had gone somewhere. He never left a forwarding address for business mail; this fortnight of holiday was too short, he said. If he had started for the camp—had been hurt—she could see him flat on a high iron hospital bed, that secretive glaze sealing his face—

Then, suddenly, without volition, all her dizzy tail-spinning and flight landed her upright on a fact, a bit of hard, high ground. Geoffrey had never meant to go to Beauchamp's Camp. He had said, "They're meeting me at Quebec." No one had expected him there. He had not been thwarted by any accident. He was precisely wherever he had planned to go. The view from the hard, high ground of this fact was ugly; the light hurt her eyes. But she stared, drawing a long breath of the thin air. He had lied. She could see how proof against discovery the plan must have seemed. Last year they had separated, agreed on silence for the days they were apart. "I am sick of writing anything," he had said. "I'm going to be a clod, an animal." Amy had left the children at a farm near their cottage, had gone herself to an island off the Maine coast, where days long she had lain in the sun on the beach, lovely empty hours in which no one cared where or what she was. Geoffrey had counted on a repetition of that silence. Ruthlessly Amy turned herself in the cold light. It had been an illusion, that enjoyment of a solitary self, a game she played between realities. Fundamentally she had no separate self now. She remembered one still golden morning when she had leaned against a rock, watching the tide creep toward her with soft, swinging water. She had thought, this is I, truly myself, only alone do I feel my own rhythm, undisturbed by sliding, slipping, warring rhythms of other people. Oh, folly, folly! Underneath she had known that Geoffrey, the children, waited for her, that at a further point she would merge with them again.

"This year, I was frightened." She spoke just under her breath, forming words slowly, "and so I found him out. I was frightened of his lie before I knew it." Bleakness settled over her. If she looked another moment at the lie, she might know what lay beyond it.

The telephone bell rang, so close it seemed an insolence. Emma, incoherent in her excitement. "Who is this? Oh, Amy! Why didn't you tell us? Isn't it terrible! Why, just yesterday I was in there, talking away to her. Mamma says she'll come right down, if there's anything she can do. You should have told us. Letting us hear from the Vet! Yes, our best cow is sick. Laurance says he'll come right away if you need him, but the Vet's here. He heard it from Charlev, he says. I'm so upset."

Amy found a piece of her mind admiring the alertness with which another piece leaped out of unseemly personal absorption into handling Emma. There was nothing to do. Father and Dewitt were taking care of things. Yes, she just slipped away in her sleep. No, the funeral hadn't been decided. "I really don't see what there would be for your mother to do, Emma. But come in when it is convenient."

She left the telephone, resenting Emma's unconscious delight in the drama of sudden death. Grandmother had never been part of Emma's intimate affairs, of course. She had been just a figure on the outer edge of the circle. Mamma would like a finger in the pie; she was so good at funerals, Emma had said.

She stood at the doorway, watching a group emerge from the other house, break into individuals. Henry started away, an irresolute gesture of farewell trailing from his loose hands. A passing car slowed, and curious glances pried at the house. Her father and Dewitt came slowly over the grass, intent, worried. Around the house moved Curly, trundling his hose cart, and Lavinia darted out at him, shaking a fist, expostulating, till Curly turned, sluggishly, and dragged the cart away. Alfred had observed the pantomime from the steps. He looked up at Amy, frowning.

"He doesn't know what he's about," he said. "Watering after that rain. Lavinia is sure it's all right for me to go off and leave him. I don't know. Henry thought he had to get back to Mary. I tell you, call up Tom. No." They had each recalled last night too clearly at the boy's name.

"He'll be all right." Dewitt pulled nervously at a fold of sallow flesh over his jawbone. "We've got to get along." He twisted his wrist to look at his watch. "My God, Alfred!" In the sunlight age suddenly dusted over his dark, lined face. "My God! It's long after twelve. I promised the bank— This is Saturday. They're closed." His tall body settled, and he moved his feet wide apart, as if to keep his balance.

"Well," said Alfred, "they'll have to wait. When they hear—"

Dewitt shook his head. "What difference will it make to them, death?" He stared at them through his thick glasses, a tiny fork of bloodshot veins magnified at the corner of one eye. "You know, I've thought about it every instant the whole forenoon. But it seemed—irreverent—not what a son should do—if I so much as looked at my watch to see the time. How do you account for that kind of foolishness?" He moved in bewilderment, asking them to explain him to himself.

"Come on." Alfred moved toward the garage. "Bisby's expecting us. He's got to order the casket right off, or they won't deliver it till Monday."

Dewitt waited until Catherine came near. She walked slowly, but her step had confidence, like the angle of her head.

"Will you call up the house? If you can get Isabelle, tell her about things. I don't know when I'll get home. Ask her about wiring Sophie. I think she ought to come. She's just tearing around, enjoying herself."

"Don't you want luncheon before you go?" Alfred drove up, and she laid her hand over his knuckles on the wheel a moment. "No, perhaps you better not wait. I'll have something whenever you're through."

Curly appeared again, this time with a splaying broom of fiber, a rake, a basket. He stood, his arms clasped about his weapons, inspecting them, his face contorted as if he tried to think, perhaps to remember. Not until Alfred and Dewitt had driven away did he set to work, sweeping the grass with long, methodical strokes.

"I think he'll be all right." Catherine came into the house. "Your father's worried about him. But what can be done? To send him away now seems a kind of defiance of Mother. You know"—she stood close to Amy, not looking at her—"I suppose it's a superstition. But I feel that she hasn't got very far away yet." Color rose in her face as she spoke. "It's hard to believe in death, to believe that overnight she'd let go of everything here she was so concerned in. I think it would take her a while to get used to being dead. She never liked to travel." Catherine looked up, an admission of helplessness in her delicate smile. "Wouldn't you think some one would have found out about death by now? I always hope it feels more natural to the person who dies." Her hand lifted to brush back her hair. "I must tell Lulu about luncheon—and call up Isabelle." At the end of the hall she turned. "Did you get Geoffrey?"

"No." Amy had to add something to that monosyllable. "I'm afraid I can't reach him in time. He's not in camp."

"Oh, I'm sorry. I suppose he's off in the woods."

"I don't know where he is."

"It doesn't matter, really, does it? There are so many of us."

"He admired Grandmother." How hard to keep her voice quiet, not desperate! "He'll be sorry, I'm sure."

"If you left word, he may get back in time."

"I'm afraid not." Amy stared at the empty door-

[186]

way, after her mother had gone, her eyes hard. She'd
have to say this over and over. They'd all ask, "But
where is Geoffrey?" He had a plan he wished to keep
secret. That meant it concerned not himself alone.
Past that point she would not look. From now to
the moment when, finally, she would know, the days
would move. Cold, glacier-slow, the days would crawl,
bearing her frozen into their green-white breast.

2

To concentrate upon Geoffrey would have been impossible, so crowded and diverse was the rest of that
Saturday. Isabelle, reanimated by death, drove over.
What were they going to do about mourning? She had
telephoned straight into Madame West's, in town, and
the head fitter was coming out to-morrow, even if it
was Sunday, with models for her and Sophie. Yes,
Sophie would arrive by noon. "I can call her again,
and have her bring dresses for you and Amy." She
appraised Amy, her eyes squinting. "You're a small
thirty-six, aren't you? Just about Sophie's size, only
Sophie's slim as a reed. Of course, having children—"
"I don't want a black dress," said Catherine. "I
shouldn't wear it again. Mother wouldn't like it."
"Well," said Isabelle, lips pursed, "if you don't care
to show proper feeling!"
Lora trailed across. She had seen Isabelle's taxi
arrive, and thought perhaps Geoffrey had come. A
handkerchief at her red eyelids, her waved hair upset
into a relief map of a dark continent, she cried again.
"Do try to control yourself, Lora!" Isabelle re-
proached her with her own plump calm.
Lora went on crying, but between sobs agreed to have

models sent out for her. Harriet had a black suit she could wear. Into this discussion broke Emma and her mother, Mrs. Miller bulging at various spots in stiff, bright blue silk. The Vet had driven them in, and Laurance would come for them by and by. He'd had an awful day with the cow, but now she was all right. Mrs. Miller sat well forward on her chair, her small blue eyes hurrying about for details. When was the funeral? Not till Monday afternoon? Well, with old people you didn't have to hustle so, even in summer weather. She nodded smartly at the silence which followed that remark. "It's true," she insisted, "unless they're awful fat."

"How can you sit there and say such dreadful things?" Lora disappeared behind a fresh handkerchief.

"I don't see anything dreadful in facts," said Mrs. Miller. "Where you going to have the funeral? Oh, I supposed you'd have it in the church." Her tone disparaged Westover customs.

"To-morrow afternoon people can see her." Catherine had a buffeted look, as if her flesh took the impact of these diverse personalities. She didn't know who would be pallbearers. Alfred and Dewitt were arranging that.

"I hope she's left things divided up fair." Mrs. Miller stared hard at Isabelle. "I think it's time her grandchildren got something, as I was saying to Emma. If her children haven't helped themselves to all of it already." Emma, flushed, whispered, "Sh-h!"

"That's all you can think about. Money. Why, she hasn't been dead a day yet!" Lora blew her nose aggressively.

"You can't tell me you aren't thinking about it, too."

Isabelle rose, her heels tapping on the floor. "If

you mean that Dewitt has had more than his share," she began.

Catherine stood up swiftly, the dignity of anger making her erect and tall. "Oh, hush, all of you!" she said. "Don't squabble to-day. You're all forgetting what has happened!"

In the silence that followed Mrs. Miller sniffed once or twice, and then decided to call on Mary. She hadn't seen the new baby, and Laurance could be sent there after her and Emma. Emma ran back to take Lora's hand, to hold it in spite of its limp struggle. "Laurance said to tell you he'd see you to-night. I know you feel bad. Honest, I'm awfully sorry. We'll bring some of those late roses to-morrow." Then she was off, like a child who has spoken a piece.

"I don't see why they keep that awful woman with them," declared Isabelle. Her plump, soft fingers pressed her temples. "My poor head!"

Lora, tormented between two antagonisms, sobbed out, "She's her mother, I suppose."

Presently Isabelle had gone, driving home in the car Dewitt had left in the street that morning. Lora went back to lie down again. "Wouldn't you feel better if you went home?" urged Catherine. But no, Lora was sure her mother would have wished her to stay with Lavinia. "Although she is so noisy. She's cleaning the whole house, and won't listen to a word I say."

Later Harriet came over. Amy was alone in the living room, with a letter from Buff which the postman had brought, a letter so young and gay in its misspelled enthusiasm that Amy finished it through tears. "Yesterday I wun the crall stroke swimming race and made second on form when I dived."

"Could I use the 'phone?" Harriet lighted a cigarette and took a famished puff. "If I 'phone over there, Mother will listen to every word, and I won't hear the last of it for days. Aunt Catherine won't mind, will she?"

"I suppose not." Amy tried not to imitate Lora in eavesdropping, but the girl's voice had a husky eagerness which demanded attention.

"It's Hal, darling. Listen, I can't come. My grandmother died this morning. No, *grand*mother, I said. I'm terribly upset. No."

Amy moved impatiently to a window, to escape the voice. She read Buff's letter again, smiling over the "couseler who is the sweetest thing and all the girls are crazy about her, and another scares you first she looks so strick but she really is very nice."

"Do you mind if I stay for another cig?" Harriet lounged into the room, her gaze at Amy deceptively intense. Just like a pigeon, thought Amy, near-sighted and concentrated on her own projects; her head moves on her neck like a pigeon. "Lavinia caught me smoking, and did she bawl me out! It's awful, staying over there. Lavinia doesn't want Mother around, and Mother doesn't want me, but we both have to stay. I just broke an engagement for to-morrow, a really important one. If my staying did any good! I said to Mother, 'Where is Tom? Why don't you rope him in?' But did she listen to me?" She sat down, crossing her thick legs, lighting another cigarette.

"Where is Tom, anyway?" Amy stood in the window, half aware of bird notes around the stone bath, wondering whether any one had filled it. She'd look when Harriet went.

"Who knows?" Harriet shrugged. "I haven't seen him to-day. He probably hasn't even heard the news. You know"—she set her feet in their flat-heeled

Heat Lightning

oxfords squarely together—"there's lot of hypocrisy about death, isn't there? Grandmother never liked me, and Tom could get away with anything, just by toadying to her. And to-day he's off doing what he pleases, and I can't even have to-morrow." The ash from the cigarette made a gray smear over her tie and she dabbed at it angrily. "Brooks, that's my friend, just hates to have her plans upset. She's temperamental. She'll take some one else." Harriet ground out the cigarette with a loud, "Damn!" and rammed her hands into her jacket pockets. "I don't know why I tell you all this."

"I don't know, either," said Amy, crisply. In spite of herself she felt a kind of pity for the girl. She looked beset, if grotesquely so. "Surely, for a few days, your friend will understand."

"She knows all about my life here. She knows I didn't care about my grandmother. She knows no one cares a snap about me." Suddenly Harriet's face began a series of grimaces, and she flung one arm up to hide them. "I wanted Grandmother to like me," she cried. "I was afraid of her. And now, you'll see! She'll leave Tom enough so he'll be independent. She told him so. And what'll I get? Nothing." She peered at Amy over her shielding arm. "You pretend you think I'm awful, talking about what she's left. But you've got away." As Catherine came in, she broke off, fumbling for another cigarette.

"Felice is here. She's been talking to 'Viny. Theodore has gone in town with your father and Dewitt, she says."

Harriet got awkwardly to her feet. "I'll move on," she said. Her glance at Amy tried, ineffectually, to push a cover over all the squirmings of her uncomprehended self.

[191]

Heat Lightning

Felice walked straight to Catherine, laid a hand on each arm, and after a moment strained on tiptoe to kiss each cheek gently.

"I feel most bereft," she said. "And I had known her only so little a time. She leaves a great emptiness."

Her words pushed open a door into sweeter air. She and Catherine sat together on the divan, Catherine's hand relaxed in Felice's firm, quick-fingered grasp, and Amy, leaning against the window, listened to the quiet that settled in the room. It's the first time today, she thought, that I've really felt what has happened. Felice dares think about her, about death itself. All the others go skittering away, tripping over themselves. Not Mother. Only she hasn't been allowed time to think till now, when Felice clears a space about her. I'm one with the silly others, embroiled in myself.

"But she had a grand life, that one," Felice was saying. "We were talking of her last night, 'Dore and I, as we lay in bed and heard the rain. I said she was strong, and so lesser people crumpled, giving way at their weakest spots. But you, being strong in a different way, stood quite straight beside her and loved her. And then," her dark eyes asked them to share this, humorously, "while I was telling 'Dore other most important things, he fell asleep."

"I did love her." Catherine's eyelids glistened. "I remember when I married, people said it was foolish to settle here, next door. But Father had given us this house, and no one knew how scrupulous Mother was about letting us alone. As long as Father lived she was absorbed first of all in him. She kept a careful formality especially those early years. Amazing, isn't it, along with that strong will of hers?"

"She had so much in herself she had no need to

walk around in the lives of others, interfering. And yet, when they took their little affairs to her, like this Tom last night, then she would act. Formality is a good quality." Felice nodded gravely up at Amy. About her brow and mouth lay faint signs of intensity, as if she held this quality up, fitting it into innumerable instances. "It gives a certain elegance which we lose if we go prying too closely."

"Some of the family might do well with a little of it," said Amy. "It's a quality that's out of style, isn't it? It used to belong to gentle-folk, and now we don't know what our code of behavior is. Good manners are artificial, and reticence is dangerous repression, and we're all in a dreadful mess. I know what I'm trying to say. We've lost more than Grandmother. We've lost her whole way of life. She knew what her own standards were, and we go fumbling along."

"You feel that, too?" Felice studied Amy's restlessness. "I thought it was perhaps that I come from a different country, another race."

"We all come from different races. Look at us! That's one trouble." Amy stopped, at the perplexity in Catherine's face. You've knocked to bits the peaceful moment Felice gave her, she accused herself.

"I don't know what you girls are talking about," said Catherine. "My head's too heavy to follow you. But I know what I think we've lost. Mother kept us together. She was a center from which we all ran off in all directions. A band about a bundle of sticks. The band is cut, and all day I've felt we were farther apart, separated by sharper animosities. I don't like it—" her hand made a baffled, uneasy gesture—"I hope I'm wrong."

Amy looked down at her mother, startled. Why, that was her thought, that wide and wider scatter-

ing,—Geoffrey's word, entropy—with never any return to a center—life breaking constantly into new
combinations, dissipating itself steadily, until—

"At least,—" Felice brushed away their abstractions, lifting Catherine's hand for a warm moment to
her cheek—" at least, me, I have no animosities to
you, my dear, nor to Amy." She stood up, her stocky
figure alert and unhurried. "Perhaps I feel less
cousinly to, well, to Emma. Who can say? You will
let me know if I can do anything? Theodore will tell
me all the plans when he comes to-night."

Amy walked out to the veranda with Felice, watched
her pull a béret carelessly over the silvered crest of
hair. "I was thinking, too," said Felice, "about Tom,
and Uncle Dewitt's affairs. They are patchwork, unfinished, the needle sticking in the seam. And no doubt
many others we do not know about. But she would
always have left unfinished blocks, would she not?"

As they spoke, Laurance drove up in his truck. He
came up the walk, a reluctant awkwardness in his tall
body.

"Emma and her mother are at Mary's," Amy answered the first query.

"Oh!" Relief flowed over him, untying rigid
muscles. "Then I'll run in a minute to see Mother.
Where is she?"

Amy pointed. Laurance wasn't obtuse, then, for all
his Emma. He'd see Lora with the Millers as audience if he must, but how unwillingly! "She's staying there on Lavinia's account," Amy explained.

"I suppose she's taking it pretty hard? Of course,
it's a shock, coming with no warning. But after all,
Grandmother was pretty old."

Poor Lora. Amy detected a Miller echo in his
words. No, worse than that, a macabre hint of the

[194]

day spent with the Vet, saving the cow. Birth and death lost their mystery, in terms of live-stock. Her mouth puckered at the astringent thought. "When is it time to die?" she asked, and took a small pleasure in the interrupted look his eyes wore at the question. "I'll have to move along. No telling what the kids'll be into, left alone."

He went, easy swinging, toward the other house. Why, he'd changed from khaki work clothes into a neat dark suit. He didn't take death entirely as a piece of the day's work, then.

"He is so very much older than Tom," remarked Felice. "But you must not interfere with his sensible attitudes by foolish questions." Her glance caught Amy's with sly perception of the undertones of the scene. "Now I must go. It is good you are here, as Catherine has so much the brunt of all this." Off she went, her arms swinging with her brisk, terrier-like trot.

Amy started into the house, and hesitated, her hand on the door. That remark Felice had left with,—was it a challenge? Did she, for eyes as shrewd as those with which Felice looked about, wear some sign of anxiety, of preoccupation warring against a complete sharing of this present experience? Felice hadn't asked about Geoffrey's coming. She floundered in her doubt, her ears burning. "You think you're the only one who notices things," she stormed. "Watching them,—Felice so serene and firm, identified with Theodore as close and smooth as—as kernels in one shell. Emma and Laurance. Even Mother with Father." She struck one fist into the palm of the other hand. What tokens did she leave about for betrayal of herself? She remembered one evening, and a doctor boasting of the signs of illness each stranger wore, imperceptible to a lay eye, but plainly there to read. Was disunion, distress, struggle, written on her forehead, implicit in her gestures? That would mean the whole world ran around with life histories visible to any observer. She tried to shrug off the dismay she felt, as if discovery of her troubled state would set it immovable, would label past all recovery her failure in love. She noticed these others because she had need of sustenance; seeing that thus and thus and thus was true, she had a lesson for her stumbling self. For the most part, luckily, people were up to their eyebrows in themselves, and stigma went unread. Felice had made a casual, customary remark. Or, if not, Felice was different.

The telephone rang again. Catherine was at the terrace door, talking with some one, a neighbor, perhaps. Amy answered.

"Who is this?" The voice was faint, guarded. "Oh, Amy! It was you I wanted." The voice was Tom's. "Listen, I gotta see you. I can't come to the house, see? But I must see you. Where's Mother? I tell you I can't come there, you ought to know that." His words ran up and down crazily. "You meet me somewhere. I don't want to see anybody else, see?"

"But, Tom, what do you want? I haven't any money, if that's—"

"Oh, God! It isn't cash. Listen, Amy,—" She could visualize the hugging curve his loose young body must make, urging huskily from some drug-store booth. "I gotta see you. You start down past the church, and I'll drive along and pick you up. Will you?"

"How absurd, Tom. You'll have to come here. I can't trail around the street to-day just because you ask me to."

"Good Christ, can't you see—" He broke off, and

Amy could hear a queer sound, an inarticulate puffing over the wire.

"See here, Tom, if you want to see me, come around this evening. No one need know. I'll meet you in the garden, in the arbor." He sounded youthfully desperate, but Amy felt distaste for his implications. Louder than his voice she could hear her grandmother, "He shouldn't have said that." He was silent so long that Amy said, curtly, "Are you still there?"

"I suppose you're down on me, too," he accused her. "I wouldn't ask you, but you're the only one that knows. What time?"

"Any time."

"It's dark by nine. I'll be there."

Well, thought Amy, pushing the instrument back on the small table, I have to take a stitch in that unfinished patch. Her eye caught an impression of movement at the margin of vision, and glancing up at the mirror on the wall, she saw, just as it disappeared, the smooth, fair hair of Lulu's bent head. Uneasily she ran back over the conversation, feeling the discomfiture of an uninvited intrigue. Had the girl heard— and how much?

"People mean to be kind." Catherine followed Amy into the living room. "But they do talk so much. Weren't you at the 'phone, too?"

"It was Tom."

"Poor boy." Catherine lowered her voice, aware of Lulu setting the table in the next room. "He must feel wretched, after last night. I know it doesn't really matter, but I can't bear to think her last evening had that—" She waved toward the dining room.

"He sounded more excited than repentant," observed Amy. "But you know, I am sure Grandmother must have been glad to go out of the middle of things, no matter how disagreeable they were. Like a general with his boots on."

Harriet appeared, out of breath. A reporter from the city paper. Would Aunt Catherine come over? Mother was no use at all.

Amy sat down at the desk. She would write to the children. She paused, after she had written Dear Bobs. No, she wouldn't tell them, until she saw them again. She couldn't send death, incongruous and foreign, in a letter to a child. When she told them, it wouldn't matter greatly. A good proctective device, that near vision of childhood, she thought.

Later her father drove past the windows into the garage. She heard him close the doors and come slowly into the house. His shoulders sagged, and he looked grimy with fatigue as he drank the highball. Catherine mixed him.

"Dinner is ready, Alfred." Catherine stood off from him, alert and undemanding. "You want to brush up first?"

He didn't want any dinner, he said. Catherine propelled him to the stairs, and went out for some final word to Lulu.

"Now don't tell me things until you've eaten." She looked across the pleasant table at him. "After dinner I must go over to Mary's. Henry called to see if I would come. She feels bad to be in bed. I'm afraid Emma and Mrs. Miller tired her, rather."

"They would," said Alfred. He served them silently.

Amy noted that her mother had ordered a special dinner, food that Alfred liked. When had she found time to think of that? And why should homely things like bread and meat offer comfort? They did, as if hunger spoke up to say, "Life goes on. Eat. Even grief whets the edge of hunger." And Lulu served

them with solicitude, having nothing to give except that
domestic care, and yet wishing to do something.

When they had finished, Alfred said, "Everything's
seen to, I think. It was awkward, this being Saturday.
Bisby's a competent fellow. I saw Clement, too.
Mother liked him best of the preachers, didn't she?"

"I don't see how you got so much done." Catherine admired him, healingly.

"I must say Dewitt wasn't much help." Alfred
wanted to spread out his day like a map, tracing every
step of his difficult progress. "He would have left
everything to Bisby, he was so eager to be off on his
own affairs. If Theodore hadn't been along, I don't
know what I mightn't have said to him. Cathy, he
wanted me to advance his share of the estate. To-
day! I did call him a vulture. His share! Good
Lord, he's had more than his share, just this past
week. Ted made me shut up, and he went off in a
rage. If he tries to borrow on his prospects— He's
had his prospects. Mother told him so."

"Ted was right, not to let you quarrel. Just because you were both wrought up." Catherine slid an
ash-tray near his hand before the inch-long smooth
ash of the cigar fell. "All day I've wanted to say
horrid things."

"I was thinking, as we drove back from the city—
death sends you back so far—about a birthday Mother
had, when we were kids. Did I ever tell you? Dewitt gave her—we had saved out of our allowances
to buy presents—an air-gun. Very proud of himself
because it cost a lot for those days. I thought he was
uncommonly smart, because we'd both wanted one.
And she said, in that dry way of hers, 'You didn't
count on borrowing it, did you?' I can see him now,
squirming one leg around the other and getting red in

the face. She put it away, too, where he never found it. But he didn't learn much from it."

"We all give people things we like, don't we?" Amy detected a pathetic undertone in her father's words; he didn't to-day wish to feel hostility toward his brother. "Bobs and Buff give me the funniest things. It's a wrench ever to realize that anything, a toy, an event, can feel different to some one else. Even death. All day I've seen death being a different feeling to each one of us. We can't help it, can we? I suppose Dewitt is so tangled in his business he can't come clear of it, the way you can. Even if he did love Grandmother."

Catherine's swift glance warmed Amy, hinted, "Thanks for helping smooth him down." Alfred stared under heavy eyebrows.

"Death ought to be the same thing to everybody," he said.

Lulu pushed open the door, and Catherine called to her, "We're through, Lulu. We're just going."

"I ought to have a talk with Lora." Alfred stood in the living room, twiddling the stub of cigar. The evening paper folded on the stand by his chair lured him with the comfort of habit. If he could sit down, to read and smoke, the evening might take on a tinge of ordinary life.

"Can't you wait?" Catherine saw the pull of habit.

"No. I'll see her first. And Curly. I haven't done anything about him. By Jove, it won't be safe to have him there when they bring—when they bring Mother back. I tell you, for a minute this morning I didn't know what would happen."

"He's been all right to-day." Catherine spoke uncertainly. "He's just puttered around the grounds."

"How did he know what had happened?" Alfred

moved to the table, laid his cigar on the tray, let his hand hover over the paper. "Or what did he know? You ought to realize we can't have him about with a funeral there. Suppose he— And yet, with Mother's feeling about him—she'd hate it, if I had him taken off, wouldn't she?"

"Alfred, dear!" Catherine's voice trembled. "Can't you leave that till morning? And Lora will weep all over you. Must you see her?"

"Yes, I must." He stalked off, somberly.

Catherine sighed. "It does look complicated," she said. "Do you want to come to Mary's. I'm going now. I won't be long."

"I told Tom I'd see him about nine."

"Don't let your father see him to-night. He's forgotten about that, for to-day. He didn't even look at Lulu." She hurried out through the side door, only to reappear. "Your father's locked the garage. Amy, you run over for the key, please."

Amy, crossing to the other house, thought: I forgot to fill that bird-bath, and, how strong that grass smells, wet and green. The dew is heavy. Mother didn't want to intrude, as if she thought Father stepped back into a long past relationship with his own family, with his sister.

The curtains were drawn at the windows; the house looked dark except for pencils of light and a glow through the frosted pane in the front door. Lavinia darted into the hall, dustcloth in hand. Her eyes blinked at Amy.

"Will you ask Father for the garage key?" said Amy. "Mother wants the car."

"I just got that Curly to bed." Lavinia scowled and ran the cloth over a shining table. "He's been

looking for her all over the house, listening at doors,
till he had me crazy. Yes, I'll ask him."

She scurried up the stairs. A door opened above,
let out a murmur of voices, and shut again. Lavinia
hurried back, the key in her crooked fingers.

"I must say, Lora'd better go home. What she's
camping out here for is more'n I see. Amy"—the
wrinkled face came close to Amy's—"you don't s'pose
she's planning to live here, do you?" Dark and
troubled, the fear of a future altered from all the past
looked out from her puckered eyelids.

"She hasn't any plans, 'Viny. She just didn't want
you alone, you and Curly." Amy took the key, cold
in the spare, clutching hand. "You must go to bed.
You don't want to make yourself sick, do you, the way
you're working?"

"I don't dast to stop. No, I'll go to bed. Get 'long.
Only if they try to put Curly anywhere, I'm going
with him."

Amy delivered the key, and when her mother had
driven away, she sat for a while on the front porch.
She could hear Lulu in the kitchen, and an occasional
abrupt buzz of a mosquito against the screen. The
rain brought them, she thought. Could they hatch,
so quickly? What silly ideas hopped into one's head!
Noiselessly, lest Lulu hear, she unlatched the screen
door, and felt her way past indistinct shrubs toward
the entrance to the formal garden. In the short time
since she went for the key, the earth had swung out of
the last dim edge of twilight. The dark sky had a
different texture from the past nights; the rain had
washed the upper air clean and the stars had multi-
plied. Like mosquitoes, propogating in rain. How
heavy the dew was! She tasted a finger, wet from
brushing leaves.

Heat Lightning

"Amy?" The whisper startled her, and her eyes, focused to the darkness, could see movement at the end of the arbor. "I was just going to whistle for you. I thought you'd never come. I saw you go over there." He spoke with a curious deliberateness.

"It's not nine yet," she said. "Is the bench damp?" She touched the rough stone with her fingers.

"Here, I've got a newspaper." He spread it, rustling, and she sat down beside him. In the dark she could not see his face, but his movements, the indefinite mass of his body hinted at tension. As he leaned toward her she caught a strong varnishy whiff. "I appreciate you coming out," he said, and she recognized his deliberateness as a heavy effort to keep his words from sliding down alcoholic byways. "I certainly appreciate it."

"What do you want, Tom?" No use upbraiding him.

"I want to know something. First I want you to know I appreciate—"

"You said that before. Hurry up."

Tom drew himself up in dignity. "If you're down on me, too, I won't—won't detain you. Thought you'd be more broadminded. Couldn't expect much of m'mother'n sister."

"Tom, you might have stayed sober, if you wanted to see me. You must hurry. I'm not sure Lulu won't join us. She must have heard me at the 'phone."

"Perfectly sober. Just a little snifter. I—" Suddenly his defense capsized, and he writhed into a heap on the bench beside her, pounding his head against his fists, choking, sobbing.

Amy caught his fists in her hands, held them in spite of his struggle, made out the words in his outburst.

"You saw her last. You went home with her. I

tell you, I have to know. What did she say? I never meant to say that about Curly. I was half wild. Did she hate me? Did she die, hating me? Amy, she was always such a brick to me—"

"Yes, she was." Amy shook him, as if he were only the child he acted. "Now sit up and stop your noise. Here, wipe your face." She pulled a handkerchief from his pocket, heard his miserable snuffle.

"What did she say? I got to know. I thought to-day I ought to shoot myself."

"And instead, you go get drunk. You'd do better to brace up."

"I had to do something." Tom shivered. "You don't know how awful I felt. What did she say?"

"She took off a brooch she was wearing," said Amy, slowly. This might be important, if the boy had any real feeling, if he was capable of anything past a maudlin sentimentality. "One Grandfather had given her. She held it in her hand"—an intolerable ache crept behind her dry eyelids as she saw the old figure—"and said, 'He shouldn't have said that about Curly.' She was thinking less of you than of Grandfather. She thought you did him great injustice, implying he was like you. She said, 'Alfred would have understood I had to speak out about Curly.' You see, Tom, she meant to protect Curly, not to betray Grandfather. She expected us to fit that small item into his whole life, the way she had always done. You suddenly waved it as justification for yourself, quite as if Grandfather had never been anything else but—well, your sort of man."

Tom groaned, laid an arm along the back of the bench and rested his head on it.

"I gave it to you straight," said Amy. "Grandmother was fond of you. The first day I came she made excuses for you. Why, she said, 'Tom's all right.' "

"She always was a brick to me," muttered Tom. "What'd she have to die for before I had a chance to straighten things out? I never meant to make her feel bad."

"You didn't much care, I'd say."

"That's right, lay into me. You got me down all right."

"You wouldn't listen if I minced words," said Amy, wearily.

"You think I'm just a rotter, do you? I'll show you. I'll show 'em all. I'll surprise 'em. Mother sniveling about my father. God, I didn't pick him, did I? Laurance so damned smug. Grandmother was the only white one in the bunch." He jumped to his feet, his mood veering precariously. "I'll tell you what I'll do. I'll marry Lulu. That's what I'll do."

"That would be wonderful," cried Amy, her tone rising to meet his. "What would Grandmother think of that?" Weariness crept in her, urging her to let him go. Why should she feel responsible for him? He would go, at all events, where he pleased, and no words of hers would touch him for more than a breath. "You think she'd like that?"

"I don't know." He stopped, surprised. "Oh God!" He sank down again, his head almost to his knees on limp hands. "What a vile mess!"

Silence followed, and Amy listened to light sounds near them. A mosquito twanged near her face and retreated; the leaves sighed, turning in their sleep; a twig snapped. Why did she feel that some one listened? Almost that she could hear Grandmother's determined tap, tap along the gravel. Suppose her mother had been right; how far would one day take the old woman from all she had loved? She never liked travel—I haven't done very well with your patchwork, Grandmother!

"Go on home, to bed, Tom," she said, more gently. "The piper has to be paid, even when he pipes a death march. Marrying Lulu would only make a worse mess. Grandmother knew that. You might brace up and be your age."

He stumbled after her as she walked slowly to the front steps. In the light from the hall she saw his face, the features loosened, unrelated to his will, tears running down his cheeks.

"It won't do any good to say it," she finished, "but if you'd lay off that stuff you drink, you wouldn't feel so sorry for yourself. Good-night."

"I'll see you to-morrow." He fumbled for a vanished dignity. "Good-night."

As Amy let herself quietly through the screen door, she thought: after all, he's precisely like Lora, translated into a different sex, a different age. They both expect never to have results catch up with them, and if they are caught up with, they feel abused. She stopped. At the other end of the long hall stood Lulu, one hand pressed against the door, her body frozen into heavy passivity, as if she wanted in spite of every desire to fly.

"Mother isn't back yet?" Amy seized the first stray thought. Lulu moved her head in slow negation. Reluctantly Amy stepped toward her, drawn by the force of the evident necessity which held Lulu poised there.

"I been listening," said Lulu.

"Yes?" After all, hadn't she half known it?

"Will you tell him something?" The girl folded her arms across her womb in a proud, instinctive gesture. "I was afraid mebbe he would ask you to do what he wanted. Get rid of it. You tell him I would not marry him, ever. Not if he asked me. He is no good. I heard him say that. I am going away, after they have the funeral. I will have my baby." The smooth column of her throat swelled as she lifted her head. As suddenly as an animal she slipped through the door and fled.

3

In the night a bell rang. Amy heard it deep in sleep; a fire signal, terrifying; she fled in panic down long corridors where smoke writhed, searching for Geoffrey, trying to scream his name. A nightmare which moved swiftly at an angle to time, projected endlessly in a spiral between seconds, so that her final terrific effort to scream brought her upright in bed, the bell still ringing in the dark house.

She heard her father speak, heard a light snap on, heard him padding down the stairs. Her knees unsteady, her heart beating crazily, she followed, clinging to the railing. It was a messenger; she could see his cap.

"Is it for me?" Her voice was too feather-light to drop as far as the hall below. She saw her father tear open the yellow envelope, read the message, and with a grunt turn off the light in the hall. He climbed the stairs, yawning, dressing gown waving back from striped pajamas. "It's not for me?" repeated Amy, faintly.

"Why, Amy, what you doing up?" He caught a second yawn halfway. "No. Just condolence from the Bennetts. They're up at the lake. I told the boy he could keep any more till morning."

Amy curled her fingers into the palms of her hands, to keep from snatching the yellow square. It should be from Geoffrey!

"What is it?" called Catherine, and Father explained again. "Is Amy up, too?"

"I was so sound asleep—" Amy stopped at their door; she felt confused, hurled too suddenly upright. Her mother was sitting up in bed, her shoulders smooth and white above the pink silk gown.

"Poor child, you are worried about Geoffrey. He's off in the woods somewhere," she added to Alfred, "and she can't reach him."

"I'm not worried. I just jumped up before I was awake. Good-night." Back in her dark room, the door closed, she sank down on the bed, as weak as if the fright of the dream had been real. Oh, you fool! she accused herself. It was real. That's how you feel. You don't know where to find him. The rhythm of the old nursery rhyme mocked her. Little Bo-peep had lost her sheep. She pressed her hands over her ears to shut out the murmur of voices from the adjoining room.

Sunday began early. Amy tried in vain to stay asleep. The day would be endless, once it had started. But the morning insisted on entrance with heavy feet and peremptory voices. Lora and Harriet came in for breakfast. Lavinia had said she couldn't be bothered. She was fussing with a black silk dress, one she said Mother had given her, pressing it, turning up the hem.

"Tom hasn't been near me," complained Lora. "Did any of you see him yesterday? I left word for him to come over."

Amy caught a glance from her mother, another from Lulu who was setting down a platter of eggs and bacon. But Lora would find it inexcusable that Tom had been outside the house and hadn't gone in. Luckily she did not linger for an answer.

"I didn't sleep a wink all night," she continued. "I don't see how you manage to look so fresh. Almost as if nothing"—she reached for a handkerchief—"had happened. If children realized how they'll feel when death comes, and they can't do anything for their mother—"

"Lora, please!" Catherine jiggled her elbow, pushed a cup of coffee nearer. "We all have to get through the day, you know."

Poor Harriet, her ears red, her face sullen, looked as if she might have heard much of the same through the night, thought Amy.

"What time are you going to Isabelle's?" Catherine pushed valiantly through the threatened shower.

"What you going there for?" Alfred looked up quickly. (Property, ticked Amy's mind. He's suspicious of Dewitt. Thinks he's plotting with Lora.)

"To see about proper mourning." Lora sipped her coffee with determined fortitude. "Isabelle's having some dresses sent out from town."

"Bisby's coming this morning, to arrange things at the house. The fewer of us around the better. He'll have his men, and they know just what to do."

"I don't intend to be in any one's way." Lora hinted at tears again.

"Why don't you take the car? Or will Tom drive you over?"

"We can walk. I wouldn't think of bothering any one."

Catherine's lids sheltered a comical despair. "Suppose I call up Tom. You try, Amy."

"Ask him if Ming is all right. I can't have him

here"—Lora was self-sacrificing—"because that cat torments him so."

Amy waited, after she had given the number. After all, Tom couldn't stay entirely clear of the family, even if he did have a woe of his own to nurse. "It's Amy." He expected some sequel to last night! She heard the quickening in his voice. "You'll have to be useful to-day," she warned him. "Your mother wants to see you, and she needs you for chauffeur, too."

"I've got an awful head."

"I'll tell her you'll be along soon. Tom, it's the least you can do."

"Okay. I'll snap around."

"That's a good boy." She wondered a little at the softness she felt for him this morning. Perhaps his confusion, his footlessness gave her a temporary illusion of wisdom, and so she liked not him, but the way he made her feel.

"He'll be over soon," she told them from the doorway. She wouldn't be drawn again into the group about the table. Presently they all drifted into the living room. Harriet lighted a cigarette, ostentatiously. Lora sighed toward her, but said nothing. Alfred fingered the fat folds of the Sunday paper, plunged his hands into his pockets.

We're like a slow motion picture, thought Amy. Every moment is dragged through thick air, is too apparent. That's what this interim feels like, between death and the end. All natural tempo is destroyed by it. We ought to make a death tableau, and we can't hold it three days. Lora reached for the paper. "There should be something here about Mother." They all waited as she rustled through countless pages.

"Here, let me have it." Alfred couldn't endure her fumbling another instant. The telephone shrilled and Amy went to answer it, glad of any imposed activity. Mrs. Parsons, explosive, hissing her steam-puffs of surprise, distress; she couldn't believe it when she heard it. If they could do anything, even a little thing? When could they view the body? Did Mrs. Dewitt take it hard? She had seemed so nervous.

The boy from the telegraph office shadowed the door, and Amy could break off the endless bubbling. A handful of messages, smooth and leering as they slid through her seeking fingers. Nothing for her. She took them in to Catherine. Alfred stood with the paper spread in outstretched hands, and Lora dug her chin into his shoulder, determined to read with him. Mary Stone Westover, born 1847, died 1930. Widow of Alfred Westover, pioneer of Flemington, founder of Westover Plows. "They gave her a long column," said Lora, proudly. "Look at the list of things she's done for this town. I'd forgotten some of those early ones."

"The reporter yesterday had most of them," said Catherine, soberly. "He said they'd had the write-up quite a while. Since Father died. He wanted to bring it up to date."

Amy read it, the fine print sliding through inexplicable tears. "They make it sound as if she was chiefly a widow," she cried. "They don't half do her justice."

Alfred looked at her, sunlight dancing in the curly hairs of his eyebrows, contracting his pupils until his eyes looked solid lapis blue. "Who could?" he asked. Then Lora gurgled, and he turned on her. "If you're going to Dewitt's, there's one thing—don't you listen to him about advancing any of your share. He'll try to talk you into it. He began on me yesterday, until I shut him up."

"How can he think of money, with Mother not even in her grave yet?"

"You'll see how he can. I'm just warning you. For all I know, he may have gone to Ripley yesterday. He's in a jam, and thinks he can't wait."

Lora blew her nose huffily. "Well, he may be my own brother, but with all he and Isabelle have had—I'm sure he ought to see I can't risk my pittance. Why, it's all that stands between me and starvation—and the children, too."

"Tell him that. I know it." Alfred folded the paper carefully, the obituary page inside, in order.

Tom sounded his motor horn from the road.

"It's much too early," began Lora, but Harriet interrupted. "Oh, come on, Mother. We have to stop at the house and dress." Departing, they had the same air of relieved acceptance of activity imposed upon them which Amy had felt earlier.

Alfred sat down in his armchair, his hands spread over his knees. "I just hope Lora isn't planning to move in next door," he said, grimly.

"Oh, Alfred!" Catherine looked up from the pile of magazines she was straightening.

"It's all right to say, 'Oh, Alfred!' I told you she was hinting at it last night. Talking about her house being too small and hinting that Mother promised her the place. It's funny"—he stared at his wife—"that we haven't one of us the slightest idea what Mother did, in her will. She could be tight-mouthed about her affairs when she chose. We'll have to get Ripley in early this week."

"What would happen if there is no will?" Amy turned from the window, having watched Lora and Harriet stow themselves beside Tom. She had waved to him.

Heat Lightning

"There is. I know when Mother made it." Before Amy could harden her indecision into words, her father pushed himself up from the chair. "I must call up Bisby, to see what time he's coming. We've got to do something about Curly before then." Before he reached the hall the telephone rang. "Yes?" he said. "What? Oh, all right." He sounded exasperated. "It's Lavinia, of all things," he called. "She wants some one to come over to pin her up. Now has she gone crazy?"

"Oh!" Catherine made a small dove-note of pity. "Poor 'Viny! It's that dress she wants to wear. She can't sew—"

"Let me go." Amy slipped quickly out of the house. You shouldn't run, a tiny voice, like a child's, spoke inside her. Not to a house where— She stood still, the sunlight moving in circles on the grass through the thick leaves. She hadn't seen it before, the wreath of laurel on the closed front door, trailing its somber weeds of black. She went on slowly, entering through the porch where she and Grandmother had sat. Lavinia met her in the dining room, a queer figure with black silk voluminous about her spareness, her hands gathering up its folds.

"I can't seem to get this fixed right," she exclaimed. "I sh'd think some one might help me get ready."

"It's too big for you, Lavinia. Haven't you something else?"

"It ain't a mite too big, once it's fixed. She gave it to me for a best dress and I been saving it. I didn't know what for."

"Let's go upstairs to the sewing room. Perhaps I can help." They couldn't stay here. Bisby was coming, with his men, and they'd walk through the house, businesslike and prompt, setting chairs in order, carrying in the casket—nothing's too good for her.

Lavinia climbed ahead of Amy, her arms hooked around puffing taffeta, the pungency of moth-balls floating behind her.

"I don't know where Alpha is," she said, peering around. "I called him, but he never came. Some nights he does gad, but I thought he'd be back this morning." She sighed. "I had my hands so full I told Lora she could go home for breakfast. Curly was set on painting the tool shed. I told him it was Sunday, and he wouldn't listen. I hid his paint brushes, too."

"Where is he?"

"You'd be surprised." Lavinia opened the door of the rear room in which the old sewing machine was kept. Boxes stood in corners, an old pier glass tipped from one wall, and near the window, a sunbonnet grotesque on the headless neck, stood a wire dressmaker's figure, robust if incomplete in its black lining basque. "Charley came and got him to go riding. He knew how Curly loves riding in a car. Curly likes him real well, too."

Curly was out of harm's way, then, for a while.

"It's no work for Sunday." Lavinia screwed her head around to see what Amy was doing at the small of her back. "But I got to have me a black silk. You know that?"

"Yes, 'Viny. Now stand still." Amy found a paper of pins in a drawer, closing the drawer before she looked too closely at the other contents,—an ebony shuttle for tatting, an ivory crochet hook—evoking hours of her childhood, with Grandmother teaching her, patient over the clumsiness of young fingers. She snipped threads that held the sash, pinned over seams, adjusted crisp folds. "This style doesn't have to fit tight."

Lavinia eyed the mirror suspiciously. "I don't aim to be too stylish," she said. "I don't want it looking like two dresses on me, that's all."

How small she was! All energy, not even many bones, thought Amy. She knelt to adjust the hem, and finally sat back on her heels while Lavinia wheeled, slowly.

"I'll run the hem in with long stitches, so it'll hold. You can hem it some day, if you like."

"I got a black lace collar." Lavinia picked at the white chiffon folds about the neck. "Wait till I get it." Amy, still on the floor, heard her rattling drawers. She snipped out the white folds, and they fitted in the boned lace collar.

"Now slip it off and I'll sew it for you."

"I can't strip here in front of you." Lavinia scurried off again, and was back impossibly soon, buttoning up a black and white percale house dress, spreading the taffeta over a chair. "You sure you got time?" she asked, anxiously.

"Of course." Amy had heard cars stopping. "Now you shut the door and sit down here, in case I need you for a fitting." Lavinia had heard the cars, too, heard men speaking softly in the hall. She clapped both hands over her mouth and her eyes ran in a suffocating wildness to meet Amy's. Amy nodded. "Yes, 'Viny. They're coming. But they don't need us." Slowly Lavinia closed the door, cautiously she perched on a chair.

"You don't think I oughta go help?"

"Father said we'd just be in the way. You stay here and help me finish your dress. You want it for this afternoon, when friends come, don't you?"

Heat Lightning

Lavinia settled in the chair, her feet primly together on the floor, her head up against the straight back. Amy threaded a needle with a long black thread and began to baste the hem of the full skirt. The room, with the door closed, grew warm; the muslin curtains hung in straight limp folds at the windows. One by one, like timid mice, queer old odors crept out and in the stillness of the air, gained boldness. Camphor balls, a hint of lavender, the dry, stuffy smell of matting, dust and oil from the sewing machine, even the rotting leather of its treadle strap, lavender again. Amy thought: it's like a spell. They live here, and if I move too quickly, I'll frighten them into hiding. Louder than the stir downstairs in the house ran the busy prick of her needle through the stiff silk. At a sigh from Lavinia she lifted her head. Lavinia had fallen asleep, her sharp chin tilting up, her hands crossed at the wrists. Poor 'Viny; she probably hadn't even sat down since yesterday morning. How defenseless she looked, the thin eyelids closed, the sparse light lashes making no accent, all her little bristles folded away. Even in sleep she was neat and restrained, keeping her balance so properly there.

Amy shifted the silk carefully, lest its rustle wake her. Lavinia wouldn't like to be caught asleep. She broke a new length of thread, holding her arm out in a slow, trance-gesture, turning her head to see the shining eye of the needle, sniffing at her finger tips as she made the knot. Dye smell, and machine oil. The thread must have lain a long time in the drawer.. She had no life beyond the uneven rhythm of the needle, pricking through the silk. Perhaps that was why women sewed so much; they didn't have to think. Your hands moved, and stray things like odors, like awareness of Lavinia, sleeping, came close to you.

[216]

Heat Lightning

You didn't think about them. You were absorbed in busyness, which walled you in *now,* as if the world held nothing else. Not till the task was finished—her fingers moved slowly, reaching the point in the circle where she had started—not till then did the walls collapse about this safe and comforting now, and your thoughts picked up their shuttle motion between what had happened, what you had felt, and what was about to happen, what you would presently feel and think.

"Haven't you got that done yet?" Amy jabbed her finger at the start Lavinia gave her. "I can't just set here the whole day."

"Just finished." Amy shook out the dress, meeting Lavinia's bright, suspicious eyes without a smile. Of course you haven't slept, her bland glance assured the worried old thing. "Now put it on, and let me see if it's all right. I'll look out the window and you change right here."

Nothing to see from the window but the upper branches of an elm, the downward arc of all the lines visible through the leaves. Amy pushed back the curtain and drew a long breath of the outer air, sweet after the old odors of the room. "There's a smell of autumn in the air," she said, not turning. Behind her Lavinia shifted her feet and rustled busily. "The first time I've caught it."

"Prob'ly them dagoes burning up rubbish. Sundays they always have a fire going in the backyard. It ain't so dangerous to-day, after the rain, but it's had me worried all summer."

"It's not smoke." It was more subtle, the sun on leaves from which the sap was running back.

"There, now you can look." Lavinia's face was screwed in anxiety. "Is it all right?" She stood before the pier glass smoothing down the skirt.

"It's fine." Amy adjusted the folds of the girdle. "But, 'Viny, it makes you look so little! Must you wear it?"

"I'm not wearing this black to be handsome in." Lavinia made a hasty motion away from Amy's lingering hands. "Now it's time I went downstairs." At the door she glanced back. "Well, you coming?"

Yes, Amy was coming. The interim was over. She brushed a black thread from her white skirt and followed Lavinia.

The double doors from the hall into the drawing room were closed. Amy stared at the paneling. She had never before seen them closed. The table in the dining room was piled with florists' boxes, and her father rattled an armful of emptied boxes and tissue paper.

"I wondered where you'd gone to." His face looked stiff, his jaw very firm. "You might get vases for these. Be sure you keep the cards." He drew a handful from a pocket. "Your mother said to put them all in a box or something."

"Is he still in there?" Lavinia jerked her head toward the living room door, closed like those ominous others.

"He's almost through."

Flowers were another occupation. Lavinia almost forgot their significance in her interest in the cards, her appraisal of different offerings. Amy had to collect vases from the other house. Roses and roses and roses. Gilt baskets and sprays and wreaths with treacherous snagging bits of wire. One of Bisby's men, a solemn young fellow with red hair and huge hands, came out to see about the flowers. He went back and forth endlessly, his hands competent enough.

"He's going to leave a man here to answer the door.

[218]

No, you don't want to, Lavinia." Alfred was sure of that. "You'll have enough else to do."

Presently Amy heard the heavy doors being rolled back. Like a stone away from a tomb. Without a resurrection. Mr. Bisby, rubbing his damp round forehead with a large handkerchief, came to the dining room. He rocked softly on his toes, giving his hands a final rub before he pocketed the handkerchief. "Now, if I may say so, we are ready."

"Where's Catherine?" snapped Lavinia. "It wouldn't be fit for me to look ahead of her, would it?"

Alfred, without a word, followed Mr. Bisby. Amy could hear them, Bisby requesting approval for what he considered a fine job, her father replying in monosyllables. Lavina went, too. Bisby was leaving, with final words. "Now you haven't a thing to worry about. I've got every detail in mind. As I said, we pride ourselves. An old person does look natural, dead, I think."

Some one had to enjoy being an undertaker, she supposed. But she waited for the sound of his departing car before she went toward the open doors.

Her father had gone, too. Lavinia knelt on the floor, arranging flowers, her black silk carefully folded back. Her grandmother, between the long windows at the end of the room, looked at first as if she slept, in more elegance than had been her wont, but soundly, with folds of gray velvet trailing down from the dais, and lights in silver brackets shining down on flowers and on the domed forehead, the deep sockets, the proud old chin. As Amy stared, the semblance of sleep drifted away from the figure, banished by a difference in that mask which had been her grandmother's face, and death lay there. Amy's blood began to pound in small, violent pulses behind her ears, in her throat. Why, it was a lie that death was sleep, that it was peace. Phrases, soft, banked between your eyes and the implacable fact. Death was nothing. *Nothing.* Once you stood yourself up to that intolerable fact, without the poor buffers religion made, or poets, you knew you were frightened, so frightened the only weapon left was anger, honest, raging anger. "I hate it!" her swift blood cried. "I hate it!"

Before Lavinia should see her, Amy hurried out of doors, across the grass toward her father's house. Alpha came walking toward her, plumy tail high, light concentrated in his yellow eyes. When Amy bent to pick him up, he slipped away from her hands, mewed at her from beneath a bush, and vanished, his bell tinkling. "I hate you, too, you killer!" She paused, looking where Alpha had disappeared. What did a cat think of death? Why, animals without thought knew death for what it was, an enemy to fear and to hate. They had no silly fantasies of heavens and themselves with wings and golden harps. As she went on slowly to the house, her busy mind dragged out something Geoffrey had once said. "Consciousness is an intruder on this sphere. Without it, the process of life and death is simple. It's our being conscious of it that makes the difficulty." Hotly, like a physical ache all through her body, she wanted Geoffrey. He would understand this hatred. He would put words to it for her. Close to him she would have less fear of a coming nothingness, because she would feel more intensely alive. Suppose one of them should die, before they met again? "Oh, stop it!" she told herself. "He's off having a good time. You'll see him soon enough."

Heat Lightning

4

The rest of the day dragged past in intermittent processional. Bisby's red-headed assistant was an efficient door tender. When relatives were in the drawing room he kept mere friends and neighbors waiting in subdued groups on the porch or on the lawn. Alfred would sit down to read, and at the sound of a car stopping, or of voices, would be drawn to the doorway. "Not many of Mother's friends are left to come," he said. "She's about the last." Isabelle and Dewitt came in late in the afternoon, bringing Sophie to see Amy. Sophie, under her polite greeting, had an air of irritation, as if she thought her grandmother might have waited a fortnight. She's like Isabelle, only not pretty as Isabelle must have been, thought Amy, as Sophie with a murmur of stereotyped phrases settled the fluffy gray fox over her shoulder and selected a chair. Her eyes were like her mother's, round and dark, but her teeth, in spite of perpetual gold bands throughout her childhood, remained unfortunately large Westover teeth in a jaw too small.

"That chronium and steel makes a good casket job, doesn't it?" Dewitt lighted a cigar with nervous fingers; his eyes were restless behind his thick glasses. "Carruthers can come to-morrow, the doctor says. We stopped at the sanitarium this morning, when we drove in for Sophie. But he'll have to go right back. He needs a complete rest."

"I must say I never thought he worked so hard as that!" Sophie ended in a light giggle.

"You don't know what you're talking about," growled Dewitt. "While you've been amusing yourself, your brother's been on the rack." He got up restlessly, with a wary glance at Alfred. "But we won't go into that. Let's get home."

"There'll be lots more flowers to-morrow," said Isabelle. "From business houses. If you need any help, do let us know. Sophie can run over any time."

"What did you do with Curly? I see he isn't around." Dewitt lingered at the door.

"Charley helped me out." Alfred's tone added, "Which was more than you did."

"Charley telephoned," said Catherine, pacifically, "that Curly was out at the farm, Charley's brother's, having a good time with some new pups."

"Perhaps they'd keep him," suggested Isabelle. "You don't suppose that Charley *knows*, do you?"

"Knows what?" asked Sophie.

"He thinks he knows which side his bread is buttered on," said Dewitt, harshly. "Look at all he got out of Mother! He's counting on her having left Curly a nice slice."

"Oh, no!" Amy couldn't keep quiet at that. "Charley was fond of Grandmother. He wanted to do something for her, that's all."

"People don't do things for nothing, Amy." He stared not at her, but at Alfred, his eyes sardonic above the hard line of his mouth. "But he'll find out."

"Now what's Dewitt think he's up to?" Alfred put the question to Catherine, as the three went decorously out to climb into their car. "He's got something up his sleeve. I know that look."

Amy thought quickly, he's seen Ripley. He knows about the will. I ought to speak of it. Not to-day, when Father's the only one of them who hasn't let himself calculate. He won't see her death as his advantage. I can't jar that decency. Mother would

hate it, too, if I blurted out, "The will's torn up." She
didn't even hear me when I did say it. Even if Dewitt
has heard of it from Ripley, what can he do?

Emma telephoned. They wanted to come to see
the body, but it didn't seem respectful to drive the
truck on Sunday, and Laurance had made a dicker with
a neighbor to trade for his Chevrolet to-day and to-
morrow too, but the clutch was slipping or something.
As soon as he had it fixed, they'd come. The older
children wanted to see Grandma. Amy cried. "Oh,
no! You shouldn't bring them! Wait a minute."
She called her mother and begged her to prevent
Emma's plan. "Children shouldn't see death. It's
too terrifying."

Catherine took her place at the telephone, insisting
quietly that Mary would not like her children to come.
She looked up at Amy as she finished her brief talk,
"Emma says she's sure they wouldn't mind," she said,
drolly, "and she may be nearer right than we are.
But she agreed to leave them home."

Lora came in, clinging to an obviously reluctant
Tom. Didn't Mother look beautiful! And did they
think her dress was suitable? It had fitted so well she
had kept it, although it might be too elaborate. With
only a silver lorgnette chain she looked curiously de-
nuded. Tom kept an uneasy eye on the door. Did
she want to be driven home? No, she would stay in
Mother's house, in spite of Lavinia. Did they know
what she had done? Stripped the linen off her bed in
just these few hours! Well, she could put it right
back. It wouldn't be right to leave her alone, with
the b-body.

"I'll barge along, then. Got some things I ought to
see to. Harriet'll be over, I suppose?" And he went,
in spite of Lora's, "Oh, Tom!"

Heat Lightning

"He's been so sweet to-day." Lora settled herself, her fingers sliding along folds of black satin into the large soft bow which she pulled carefully away from the chair. "It's a French model," she added in an aside to Amy, "Paquin, I think she said, or was it Vionnet? I can wear it without the little jacket. More like my own little boy again," she went on, full voice. "He was devoted to Mother. I said plainly to Dewitt and Isabelle I was sure we'd find he had been her favorite grandchild. You know, Alfred, Dewitt didn't say a word to me about lending him money. Although I fully expected it, after what you said." She paused, impressively. *"But.* He was telephoning, I am sure it was to Walter Ripley. When I came into the room, he was positively rude. He put his hand right over the mouthpiece and glared at me. As if I didn't have a right to hear what my own brother said to my own mother's lawyer! That's why he didn't ask me for anything. He has a deeper scheme."

"Let's drop it to-day." Alfred walked heavily across to a window. "Anyway, here comes the Reverend Mr. Clement and his wife."

They were the first of a series of callers. Amy, silent, outwardly meek, sat in a corner and listened. They were all the same, like a phrase in music repeated over and over again. Enter with a low, hushed voice, a muted note, condolence and sympathy; dear Mrs. Westover, so sudden, wonderful woman, how you will miss her. Then, briskly, brightly, words about the weather, about the drought, about business, about anything! Turn our backs on death, pretend it isn't there, the implacable enemy we hate and fear. Be cheery, brave, resigned, cheery again! She rose abruptly in the middle of a wave of cheeriness.

Heat Lightning

"I think I'll walk over to Mary's." Her glance at her mother admitted a need to escape.

Twilight had come on unnoted while people talked and talked, a colorless, blanched twilight. Amy walked slowly, savoring release in the brief solitude before she came to Mary's house. She saw Felice and Theodore coming, arm in arm. They saw her, and the three came slowly together, winding up the fine thread of recognition. "Hello, where you off to?" Theodore took one hand, Felice the other, and for a moment they stood like children in a magic circle.

"To see Mary." Amy dropped their hands. "The house has been full of people all day. I'm running away from it." She envied them their unscathed look.

"You see?" Felice looked up at Theodore. "I said there would be so many you would not be missed. He had a scruple about working to-day, and yet with yesterday and to-morrow that he must give up, it was necessary to work hard."

"I did need time," Theodore admitted, grinning at Amy in apology. "It seemed heartless, but Felice said I was sentimental, as there was nothing I could do."

"She's quite right. There's nothing to do but wait till to-morrow's over. You're lucky." They'd spent all day in their own lives, ignoring death, as one normally does ignore it. Lucky indeed!

"It was a relief." Ted peered at her more intently. "You look pretty seedy," he said. "Sort of in the midst of it, aren't you? I say, isn't Geoffrey coming?"

"Apparently not." Amy saw Felice jerk at Ted's arm, a slight admonitory jerk. "I can't reach him. I don't know exactly where he is." She dared them to question further. Ted, having remembered that

Heat Lightning

Geoffrey existed somewhere, was loath to drop the matter.

"I say, that's a shame. Let's see, where was he?"

"Fishing," said Felice, succinctly, "and fish-lines are not telephone lines, is it not so, Amy?" She pulled Ted gently into motion. "Good-night, Amy. We do not stay long to-night."

Amy, walking on alone, had a moment of hot resentment. What business had Felice to suspect anything, so that she rushed in to protect Amy against clumsy questions? Oh, be fair to her! Common sense slugged the resentment off the floor. She's not prying and curious. Why, you can't even talk about him naturally. She waited a moment for a small touring car, packed with a noisy, numerous family, to whizz past, and crossed the street at an oblique angle, coming into the block which led to the village park. The electric sign on the theater blazed out, saffron yellow in the twilight, WESTOVER PICTURE HOUSE, and cars lined the street, tails to the curb, like dusty minnows along the edge of a lake. Why, to-night she and Grandmother had planned to see this picture. "I always go on Sunday." Amy crossed the street, sidled between two cars and stood at the entrance, reading a sign, hand-lettered unevenly, which hung beneath the ticket booth.

"This theater will be closed to-morrow afternoon in honor of the founder, Mary Stone Westover."

Oh, no. Don't close it. Had she spoken aloud? The girl in the booth was staring at her. Amy walked on. They ought to open it wider, inviting every one to come free. Grandmother would like that better.

The church bell began to ring, dropping its plaintive notes from the red brick steeple farther along the main street. Mr. Clements and his wife must have gone home, then. Dearly beloved. Who went to church nowadays? Around the corner swung the city bus, its warning claxon defeating the church bells. But as Amy walked on, away from the bus corner, she heard the bell still ringing, its waves of sound waiting for her beyond the noise of the corner.

The nurse, less formidable in a green and white sprigged silk, met Amy at the door of Mary's house, seizing upon her with the avidity of an ended frustration. "Now you can sit with Mrs. Chester. We've been waiting for Mr. Chester to come. You just tell her I've gone. Gracious, I thought I wasn't going to get away!"

Amy climbed the stairs, feeling a belated awkwardness that she came empty-handed. She might at least have picked some flowers. Mary was sitting up against piled pillows, little fretting lines at eyes and mouth. "Oh, Amy!" she sighed. "Thank goodness! If the nurse had come up once more to ask about Henry, I'd thrown a pillow at her! She must have had a date with her young man."

"She's flown to keep it." Amy drew a chair near the bed and sat down, looking quickly about. The room was close, in spite of opened windows, with faint annoying odors—ammoniac undertone—that rack of unmistakable white squares in the bathroom, of course—talcum powder—"Where's the baby?"

"Asleep in the next room. I hope she stays asleep. This heat bothers her." Mary sighed again. "I certainly will be glad when I can get downstairs."

Mary, recovering, had lost the traces of younger sister. She looked older, sharper, her hair pushed straggling behind her ears, and the petulance of a half-way stage in her voice and manner. What had Amy been doing? She hadn't been in for days. Wasn't it a frightful shock? Who would have dreamed of Grandmother dropping off like that? How did she look? "I tried to make the doctor say I could get up for the funeral. I've been sitting up for hours, but he says I can't stand yet. I should think I could."

"But why should you? She's dead. It wouldn't matter to her."

"You know perfectly well why I should. Sometimes you try to sound smart, Amy. And yesterday Emma's mother actually sat there and boasted that Emma never stayed in bed more than four days. I just cried after she had gone. Poor Henry was so upset. He said he'd never let her in the house again. Of course he will. He's over at Mother's, now. He had such a headache all day I wouldn't let him go out in the sun. That's why the nurse was in such a stew. I didn't intend to sacrifice Henry to her young man. I do wish you'd tell me about things. I just lie here and wait."

Amy brushed her mind for crumbs of the day. Mary's tired and uncomfortable, she told herself. Get busy and entertain her, even if she is determined to disapprove of you. Lavinia's dress, and Curly, and Lora's new dress, and the flowers, and callers. Plenty of crumbs for the simple hunger Mary felt. She just needed to share the family event. She frowned at the account of Emma's telephone call. "I suppose Lucy is old enough to go to the funeral," she said, "but she hasn't a decent dress to wear."

"You wouldn't let her go!"

"I'd like her to remember her great-grandmother," said Mary, stubbornly.

"Why remember her dead? A child can't understand death. I can't."

"They can understand that God has taken her soul

away to Heaven." Mary looked suspiciously at her sister. "You know that much, I hope."

"I don't."

"At least"—Mary leaned forward from her pillows, her chin dragging cords of her thin throat into prominence—"at least you tell your children that, don't you?"

"I don't tell them what I don't believe," said Amy.

"Do you?"

Mary dropped back, sudden petals of color on her cheekbones. "I most certainly do. That is, I believe things I know I ought to tell them. I always felt New York was a dreadful place, Amy. You've been influenced by Geoffrey, too. He scoffs at things. I've heard him."

"So much the better, I'd say." Amy was contrite; her sister's hands trembled at the crumpled edge of the sheet. "Things ought to be scoffed at. It does 'em good. Darling, let's not argue about deep matters! Did you hear about the movie theater?" She hurried into the story of the sign. It was her last crumb. If Henry would only come! "How about a nice cold drink, Mary? That rain didn't cool things off very long, did it?"

"I'd like a drink. But don't waste ice on it. The nurse said the piece was almost melted." She had forgotten God and souls in the nettles of her inadequate household. "I'm sure they leave the doors open, changing the baby's bottles so often. The nurse says the girl does." Her hands worked uneasily, smoothing the hem of the sheet.

"They certainly might let you alone about such trifles." Amy welcomed a chance to rail at something. "You oughtn't to think about ice melting, or—"

"That sounds fine. Lie here a day and see how much you get out of."

"You lie there and listen to me."

As Amy chipped vindictively at the diminished ice, and hunted for a lemon among plates of dejected scraps of food with which the ice box shelves were cluttered, she thought it as well Mary couldn't look over her shoulder. Limp, grimy dish towels, dingy oilcloth. The maid needed jacking up. She found a tray and a tall glass, draped a crescent of lemon peel over the brim. Poor Mary! It must be wretched to lie upstairs and listen to the creaking of domestic machinery. Amy marched back resolved to be patient.

"I heard you," said Mary. "I suppose the ice won't last, now, and baby's milk will sour."

"There's plenty. Here, drink this."

Mary made a wry face. "It's sour!"

Perhaps it was; she needn't suspect Mary of planning to disapprove of everything she did, need she? Amy returned with sugar bowl and spoon.

"And please just peek at the baby. I thought I heard her."

Amy peeked. Through the bars of the battered white iron crib she could see the pink blob of face, almost featureless in sleep.

"You must have heard her snore," she said, returning.

"She doesn't snore," began Mary, indignantly. At Amy's laugh she set down her drained glass, smiled just enough to indicate that she knew Amy meant it as a joke, and added, "Lucy did, but she had adenoids. We're going to call her Henrietta." She paused. "Henry says he didn't want a son, as boys have such a hard time in this world. I'm glad she's a girl. I'm so used to girls."

"You can't not be glad, can you?" Amy adjusted the torn parchment shade on the lamp, and sat down again. "It would be inhospitable to your own baby."

"Aren't you going to have any more, Amy?"

"Not intentionally." Why did Mary incite her to mockery? "They cost too much, adenoids and education and everything."

"You're extravagant, the way you manage. Camps, and private schools." Mary stared at her with visible resentment. "I suppose you buy all their clothes ready made, and you have things yourself—"

Amy made a flying grab at the heels of her resolution about patience. Mary was palming off on her the complaints she wouldn't make to Henry.

"There's my work, too," she said, gently. "I suppose that seems selfish to you, but I'd hate to give up the reviewing I do."

"Henry wouldn't let me work," said Mary, proudly. Her face altered, softening into the contours of a day dream. "Oh, Amy, if only—" She hesitated. "Ever since I heard Grandmother was dead— After all, I am named for her. Don't you suppose she may have left me something? Even if it isn't much. Then Henry wouldn't have to try so hard to get a job. He ought not to have to. He isn't fit for ordinary work. People bother him so. He wants to write a book. About his experiences in the war. He can't settle down to it while he thinks he ought to hunt for a position. But if Grandmother"—her sigh expanded into the lovely, shining bubble of her dream—"I've just lain here thinking about it. Sh!" She lifted a warning finger. "There he is. Don't say a word. I think he guesses what I hope, but I wouldn't speak of it."

Henry was coming upstairs, with the subdued, cautious tread of a man trained in the ways of sleeping children. His patient face lighted as he saw Amy. "That's nice," he said, standing at the foot of the bed. "I hoped you were here. Mary hasn't had much company the last few days." His glance set Mary where she should be, at the center of the universe, and rebuked mildly the vagaries of fate whereby death could draw attention away from birth. "It was lucky she didn't get in to the hospital, or none of you would have found time to see her."

"Isn't Mother coming to-night?" asked Mary, promptly.

"She sent her love, and said she'd come in the morning. Laurance and Emma and Mrs. Miller were there when I left. They're going to bring Lucy in to-morrow to stay with you during the funeral. I told them no one realized how hard it was for you to lie here, neglected."

"Henry, you didn't say that!"

"Well, perhaps I didn't say neglected, exactly. I meant it. To lie here while your own grandmother that you were named for was being buried." He looked at Amy, pressing his lips firmly over a final puff which rounded his sagging cheeks. "And that Miller woman didn't have a word to say!" he finished, triumphantly.

"Oh, Henry!" Mary glowed at him.

Thus they sustain each other, thought Amy. It's amazing. She rose, jarring the table so that only a hasty movement caught the rocking lamp. She settled the rickety shade again, and bent to kiss Mary. "Good-night. Sleep tight," she said. "Good-night, Henry." He held her hand as a thought jerked at his muscles.

"Oh, by the way, there's a telegram for you. I might have brought it, but I wasn't sure— It came while I was there. Geoffrey, probably."

Heat Lightning

Every nerve in her body leaped for a mad rush toward the point in space where that message waited. "Why didn't you bring it?" she cried, and then had to withdraw her hand properly, to descend the stairs one step at a time, to walk along the street, holding herself back into a walk that broke its swift motion into little running steps now and again. How far it was! Would that be a short cut, down the alley behind the garage? No, she might find the other end closed. She brushed past groups of people littering the sidewalks; the movie was over. The final blocks were like the last stages of a long swim, when you set yourself a certain rock past the point your usual skill can reach. She floundered, her heart pumping, and came up at the door of her father's house. A moment she waited there. She couldn't rush in, betraying herself. She tried to smooth down the tattered rags of her anxiety, to draw a long breath. Between her breasts cold perspiration slid in ridiculous, tickling drops. She couldn't wait.

Her mother and father were alone in the living room, her father leaning forward in his chair, her mother standing beside him, one arm over his shoulders. The posture, the gesture, conveyed some emotion, but Amy couldn't delay for that. "Henry said I had a message," she said.

"Oh, yes." Her mother withdrew her arm. "Where is it? No, those are just— Oh, there!" She pointed at the mantel shelf. "I put it there so it wouldn't be mixed up with the others."

Amy's fingers tore it open. Just two words. *Coming. Geoff.*

"Is it Geoffrey?"

Amy nodded, still looking at the sheet. "He just says coming. He might have told me when."

"Let's see it." Her father lifted a hand for it.

"It's dated seven at New York. That's too late for one of the through trains. He must mean he'll be here to-morrow in time—"

"He doesn't know what time," cried Amy. "I haven't known where to reach him. I don't, now."

"Well, he's been in New York, and that's nearer than Canada. He's on his way." Her father returned the flimsy square to her, and she turned it aimlessly between her fingers, as if she could press more news out of it. "Sit down a minute, Amy. We were just talking—"

She looked at her father, dragged from her concentration by a flat, dry note in his voice. Her mother stood beside the table, shuffling into piles the mass of condoling messages. Her father's floridness was drawn into blotches under the skin.

"Ripley's been here." He stared down at his hands, rubbing the thick balls of the thumbs round and round. "He says you know about it. Did you see Mother tear up her will?"

"Yes." Curious how old patterns persisted; in spite of herself Amy dropped into a pit of guilt, like a child confronted with some fault, innocent from the child's intention, but serious to the adult. "I tried to speak of it, but Mother didn't notice." Oh, silly, to make excuses! She hadn't committed a crime. "You and Mother were the only ones decent enough not to look ahead past her death to what you'd get. I couldn't bear to bother you. Does it matter so much?"

"I knew it must be something like that." Catherine laid her hand again on Alfred's shoulder. "Amy couldn't possibly take sides with Dewitt."

Amy made a violent movement, dragging her feet back under her chair, straining forward. "You thought that!"

Heat Lightning

"I couldn't understand the matter." Her father stared under shaggy brows, pushed one hand through his stiff hair. "If you knew, and didn't warn me—"

"I don't understand." Amy's lingering guilt sharpened into indignation. "It didn't seem to make any difference, until you had to settle up Grandmother's affairs. What kind of warning should I have given?"

Alfred let his hand drop heavily.

"It's Dewitt," said Catherine. Her eyes added, "Don't be angry with your father!"

"After all—" Alfred leaned back. "If I had known, I couldn't have done anything. But Ripley decided I didn't know what my brother was up to. He went there yesterday, straight from ordering her casket. Got it all out of Ripley. About the will. He's had, this past week, thousands of dollars from Mother. I don't know how many thousands. More than a third of the whole estate. He's calling that a gift, made freely before her death. Why, he'd got her to turn over some of her best securities, and he put them up and lost them. And now he's claimed his third in what's left, after he's stripped it. Ripley says there's no way to prevent his taking it."

"It doesn't matter so much to us," said Catherine, placatingly. "It's bad for Lora."

"It does matter to me. It's a bloodsucking, dirty trick, for one thing. That matters, if you find out your brother's that sort of scoundrel, doesn't it? It's not what Mother wanted. He'll even force the sale of the old house. He'll have the factory, too, if I don't watch out. I haven't any funds to buy him off."

"Alfred, he isn't a criminal, after all."

"He's demented, like all these other fellows who are being swept off the earth. Crazy. But you can't shut him up. Crazy!" Alfred gave a short, ugly

[235]

laugh. "It was because I wanted to shut Curly up, and Dewitt was willing to truckle to Mother, that he got the money out of her. And then she was going to write a new will, to force my hand about Curly. Ripley didn't like it."

"No." Amy crumpled the telegram between her palms. "He wanted her to sleep on it. And instead—"

Her father pushed himself up to his feet. "Instead, she's dead. I won't insult her with more of this to-night. Nor to-morrow. Whatever Dewitt has the black heart to do before she's buried, he can do. Not another word. Not until to-morrow is past." He looked sternly at Amy, as if she argued the matter, and with a determined briskness left the room. His feet on the stairs had the same firmness.

"It's too bad." Amy tasted tears on her mother's cheek as she held her tight for a moment. "It's—unmentionable."

Catherine tipped her head back, blinking swiftly. "I mustn't cry," she whispered. "He feels bad enough already. There." She dabbed a handkerchief at her eyelids. "He's always helped Dewitt so much. That's why this is so terrible to him. And when you already are stripped open by one strong feeling, other things get farther in. Well—I'm glad Geoffrey's coming. Don't tell him about this—till later. Your father's right. It would be intolerable to have every one thinking about this to-morrow, when they should think of Mother. Good-night, my dear."

She couldn't stay a moment longer, thought Amy, hearing her swift ascent. She must run, run after Father, bearing him whatever solace she can. As for me—she sat down again, spreading the crumpled yellow paper on her knee. *Coming. Geoff.*

Heat Lightning

5

Through the next morning Amy played a game with herself against time. She moved hope, like a checker, to a definite hour, saying, If Geoffrey did catch the Limited, he will be here by ten. I will not think of him till ten. And at ten she moved hope along the face of the clock to eleven. He might have caught that special night train to Detroit.

"I wish we knew which train Geoffrey is coming on," said Catherine. "It would be nice for you to meet him."

"That's his loss." Amy pretended she hadn't been pushing against the sluggish minutes. "He'll come straggling in sometime to-day."

"You don't want to drive over to Mary's with me? Henry seemed to feel she was unhappy, we were all so busy."

"So I gathered. Well, you do want attention when you've just had a baby. No, I won't go. You might give that hired girl a talking to. I never saw a worse looking kitchen."

"I don't dare." Catherine smiled. "She'd leave on the spot. She was going to leave Saturday, because the nurse complained—the toast was scorched, or something. I had to appeal to her better nature. If you aren't coming"—she drew on her driving gloves—"perhaps you'll keep an eye on Lavinia. She's likely to decide to wash, this being Monday. I saw her scrubbing the back steps before six this morning."

"I'll go over." Amy got to her feet, shaking her hand until her wrist watch slid beyond the cuff of her sleeve. Only ten after ten.

A small truck stood in front of the other house.

Heat Lightning

Mr. Bisby and the red-headed assistant were rattling folding chairs, the young man whistling as he worked. What was the tune? Some current jazz thing. Amy found herself keeping time as she walked through the quiet haze-gilded sunlight. Bisby threw a harsh word, and the boy looked up, lips puckered, the whistle expiring. The tune ran on in Amy's head. You shouldn't whistle, she thought. Remember what you're about. Bisby's training you. If you want to grow up to be a good undertaker—

Lavinia was in the kitchen, sitting upright in her rocker, feet square on the floor, hands idle in her lap, the black silk flowing down in a pyramid from the small gray head. Her face, expressionless, red about the eyelids, looked just as time felt; she had run down.

"You aren't sick, 'Viny?"

"No, I ain't. I made up my mind I wasn't fooling myself any by working, and I'd set down and give in to it."

Amy glanced at the clock on the shelf above the sink. "Geoffrey's coming," she said.

"I should think he might." Lavinia tipped her head, listening. "They make too much noise with those chairs. That Bisby acts as if he invented funerals." Malicious humor flickered among the wrinkles of her face. "Did you hear him and Charley this morning? They had a set-to, in the front hall. They didn't see me coming down the stairs. Charley wanted to drive the hearse, and Bisby said it wasn't regular, especially not to pay for it, and Charley said nobody could pay him for that. Then Bisby said as how he made a flat price for everything and how could he take some out, and Charley said all right, he'd charge more for the cars to follow. Then Charley saw me, and they shut up. That Charley's a good

[238]

man. He'd come to tell me Curly was all right, and I wasn't to worry about him. He got the best of Bisby, anyways. When he first come here, Charley, I mean, he couldn't even speak English. Your grandma did a lot for him. He knows it, too. He's not like some I could mention, already snooping about to see what they can pick up."

Amy took down a glass from the cupboard and turned the faucet. She watched the water, twisting like a ribbon, making a pleasant sound against the porcelain. Waiting was thirsty work.

"You needn't say I told you, but Lora's been in her room, picking over things in her drawers. It's maybe none of my business, but I should think she could wait."

Poor 'Viny! She had, so many years, relished her skirmishes with Lora, because they were part of her protective loyalty to Grandmother. Any small triumph over a mere relative satisfied her jealous devotion. And now, with death, she was reduced to an outsider, and Lora triumphed because she was a daughter. Grandmother would have made some provision for her,—Amy set down the glass with a thud —but she had destroyed her own provisions.

"You might wash that and set it back," said Lavinia. "I don't want my kitchen all messed up." She watched Amy obediently rinse and dry the glass. "I don't think your Grandmother would of been any too pleased to see Dewitt ransacking her desk, either. I'd like to tell 'em just what she'd think of them but—" she pulled her lips between mumbling teeth, and looked up, her eyes harried—"they wouldn't care, would they? I have a feeling that everything's going to be different. All busted up. I ought to be glad she died so easy, without being sick or helpless, the way some old folks are. I say to myself, Lavinia, she's in Heaven, and you ought to be glad of it. But—" Her voice ran off in a thin wail— "Heaven's such a big place!"

"Oh, 'Viny, darling!" Amy tried to find some word real enough to offer Lavinia's lonely fear. "Things aren't all busted up. Different, yes. But with Mother and Father right next door— They won't let anything happen to you."

"I'm not worrying about myself."

Amy pushed back the blue checked sash curtain; had she heard a car next door? Only Bisby driving away. Not half past ten yet. The little sound, the quick hope, sponged off her sympathy for Lavinia, her brief perception of the other's mood. She leaned against the window sill, fingering the curtain, shrunk into a hard pellet of concentrated waiting. When would he come? Her imagination did not move past that moment of arrival, and she felt the coming not in any visual image of Geoffrey, but as a moment when intolerable constriction could be relaxed.

"I guess they've gone," said Lavinia. "I'm going to sit by her, now it's decent and quiet."

When she had gone, with a dry rustle of her black silk, Amy turned from the window to stare at the oblong wooden clock on the shelf. Behind the worn painted landscape on the lower half of the door the pendulum showed fitfully, and the irregular ticking was like the sound of some one sewing in the quiet room. Time, running up a seam, thought Amy. You mustn't watch, or it will never reach the end.

Some one was coming, and she lost the faint ticking. Harriet peered in, and immediately followed her near-sighted glance into the room.

"Where is Lavinia?" She nodded brusquely at Amy, her fingers busy with the black knotted tie under her collar. "I borrowed this of Tom," she said, "and it won't lie smooth. I always wear a figured tie with this suit, but Mother said it had to be black to-day. She wants some tea and toast."

"I'll make them." Amy moved eagerly into an occupation. You could cheat time with small tasks, like filling the kettle, lighting the gas, cutting bread.

"Where is Lavinia, anyway? She drove us wild yesterday, tearing around, and this morning she won't do a thing." Harriet lounged against the table with an air of masculine helplessness.

"She's in with Grandmother."

"Well, as Mother says, if we do move in here, how can we keep her? She's been so spoiled she thinks she owns the place."

"She's been here years and she worshiped Grandmother." Amy frowned over the toast. "Haven't you any imagination?"

"Of course I have." Harriet retreated into her defensive sulkiness. "I can see how impossible she'd be."

"Will you get the butter?" Amy set dishes on the tray, bidding herself keep silent. The kind of anger Harriet stirred in her could have no useful outlet. It's worse than speaking in different languages, she thought, trying to get through that egocentric dullness of hers. "There, I think that's ready."

Harriet had the last word, triumphantly, as she bore away the tray. "It isn't as if you were the one to put up with her, you see. You go back to New York in a few days."

Amy shrugged. She wouldn't look at the clock until she had set the kitchen in order again. There. Not yet eleven! The telephone rang, and Amy hurried to interrupt its unseemly clatter in the still house. Tom.

"Oh, Amy? Say, tell Mother, will you, that I'm here at home, in case she wants anything. I won't come over, not till the funeral. She needn't ask me to. I can't stand it, hanging around there. Say, Amy, have you seen Lulu?"

"Of course."

"Listen, what's she up to? She hasn't said anything—"

"She's doing her work as usual."

"I didn't know whether they'd keep her on, but I suppose—"

"Lulu has been postponed, Tom. That's all." Amy glanced up conscious of a sound. Harriet blinked at her from the doorway, her mouth pursed avidly.

"Her old man'll be after me again to-morrow with a shotgun." Tom groaned. "And what'll I do? Listen, Amy, would you sort of sound Mother out?"

"I would not." Amy hung up the ear-piece and looked at Harriet.

"I came down to answer the 'phone," began Harriet, defensively. "Wasn't it Tom?"

"He'll be over at two," said Amy. "In case Aunt Lora wants anything, he's at home."

"But, Amy—" Harriet had ducked her head, and Amy could fairly see the few words she had overheard rolling round and round in her mind, trying to connect with other words, to increase in meaning. "He was asking you about Lulu. What on earth? You might tell me, I should think."

"Ask Tom." Amy started back through the kitchen. Harriet hurried after her, seizing her arm.

"I bet he's mixed up with that girl! I know he's in some kind of jam. Is that it? Well, you needn't tell me. I know!" Her face had flushed, and she

[242]

breathed through her words. "The filthy little beast!" she dropped her hand.

"Harriet, if you go running to Aunt Lora now, with whatever you suspect, you'll be a worse beast than Tom! Let it alone until Grandmother's safe in the ground, at least."

"Tell me, then. I won't say a word."

"I have nothing to tell. But if you don't keep still—"

"I'll postpone it—like Lulu." Harriet thrust her hands into her coat pockets, her mouth hard in speculations. "I'll find out, though. The little squirt, pulling the wool over Mother's eyes!"

Amy left her. In the space between the houses the noonday sun defeated the shadows; through the windless haze a leaf, too light to fall, drifted in lazy spirals. Harriet, with her clumsy jealousy, her stupid hungers, was like a dry shadow behind Amy. And Geoffrey hadn't come yet. At twelve he would come, surely.

But at twelve he hadn't come, nor at one. "Shall we make the hour later in the afternoon, in case he gets here?" Alfred asked. He and Theodore had just come in from a final conference with Mr. Bisby.

"Oh, no!" Amy was firm. "He may walk in any moment. And anyway—" Her game with hope was played out, and a dull anger against Geoffrey's inconsiderateness had followed.

"Dewitt wasn't home this morning. Bisby called him up." Alfred had turned to Catherine. "There'll be the six of us, six men of her family, for bearers. If Geoffrey came, he and Henry would make eight."

He means that Dewitt was up to schemes, even this morning, thought Amy. She looked at him in a rush

[243]

of warm affection; his face had a peculiar stiffness, as if he held aloof from thought.

They ate luncheon hurriedly, absently. Henry appeared at the doorway as they finished, his thin hair slicked back, one eyelid twitching. Dewitt and Isabelle and Carruthers had just gone in next door, he said. Laurance was coming as soon as he had left Lucy with Mary.

"We'd better go over, then." Alfred rose, his hands busy with the square of napkin. He folded it, tried to fit it into the silver ring, fumbled at it, and Felice, with a soft noise in her throat, took ring and linen from his blind fingers. "We'd better go over," he repeated, his eyes seeking Catherine.

"I'll follow you at once." Amy went up to her room for a dark coat and hat. She stood before the mirror adjusting the hat, pushing back the waves of dark hair. Her face looked small and white between the black brim and the soft frilled collar of the silk coat. Sorry for itself, thought Amy. She looked from the landing window of the stairs; the procession of cars waited, shining beetles in the sun, Charley's new hearse drawn back from the entrance, the others tailing off around the side street toward the brook and Joe's house, the drivers lounging in little groups, and several small boys, probably Joe's, hovering in anticipation across the road. A small car stopped, its nose against the hearse, Mrs. Miller and Emma emerged, Laurance thrust out his head for a brief word with Charley, and the two women waited, round and solid, while Laurance drove into the yard directly under Amy's window.

"I don't want to go over there," she said, forlornly. But her body, more decorous than her mind, moved down the stairs and into the yard.

Heat Lightning

The others were already taking their places on chairs set in rows in the living room, with creaks of wood and metal as the folding apparatus yielded to their weight. Mrs. Miller edged plumply through the rows to a front corner, next to Lora, who immediately turned away, drooping toward Tom, in the next chair. That unfamiliar head, thin, long, sleek, above ostentatiously well tailored shoulders must belong to Carruthers. They were all there, the men and women who carried in their flesh whatever lived of the old woman who lay so indifferent beneath the blanket of roses, and the few others who mixed their flesh with Westover flesh. All except Mary, and the children of the fourth generation. And Geoffrey. Amy took a chair near the door, and Lavinia, a black sailor sliding precariously on her thin hair, came to sit beside her. From the dining room came a subdued murmur. The Reverend Mr. Clement, consulting with Mr. Bisby. The heavy pot-pourri of many flowers and of death flowed about Amy, and underneath, the faintest note, the white camphor smell from Lavinia's silk.

Mr. Clement came from the hall into the drawing room, his broad face solemn, his hands clasped over a Bible. Before he began to speak a quick step crossed the porch, a quick voice sounded in the hall, and Amy's heart climbed into her throat to beat so loudly she could not hear the voice. Bisby slid another chair through the door behind her, and Geoffrey was there, leaning forward, his two hands meeting around hers, warm over the pallid fingers that lay in her lap. For an instant Amy turned her face, and his hurried breath touched her cheek. Through the room moved a stir of quick glances, aborted greetings. Mr. Clement waited a moment, opened the Bible between half lifted palms, and began to read.

[245]

Amy closed her eyes, not listening to the cadences of his words. She wanted to look at Geoffrey, to hurt him with arrowed glances dipped in the dark brew of anger, of hope fermented into frustration, of disdain at his late, dramatic entrance, and she could only sit there while her heart beat less slowly, seeing on her tight eyelids the black torches, images of the lights that burned above the casket. Some one was crying, a low, continuous accompaniment to the stately phrases. Lora. Amy opened her eyes, and saw Tom put his arm awkwardly about his mother's shoulders, saw Mrs. Miller's broad, small nose turned disapprovingly toward Lora. Old words, set down, centuries ago, ointment for the wound death made. I am the Resurrection. What had Grandmother believed? Words about her life, surface praises, not cutting down to reality. A prayer. Now if the family will file past for a final look. In the rustle of movement, the creaks and rattles of the chairs, Amy could turn at last to Geoffrey. His glance came down over her search, defiant, tender, and his hand shut hard about her fingers.

"Poor girl," he whispered. His face looked strange, as if for a long time she had not seen it, the deep eye sockets, spaced wide, the strong spring of the nose, the lean cheeks with lines past the corners of the wide, mobile lips. Quite suddenly it changed, and she knew it in her finger-tips, the feel of the forehead, fine skin over hard rounded skull, up to the v's in which dark hair grew over the temples. Geoffrey. Hand still shut in his, she moved slowly in the file past the casket. She felt his grasp quicken; he knew about death, its anger and its fear. Her grandmother's ivory mask took no color from the roses; the mouth was queer, waxen lips never meant to part. This was just an effigy kept for the ceremonials life insisted upon. "If you and Mr. Chester will act as one pair," Mr. Bisby was whispering at Geoffrey, prying him away from Amy.

Then she stood in front of the house, while Charley, his cap unnaturedly straight on his yellow head, climbed to his seat and started his car. He moved as far as the end of the block, and men carried out flowers, wreaths and sprays and blankets and elaborate designs of harps in lilies, already drooping in the heat. The eight men rode in one of the large limousines. Amy found Lavinia clinging with claw fingers to a floating end of her scarf, and said, "Yes, you can ride with me."

The cemetery lay on a sloping hillside beyond the tracks at the edge of town, the stones brittle and white in the sun. The artificial turf spread over the dusty gulf of the new grave, the sober awning erected on the grass, the casket glittering, tight sealed, sliding down its canvas bands among branches of fir and myrtle,— it's like a scene in opera, thought Amy. The polished granite monolith caught sunlight in the deep letters that spelled Westover. Plenty of room for all of us here, room for all who come. It was over, and they could walk back to the waiting cars. Alfred and Dewitt stood side by side a moment; they looked like brothers, some obscure hint in the way their heads grew out of their shoulders, for all their unlikeness. Alfred stared at Dewitt, intently, and thrust out his hand. To Amy, behind them, it seemed a curious farewell, as if they broke a truce they had kept for the day.

They were no longer part of a ceremonial procession. Charley drove away first, his eyes red. Bisby and some of his men were staying, and Amy saw, discreetly loitering at a distance, workmen in overalls the color of the dry earth. They were no longer unified; they separated into families, Dewitt marshaling his wife, Carruthers, and Sophie into one car, Lora supported by Tom, and Laurance sharing a car with Mrs. Miller and Emma; Lavinia and Harriet and Henry, like remnants, drove away with Theodore and Felice.

Alfred and Catherine turned to Geoffrey, while they waited for the last car to drive to the gate where they stood.

"We had given you up," said Alfred. "I didn't see you come in. It gave me quite a start, seeing you with Henry." And Catherine, "I am glad you got here, Geoffrey."

"Funny thing." Geoffrey had flung back his coat, rammed one hand into a pocket. "I had a hunch I should hurry. I hadn't heard directly the funeral was to-day, you know. I just happened to stop at the office, and found a wire. Too late to catch a night train." He didn't look at Amy, but she knew; he was telling her, through her father and mother. "I knew a fellow on the *Post,* who got me a seat on a night plane as far as Cleveland."

Alfred nodded approval.

"Only then I had a deuce of a time. Local trains, finally a jitney out from the city. Here I am."

"You flew?" Catherine was interested, as if he had sprouted his own wings. "Well, I'm glad Amy didn't know what you were up to."

Amy, settling herself into the car, sighed. It was characteristic, wasn't it? First he was late, and then he distinguished himself by special haste, arriving at the final moment.

"It was so baffling, knowing you were somewhere in

the woods, and not being able to reach you," Catherine went on, warmly.

Now, thought Amy. But Geoffrey only said. "Yes? I hope you didn't worry. Of course you wouldn't."

"Amy didn't worry us about it, at least," said Catherine. "It's been wonderful for us, having her here. Although I'm afraid, when she came for a rest—"

"I saw Grandmother, before she died," said Amy.

Then they were silent, the car running swiftly away from death, back to town, back to life, with gusts of hot, dust-laden air striking their faces. Geoffrey sat on one of the small folding seats, half turned toward them, his long body in a relaxed bow, one hand dangling. Amy stared at the hand, the veins prominent in ridges under the brown skin, the long, uneven fingers spread tensely. His hand betrayed him, for all his easy posture. He turned for a moment, and again his glance rode hers down, with that mixture of defiance and tenderness. Amy pushed her shoulder against the upholstered back of the car, and panic moved its soft, furred wings all through her blood. Waiting had an end, now, and presently she and Geoffrey would be alone, trying to put words to the darkness between them, like lifting puny candles in a black night where wind blew down the flames in spite of sheltering fingers.

"You know," said her father, abruptly, "I thought I saw Curly out there. Over beyond a monument. It must have been a workman. I should have asked Charley about him."

"He's safe with Charley's brother till to-morrow." Catherine laid her hand on Alfred's knee.

Geoffrey listened, with an unprying alertness; he never had need of questions. Casual words, hints of situations, fell together in his mind with amazing precision, so that often his post-comment on an experience, on a person, had more meat than the experience itself. By the end of the day, for all he had come so late, he would know with a sharper truth than all her own watching had given her, the temper of the family affairs. Amy stared resentfully at the hard line of his jaw. He was like one of those paleontologists, if that was the word, constructing a whole animal from the scratch of a toe-nail on rock. She remembered— had they driven together, the four of them, that time? —the anxious pride with which she had first brought him to Flemington, to introduce him to the family. He wasn't easy, socially. He wouldn't bother to conceal himself, although neither did he impose himself. She had been afraid they might not like him. Grandmother had taken a great fancy to him; Father and Mother had liked him. Not all of the others. Mary —well, as she had said, she thought he scoffed at things. Only the clever ones liked him. The rest suspected him. She looked away from him, at the street. Already they were passing the triangle of park. Was he, at this very minute, lying behind the blank wall that had risen between them, scoffing at all he knew of her? It wasn't fair!

They all stood for an uncertain moment at the entrance to the house, until the car had driven away. Bisby's small truck was at the side door across the lawn, partly loaded with chairs, their varnished legs making a diapered design yellow in the sunlight. The red-headed boy came out, more chairs piled in his arms. "What do we do next?" asked Catherine's silence, her mouth quivering.

"I wonder if Theodore came back here. Some one's in the house." Alfred moved stiffly up the steps.

"That scene is over," said Geoffrey, "and we've all forgotten our cues for the next one."

"That is the way it feels, isn't it?" Catherine nodded. At first Amy thought the entire family must be calling, the living room seemed so peopled. But Dewitt with his three had not come, nor Henry. Emma at least knew her cue. The funeral was over, and she expanded into chatter. They must run along, gather up Lucy, and get back to the farm. They'd just stopped to see if they could do anything. Laurance was in an awful rush to get back, he'd let so many things slide the last few days, not that they minded, of course, they wanted to. She made round blue eyes at Geoffrey. Where had he been, the naughty boy, not coming till the minister had actually started? She wouldn't let her husband treat her that way. She giggled softly, made a pounce at Laurance, hooked her arm through his, and tipped up her chin so that her round throat gleamed fair above the dark figured silk she wore. She was actually flirting with Geoffrey, preening herself like a bird. Mrs. Miller, bulging over a chair, fanned her crimson face with a folded newspaper. "I said there'd be nothing else to do here, not to-day, but they wanted to stop."

"Tom wouldn't come in," complained Lora, feebly, from the couch. "He insisted on our going home, but I can't leave everything to Lavinia."

Harriet, sitting awkwardly at the foot of the couch, looked at Amy, her eyes too knowing.

"I'll have Lulu make some iced tea." Catherine disappeared, and Amy followed, dropping coat and hat in the hall. The kitchen was empty, and no answer came in response to Catherine's call up the rear stairs. "Now what—" she began, and her eyes met Amy's in a flash of certitude. "She's gone, Amy."

"Poor girl. She had to go sometime, I suppose."
Amy lighted the gas and set on the kettle. "I wish
they'd all go. Hanging around when you are so
tired!"

"At least she filled this pan, so we have plenty of
ice cubes." Catherine dislodged them, chinkingly, into
a large pitcher. "I can't seem to think what we ought
to do about her." She held the checkered pan between
her hands, her brows puckered. "Isn't it queer, how
my thought just then was that it was too bad Mother
didn't see to it before she died. She would have done
something. It will have to be money, of course. Lora
will have to know. Make that tea good and strong,
Amy, so we can cool it."

"If she's really gone, why couldn't Lavinia come
over here?" Amy knew how her mother felt; she was
too weary to gather herself for hurdles along the
course. They loomed ahead, insuperable: Tom and
Lulu, Dewitt, the property. "She's sort of set and
crochety, but she likes you. She can't get on with
Lora."

Catherine shut the refrigerator door on the refilled
pan, and the motor churred busily. "But if Lora per-
sists in staying over there—" Absently she arranged
thin cookies on a plate.

"She won't, if she has no one to wait on her."

Amy carried the tray with black-footed tumblers into
the living room, and Felice cleared a place for it on
the table. Theodore, her father, and Geoffrey stood
at a window, talking in low tones. Mrs. Miller observed shrewdly the details of the service, the long hollow stemmed glass spoons, the tumblers. She would,
thought Amy, suggest that Emma look at the ten cent
store for something of the sort. Finally Laurance
dragged them away, and Alfred decided to drive to the

[252]

office for his mail. He would drop Ted and Felice on the way. Geoffrey could come along.

Catherine had gone upstairs. Lora, after a third glass of tea, drooped among the pillows. Harriet sat near the window, smoking. "How soon will they read the will?" she blurted out.

"I think they should immediately." Lora poked her head forward. "With Dewitt in such a state about his affairs."

It's not my business to tell them. Amy walked restlessly to a window, looking out at the street where dust hung from the vanished cars. Geoffrey needn't have run off—

"Not that I expect a cent," went on Harriet, significantly. "I'm just curious—about Tom."

Catherine came back. She sat down near Lora, her fingers tucking in stray curls at the nape of her neck. "I'm in sort of a plight," she began, mildly. "Lulu has gone home. Cleared out, bag and baggage."

"Good Heavens!" Lora sat upright. "You better count the silver."

"What'd she go for?" Harriet pounced upon a clew, but Catherine made no answer.

"The more you do for those girls, the less they thank you!" Lora spoke emphatically. "I always thought she was sly. Leaving now, when you have Amy and Geoffrey here!"

"She must have had a good reason," insisted Harriet. For a second Lora's attention wavered to her, but the habit of ignoring her daughter's remarks prevailed.

"You can't depend on any of these foreigners," she stated.

"The point is, Lora,—" Catherine dodged away from the hurdle of Tom and Lora's discovery, breathless lest Harriet should corner her, force her over it—"I think Lavinia would help out. Not, of course, if you stay at Mother's house. But you'll be going home now, won't you?"

Lora shook her head, a flutter moving the neat ridges of metal-black hair. "You're trying to drive me out! I never would have thought it of you, Catherine. Trying to throw me out. How do I know what would happen to things? I mean, some one ought to stay."

"It would be better for 'Viny, too."

"If you wish to consider her before me!" Lora's face quivered in a preliminary arrangement for tears.

"Your staying can't make any difference. There will have to be a settlement."

"If I go, I'll be tricked out of everything. The one that's on hand gets things." Lora was crying now. "With Mother gone, who's to look out for me?"

"You know Alfred will." Catherine rose, flushing in indignation. "Do as you like. But I shall ask Lavinia to help me out. You can't keep the house by moving into it, unless it comes as your share. Dewitt's making trouble enough for Alfred. It isn't decent, this grabbing, as if the only thought we could give Mother had to do with what she left behind."

"I'm not grabbing! It's—" But Catherine walked quickly out of the room, and Lora had to fling her tearful protests unsatisfactorily at Amy. "I don't know what's got into Catherine," she ended. "Talking that way to me!"

"We're all tired out," said Amy, "and ought not to speak to each other, not till to-morrow, at least."

"We ought to comfort each other." Lora veered into a new wet tack. "She was my mother, and I miss her more than any of the rest."

"Oh, come along, Mother." Harriet laid a firm

hand on her mother's wrist and urged her to her feet. "Let's get out. Aunt Catherine doesn't want us here. Nobody's going to carry off that house over night. You'll feel more natural in your own bed. Come along."

In a moment she slumped back from the porch. "She won't walk. Says every one will stare at her. I'll call a taxi." When she had telephoned, she came back to the living room. Amy looked up at her from the low chair where she had flopped. The girl's chin trembled over the black knotted tie; her sullen, heavy mouth, her shallow eyelids had a stubborn preoccupation. "Amy, you might as well tell me," she said. "Has Tom got that girl in trouble? I could see you weren't surprised, you and Aunt Catherine, that she had gone. That's the reason, isn't it?"

"Ask Tom," said Amy.

"He seems to have confided in every one else, except his own family. I suppose he was drunk. Aren't men disgusting! You might tell me about it. I'll have a sweet time when Mother finds out."

"He didn't tell us anything." Amy had to lift a slight cudgel in Tom's defense against the animus-ridden glee in Harriet's face. "He went to Grandmother for help. Money, of course. She came straight over here, as she would, to confront Lulu. That's how we knew. It was that last night, before her death. Lulu had locked her door, so—"

"Whee-oo!" Harriet whistled. "I bet that was a scene. So Mother's little boy is in a real mess. I say, Amy, will he have to marry the girl?"

"I wish you wouldn't smack your lips so over it!" cried Amy.

"What?" Harriet shrugged. "Oh. You mean I should be a loving sister, shocked, tearful. All his life he's had everything, people liking him, freedom, cash. I'm not shocked. I hope he has to pay through the nose."

"Harriet!" Lora's call came sharply from the porch. "Here's the taxi." With a defiant squaring of her shoulders, snug in the dark jacket, Harriet walked away.

Tom would have a nice time, thought Amy. Poor Harriet was a muddle. Her well of loneliness had brackish waters. Laurance was the best one of that family, because he was older, because Emma had pried him well away from the others. Lora and Tom Blake senior had done that for their children, hadn't they? Mixing them all up. Who was responsible for what one was, anyway? Amy felt protest stiffen along her spine. If you bore children, fed them, clothed them, shouldn't that be enough? Must you give them your emotional life, too, like a solution in which they floated, held steady against jars and warpings and bruises? I won't be to blame for Bobs and Buff, she said, under her breath. I have to live, myself. I can't be a solution. It's like carrying a child all his life in a womb you make not of your body, but of your very self. Anyway—she flung her arms over the low arms of the chair, let them dangle. You can't make that kind of womb alone. It's impossible. No one would have wisdom enough to make a perfect solution in which a child could float. If you had rules, like a formula in chemistry— But nowadays there were no rules. Life inched along, in random spurts, and you never saw the path it took.

Amy relaxed, her hands quiet along the wide arms of the chair. The heat of the late afternoon pressed down her eyelids, and her consciousness withdrew to that uncertain margin between sleep and waking. The

Heat Lightning

image of her grandmother came close and triumphant upon her, the proud, hooked face, the silver knobbed stick, an image altering with the swiftness of light not in visual changes, but in fleeting moments of relationship to other people: the brooch that was a peace-offering, Curly afraid of thunder, even Alpha, arching against her foot, countless moments, disconnected, forgotten, and in all of them the same gallant assurance, the same valiance. She knew what she lived by. Amy stirred, and the shallow wave of sleep ebbed away. There had been truth in that half dream. Her grandmother lived with sureness, knowing her own code.

It had been Lavinia's voice that woke her; she stood at the door, her hands tying a white apron over a print dress. "I said, you'd rest better if you lay down."

"Yes, 'Viny."

"I told your mother I'd be glad to help out, if she'd turn the key over there. I couldn't leave it for snoopings around." She stood at Amy's elbow, rubbing an inquiring finger over the polished table. "I guess I needn't dust up. That girl ought to be ashamed, clearing out without a word. But you and your husband make too much work for your mother, that's all." She picked up a thread from the rug, and with proprietary steps, retreated to the kitchen.

She owns the place already, thought Amy, amused. Poor Lavinia.

Amy and her mother sat on the terrace, listless, becalmed, with a twilight sky milky-pale behind the quiet trees.

"This weather hurries things so;" Catherine paused, at the sound of a car. But it droned past. "Alfred must be showing Geoffrey the town. He'd left the factory an hour ago. I called to see." After a mo-

[257]

ment she went on, "There won't be a flower left in a
week. They wither into tight seeds almost the minute
they bloom."

"They must propagate before they die." Amy
stopped the slight motion of the hammock with a lazy
toe. "Like men in war-time. Funny, when you think
of it, isn't it? The harder the conditions of living, the
stronger the sex-urge."

"Can you call it that in my poor gladioli and nasturtiums? Yes, Lavinia?"

Lavinia had appeared again at the doorway. Her
preparations for dinner had been chiefly a series of
inquiries as to what on earth that girl had done with
something. Her disapproval of the places chosen by
Lulu to secrete utensils and condiments had a strong
moral tinge. Silver polish, this time. The coffee
spoons were a sight.

"Must you polish them to-night?" Catherine rose.
"Oh, there they are!" Not the spoons. Alfred and
Geoffrey were driving into the yard. "Never mind,
'Viny. The spoons will have to do. Alfred needs his
dinner at once."

She went through the house to meet the two men,
and Amy pushed the hammock into gentle motion.
She wouldn't rush at them. Geoffrey could search
for her now. She could hear her mother in the hall.
"It's the second door on the right, Geoffrey. You'll
find your bag upstairs. Dinner's ready as soon as you
two are." And Geoffrey, "I won't be a minute."

At the casual words in Geoffrey's low, deliberate
voice, Amy leaned forward, intent. He said nothing
more. Why should just the tone of his voice penetrate
her with a sharp awareness of Geoffrey, of Geoffrey-
essence, opposed to herself, so infinitely more real
than her thoughts about him? Perhaps voice, being

insubstantial, coming from the whole instrument· of the body, could drop down in crevices between the atoms of yourself, setting up a new rhythm that had a quality of the other self. You can't ever think out a person, coldly, separate from him, because you are different, yourself, when you are apart. She rose hastily and crossed the flagged terrace to the doors of the dining room.

"Hello." Her father looked after Lavinia, who had just whisked out of the room. "What's she doing over here?"

"Lulu left." Catherine spoke lightly, unfolding her napkin with a gesture of shaking away the whole situation. "So I asked Lavinia to help."

"You mean she just left? Without saying anything?"

"She was gone when we came home. Geoffrey, you sit there, opposite Amy."

"Oh, there you are!" Geoffrey's glance challenged her.

Amy could see her father, obedient to the little lift in Catherine's eyebrow, swallow further questions about Lulu. "Are you going to keep Lavinia?" He dropped his voice, discreetly. "I'd been wondering what she'd do."

"I don't know." Catherine laughed. "She'd make us eat oatmeal for breakfast every morning. She's always felt herself a deputy of Mother, you know," she added, to Geoffrey.

Lavinia poked open the door. "When you're done with that course, you fetch out the dishes, Amy. I can't leave this steak."

"You see!" Catherine was delighted, less, thought Amy, at Lavinia, than at any pretext for an easing of the heavy day. Amy carried out the bouillon cups,

finished mixing the salad dressing, held the door while
Lavinia bore through the parsley ornamented steak.
"That smoke's from the sides of the broiling oven."
She stood behind Alfred, after she had deposited her
burden. "It's a wonder that girl couldn't ever scrub
them. It'll take me a week to get things in shape.
That other side's for you and Mr. Geoffrey. It's
rarer done, the way a man likes it. Now eat a lot.
You look as if you needed it."

"Lavinia thinks I neglect you." Amy let a sly glance
slip from Geoffrey to Lavinia.

"She does, too!" Geoffrey was waiting for her to
look at him again. Amy ignored him, serving the crisp
lettuce.

"Well, I don't know." Lavinia started toward the
kitchen, loath to leave them. "Men take an awful lot
of coddling."

Through the rest of the dinner they tried to make
talk of trivial things. But trouble, like a stubborn dog,
rushed after the thoughts they tried to throw away,
dragged them back for each of them to stumble over.
Alfred asked Geoffrey about business in New York.
Were things really bad there? And Geoffrey, inno-
cently, had a story of a brokerage house that had failed,
of a member of the firm who had thrown himself from
a window. Back came the hound Trouble, wagging
its tail over the suggestion of Dewitt. Alfred turned
to fishing. What about trout in the Canadian streams?
Geoffrey, the hollows between cheekbones and jaws
deepening, looked straight at Amy as he answered,
"I don't know, not about this summer. I hear the
drought has affected the streams. I didn't get North."

"Oh, I thought that's why Amy couldn't reach you."
Catherine was waiting, too, for his answer.

"My plans changed suddenly. I hope to get away later."

"Shall we have coffee in the living room? It may be cooler." Catherine rose quickly, breaking the strained pause. Amy offered to carry in the tray.

The kitchen was empty. She set the silver service on the tray and poured the coffee slowly into the pot. Lavinia scurried in. "You know, I can't sleep over here to-night. I can't get that cat to come over. He's mewing at the back door. I took him his supper."

"You don't want to sleep there alone, 'Viny."

"Alone's alone, whatever roof you're under. I got my own bed there. You tell your mother I'll show up bright and early." With a mutter about never seeing such dish rags she began a clatter of plates at the sink, and Amy retreated before the ruse against argument damaged china.

"We're late to-night." Catherine poured coffee into the Italian cups. "Sugar, Geoffrey? You two were rather late about coming home. Did you drive somewhere?"

Alfred looked up from his cigar, his eyebrows meeting. "Did we?" he asked, drily. Geoffrey nodded at him, a friendly, conspiring nod. "I warned Geof not to bother you about it before dinner. We had to hunt up Curly."

"Oh—" Catherine's murmur had involuntary protest at another task imposed on Alfred. "Oh, my dear!"

"Yes. You know, I had a notion I saw him? Well, I did." He drank the coffee. "On the way to the factory, Charley shouted at me. His brother'd sent word Curly had disappeared. Charley didn't get the message till he drove back to the garage, afterwards. He didn't know where to look. We came back to the house, parked down there by Joe's. I thought you'd had enough, without worrying about that. One of Joe's kids told us he'd seen Curly running up the road after the procession. Parade, he called it. Cathy, he chased us, Curly did, the whole way out to the cemetery. We didn't go fast, I suppose."

"We found him," said Geoffrey, quickly. "Don't look so stricken, Mother."

"Yes, we found him." Alfred set his cup on the table, and walked to the window. "He was helping—" he turned a moment, his face contorted—"helping fill in the grave. He didn't want to come away."

"Did he—" Catherine choked—"did he know?"

"I don't think so. How can you tell what he knows? He'd run after us, and then—I think he just picked up a spade, that's all."

"Charley's a good sort," said Geoffrey, quietly. Amy felt warmth brush over the chill her father had invoked, with the macabre spectacle of Curly, a spade in his hands. "He'd followed us in his own car, and he persuaded Curly to go along to feed the pigs. Talked to him a minute, and off went Curly, cheerful as could be."

"I suppose he just got it into his head he wanted to come home, this morning. It's a long way, luckily, so he didn't get here—too soon." Alfred flung aside the folds of curtain his hand clutched. "What are we going to do with him? Johnson can't keep him indefinitely, especially if he takes to bolting. I told Geof about it." He ran his fingers through his stiff hair. "My God! When I saw him making the dirt fly—it was like a nightmare."

"And yet," said Catherine, "it would be worse if he realized what the grave was. I'm glad he couldn't.

Heat Lightning

That first morning he was frightened, as a dog might be, by strangeness. This draws a line past which he can't go, you see. If he comes back, he'll look for her around the house, in all the places where she used to be, and then he won't look any more."

"For all we think we're so much smarter," began Amy, in a dry rush of words, broken midway by the startled gesture her mother made to silence her. No use bothering her father with bitter phrases about how little they knew. If he found any precarious comfort in ministers and rituals, let him keep it. That was what Catherine meant.

Alfred pushed his chair nearer a lamp and sat down, unfolding the paper. They were all silent, waiting for a hint of the world outside the house to release them from the ashy emptiness in which the day had left them.

"They're praying for rain in Kansas," said her father. "In spite of all our science, men take to primitive measures in time of stress, don't they? Corn crop shriveling in the fields. You know, men will starve next winter if something isn't done. Men will face hard times, and Mr. Hoover's reassurances won't feed them."

"Can't you find something cheerful?" asked Catherine, piteously. "I don't want to think about hard times."

Alfred tossed the paper to the floor, the loose sheets rustling down in an untidy tent. "Sorry," he said. "Guess I'll go to bed. Good deal to see to to-morrow. You don't mind, Geof? You couldn't have had much rest last night, yourself."

"I'll set these away." Amy piled the small cups and saucers on the tray, the spoons rattling under nervous fingers. She brushed past Geoffrey, not looking at him, and carried the tray to the kitchen, her heart hurrying in her breast. In the dark she felt carefully for the table, and let the tray down. Lavinia had gone home. Alone's alone, whatever roof—I'm afraid, she thought. I want to run after Lavinia, to hide away.

"Don't you need a light, Amy?" Catherine held the door ajar and fumbled along the wall for the switch. "There. Did 'Viny go back?" She sighed. "I couldn't persuade her to stay. I didn't have energy to argue."

"I'll go stay with her," said Amy, eagerly. She was climbing out of her panic on a slippery bank, but her mother pushed her back.

"What nonsense, Amy!" She stepped nearer, dark smears of fatigue beneath her eyes. "Amy, you and Geof—" she brushed Amy's wrist, her sensitive fingers not steady—"is something wrong?"

"Darling, what an idea!" Amy kissed her, on the little worried place between her brows. "Let's all hurry to bed and end this long, unhappy day. Come on." She snapped off the light and led her in to the stairs.

"Is the front door latched?" A moth thudded against the screen, its gray wings a blur of motion. Amy turned off the light, and they climbed the stairs arm in arm. "Now don't talk all night, when you're both so tired," her mother said. "To-morrow we'll all feel better. Sleep well. I put Geoffrey in Mary's old room, next yours. It's a little cooler than the guest room."

Because her mother waited a moment, solicitude worrying at the edge of her smile, Amy had to walk straight through the barrier of her own reluctance, to close the door upon herself with just the proper casualness.

Heat Lightning

"I say, Amy!" Geoffrey called from the adjoining room. "Lend me some toothpaste, will you? And soap. Where's the bathroom?"

"Two doors down. You'll find them on the shelf."

"I'm filthy, after the trip and all. You want a bath first?"

"No. Go along."

Amy stood motionless, buffeted by the sounds of Geoffrey's slapdash preparations: the thud of his shoes, the scuffle as he scrambled out of his trousers, the plop of a garter, and the low, tuneless whistle as he padded away. Dear God, why should they ache so in her, those ludicrous, natural sounds? That was it; they were too natural, evoking an intimacy gone hollow. They frightened her.

Hastily she undressed, peeling off silk that clung to her warm flesh, flinging it aside. Standing before the mirror, knotting a ribbon about the waist of the flimsy silk gown, she thought: it doesn't matter how I look. There must be a me Geof sees which isn't that —she stared at the pale, pointed oval of face, and brushed back with hard strokes the dark hair. She dropped down on the low chair, her shoulders drooping. After you loved a person, you stopped looking at him. Small things, the way fingers lay together, the way a smile began, the swing of shoulders in walking, the arch of ribs under smooth skin—you had those. Presently you had not those details as signs of the man, so much as yourself returned through him. Yourself enhanced, steadied, made proud and assured. And then—what happened?—what cruel sun, striking too fiercely on the mirror, melted the quicksilver, mottling the surface, and your self came back distorted, belittled, wavering. That's what we've done, thought Amy, dully. I don't know how. Geoffrey was coming past her door. What had he been thinking all day, behind that occasional glance in which their eyes had met? The defiance had been his own self, armed; the tenderness no doubt little more than admission that death was a difficult business.

She slipped out of the room without reply to Geof's questioning, "Amy?" Locked into the green bathroom, she had brief respite. Geof had folded his towels with care, like a small boy on his best behavior. On the thick mat was the print of his wet foot. As the water ran into the tub Amy shook off her mule and laid her foot on the print, in a queer caress. She lay in the scented water, her eyes closed, and thought it would be easy to drown, just to let the muscles of her neck go soft, to lie back—

When she came into her room again, the lights were out, and Geoffrey, a dark figure at the window, said, "Hello. Do you need a light? It's cooler without them."

"No."

"I drew a chair up here for you. Unless—are you dreadfully tired?"

Amy moved toward the window, a hand out in the darkness brushing over the smooth footboard of the bed as she passed. She found the chair. Geoffrey was sitting on the broad sill of the window, and as her eyes focused to various degrees of darkness she could guess at his posture, crouched forward, hands twisted about his knees.

"It ought not to be so hot in the middle of the night," he said. "The earth must be baked to the core. I can smell it scorch. Dry leaves, dry grass, dead flowers. New York's worse, though. Melting tar and dirty humans and motors belching gas."

"Yes," said Amy. And then, without volition, she heard her voice add, "You were there all the time?"

"No." Geoffrey leaned against the frame of the window. "No, I wasn't."

Amy waited; she pushed her feet hard, hard down on to the floor, to stop the dreadful trembling of her body.

"You want me to tell you?"

At the warning in his low voice she flared in anger. He would make her responsible for whatever unhappiness he delivered, would he? "As you like," she said.

"I don't like at all." He was bending toward her, but she would not reach for the hand that groped for hers. "Not this way, by being caught out in a lie. Your mother said you telephoned the camp. I did intend to go there."

"The camp hadn't heard of it."

"No." His tone altered, responding tensely to her anger. "But as I said, I meant to go there. I got off the train, though, at Albany, because I couldn't figure out what we had quarreled about, and I thought I'd come back. Then you had cleared out. I didn't know where. The elevator boy told me you left with Preston carrying your bag."

"He went to the station with me. Geoffrey!" Amy tried to see his face. "You couldn't have thought I went off with Preston!"

"Why couldn't I? I always hated him. I felt damned ridiculous, tearing back all repentant, and finding an empty house. If I must be honest—" he answered the choked sound Amy made—"I rather hoped you had gone with Preston."

"Preston!" Amy's laugh had the high pitch of almost hysterical incredulity. Images of Preston blundered against her confused mind, his plump, pale face, his thin, reddish hair, his plump white hands, his gentle, absent-minded manner,—he had rushed off the train to buy magazines for her, and had come running along the platform after the train started, waving them ineffectually at her window. "Of course you know he'd come about some reviews he's doing till I feel like work again. If you had such a grotesque notion—hope, you said—"

"Wait. I'll explain. I couldn't sleep that night. The apartment was beastly. Empty, noisy, hot, dust gritty on everything. I went along to the office next morning. Cooper was sick. So I could cut out all notion of a holiday and buckle down to work. The boss wouldn't okay that last lay-out I'd done, the big fall motor ads, and for God's sake couldn't I get some decent ideas? I felt crazy. Well, Nina telephoned that afternoon. When she invited me over, I went. And stayed."

"So—she got you finally." Amy shut her eyelids tight, but her hot tears could not drown Nina, sleepy white eyelids and soft reddened mouth, her hands brushing Geoffrey's; Nina in spangled black evening dress leaning over his shoulder, inviting his exploration of the clever way she fastened on so sketchy an amount of dress above the waistline. Nina, an obvious, amorous, persistent cat. "She'd almost given up hope." Amy thrust her body downward in the chair, knees crushed together, arms hugged to her sides, as if she could drive herself farther into the pull of gravity, could add weight enough to put an end to the dreadful trembling that threatened to scatter her in separate atoms. "Oh, if it had been some one I didn't know I could stand it!" she cried out.

"No. Because you do know her you should understand what happened to me. Like getting drunk, Amy.

The same kind of wiping out of troublesome reality.
The same kind of morning after. Bad taste, awful
head,—you'd be ashamed, perhaps, if you bothered
to look. What's the use? It's over. And by God,
you've escaped for a while!"

Amy held her body rigid except for her hands, which
quivered uncontrollably from stiff wrists. Silly clichés
rocketed in her head, phrases about "How could
you?" and "Do you expect me to forgive you?" She
shut her lips upon the words; they were out of dramas
of betrayed wives, not her own feeling. She didn't
know her own feeling yet. Ridiculous, the way words
tripped along like—like fatuous movie captions—and
unless you waited, careful, quiet, you never knew what
lay at the bottom of your heart. Geoffrey was trying
to give her honesty; his low voice had a white simplicity.

"Escaped what?" she asked. She had to know, even
if he answered *You*.

"Everything. Failure, dullness, knowing you aren't
getting anywhere, that there isn't anywhere to get,—
your puking, driveling self. You turn for a moment
into the fine fellow you used to be. It's a kind of
temporary death. Always with a penalty when you
crawl back into consciousness again. It's as if the very
cells of your body loathed death, feared it so much they
wouldn't stand for your getting off even for a few
hours. Did you ever realize that, Amy? There isn't
an opiate you don't suffer for, from drugs to a clout on
the head. The decay of the flesh is the final ghastly
penalty for complete escape, isn't it? Life's a third
degree system; a glare of light in your eyes, a blare of
sound in your ears so you shan't slip off a second."

Amy pressed her hands together, the fingers wrench-
ing until the knuckles ached. Geoffrey's words floated

about her like a vague sea of diffused misery. She wanted his head against her breast so that she might comfort him, might rock him there. Fiercely she needed a focus for the very diffusion of pain. "What has this to do with Nina?" she flung at him. She heard his quick movement of withdrawal.

"Nothing much, if you won't see. Nina—or any other woman—I wanted an opiate. That's all. How can I go on prating, with you so cold and still? What did you run away for? It was running away, your coming out here. It was time we did something violent, one of us. Perhaps I just wanted to hurt you, to make you look straight at me for once."

Amy moved in her chair; she had no more strength to hold herself heavy, weighted. At her motion Geoffrey stood up, his figure opaque darkness blotting out the different darkness beyond the window.

"I'll go along. I can't stand your saying nothing. You might chalk up with your grievances this. It's the penalty I was talking about. Going off with Nina made it too damned clear." His voice grew louder, exasperated. "I can't even make love to another woman, Amy. I'm tied up. I love you."

Amy flung out her hands, caught at his sleeves. "Why didn't you say it sooner?" She shook his arms. "Geoffrey, Geoffrey!" He stumbled forward, and somehow got to his knees beside the chair, one arm lifting her away from it, her hands pressing his face down against her throat. For a long time they did not move, except for shivering sighs that Amy could not stop, except for the curving of fingers over his hair. "Poor boy," she said, finally, letting her hands drop. He lifted his face, brushed her cheek in a faint caress, and dragged himself around until he sat against her chair, one hand on her ankle.

Heat Lightning

"You know," he said, "I feel quite empty, and a little holy. Now that's funny, isn't it?"

"So do I. Geof—what have we been doing to each other?"

"Never mind. Let's not do it any more."

Her hand crept around his neck, until a finger lay in the hollow at its root. "I did run away," she said. "I thought first I might never come back. I couldn't stand it, the way we got on each other's nerves."

"Don't talk." He lifted his free hand and laid a finger on her lips, sealing them. "To-morrow will do, if there's more to say."

Peaceful, like the autumn night, dark, without wind, through which a leaf might drift, too light to fall to earth; peaceful as air, so still a candle flame could burn, its golden tapering tip steady, unwavering.

Amy scarcely heard Geof's low, "Are you asleep?", scarcely knew he led her to the bed, lifted her heavy feet, spread the sheet over her breast. She slept, peaceful as air in which a flame lifted a golden, tapering tip.

Book Three

THE morning sounds of the household threatened the heavy sleep in which Amy lay; as she stirred, another wave of sleep would seize the sound, rolling it under and away in a dream. Geoffrey looked in at her, and he too became a dream. But she was a shore from which the tide receded, in spite of soft reaches of sleep waves, and presently she knew, reluctantly, that she was awake, a shore exposed to wind and sun. She stared up at the ceiling, where an aureole of light shimmered in a flattened bubble. What made it? "I'd have to put my eye to the ceiling to tell," she thought, and laughed at her own silliness. The door into the adjoining room was closed. Geoffrey hadn't wished to wake her. She sat up. Yes, there stood the chair, close to the window, and the end of the frilled curtain was plastered against the sill where Geoffrey had sat. The hot sunlight streaming in upon the properties of the scene made a diaphanous unreality of what had happened, like sun beating through a candle flame. Amy slid out of bed, shook out the crumpled organdy curtain, and looked at the low chair. Had it been only an illusion,—not peace so much as exhaustion in which feeling ceased to live? Hurriedly she pushed open the door into the next room. Cigarette smoke, pajamas in a heap on an opened suitcase, brushes and a discarded collar on the white dressing table that had been Mary's, but no Geoffrey.

No wonder. She held her wristwatch to her ear to be sure it was running. Half past nine. As she dressed she stopped a moment, her hands clasped at her throat, her arms pressed hard against her breasts. It must be real, she thought. I'll have it real! But why, began her mind, hard and bright as the sun, if your husband says he's been unfaithful, should you then think you have moved closer to each other than in any moment, even of dark passion? It's true! There are things you can't know with your mind. But he might have waited till she woke. All day they would move separate, insulated from each other by the presence of other people. We aren't safe, yet, she thought. We only hope we may be, if—

She clasped the scarlet belt around her waist, ran a comb through her hair. At a sound in the hall she stopped, her eyes darkening in expectation that tried to beat down fear.

"Amy?" Her door swung cautiously open, and into the mirror behind her own reflection, came Geoffrey. "Why, you're dressed. I came to suggest breakfast in bed."

She turned slowly. His voice had a superficial gayness, but in his eyes, in the tensing of his jaw, she read the same fearing expectation she felt.

" 'Viny said if you were sick, she might fix a tray. Amy—"

She ran toward him, her hands clung to his shoulders, and they kissed, a hard, quick kiss, from which they stood apart to look at each other.

"You slept so quietly, like a child," he said. "I was afraid to have you wake up. I thought perhaps last night you had been so worn out you didn't care, and this morning you'd be shut up tight, away from me again."

"No." She poked a forefinger into the palm of his hand. "I'm cracked so wide open I'm falling apart." She pushed his fingers over hers.

"Is she up yet?" shrilled Lavinia from the hall below.

"Yes. We'll be right along." Geoffrey jerked his head in an impatient gesture. "I suppose we must. How long do you have to stay here, Amy? Will you come with me, to-night? I've got to get back. I want you with me. We've been so damned unhappy."

"I don't know." Amy disengaged her finger and moved toward the door. "I haven't thought about it. Mother may need me here. I don't know." His impatience blurred the clarity of her response to him. "I don't know whether I want to come with you." He shouldn't think it was as simple as taking a train.

As they went down the stairs Geoffrey caught her hand again. "I know you can't tear off this minute," he said, quickly. Amy felt a revelation explode like a sky rocket into bright stars, sharper and swifter than words. That's one of the things you've done, it showed her; retreating in absurd irritations instead of seeing why he did things, letting him see why you did them, what you wanted. A duplication of sensitiveness, swinging them apart on diverging tangents. She felt it as a reiterated pattern of their way together, something important that she must take out later, when she was alone, to look into. Now she had it only as a troubling flash.

"Oh, Amy!" Catherine paused on her way through the hall; Amy recognized the abstracted, intent expression on her mother's face as purely domestic, concerned with linen, ordering, planning. "I was just going to see if you were awake. Mrs. Maguire is here, washing, this morning. Haven't you things you'd like to put in? You'll have to hurry; she's almost through the white things."

"Does she do silk all right? I need a clean frock."

"She's pretty good. I'll ask her to be careful. But you must get it now. She's out of humor, because Lavinia made too many suggestions." Catherine's quick smile invited them to enjoy that picture. "You know," she added, "I didn't like the way she asked where Lulu was. Do you suppose she knows? Have you told Geoffrey about that? He might have a suggestion. But I mustn't stand here talking this time of day." She went on with her purposeful step.

Amy, gathering a few garments, hurrying to the kitchen with them, thought, I must hurry, because yesterday was wash day, not to-day, and we must get back on schedule again, no matter what interrupts. All the routine of living was a kind of moving sidewalk, carrying you along past graves, past grief, past any kind of feeling.

"Where you going with those things?" Lavinia pulled at a floating tail of silk. "You aren't giving them to *her* to do? I wouldn't put it past her to boil 'em up with towels."

"Mother said to, 'Viny."

"Now, Lavinia!" Catherine extricated the silk from Lavinia's grasp. "You aren't to talk any more about the way I have my laundry done. No matter how terrible you think it is!" She vanished down the stairs to the basement.

"I could do it myself," muttered Lavinia; the crisscross of wrinkles around her mouth and chin twitched.

"Your mother thinks I'm too old, that's the whole trouble."

Poor Lavinia! It was fear that bit in fine lines, fear of age, of uselessness. "Don't be silly," said Amy, heartily. "Mother's always had Mrs. Maguire, hasn't she?"

"You better go eat your breakfast, I should think." Lavinia seized a broom. "Or you'll be eating on top of lunch."

Geoffrey stood on the terrace, smoking. He looked in as Amy sat down at the table, and then as Catherine followed her into the room, he wandered out of sight. Guest fidgets, thought Amy. "Where's Father?" she asked.

"He would have taken Geof with him." Her mother answered the implication that a man was lost, stranded in a morning household. "But he had to see Walter Ripley this morning. Is that coffee hot enough?" She laid her hand on the percolator. "I'll heat it." The long cord dangled in her hand. "Oh, Lavinia's taken it out." She stooped beside the buffet, fumbling along the wall for the base socket. "I told her not to." Her face, when she came back to sit beside Amy, was flushed. "What shall I do with her! She said houses caught fire from electric doodads left around. If only she didn't have her own way for so many things!" Catherine sighed. "She got your father all stirred up at breakfast, too. She brought the keys over, and said she wouldn't be responsible for things in the house with so many snooping around. Alfred asked what she meant, and she said she meant his brother and sister. I've never seen your father look so—so stricken. Dewitt was there early this morning, Amy, and he didn't come over here at all. Rummaging, Lavinia called it, through everything in the library he hadn't got into the other day."

"What can he expect to find there? Ripley told him about the will." The clucking of the percolator caught Amy's ear, and she got to her feet quickly to detach the cord. She looked down at her mother; a little gray curl, escaped from the knot, lay on the smooth, drooping neck, and one hand moved a square of Italian cloth back and forth on the table.

"I don't know." She lifted her head, the line of neck altering into its familiar poise. "I just mind Alfred's being pulled this way and that by his feelings. He won't care half so much about losing money as about losing a brother."

"Of course—" Amy poured coffee into a cup and sat down again. "You don't lose a relative, no matter how he behaves."

"Yes, you do. You lose the way you've always felt about them. Dewitt's not acting the way Alfred supposed he was, you see. If he's a different sort of man— It destroys so much of the past. That's why it's difficult. Perhaps it can be worked out. Your father's going to ask Ripley what the old will provided for, and what it was Mother wished to do, that night. He'd like to take care of things as she would have wished."

"You both are grand," said Amy, soberly. "With every one else yelping about what he can get—"

"I must admit, Amy,—" Catherine screwed up her eyes ruefully,—"that when I made Lora go home last night, I felt actually mean. Not a bit decent. I was as cross about her trying to put in a claim as—why, as Dewitt might have been. It's hard to be decent and fair about property. All this morning I've had that little mahogany sewing table of Mother's in my mind. She told me I could have it, and Lora will grab it. Now you see your own mother isn't very grand."

"Is that the worst you can do in the way of coveting?" Amy jeered. "I'd go right over and carry it home if I were you."

"And make it the very piece Lora especially wanted? Not me." Catherine rose as Amy piled her dishes together. "I'll take those out. You go see what Geoffrey's doing. You didn't eat much breakfast. But you do look better." Her quick glance had the quality of delicate pressure against a door behind which Amy and Geoffrey lived, and her retreat to the kitchen was withdrawal in haste before the door opened. Amy sat still, her finger brushing sharp toast crumbs into a pile. Suppose she had told her mother what Geoffrey had said, last night. She could feel embarrassment, like an astringent drug, pucker her throat. Extraordinary, the degree to which sex couldn't exist, in a relation to a mother or a father. Like a primitive taboo, the silence you must keep. An insistence on the first stage of that relationship, in which the child was ignorant, and innocent of sex, himself. Would she do the same thing for Buff and Bobs, in spite of fine theories about frankness and truth?

She went to the opened doors. The heat curled in beneath the taut, dry awning; the grassblades at the edges of the flags were brown. Was it prudery, this taboo? Or a sorry desire to seem wiser, as a parent, than any human being could really be? She leaned against the wooden frame of the doors, a finger pushing idly at a blister of white paint. Wasn't it an instinctive indifference? All this struggle between her and Geoffrey for some kind of happiness—what, after all, did it matter, years from now, to Buff or to Bobs?

We're only tools, by which they shoot off into their own separate existences. Her loving Geoffrey was her own life, not theirs, except as a medium for their tender years. Emotionally, children were by-products. She was a by-product for her father and her mother. If there were no taboo, she would be in a worse muddle, being just a casual result for them and trying at the same time to be her separate self. Mother couldn't come far into her life without revealing her own. Amy felt herself drawn down to a point of intense light, in which whirled the shadow of a new realization. You gained your own identity only by cleavage. Reproduction of selves, souls, whatever you liked to call them, by—what was the term?—fissure?

The telephone bell jangled, scattered her thoughts just as the fragments had almost cohered into a tangible whole. She waited, but no one else answered, and reluctantly she went into the hall, wondering whether she would catch back that almost captured idea, wondering too, whether the excitement had been only illusory, and not that rare feeling of truth coming into vision.

Lora's voice babbled at her ear. "Is your father there? Where is he? I called the factory. I've got to see him. Tell your mother I must speak to her. No, go away, Harriet! I won't keep still. Sending that girl home! Are you there, Amy? Call your mother! Somebody's got to do something."

Amy balanced the ear-piece gingerly beside the telephone, and went to the kitchen. "Where's Mother?"

Lavinia scraped new potatoes busily. "I guess she's down in the laundry. Keeping an eye on that Mrs. Maguire."

Amy called down the stairs, and waited till her mother appeared.

Heat Lightning

"It's Aunt Lora," she said. "On the 'phone."

"Which is it?" asked Catherine, as she let the kitchen door swing behind them. "The will or Tom?"

"Tom, I judge," said Amy.

Her mother's end of the conversation was chiefly monosyllables, accompanied by the steady, indistinguishable twang of the instrument. Finally Catherine said, sharply, "I can't come over now, Lora. I told you Alfred had the car. When he comes, I'll tell him. I don't see what Laurance could do, if you did send for him. Of course I'm distressed. I didn't send Lulu home. She went." With a gesture of final impatience she hung up, silencing the twang.

"Lulu's father called on Lora," she said dryly. "Lora seems to think I'm to blame, first for making her leave Mother's house, so that she was home when he came, and somehow for Lulu, too, since she worked here. I suppose it is a shock."

"Lora'd never think of blaming herself, would she? Or Tom."

"What for?" inquired Geoffrey, as he strolled in. "Or am I butting in?"

"No, come in, Geoffrey." Catherine turned to him in quick, feminine relief, at which Amy smiled. "Perhaps you can suggest something. It's that business about Tom. Didn't Amy tell you? Oh, I thought— I mean, I heard you talking so long—"

"I haven't told him a single family scandal." Amy hurried on before her mother could be hurt because of this neglect. "It's Tom, going to have a baby. That is, Lulu is. She was Mother's maid."

"That blond Slovak who let me in yesterday?" Geoffrey nodded. "I see. How careless of him."

"Don't be flippant!" Sudden anger pinched at Amy's heart, so that her eyes, wide and hard, cried

[283]

out at Geoffrey the words she subdued in her throat.
Tom wanted escape, too; drink, and a woman!
"I'm sorry." Geoffrey's glance recognized her
anger, as he turned to Catherine. "But he isn't your
problem, is he?"
"Lora's so helpless. She's just found out. We
didn't know about it till the night before Mother died.
The father's been around to see Lora this morning.
Poor Lora, it must be hard on her. She broke with
Tom Blake for just such things."
"Oh, yes, I remember."
Geoffrey wouldn't look at Amy. He bent near her
mother, listening, offering her a subtle promise of
able, male assistance. Amy moved away from them,
into the living room. I couldn't help it, she thought.
At least I said nothing. An outraged self, buried in
mud, had spat. I know he's not like Tom.
"As long as the girl's that old—" Geoffrey and her
mother came into the living room. "If she were under
the age of consent, it would be another story. What
did the father say?"
"He doesn't speak much English. He used to come
here once in a while, for part of Lulu's wages, I suspect, so I know him. He probably didn't have a
chance to say much, when Lora discovered his errand.
She locked the door on him. Tom wasn't there. He's
never there. I always wondered where he found places
enough to go as much as he went. But I see he isn't
overly particular." Catherine offered Geoffrey the
problem in a gesture of open hands. "I'm not as
shocked as I should think I ought to be. People seem
to get over such things so quickly nowadays. But Lora
will just moan, 'Oh, Tom, how could you?' and Tom
will find excuses. So some one of us has to do something."

Heat Lightning

"Grandmother was probably right," said Amy, bitterly. "Give the father money enough to buy a husband for Lulu. And Tom's baby will be the first of a raft of them in a shack down below the tracks."

"That sounds sensible." Geoffrey answered her tone rather than her words; his eyes were cold under the long straight fold of the lids. "The first child will be the best of the lot and support Lulu and her husband in their old age."

"Maybe it will be like Curly." Amy stopped, at the sharp exclamation from her mother. "I'm sorry." (How tell her mother that she was crying out against the male casualness in Geoffrey's attitude, casualness that rubbed salt in a wound she had scarcely known she suffered?) "But it's so mixed up."

"It would be much worse if Tom were married." Catherine spoke with an access of hopefulness. "He may learn something—although if he's helped out of this, as he always has been helped out of messes— And he'll have to be helped, to keep it hushed up."

"Cupboards locked on all family skeletons," said Amy. "Yes. What a lot of trouble it would save if we had a public bone pile where skeletons were dumped. It isn't as if all families didn't have their own."

"Don't you talk that way to your father," cried Catherine. "He's too proud of the Westover name." She jumped to her feet, her color heightened, her hair ruffled like agitated crest feathers. "It would annoy him terribly. You don't sound like yourself, anyway."

"Darling, I won't." Her mother's intensity shook Amy out of her murky undercurrent. "I'll be good."

"He'll have the brunt of this," Catherine hurried on. "As he always does. Laurance can't help. The Millers won't let him. And Dewitt—" She drew a

long breath and lifted a hand to smooth her hair.
"There!" A car ran past the window. "There's
your father now." With a warning, protective glance
she hurried away.

Two long steps brought Geoffrey so close that Amy
had to let her head lie back against the chair in order
to look up at him. The posture strained her throat,
exposed her breast where her heart began to beat so
quickly, stretched her helpless for the hard, cold
weapon of his eyes.

"What were you trying to do, Amy?" He laid a
hand behind her head, on the chair. "Quick! They'll
be right in. You were throwing bricks at me, weren't
you? What do you want to say? I prefer it straight,
not nasty undercuts."

She could see the contraction of muscles under his
cheekbones; the long folds of eyelids made hostile
strokes under tense brows.

"I don't know." Her words hurt her strained
throat. "Why did you follow me in here? I came
away."

"Your mother naturally wanted to include you in the
discussion. Why, she noticed something was up."

"It wasn't exactly fair, was it?" Amy pulled herself
forward in the chair, away from his hostile eyes, one
hand up to ease the strain in her throat. "Taking
digs in public. But you made me furious. I hated
you. Not just you. All men. Men and women trying
to live together. I don't exactly know."

"But why? Because I wasn't horrified about your
cousin? I suppose he's a young rotter."

"Something you said—linked you with him. Worlds
separate from me. I think—" Amy spoke slowly,
half waiting for her words to show her what her
thoughts were—"it was jealousy. Oh, not of Nina.

Deeper than that. Of your being different. Able to escape so easily. Male." She was aware of his sudden movement, as if he rejected her words. "After all, Geoffrey—" she leaned back again, mockery in her voice—"I need a little time. We both do. If you swallow something whole, or bury it alive, it kicks for a while." She reached behind her shoulder, and drew his hand against her throat. "This is me," she said. "Feel it? And those bricks I threw—they're stray bits of underpinning. I don't know what. The trouble with us—why, Geoffrey, that's what we've always done! Chucked things at each other, and not known even where we picked them up. And all the time—" She felt his hand change from its reluctance into warm volition, the fingers moving along her throat until her chin rested in the vise the thumb made.

"All right." He bent over her, steadying himself with his other hand on her knee. "I like the sound of your voice, if I don't know what you're talking about. But—" Some one spoke loudly in the hall, and with a low "Hell!" he pulled away.

2

"It'll do no good to look." Alfred's voice burst over a low murmur from Catherine. "Don't you see that was what Dewitt was after? He knew Mother had those securities at the house. He must have seen them when she made him that loan."

"I can't believe he'd do that."

"Give me the key. Lavinia had the right idea, locking the house. Only she locked it too late. You'll see." Alfred let the screen door slam, and the vibrating wires echoed the note in his voice.

Amy went quickly into the hall. Her mother watched the other house, her shoulders well back as if she waited for more doors to slam. Up the steps came Henry, squinting to see who stood there behind the screen.

"Good-morning." He came in, removing his straw hat, wiping his high forehead with a folded handkerchief. "It is hot, isn't it? But of course, walking's good exercise. If you haven't got a car." He smiled uncertainly.

"Why, Henry!" Catherine stood aside for him to enter. "Mary's all right?"

"Yes, yes." His eyelid twitched and he hurried into words, swallowing at his Adam's apple. "She sent me over. That is, she was lying there, getting anxious, and I said I'd come. Since she couldn't very well, herself. It's about the will. You know anybody lying in bed gets to thinking along a certain line. Mary's built up quite a lot of hope, something her grandmother promised her. At least I think it was a promise. She didn't want me to telephone about it. People do listen in, sometimes. But she thought you'd know about the will to-day."

"I didn't know Mother had promised her anything." Catherine had stepped back into the doorway, where she could see the other house. She spoke absently, humoring a child's fancy.

"Well, practically, I think. As her namesake." Henry hesitated, turning his hat under his elbow. Amy remembered her sister's face, soft with light reflected from the bubble she had blown; she saw suspicion twitch at Henry's eyelid, saw fear wipe off the diffidence he had worn for his errand. "You wouldn't disappoint Mary?" he asked. He jerked his hand out to compel Catherine's attention; his hat tumbled to the floor, wobbling in a circle before it fell. "Mother, you don't mean she hasn't got anything in the will? Nothing at all?"

Alfred was coming back, slowly, his head thrust forward. Catherine brushed off Henry's plucking fingers. "There is no will," she said. "Mother destroyed it. Mary had no business to count on it. Oh, it's dreadful, the way decent people turn into buzzards!"

"But if there isn't any will," began Henry, desperately, just as Alfred reached the steps.

"Oh, you're here." Alfred stared under the tufts of his eyebrows, strained white patches beneath his eyes. "Will, did you say? You've begun your grabbing too late. Why, my mother's been dead since Saturday, she was buried yesterday. You shouldn't wait till the corpse is cold."

"Alfred!" Catherine pushed Henry aside and laid her hands on her husband's arms, her whole person insistent that he look at her, that he heed her. "Henry hasn't done anything. You mustn't blame the rest of us—"

"I didn't intend—" Henry murmured, unheeded as Catherine went on.

"If Dewitt has taken the rest of the bonds, what of it? We don't need them. Don't hate it so much, Alfred."

"I found that little steel box, the one Father used to keep in the office safe, Cathy. Would you think a man could steal from that box? I think my fingers would shrivel before they would do that. Empty. It's funny, isn't it? Do you know what Ripley thinks? He implied it was a smart trick on my part, to avoid inheritance taxes."

"You didn't tell him?"

"God, no! He still thinks Westovers are decent

men. He said to me, 'If it was some families, I'd be worried at no will. But with you folks—' He'd made a list, what he remembered, of small things Mother had mentioned. Like Lavinia, and the scheme about the park. He knows we'd want to carry them out. Why, except for the house and the land for the park, there won't be enough left to pay the funeral bills."

Henry stood on tiptoe to peer over Catherine's shoulder at Alfred. "But if your brother has taken what wasn't his—"

"Please, Henry!" Catherine gave him a swift, silencing glance.

"At least it wasn't yours!" At Alfred's bellow Henry jumped backwards in a startled dancing step, and with a deprecating gesture, edged for the door. "You're no worse off than you were," flung Alfred after him, and Henry darted for his hat and hurried away, his shoulders stiff as if he expected Alfred to throw after him some devastating phrase about his insecurity.

"Another minute and I'd have told him what I think of him as my son-in-law." Alfred shook off Catherine's hands. "I can't seem to hold my tongue. If I could get hold of Dewitt—"

"I'm just as glad you can't!" said Catherine.

"I tried. But he's not going to let me find him till he's thrown away everything he can get his hands on. You're right. I couldn't do a thing if I found him. I couldn't choke it out of him with my hands. I can't prosecute my brother for rifling his mother's strong box." The choleric tenseness of his body sagged into apathy. "Brother against brother. The children's teeth on edge. It began with Curly, didn't it? Mother lugged the box home to buy Dewitt to her side. Curly had to be paid for, didn't he? He was a sin, smoothed over. This is part of the reckoning."

"Oh, no, Father!" Amy cried out, involuntarily. "You can't call it reckoning, if Dewitt needed money so much he didn't care how he got it. Whatever Curly was, Grandmother hadn't smoothed him over. She'd taken him, knowing who he was! She must have paid, and Grandfather, too."

"It's a part of the reckoning." He looked at Amy almost pityingly, and Amy thought in a sharp twist of feeling that he seemed much older, as if the death of Madam Westover had moved him on a generation. "You younger people like to pretend there are no consequences. Why, sometimes I think there isn't anything else. Those old Bible fellows were smarter than you are. How does that go, Catherine? About the fruit of the fathers? Never mind." He started slowly toward the door.

"Where are you going?" Catherine caught his hand as it moved the latch.

"Just to Lora's. I have to tell her." He went out slowly, his movement sluggish with thought.

"I say!" Geoffrey's voice behind Amy startled her. "Some one ought to tip him off. He doesn't know Aunt Lora's already had more consequences than she can handle, does he?"

"You go with him." Catherine's eyes, bright, flurried, besought Geoffrey. To his demurring she added, firmly, "Go along. You're a man, and may have some advice. Anyway, Lora won't be so bad if you are there. She can't blame you for anything. Not that I can think of. Hurry, he's started the car." Her ardor shot Geoffrey down the steps. "I'm glad I thought of that," she said, after a brief pause to watch

the car drive away. "Lora can't be quite so sentimental and desperate."

"I'd rather Father would stay angry," declared
Amy, "than talk about reckoning and consequences. It
sounds so old and helpless!"

"No." Catherine had started toward the kitchen;
she stopped, her head averted. "No. You're wrong
if you think that. He liked finding a reason for things,
even one like that. I don't mean he's reconciled. But
if he sees a sort of plan, he can stand it. He likes
order and reasonableness."

"You don't believe it," begged Amy. "You don't
believe that Curly was a sin, and therefore Father has
to suffer, do you?"

"What I honestly think——" Catherine's mouth
made a wry grimace of confession——"is that Isabelle
drove Dewitt too hard. My mind is small enough
to go just that far. But I don't want your father
staying angry."

The door at the end of the hall popped open, and
Lavinia appeared.

"Did those men go away again?" she demanded.
"I got lunch ready to set on."

"Lunch will keep, Lavinia. There are things to
see to, to-day."

"Did he find what his brother was hunting for over
there?" Lavinia flapped her apron. "I saw him
a-running over. I don't mean to pry, but I can't help
knowing things are going on." She closed the door
firmly behind her. "That Maguire woman's got long
ears," she said. "I might as well tell you. There
ain't any use looking for a will. Your mother brought
the waste paper basket out that night, to empty it.
Scraps and a piece of red seal. She was real put out
about Curly, and she had a plan. She was going to

leave the house to Curly and me, as long as I'd stay
and take care of him. But the Lord had another plan.
I wisht I knew what it was." Lavinia's face creased
into tight wrinkles, fear squeezing it in a cruel fist.
"I s'pose I got a few years of work left in me. That
first day, Saturday, I kept thinking, this is my house,
she meant it to be mine and Curly's, and if I spoke up,
you'd want to carry out her plan. But you wouldn't,
I see now. Money makes an awful itch, even in good
people's fingers. I haven't got a claim. The only one
I had was on the way she felt to me, and she's not here
any longer."

"We are," said Catherine practically. "You've got
lots of claims on us. But that plan would have made
a lot of trouble, 'Viny. Even Mr. Ripley didn't like
it. And Lora and Dewitt— Mother would have seen,
after a day or so, that you alone with Curly in that
big house, with Curly growing more difficult—oh, no.
You couldn't have done it."

"I can't now, anyways. I got that much sense."
Lavinia jerked herself into her usual truculence.
"That's why I say the house ought to be locked up till
things is settled fair and open. The worst a family
ever acts is over property. I know. I got a little
something laid by myself. I don't want any charity."
She thrust out her chin and bolted for the kitchen.

"So that was Grandmother's scheme," said Amy.
She recalled Harriet's complaint, at the end of that
long Saturday, that Lavinia acted as if she owned the
place. Poor 'Viny! She had been pretending that she
did.

"It's too bad Mother told Lavinia. Now she'll
always feel she has lost something."

"That links her with the rest of the family, doesn't
it?"

Heat Lightning

Catherine, with a slight gesture, brushed aside Amy's mocking reflection. "Would you mind putting the rooms in order upstairs? Yours and Geof's. I can't seem to get things done this morning. I haven't ordered dinner yet." Domestic preoccupation settled around her, as if she came breathlessly from bleak outer space into a small, safe room. "There'll be time before lunch."

Amy started obediently up the stairs. Hand on the rail, she leaned down to say, "Geoffrey has to go back to-night."

"He does?" Catherine returned from a foray into the dining room. "So soon? I thought he had a vacation now."

"A man in the office is sick." Amy hesitated; she owed something to the concern Catherine had hidden. "That's why he didn't reach the camp, you see. He wants me to go back with him."

"Why—" Catherine's face tipped up toward Amy, dismayed. "I hadn't thought of your going." She smiled, almost in apology. "I must have felt you were just my daughter again. Of course, if Geoffrey needs you—"

"I shouldn't say that." Amy climbed a few steps. "If I were any use here, until some of the messes clear up—"

"They aren't your messes." Catherine's inflection quoted the word, with distaste. "You aren't responsible for them." Amy had a perception of the swift process in her mother's attitude. She had lifted Amy out of the center of her own life, where the quick, shifting emotions of the past week had placed her, and had moved her to a more distant spot, with threads still dangling, to be sure, but still a place remote, encompassed by husband, children, unrealizable details

[294]

of her adult life. "I just hadn't considered your going. You have to go sometime, and if Geof wants you—"

I'm as good as gone, thought Amy, ruefully, as she finished the stairs. For all I've been feeling so— well, if not helpful, at least an indispensable part.

She folded the sheets from Geoffrey's bed, and smoothed the taffeta spread into place. She set his limp leather bag to gape on a chair, and dropped in brushes, collar, pajamas, trying to hold herself aloof, as if these were just things, not objects capable of stirring her because they had a part in Geoffrey. On the table near the bed was a manilla folder tied insecurely about its paper contents. She poked a sheet inside, and the words scrawled in pencil, insignificant as words, had in their very shape the feeling of Geoffrey's hands, the long, uneven fingers, the ridges of veins, the temper of his muscles. He'd brought work along. She held the portfolio between her own hands, hearing those heavy words of his, last night. Failure. Knowing there isn't anywhere to get. He hated it so abominably when they chucked a piece of work back at him. He had a sardonic twist in his attitude toward himself as clever advertising man, so that he tolerated the work calmly enough when it produced approval and praise for him. But criticism ruined the slight palatability of the whole job, and he fell into ugly self-depreciation. This past year, with the strain of losing accounts, with fiercer competition,—Amy laid the portfolio in the bag. Hadn't she been hard and bright against his blackness, as if by ignoring a mood you negated it? Thinking her hands were full enough, with her petty reviewing, with the children? Accusing him,—oh, not in words, so much as in chilly dignity,— of having small concern about her difficulties, of grouching needlessly.

Heat Lightning

She went into her own room, moving slowly, lest her thoughts be jostled into hiding. She had never before tried to stand him away from her, away from personal relation to her, to look at him separate, as a person. Not since those early, first encounters, and then interest in him had so quickly been drowned in passion for him. Perhaps love always ran that course. You loved a man, you lived with him, tried to make a sort of life with him, and you ceased to look at him except as he affected you. Was it sorry proof of her own egoism that this had happened? Or was it the way love went? You responded to inflections of voice, to overtones, in terms of your own desires and failures. And the man you loved became a sort of scape-goat for the difficulties not in love, but in the whole business of living. Had Geoffrey done the same for her?

When you first loved, you were young and vainglorious, cocksure, headed for the promised land of victory, achievement, with the world a small place, exciting, to be sure, but little more than a ball spun under your proud feet, like a circus performance. Growing older was in part a painful shrinkage of yourself, into a speck in the cosmos, and the promised land you hurried toward was not unlike the other dusty stubble fields you crossed to reach it. You didn't see yourself shrinking; you only felt discomfort as your ego was squeezed down. And you took it out on love, resenting the sad fact that days were no longer glamorous.

She had thought she knew so much about love, in a modern, sophisticated knowledge that the first absorption must lessen, that passion must lose its intensity. She had known too much, and far too little. When you grew older, and a day wasn't a dazzling space of sun between two darknesses, then you should know your lover had his own dusty road to travel. What had Grandmother said?—a lifetime's too short to find your way about another's heart. And she, poor stupid fool, hadn't tried. She had thought: he's irritable and moody; he's not concerned in what I'm doing; he's critical of me; he's ridiculous the way he swells up when women flirt with him. Never once had she wondered what he was thinking of her, or of himself.

She looked at the window where he had sat last night. Time one of us did something violent, he had said. She hated Nina; the worm jealousy set up its ugly undulation in her blood. She drew a quick breath; it was hard to be as honest as she tried to be. She knew Nina as inconsequential, and she could match Geoffrey's candor with comprehension, at least. She had known her own hasty, sensual responses to other men. Flesh had its impersonal, less selective way, whether or not you admitted it. That she hadn't gone farther than recognition of the impulse might be chance. Or some deep element of her relation to the children, protecting her through its very chastening of flesh from vagrant impulses.

Her mother's quick entrance startled her; her blood sang in her ears, released from an intensity of thought which had suspended ordinary bodily processes.

"Are you packing, Amy? I've been thinking it over, and after all, you might as well go with Geoffrey, instead of waiting a few days for the end of the week. The trouble here will just have to work itself out. I called up Felice, and she and Ted can come in for luncheon to see you, or a sort of late meal, early afternoon dinner." She moved competently about the bed, shaking off the smooth sheets, snapping them into folds. "I was stupid when you spoke of it. There."

She drew the tufted spread into place. "Now I'll help pack your bags. You'll have to run in to see Mary this afternoon, and you ought to start for town by six, you know."

"I hadn't decided," protested Amy.

"Of course I wish you both could stay. But since you can't—"

"You're really driving me home." Amy pulled a suitcase from the corner. "I can throw things in. You have enough else to see to."

"If it was Alfred, I'd want to go." Catherine sat on the edge of the bed, the sheets flopping over her arm, one white canvas pump beating a tattoo. "I told Mrs. Maguire to iron your few pieces right away." She pushed her restless foot against the floor and added, "Amy, aren't you doing too much, with that outside work—"

"You mean the few reviews I write? About a column a week?" Amy looked up from the dress she was tucking into place.

"I thought perhaps—" Catherine's color deepened —"I know I'm old-fashioned. But I worry about you. You seem nervous. I wonder if you find time enough for Geoffrey and the children. I know this week's been hard."

"Perhaps I don't find time enough for them." Amy's movements increased in jerky speed. "I don't devote myself, the way you do to Father. But I like reading books and talking about them. We need the money, too."

Curious how part of her leaped up, wary, at a threatened tether, in her mother's mild comment. A survival of those heady days of adolescence, when she lived in exaggerated rebellion against any hint of coercion. She

[298]

must remember that Buff and Bobs, presently, would move into that stage of feverish autonomy.

"It's difficult for a mother to give up the habit of offering advice, isn't it?" Catherine laughed, at herself, at her detection of Amy's mood. "For all we know no one wants it. Of course I'm proud of you for being so clever. I just want you happy." She rose, tucking the burden of linen under an elbow. "It used to be almost a handicap for a woman to be too clever," she added, thoughtfully. "It made her restless. I suppose then she started a woman's club, didn't she? I remember a woman here, Mrs. Wycombe. But her husband ran away with another woman!" Catherine's mouth lifted in a droll smile. "And people said it served her right."

"Nowadays probably Mrs. Wycombe would run away first," said Amy, lightly.

"She did make eyes at your father." Catherine's tone had a reminiscent, youthful relish. "He was quite enamoured of her for a while. Mary was a baby, and I wasn't getting out much. It didn't last long. I bought a new dress, and we joined the whist club."

"You darling innocents!" Amy dropped her writing case into the tray, and seized her mother in an impetuous hug. "I wish life was as simple as that nowadays."

"It didn't seem simple. But I know what you mean. When I think about you—with the children off in camps or in schools, and living in an apartment without any yard, and you writing articles full of long words— But I promised myself not to say another word about that. After all, none of it matters, if you find out in time what things are important. My mother would have thought I was terrible, because I had a washing machine and bought canned goods. So you see?"

"What is important?" Amy kept her arm about her mother's shoulders; in her mother's tone, in the acceleration of her speech, she felt a desire to communicate fully and quickly, as a fending off of approaching departure.

"To me, now, just two things. Your values alter so, as you grow older. You let go of lots of things you struggle at first to get. I think Mother's death made me think about it, what I consider important. Death stops you, turns you inward. Well—" she sighed, and swung open a secret door—"one is acting so I don't feel ashamed of myself, so I feel comfortable with myself. Sometimes I'm driven into saying or doing things I know I'm going to be ashamed of. The other—that's people. Loving them. Loving them enough, now, so you feel alive. Not a general, vague love for everybody. That's nonsense. But for your special ones." The color lay bright on her cheekbones, her eyebrows lifted into the little triangle of concentration above her delicate nose. "I can't explain any better."

Amy was silent; words with rude breath might blur the surface of the treasure her mother exhibited so diffidently. With a shrug Catherine moved away from Amy's arm, swinging fast shut the secret door. "It can't seem very much, till you find it out for yourself," she said, her tone altering to prosaic dryness. "Some people wouldn't agree with me for a minute. Look at Dewitt. Isn't that the car, now?" The metallic slam of a car door came from the street. "And I've been a garrulous old woman, instead of attending to my work." But before she went, she leaned a moment toward Amy, and kissed her, setting a signature and seal to finish her confession.

Heat Lightning

3

Amy, collecting final odds and ends for her bags, carried on an erratic monologue, answering her mother. How do you know when you ought to feel ashamed of yourself? That's conscience, I suppose. Nowadays you think, ah, there's an inhibition! That sense of guilt comes from some standard thrust upon me when I was too young to resist. (I might as well change into that traveling suit now. It will be beastly on a train to-night.) Yes, we distrust what used to be called our consciences. We don't know what we live by, nor what we believe. That's why it's so hard to behave well. We haven't any code. Grandmother had one, a steady framework. Mother has one, more personal, not so rigid, perhaps. Here's Father, insisting on duty and stern consequences. But for me, and lots of us, the demolition company has moved in— (she could see a street, with an ugly gaping hole, scars of old roof lines, dangling plaster and bricks).— But there's no plan drawn for any new building.

We're too many kinds of people. (She stripped her dress over her head, and stood still a moment, waiting for the rest of that idea.) We come from too many races, too many countries. Past her whirled a rapid, fragmentary impression of the past week here, of days in New York, with bits of faces, of voices, of blurred hints of streets or restaurants or some one across a table, looking at her, quite as if a river bore them down too swiftly for distinct vision. That's it, cried her mind, triumphant. Nothing homogeneous in what we disbelieve, we're all smashing different idols. Look at just this family—bits of flotsam in the down-running current of impressions—Emma, Felice,

Heat Lightning

Curly, Isabelle, Lulu, and all the rest of them, each with his own code, derived blindly from distant soil. We're making a new race, she thought. She pounced at her blouse and skirt, and dressed with hasty, excited motions. This hitting upon a comprehension for yourself made a heady moment. Plenty of other people had no doubt seen it; realization for yourself was another matter.

That's why it's a hard time to live. We are, actually, having to make a new code to live by. Now that's a large and impressive idea! She snapped the locks of the suitcase, and ran across to the dressing table, to sweep the toilet articles into the handbag. Just what do you mean, when you come right down to it, to your small self? She bent toward the mirror, and powdered her nose reflectively. Was there a new code? What, at the very bottom of her heart, did she believe in? Did it differ, fundamentally, from her grandmother's set of values? Courage, love, loyalty. The scene shifted, but there were no new virtues. Who needed any new ones?

Here she was, packed and ready to go home with Geoffrey, without having at any definite moment reached a decision. All the moments since she had come to Flemington had been working toward that decision, hadn't they? Not a conclusion arrived at coldly, by balancing advantages; a necessity which was left after the agitation of the week had broken up her dull and apathetic surface. It was queer to feel more alive because of death and fear and hatred; perhaps intense feeling was a kind of electric disturbance in which old sluggishness and stupidity were consumed. Heat lightning, revealing flashes in a murky summer night.

"Amy!" Geoffrey was taking the stairs in a rush.

"Mother says you're packing." He sought confirmation in a glance at the bags, at Amy.

She nodded. If he should look triumphant, as at an easy victory!

"I'd made up my mind to wait till you would come," he said. The subtle change in his posture was relief, not triumph. "Luncheon's ready. Felice and Ted are here. A great pair, aren't they?" He postponed their own affair.

As they went down the stairs, Amy thought: a week ago I should have resented that, thinking he meant to compare us, to say, see how Felice lives in your brother. I can't be like Felice, but it's me Geoffrey wants. She sighed, and Geoffrey turned.

"What is it?" he asked.

. "I can't tell you now. There's no time. Geof, would you like a wife like Felice?"

"How do I know?" Geoffrey was laughing at her, the lines from nostrils past lips lifting into parallel accents with the straight lines of his lids, his eyes warm. His hand closed over hers for an instant before they entered the dining room. Oh, thought Amy, with half a chance we'll make a go!

Felice stood at the buffet mixing salad dressing, her firm shoulders and gray crest intent on her task. Alfred and Theodore strolled in from the terrace, discarding cigarettes and discussion at the door. Catherine came from the kitchen, bearing a large glass pitcher of amber tea in which ice clinked.

"There. It will not be stiff a day so warm as this." Felice poured the dressing over the curled leaves. "I am sorry for you two, going on a train such a night."

"I begin to think this weather's responsible for lots of trouble." Alfred took his seat at the end of the table, the strong light under the awning exaggerating the white circles beneath his eyes. "Dries up all decent human sap. Nerves get bad, business gets worse, crops are ruined, people do crazy things, all because of the drought. Might as well close the factory. Have to have rain to sell plows."

"It is nervous weather," said Felice. "Lettuce is excellent for nerves." She pushed the bowl toward Alfred. "But I think it is other people who are dried up, and then you must run around trying to help them."

"That's what I've been saying," said Theodore. "Father's taking the burden of the whole damned family. I'm not much good on business, but how about using me as a buffer? Let's have a conference."

"Geoffrey made a good buffer this morning." Alfred's face loosened into amused recollection. "Lora was torn. She didn't know Geoff quite well enough to let go, sort of kept wanting to impress him, I guess. And yet here he was, part of the family."

"She hinted I might go hunt up Tom," said Geoffrey. "But I didn't know his haunts, and anyway Father gave me a high-sign to stay. The two things, Tom and the lack of a will, seemed to counteract each other. They split up the tragedy, so each got only half the possible emotion."

"And that was plenty, if I know our Aunt Lora," said Theodore.

"Harriet didn't help any." Alfred speared a slice of ham, laid it carefully on his plate. "She was incensed, thought Tom ought to marry the girl. She's a queer piece. There's one good thing, though. I had suspected it was Mother who was sending Tom to the university, and it was. Lora hasn't much income. So now"—he waved his hand negligently—"Tom can get to work. And it's time."

Heat Lightning

"Let's put them all off till after lunch," begged Catherine. "I know I always say that, but I can't eat and think about problems."

Felice came alertly to her aid, and the talk moved in fitful eddies from one casual suggestion to another. Alfred sat in silence, and when some remark from Geoffrey started Theodore on a technical discussion of the latest physical theory, Amy sank lazily into her own thoughts. Theodore's sunburned forehead wrinkled earnestly, and he sketched formulæ in the air with a fork. "A hundred years from now we'll have a different philosophy, just catching up with mathematics to-day. You'll see! We know now we can never reach exact knowledge. That's an admission your mechanistic philosopher won't face. You can't look at an electron and see it as it is. Its act of permitting you to see it alters it. Don't you see? Every element of permanence, of staying put long enough to be perceived, of existing according to any of our sacred laws, every element like that lies nowhere but in the mind that invents it."

Amy listened, caught out of her drifting thoughts by his seriousness.

"You can't build a social philosophy out of that theory of elusiveness," said Geoffrey. "We act as if this table would hold up our luncheon, and it does. It will be a table to-morrow, too."

"Oh, your as if's! Men acted as if the earth was a flat plate with a revolving sun, and they got along for centuries. Then they acted as if they'd soon have the last crumb of exact knowledge, and now they admit, some of the wise ones, that we are at the end of knowledge, and it breaks into mystery, never to be captured. A few years ago man was a bunch of conditioned reflexes, and you could tell the world his story in a few words. Now, by all that's holy, you can't get your eye on what we call matter, not the most infinitesimal scrap. How's that?"

"It doesn't affect the way you behave, does it?"

"I don't know." Theodore looked at Felice, and rumpled his sandy hair in a vague gesture. "Does it? I don't know how I behave."

"Tell us, Felice. Does your husband act on the assumption that you are a vast collection of uneasy electrons pursued by electrical disturbances, or however else he'd describe it?"

"Sometimes," said Felice, promptly. "On the whole he would expect me to be much as I was a few minutes ago. Although in my mind I have made a comparison between people and these electrons, which alter themselves in the act of being seen. It is that we, too, alter ourselves when we show ourselves to others. But poor Father! He is most politely bored."

"Huh? Oh, I wasn't listening." Alfred stood up, letting his napkin slide to the floor. "I must call up Ripley. He may have heard from Dewitt."

"And what use," asked Geoffrey, as Alfred walked away, "is your theory of matter in the case of the missing securities?"

"None, because we live *as if*," mocked Theodore. "Don't look so worried, Mother. We won't insist on abstractions any longer. Come on in the other room."

As they rose, Catherine, with a startled sound, stepped out on the terrace. Circling the old house at a slow amble, the black cat marching behind, was Curly; he tried the porch door, and pushed through the shrubbery to lay his face close to the study window.

"He's tramped all those miles in the heat." Catherine's voice was dismayed. "And the house is locked."

She went hurriedly to the kitchen, and a moment later Lavinia darted across the lawn.

Amy couldn't hear what she said, but Curly listened, shaking his shaggy head, and then came back with her to the kitchen door, Alpha at his heels.

"He must come home," said Felice. "Only if they lock him up will he stay."

Alfred's voice boomed at the telephone, and Theodore, with a whistle, strolled into the living room.

"Go on, you two," said Amy. "I'll see if there's anything I can do." She made a pile of crystal fruit plates and carried them out to the kitchen. Lavinia was cutting a sandwich, her elbows jerking in her haste, and Catherine stood at the door, talking to Curly, who sat beneath her on the steps, head bent, blue shirt dark and wet across his broad back.

"Mother's gone away, Curly. That's why we locked the house, and Lavinia came here. There's nothing wrong. Don't cry."

Alpha rubbed against the screen, purring.

"He'll feel better when he gets some food in his stummick," Lavinia said, briskly. "Here." She carried a glass of milk and the sandwich, shoving the door ajar with her foot. "You eat this up. You want to be sick, running miles in the dust this kind of a day? The idea!" He turned his head docilely, at the accustomed scolding, his bewildered, dust-smudged face lifted toward Lavinia.

"Don't fret about him, Catherine." Lavinia shooed her away from the door. "When he gets cool, I'll set him to work. Then he'll be all right. He just got upset, finding the house shut. And I don't want any fussing about those dishes. You clear out, both of you, and leave me be." She poured a saucer of milk for Alpha and set it outside on the top step. "It's the first time that cat's come over, too," she added.

"Well," said Catherine, as she and Amy left the kitchen, "I must have hoped Curly would stay out there with the Johnsons. Now what? And Lavinia's delighted he's come back."

"So's Alpha." Amy tucked her hand under her mother's arm. "Just because they're all that's left. I'm afraid you've inherited all three. Father's decided Curly's a consequence."

"I can't turn them out, can I?" Catherine's mouth puckered, tasting future minor conflicts with Lavinia, perhaps. "Isn't that the way things go? While you try to decide what you ought to do, the problem moves in on your own doorstep, and settles itself. If Lavinia were less—"

Alfred burst through the door, colliding with them. "Oh, Cathy! I'm off to the works. Dewitt's to meet me there."

"Why not here?" Catherine's hands flew out to detain him. "Alfred, I'd so much rather he saw you here."

"Too many folks around. He wants to see me alone. Oh, don't worry. We don't fight with our fists."

"You'll come back early? Amy and Geoffrey are going, you know." Catherine pursued him to the door, her anxiety spread like a net to delay his going.

"Yes." He held the thin disk of his watch between his fingers. "Over two hours. I should get back. Otherwise you call up, and I'll send back the car. You could drive them in. But I should be through. I tell you, Cathy, you aren't to worry. It'll be a relief to get to the bottom, whatever the bottom is. Now I've seen Dewitt as part of a reckoning up—well, I don't feel so furious." He drew his fingers along his jowl, his eyes reflective. Then, clapping on his hat, he left them, his gray coat crinkling between his squared shoulders.

"You see?" said Catherine, with a hint of pride. "I told you if he could put some reasonableness into things, he could face them."

"What I see," replied Amy, "is that he'll probably give Dewitt what he asks for. And you won't lift a finger, if you think Father feels more comfortable."

"Just the same, I do wish Dewitt had come here. Then if they got too excited, one of us could open the door." Catherine's face contracted, fine lines deepening at the corners of eyes and lips, as if she ran after the car, pursuing Alfred straight to the moment of encounter, and was thrown back helplessly at a closed door through which no sound could pass. Then with a quick movement, a shiver of dismissal, she said, "But you have so little time left. Let's see—" She lifted a hand to smooth her hair, and came with the gesture wholly into the present moment. "You must see Mary. Geoffrey hasn't been over there, has he?" She walked into the living room. "Geoffrey, you mustn't go back without saying hello to Mary."

"But Mary doesn't approve of me, Mother." Geoffrey dropped his paper, and at the amusement in Felice's eyes, played up his dismay. "In her delicate state, I'd be an awful strain."

"Nonsense. She'd be hurt if you didn't call. Why don't you and Amy take Ted's car, if he'll trust it to you?"

"He never could drive my car. He doesn't know the secret words to whisper when her heart flutters." Theodore grinned at his mother, a stanch, admiring grin which said, "Good old sport!" "I know he has a way of his own with animals, but our Pepita is a one-man dog."

"You drive Amy over," urged Geoffrey.

"No, Geoffrey. You go along. Of course Mary likes you. She may think you're a little satiric, but she really hasn't seen you enough to know." Catherine looked bewildered at the brotherly guffaw from Theodore.

"Don't crack any jokes on Mary," he said. "She always suspects jokes."

"You are hard on Mary." Felice closed her book and rose. "It is only that she is always afraid lest we do not appreciate her Henry. Come, I will show you how to manage Pepita."

"I ought to 'phone in about reservations." Geoffrey looked hopefully at Amy, but she wouldn't let him off.

"Come along, lazy thing," she said. "Ted will 'phone in for us. Perhaps they'd have a compartment car on that train. I feel extravagant this kind of weather. You ask them, Ted."

The air outside the darkened rooms of the house seemed thickened by light, offering sluggish, hot resistance to face and limbs as they moved down the walk. The car lolled at the curb, a bent fender suggesting a slouched hip, the odor of hot metal, dusty leather standing about it, visible in shimmering waves from the nickel.

"The shade has run away from our poor Pepita," said Felice. "See, you must push this so, and so. She is so hot she will start, I think."

Off they rattled, Amy sitting away from the scorched seat, her arms cradled from the blistering edge of the door. Geoffrey's chin looked stubborn, but the jiggle of the car destroyed the gravity of his expression.

"What'd you make me come along for?" he growled.

Heat Lightning

"Mother wanted it." Amy shoved her elbow under his arm. "So did I. You know Mary'd be furious. We won't stay but a minute." She smiled. Geoffrey looked so huge gathered under the wheel, and their rickety progress through the heat-emptied streets was so solitary, so ludicrous. "Mary thinks you scoff," she added. "Don't scoff, will you? No, the next corner."

"Now you wait here while I see." Amy had knocked softly, and when no one answered, had gone into the living room. It had a neglected orderliness, the box of children's toys in the corner undisturbed, the chairs at unused, accidental angles. From above came the whimper of the baby.

Amy went quietly upstairs. The nurse sat in the doorway, the baby naked across her knees, pink, freshly powdered. "There, there." She patted the squirming legs. "Oh, Mrs. Norton!" Her hair straggled under her cap, her starched manner had suffered limpness. "We've had a little wind on our stomach, that's all. This heat. I suppose the hospital would be just as hot. Mrs. Chester's lying down. She had a headache. You can look in. I don't think she's asleep."

Mary wasn't asleep. She lifted her hand, limp-wristed, as Amy peered in. Under the lowered shades the light came at an angle, emphasizing the dark rings about her eyes. "Hello. I hoped you'd come over."

"Poor kid. Got a headache?"

"Not much. My ice-bag leaked. Henry's going to bring me another." Mary pushed herself higher on the pillow. "He's in town. I didn't want him to go till it gets cooler. He'd heard of an opening." Her mouth quivered, and she laid her fingers over it. "He was awfully worked up this morning. What did

Father say to him? Oh, I think it's too dreadful, about the will. What *did* Father say?"

"He just said we weren't any of us any worse off than before."

"It's much worse, knowing you aren't to have what you hoped for. He said something to hurt Henry, too, or he wouldn't have rushed right off to look for a position."

"Geof's here," said Amy, abruptly. "Downstairs. We've got to go back to-night. Perhaps you don't feel up to seeing him."

"But Amy! You ought to stay—till they find out about Uncle Dewitt—"

"Can't. Geof—" Amy hesitated; would Mary resent a necessity that drew Geof back to work? "Shall I call him?"

Mary thrust her head up from the pillow, her hair swinging softly about her white face. "This room's a sight. The baby's been fretting all day, so the nurse hasn't had a minute. Pick up that face cloth. And please brush my hair a little. My dressing jacket's on the chair."

Amy tidied the room. She brushed Mary's thick, fair hair, held a mirror for Mary to powder her nose. "A little rouge would help."

"I never use make-up. Henry doesn't like it." Mary made a virtue of the omission.

"I bet he would, once you tried it." Amy straightened the few things on the dressing table, sighing at the comb with a broken tooth, at the discolored celluloid of brush and mirror. Poor Mary! She'd been crying, too.

"Now, you look very nice." She tied the blue bow Mary fumbled with, and kissed her gently. "Mary, don't feel so wretched about that money. After all—"

"Don't you dare tell me money isn't everything!" Her mouth quivered again. "I'd planned what to do if it was just a little, a few hundred. And then if it was more—" Her eyes had the desolate expression of a child who sees a wet smear where a moment before an iridescent bubble had floated. "I thought I knew better than to count my chickens." Her face hardened. "I ought to know better now. It was nice while it lasted. When I think of Aunt Isabelle, with that house—"

"She's got her own troubles just now." Amy gave the sheet a final smoothing, and went to the hall. "Geof, come on up," she called, softly, at the nurse's warning finger. "Sh!" As he came toward her an impulse, a shadow self, folded down out of her body, flowed to his feet and stood close, so that she waited, empty, thinking, that's my living self that runs to meet him; all these other feelings I dip into and run away from; this is my life, coming toward me with him. She pointed toward the baby, quiet now, no longer swimming to escape distress, and smiled at his humorous, male indifference. They slipped past the door, and into Mary's room.

"Hello, Mary." He took her hand a moment, and looked about awkwardly. Amy pushed a chair near for him, and perched herself on the foot of the bed. "Looks like a nice baby, what I saw of it. You're looking well, yourself."

"She is. Her name is Henrietta."

They talked a little; there was always the weather, a glance at hard times, commiseration from Mary that they must go back to the city. Then silence, a faintly hostile silence of strangers who have too much intimacy, won not by acquaintance, but by transverse relationships.

"We must run along." Amy slid from the bed, and Geoffrey rose with alacrity. "We borrowed that car of Ted's to drive over. You know, Pepita. The owners may need it."

Mary's sniff disposed of the nonsense in such a name for such a car. "Where's Father's car? He's not at the factory to-day, is he? I thought Henry said—"

"He's there this afternoon. He went over"—Mary would, on the whole, prefer to know as much as the rest of them did—"to meet Dewitt."

"He did?" Mary's blue eyes were round. "Why didn't you tell me? Then he'll find out— Oh, it's awful, lying here, while you all know just what's happening!"

"But we keep you posted. You ought to be glad you escaped some of the week just past." Amy bent over her. "Good-by, Mary. I hope you'll be up soon, and fit as a fiddle. Don't you send that nurse away till you can't stand her around any longer. It's always harder than you think it's going to be, looking after the baby yourself."

"I guess I know more about that than you do," said Mary. "I want the other children home soon. They're just running wild. Lucy told me, yesterday. But I can't do a thing about it."

"They're having a grand time. Good-by."

The door of the baby's room was shut; they tiptoed past and out of the house.

"Where's Brother Henry?" Geof fidgeted with throttles, coaxed Pepita into a spasm of throbbing.

"Hunting a job." Amy recognized a twinge of discomfort; queer how identity with your childhood's family persisted, so that any hint of disparagement ruffled you. Geoffrey had been considerate. "You were very good," she said. "You didn't scoff a scoff."

[314]

"Oh, sickness doth endear them to us," said Geoffrey, lightly. "How many kids have they got now? Five, eh? All girls. Give me our two." He felt hastily in a pocket and tossed a card to Amy's lap, grabbing at the throttle as Pepita resented the momentary neglect. "Found that at the office. I'd forgotten it."

Amy looked at the snapshot of Bobs, poised for a dive on a springboard above the lake, his thin body a taut arc in sunlight. Beneath it was scrawled, "Hello Dad here me splash." The darling, thought Amy. He wanted to show his father how smart he is! And then, I do hope he dries his ears properly, those awful earaches he had as a baby—

"Getting to be a great kid, isn't he?" Geof tucked the card back into a pocket. "In a few more years he can go fishing with me."

"I don't want them growing up so fast," wailed Amy. "It means we'll be old."

"Nothing we can do about that." Geoffrey grinned at her. "Just wheeze and rattle like this bus."

Amy dropped against Geoffrey's shoulder. The hot air pushed apart by their progress folded in against her forehead, under her hair. It was time itself, cleft by the prow of identity, folding in, *now* endlessly escaping into *then,* nothing stopping its flow until you slipped back into death.

"It's terrible, Geof."

"What?"

"Feeling time. Like a nightmare, where you fall and fall—"

"Then you open your eyes and wake up." Geoffrey shot around a corner, and they halted in front of the house. "Anyway," he added, "that's not time you're feeling. That's just growing old. Time's something curved, and we aren't clever enough to feel it. Our

senses are too dull as yet. When we do, we'll stroll
back and forth in it, and maybe we'll know what it's
all about. Just as we ride around the town now. I
must ask Theodore about time." He laughed, but
his eyes had a sudden brilliance. As they walked into
the house Amy thought: he loves it, letting his mind
swoop like a falcon after some idea. Ted stirs him
up. Dullness, routine—what hooded the falcon,
chained its feet? You had to be free to send your
falcon for a star. Your low, small, stumbling self
had to rest secure. And that, precisely, was what
love was for. That was what she wanted from Geof,
wasn't it? And perhaps, now that she saw it, she
could manage to furnish it for him.

4

As they stepped into the hall, the tone of rapid
talk in several voices pierced through Amy's absorption. "Here's where we postpone time and such trivial
matters," said Geoffrey. "Emma seems excited."

Emma broke off as Amy and Geoffrey entered, lifting a flushed face, full, soft lips parted for further
outburst. Anger trembled through her, dyeing her
throat and bare arms a deeper crimson under the sun-
burn, giving an effect of swift motion to her body as
she sat tumultuously upright on the divan. "You'll
probably be as—as selfish as they are!" She disposed
of the other three in a full swing of one arm. "Well,
anyway, I told Laurance I was coming straight in to
tell his precious family. He said I shouldn't, and I
did. He thought I couldn't walk so far. I got a lift,
part way." She swung a dusty shoe, and the column
of her throat swelled with indignity. She was so thor-

oughly an expression of her feeling that she had not a crumb of her usual coquetry for Geoffrey.

"Emma thinks Laurance shouldn't have helped Tom," said Catherine.

"Would you like it if your husband gave away hundreds of dollars to a—a skunk? When you were pinching and saving—"

"But, Emma!" Amy sank down on a chair, uncomfortable as if Emma added to the physical heat of the day. "Where is Tom? What do you want us to do?"

"I want my money back. That's what I want. I told Laurance I was going to get it, too. I don't know where Tom is, and I don't care. He's run away."

"Tom went out last night," interrupted Theodore, "and persuaded Laurance to finance his departure. I should think it was a wise move, myself."

"Laurance sneaked off with him, down in the fields, and I couldn't find them." Emma defied them. "He wouldn't tell me a thing. I was bound I'd find out. He locked up his desk. Locked it so his own wife couldn't get into it! But before lunch he changed his clothes, he was so sweaty, and he forgot to take his keys. I found his checkbook. Right while he was eating, too."

Felice got to her feet and stood squarely in front of Emma, her eyes dark with disapproval. "You should feel some shame, first to act like that, and then to tell us. Your husband is not a child. He has a right to help a brother if he likes. You come here and make a great noise about what? A little money. Mother has already enough to distress her. She has told you there is no will, no money for any one."

"Oh, you!" Emma sniffed lustily. "I don't need any French advice. I know you think I'm stupid, but

I think some things are more important than a nose in a book."

"Emma, my dear!" Catherine moved hastily, her eyebrows lifted in dismay, to sit beside Emma on the divan. "Don't tell us what you think of us, not now while you feel so angry." Her tone cajoled softly, as she might have coaxed a child. "You can't expect us to replace money Laurance chose to use. You should be proud of him that he helped Tom out. Whether it was wise or not. He must be wretched, if you told him all the things you say you did."

"I'm not proud of him." Emma's chin wriggled, and she shut her eyes tight against tears. "He was just as mean as he could be. He wouldn't even tell me where he sent Tom. Work? That loafer! I went to his mother's first, but she wasn't home, only Harriet and that pop-eyed dog."

"I'm glad you didn't see Lora. Not while you're in a temper." Catherine patted the grubby fist beside her.

Suddenly from the street came the imperative honk of a motor horn. Amy pointed between the long folds of the curtains. The Ford truck waited, drawn in at an angle beside Pepita, and on the seat, his face a comedy mask of stern reluctance, sat Laurance.

Emma had jumped to her feet at the sound, to stare through the window, her quick breath straining the silk across her breast. A conflict of visible emotions rippled over her, so that she fled for safety into hiding, she drew herself up in outraged dignity, she rushed out to encounter Laurance all in an instant. Unexpectedly she laughed, a young laugh, gay and triumphant. "He said I needn't ever come back," she said, "and then he came after me!" She looked about at them, her eyes very blue under the thick, fair lashes-

"Well, anyway, I guess I showed him. And Mamma said she'd bet old Grandma Westover didn't leave much, the way she threw money around. Let him blow his old horn." Laurance, after a second blast, swung his leg over the fender, jumped to the ground. "Ee!" Emma shrieked. "I got to wash my face. You tell him he can just wait a while." She pelted up the stairs.

But Laurance merely stood beside his car, looking stubbornly at the house. He leaned to the wheel and reached for the horn button again.

"He's too embarrassed to come in," said Catherine. "I'll tell him." She started for the door. "He ought to see Lora, anyway."

The dialogue between her and Laurance made an amusing pantomime, Catherine quiet, consoling, Laurance explosive, belligerent, and then explanatory. He finally climbed back to his seat. At some final word from Catherine he shook his head violently. Emma ran down the stairs, shouted a sanguine good-by, and went along the walk, her eagerness held into a nonchalantly lagging step. Laurance did not look at her. She seated herself at his side, and waved a careless hand at Catherine as the truck leaped backward from Pepita, and with startling speed jumped ahead and down the street.

"Emma minded the money part," observed Felice, as Catherine came back, "but far less than that her husband should defy her. So now she is in excellent humor."

"Laurance isn't. Not yet." Catherine shook out the cushions of the divan, and sank down. "Emma's worked off her temper, and they'll be all right."

"What did he say about Tom?" asked Amy.

"Only that he had to help the boy clear out. He

said Tom was in a dreadful state, and he thought
Lora wouldn't—well, you know Lora. He won't say
where Tom's gone. Some friend offered him a job.
Quite far away, I judge. He felt guilty about it, but
as he said, what good to make Tom stay and face the
music? There'll be much less music with him gone,
won't there?"

"Think of old Laurance bucking his mother-in-law
and helping his prodigal brother!" Theodore stretched
lazily in his chair, his horn-rimmed spectacles balanced
over a square forefinger. "No doubt Father's doing
the same for his prodigal brother right now. Lucky
for Felice I haven't got a brother. And young Tom's
skipped. Well, well."

"Mother's right." Amy thought of Tom's bewildered, pasty face, the features shock-blurred out of
their arrogance. "It isn't admirable, running away,
of course. But nobody wanted him to marry Lulu.
Not even Lulu. And Lora would have ragged the
life out of him. That's what Laurance saw. A good
break, I say."

"Anyway, he's gone." Geoffrey pushed his cuff up
from his wrist-watch. "We've got to get along soon.
What about a bus, if Father doesn't show up?"

"Oh, he must come!" Catherine glanced incredu-
lously at the clock. "Is it that late? I don't see"—
her gaze stiffened, its energy moving inwards in an
attempt to build the scene in the familiar office—"what
they could do that would take so long."

"Maybe Lora's there. Emma said she wasn't
home." Amy added a third figure to the scene. "She'd
take more time."

"Get your bags ready, and I'll telephone." Catherine sighed. "It's horrid, waiting. You can imagine
so many things. Father said he'd send over the car if

he couldn't come. One of the men can drive you in. You wouldn't mind if I didn't go?"

"Of course not." Amy made her reply matter-of-fact. Expect her mother to run off when Alfred would be coming home, hunting for her? "It's much too hot, anyway."

"It's not hot, driving, but—"

"Of course, darling!" Amy smiled at her. "It's too cold. But you stay here, anyway. I won't be long."

From the stair landing she looked out across the lawn between the houses. Curly, on his knees, worked along a path bordered by withered iris leaves, the long shadow of one of the elms reaching just beyond his shaggy head. Lavinia had set him at a task. Incredible that nowhere in the old brick house, behind the drawn shades, moved the sound of Grandmother's stick, nowhere—

Going away was a queer thing. You said, coldly, at such a time I must go. Then when you slipped inevitably into the moment you had set, only the cold decision had the potency to free you, not from inertia, but from a momentum concerned with staying. You became a meteor, torn off to make a plunge into space, instead of whirling along in concentric orbits with the stars of whose system you had been a part. Human relationships pulled at you, defied you to destroy your connection with them. To tear yourself away was more than an empty phrase.

Amy took a final look about bathroom and bedrooms, snapped the lock on her second bag, pulled on her hat, and silk jacket over her arm, went down the stairs. "You can collect the bags, Geof," she called. "Did you get Father?"

"He's left the office, some time ago, the girl says.

He has the car. If he doesn't come in a few minutes, you'll have to go by bus." Catherine turned from the window, where she had searched hopefully up and down the street. "I don't like to call up Dewitt's."

"I hate to go without seeing Father again." Amy listened to Geoffrey's quick tread in the rooms above.

"I know. But I'll write you about everything."

"I must say good-by to Lavinia."

"Oh, goodness, I haven't paid Mrs. Maguire. Her day's work ends at five sharp." Catherine searched the street again before she went for her purse.

Amy traced Lavinia by her chatter through the empty kitchen to the yard at the rear of the house, where she was helping Mrs. Maguire fold down the linen from the clothes wires. Amy watched her a moment, a wiry little figure slapping the square of a sheet into folds; the linen hung without motion, canvases spread to catch the dappled patterns dropped by diffused sunlight through the thin foliage of the trees.

"Fold in sunshine with 'em, I say." Lavinia shouted at a disturbance behind a sheet, which developed into Mrs. Maguire, puffing as she dislodged clothes pins. "Steam laundries is a crime."

"Amy!" Catherine let the screen door slam in her haste. "Your father's here. He says we must hurry." She ran down the path, shoving bills at Mrs. Maguire. "Amy's going, 'Viny. Come say good-by. Thursday again, Mrs. Maguire? Good-night." She seized the folded sheet from Lavinia's hands, threw it into the basket, and pulled her toward Amy. "Hurry, dear. Oh, I am so glad he got here!" The release from the long afternoon of waiting had snapped her into eagerness. She ran into the house, her voice coming back in some phrase of urgency.

"So you got to go with your husband." Lavinia

looked across at the old brick house. Her sharp chin pulled the cords taut above the neat flat collar of her print dress. "Well, it's been a sad time. I'm real glad you was here. Your Grandma was fond of you. Things'll be different, next time you come. But I ain't going to worry. I can keep myself busy."

"Come along, Amy," Theodore shouted at her.

Amy threw her arms about the stiff figure, and kissed the cheek, crinkled like paper under her lips. "Good-by, 'Viny, dear," she said. "Take good care of the folks." She turned quickly into the house. The wiry indomitability of Lavinia ached in her throat to the edge of tears.

Theodore and Felice waited on the front steps. Good-by, good luck; see you some day in New York, perhaps. Her father stood beside his car.

"Sorry to hurry you. I didn't realize it was getting so late." His face wore an impersonal calmness. "Your bags are in back, all safe."

"You're sure you want that long drive, after a hard day?" But Amy was in beside Geoffrey as she spoke.

"Certainly." He dropped the seat into place, brushing her knees, and banged the door. "Let's open this windshield." He swung the glass out at an angle. "Now we're off."

He drove rapidly through the town and struck the broad highway running between flat, parched fields to the city. The warm air buffeted at their faces, dusty, faintly tar and earth scented. Amy remembered that night drive, days and days ago, and her longing to be absorbed out of herself into a child union with these two, her father and her mother. Now, with Geoffrey lounging beside her, one long leg poked forward between the seats, she resented that earlier, tired mood of negation and escape.

[323]

Presently her father began to talk, in abrupt phrases, obviously because he felt some pressure of their common—not curiosity, surely—rather a need to know what had happened. He couldn't explain the whole matter; he didn't understand all the ins and outs himself. Dewitt had been completely frank. He was pretty well wiped out.

"He says if he'd got funds in time, last Saturday, he might have saved something. But his orders reached the broker too late. He had to cover some deal of Carruthers, too. He's struck bottom all right. Lost his house, his business."

Amy stared at a draggled farm they passed, with battered wrecks of cars piled beside the sheds.

"Not much use being hard on him, was there?" Alfred glanced at Catherine, who made no answer. He shifted gears, waiting at a railroad crossing. "He's borrowed, on his third of Mother's house. Loan shark's rate, too. We'll have to sell. That's why we sent for Lora. I'm afraid it means ruining our place, Cathy. It won't sell for anything except a garage corner, or some kind of business. It's too far downtown."

Catherine shrank down in her seat, but she still said nothing.

"I offered Dewitt a place in the factory. Father would have taken him back, any minute he'd come, of course. Well, that's all. I had to help him."

For a few minutes he was intent on driving, waiting a chance to maneuver past a huge and noisy van. Its clatter and bulk oppressed them all into sharing the driving, nosing out, falling back as a car rushed toward them, at last with a spurt sliding past and ahead into open road with the uproar a subsiding threat at their rear.

"Dewitt didn't want to go home, poor devil." Alfred eased himself in his seat. "A man ought to want to go home, when he's in trouble. I couldn't see anything we could do, though, about Isabelle. When she finds they've got to move into some little house— Poor devil!"

Catherine turned, the warm wind blowing curls against her neck and cheek. "Why couldn't they have Mother's house?"

"It's too valuable. Lora needs her share, Dewitt's borrowed his. I can't pay that off and give it to him."

"But a garage next door!"

"No one will pay what it's worth to live in it. It isn't any longer the good residential part of town. What we ought to do is to include our place." He nodded at her, gravely aware of the shock in his words. "We won't have a chance to worry about it for a while," he added. "Not till things pick up."

Catherine shifted a little farther, so that for a moment her glance met Amy's, admitting in a flash her consternation, her bereavement. Then she gave a little hitch so that she sat quite straight, and said, "Of course the house is too big for us, now the children are all gone."

"Hooray!" Geoffrey's explosion knocked him forward, an arm over Catherine's shoulder, a hand on Alfred's. "Marvelous! She takes it with common sense. I tell you, Father's a fellow who isn't afraid to come home, no matter what trouble he's in."

"He isn't in trouble," said Catherine, defensively.

"He would be, if you saw it that way."

"Don't, Geof," Amy warned him, softly. "You embarrass them."

"I suppose it's true." Alfred slowed for a slight traffic block, a piece of road repair. "If you were like

Isabelle"—he grinned at Catherine—"I'd had to put the screws on Dewitt. Not that it would have done any good. If you shook him upside down, not a copper would rattle out. As it is, I feel more comfortable." He looked it, thought Amy. His color was better, spread evenly instead of blotched, and the white patches under his eyes were gone. "There's another fellow"—he pointed across the road—"who meant to get rich quick. Look at the wreck." Just opposite the car stood an elaborate and flimsy wooden gate, from which the paint had chipped, CHARMWOOD SITES in faded red letters over the shallow arch. In the field beyond was a checkering of roads, grass in the old ruts, and rows of unfinished two-story houses, wind and sun blackened. "He couldn't raise the money to finish his scheme. That was Moody, you remember, Cathy?"

The line of cars jerked ahead, and Alfred was busy, extricating himself from the delay.

"It's a symbol of times now, isn't it?" Geoffrey asked. "Grass in the proposed streets, and no roofs over grand schemes to be millionaires by to-morrow. It makes the air we breathe uneasy, like this damned heat and drought."

"Then the thing to do," said Catherine, "is not to run around too much, and not to get excited, but to wait till it rains again!" Her eyes shone at them, pleased with her figure.

"If it will rain." Geoffrey's undertone was sucked into the current of a passing car.

They were silent, entering the monotonous dull streets at the outskirts of the city, stagnant with odors of ripening and decay under the steady sun,—not only fruit, vegetables, but fabrics, metals, asphalt, flesh itself. The outgoing traffic thickened into constant impact of passing vehicles.

"You've got your tickets? No?" Alfred cut past a trolley car. "Well, it's not far now. We've hit the homeward flow, that's all."

At the entrance to the station Geoffrey darted ahead to collect the tickets and reservations. Alfred unlocked the dusty luggage compartment and lifted out the bags. Then the three of them stood near the gate, the enormous hall dwarfing the restless human flow about ticket windows and paper stands. The slight awkwardness of a final moment settled over them, as if only momentous words should be spoken, and only trivial ones presented themselves.

"Write soon, won't you? Let us know—" Catherine reached for Amy's hand. Her firm, tender fingers completed her phrase. Let us know that you are well, that you are happy, that you think of us occasionally. "And don't worry about us."

"I won't." Amy looked at the two of them, her father square and heavy in wrinkled gray flannels, his face cleared of the harassed, almost defeated expression it had worn so many days, even his thick eyebrows more tranquil; her mother with her small head well back, her eyelids thoughtful. "I won't worry about you two."

They stood close together, a small group isolated just as other groups were set apart by their knowledge of each other, by the fact that emotion moved among them, and not from them to strangers. Amy laid a hand on her father's arm, felt her mother cling more firmly to her other hand. "But where is Geoffrey? You don't want to miss that train, now." Her father flung up a beckoning hand, and whistled. "Here we are!" Parting was too taut a string to endure much stretching. "Here, Geof!"

Geoffrey rushed up, a porter at his heels. "The train's in. Those three bags, boy. Good-by, you two." Amy kissed them. "Good-by, good-by." She turned, as she and Geoffrey ran down the slight incline, to wave at them behind the iron barrier. "Good-by."

THE END

Persephone Books publishes the following titles: